Praise for *The Secret Garden of Yanagi Inn*

"Evoking Burnett and du Maurier in equal parts, in a setting dense with the distinctive native flora and fauna of Japan—including a delightful blueberry-eating tanuki—this novel is wholly original, and both modern and timeless. We should all celebrate this introduction to the lush and fecund imagination of a remarkable talent."
—**Suzanne Kamata**, author of *The Baseball Widow*

"A lovely re-imagining of a classic tale. Amber Logan transforms the story of *The Secret Garden* into something new and fresh, yet still utterly timeless."
—**A.C. Wise**, author of *Wendy, Darling* and *The Ghost Sequences*

"Logan is a master of atmosphere and texture. *The Secret Garden of Yanagi Inn* is a haunting tale of grief and enchantment that will linger in your mind long after reading. Perfect for readers of Neil Gaiman and Genevieve Valentine."
—**Helen Marshall**, author of *The Migration*

"Lyrical and haunting, *The Secret Garden of Yanagi Inn* is a luminous retelling of a classic tale, made modern through the lens of Logan's intrepid American heroine. A story of redemption, forgiveness, and the transformative power of grief. Beautifully moving and inspired."
—**Paulette Kennedy**, author of *Parting the Veil* and *The Witch of Tin Mountain*

"*The Secret Garden of Yanagi Inn* is a puzzle box of buried memories, grief, and the love between mothers and daughters. Amber Logan's poignant update of *The Secret Garden* sits within the legacy of garden literature that explores the unbreakable link that connects people, place, and time."
—**Tiffani Angus**, author of *Threading the Labyrinth*

"[A] nuanced story about healing from loss mixed with family secrets, a mystery to unravel, and a dash of the supernatural."
—**Sara Fujimura**, author of *Every Reason We Shouldn't*

"The prose, rich in detail of Mari's feelings and experiences, builds the atmosphere with slow precision."
—**Rebecca Otowa**, author of *At Home in Japan: A Foreign Woman's Journey of Discovery*

The
Secret Garden
of
Yanagi Inn

The Secret Garden

of

Yanagi Inn

A NOVEL

Amber A. Logan

CamCat
Books

CamCat Publishing, LLC
Fort Collins, Colorado 80524
camcatpublishing.com

© 2022 by Amber A. Logan

Hardcover ISBN 9780744306064
Paperback ISBN 9780744306460
Large-Print Paperback ISBN 9780744306439
eBook ISBN 9780744306415
Audiobook ISBN 9780744306347

Library of Congress Control Number: 2022936317

Book and cover design by Maryann Appel

5   3   1   2   4

To all the brilliantly flawed and complex women in my life.

Chapter One

December 24th
Chicago, Illinois

I'd always been told hospitals were a place to heal and rest, but my mother's hospital room was an assault on the senses. The stench of decaying flowers and cloying cherry disinfectant clung to my skin, invaded my nose. A wave of nausea swept over me. I couldn't breathe, couldn't think.

"I need to get some air."

I rose to my feet before Risa could object, although I knew she wouldn't. My sister had been trying to convince me all day to leave Mom's hospital room, to go get some real food or take a walk.

"Sure, Mari, go ahead. I'll stay with Mom." Risa nodded without looking up, her short blond curls bobbing. She leaned back in her bedside chair, still absorbed in her book. I glanced at Mom, now a papery, skeletal version of the woman she once was. But at least she was peaceful, sleeping.

As soon as I stepped through the hospital's sliding glass doors, the blast of cold air sent an involuntary shiver through my body. I pulled my hair back into a ponytail, knowing the chill wouldn't last, that five minutes in I'd be sweating, my muscles warmed. Maybe the fact I already wore running shoes was fate, or maybe I'd just gotten lazy—too exhausted after so many long days split between the gallery and the hospital to care about my appearance. Either way, I'd dressed in sweats that morning and I was going for a run, damn it.

I turned north and ran down the nearly deserted sidewalk. Streetlights were wrapped with faux greenery and twinkling lights, and last week's snowstorm had left lingering mountains of gray snow on the edge of parking lots. The morning air stung my throat, but the cold was a welcome change from the stifling hospital room.

I ran for most of an hour, my pace too fast to fall into a comfortable groove. But the burn in my muscles and the emptiness of my mind renewed me. No worrying about the doctor's cryptic prognoses, about visits from the counselor who peeked in occasionally to "see how we were doing." I could just run—it was me and the cold air and the thud-thud-thud of my feet on the pavement, and all was right in the world.

But it wasn't. This was a dream, and reality waited for me back in that suffocating room. Risa would be wanting her midmorning coffee, and I, being the good big sister that I was, ordered two drinks from the Starbucks around the corner so she didn't have to settle for the unbranded kiosk in the hospital's lobby.

I expected to return a hero, sweaty but triumphant, brandishing two grande peppermint lattes as I opened Mom's door. But as I carried the drinks down the hospital corridor, I saw Mom's door was already open. My hands trembled.

I sped up.

Sounds of movement and talking inside the room. And crying— Risa was crying. I broke into a run, burning my hands as peppermint latte sloshed over them onto the pristine polished floor.

Risa was still in her chair, sobbing behind both hands, her book dropped at her feet. Two hospice nurses stood at the foot of Mom's bed, speaking in quiet, respectful tones.

Mom didn't look any different, looked for all the world like she was still sleeping.

But the whirring, dripping sounds had stopped. They'd turned off all the machines. Only Frank Sinatra's crooning "Silent Night" drifted down the hall from a distant room.

Mom had died.

And I'd missed it.

Chapter Two

Two months later
En route to Japan

The dimmed cabin lights brightened to a rosy glow, mimicking a sunrise though it was late evening in Kyoto. I wiped the drool off my lip with the back of my hand, glanced at the passengers on either side of me. The elderly woman to my right was awake, watching *Roman Holiday* on her seatback screen—Mom's favorite movie, one I'd watched with her three times in the hospital alone.

The smartly dressed blond woman on my left had her laptop out on her tray table. Her stockinged feet rested on carry-on luggage with the same floral print as the weekender bag Mom had picked up in England years ago.

An optimistically small bag for her hospital stay.

The woman was probably working. Her nails on the keys tick-tick-ticked away, knocking on the door to my brain, reminding me I should check my work email. I reached for the bag between my feet. And Risa would need to be reminded of where I'd left Ginkgo's pills. She needed to know he wouldn't take them without sticking the pills inside butter. She needed to know—

STOP IT, *Mari*. I pictured my little sister smirking at me, arms crossed, standing next to my white puffball of a dog. *Relax—I've got this.*

I leaned back in my seat, rhythmically twisting the too-loose ring on my middle finger.

The flight attendant pushed a drink cart down the aisle. She wore a fitted top and pencil skirt, a jaunty kerchief with the Japan Airlines red crane logo tied around her neck. "Green tea, coffee?" Her voice was quiet, soothing.

I raised my hand. "Coffee would be amazing, thank you."

She smiled a practiced smile, set a small cup on her metal tray, and poured the coffee from a carafe. The two women on either side of me asked for green tea.

Even over the aroma of my coffee, I could smell their tea. I'd missed it, the slightly bitter scent, the warmth of it. A scent from my childhood. Japan. *I'm really going back. This is real. This is NOW.*

I took a sip of the coffee, hissing as it stung my tongue. A sharp, cheap flavor like the instant crap Thad used to buy when he'd finished off my good stuff.

I should've asked for tea.

"*Ladies and gentlemen, we will be landing at Kansai International Airport in approximately half an hour. We anticipate a slightly early arrival. Local time is 7:14 p.m.*"

My cardigan was damp with sleep sweat. I'd take it off, but I was afraid of elbowing the ladies next to me, so I made do with pulling my hair back into a ponytail and hitting the button for my personal fan. It whirred to life, but the clicking annoyed me, and I turned it back off. In the row behind me, someone sneezed.

What the hell was I doing running away like this—abandoning my sister, my now ex-boyfriend, maybe even my job? Tears welled in my eyes and I fought them back, staring at the screen in front of me, at the image of the tiny airplane and the dashed-line trek it'd made across the Pacific Ocean. Even if Risa had made all the arrangements and basically shoved me out the door, it felt wrong to just leave. Even if it was for only four weeks.

Deep breaths, Mari, deep breaths.

At first the timing of the grant had seemed fortuitous, if a bit rushed. But the closer I got to Japan, the more reality set in and the vague details of the NASJ grant paperwork felt more and more inadequate. Photograph an old, isolated Japanese inn "for posterity's sake"? It wasn't much to go on.

Had I brought the right camera lenses? Would four weeks be enough time? It seemed an eternity to me right now, but I'd never been asked to document an entire estate, never even received a grant before. I was an artist, not a documentarian.

At least, I used to be an artist.

Maybe I should've splurged for the upgraded camera bag with better padding. I pictured the *Roman Holiday* woman next to me opening the overhead compartment and my camera bag tumbling out onto the floor. Contents may have shifted during flight.

Could she even reach the overhead compartment? She was a tiny Japanese woman—probably in her seventies. I snuck a glance at her.

But Mom was sitting next to me.

I froze, my entire body turning numb.

Mom, leaning back in her seat, was watching the movie with a slight smile on her lips. Her platinum blond hair was tied back in a loose ponytail, but tufts had fallen out and were dusting her shoulders, her blouse, like dead leaves. She sipped her green tea.

I struggled for air. The sweat dotting my skin turned cold, clammy.

No, no, no. I'm just tired, didn't get enough sleep. I closed my eyes, inhaled deep, gasping breaths. Mandarins, I smelled freshly peeled mandarins.

"Are you all right, honey?"

My eyes flew open. CEO woman on my left, with her slim laptop and flowered bag, stared at me. Her eyes were wide with concern.

I shot a glance to my right. The little grandmother had returned and was happily watching her movie, oblivious to my distress.

Am I all right? The dreaded question.

Did she mean "do I need medical attention?" Or was it more of the existential "all right" we all seem to strive for but never quite manage?

I smiled at the woman, responded with the only reasonable lie one can give to that question: "I'm fine."

Deep breaths, Mari. Deep breaths.

The flight attendant in her perfect pillbox hat and red bandana came by again, this time with white gloves and a plastic trash bag. I handed her my half-empty cup of coffee with an apologetic smile.

I should've asked for tea.

Like an orderly river, we flowed off the plane and down the jet bridge, then spilled out into the brightly lit airport. I squinted, one hand carrying my camera bag, the other pulling my square carry-on luggage.

The stop at the bathroom with its private floor-to-ceiling stall doors, the polite customs workers, the wait for baggage—it was all a blur. A foggy-headed, clips-and-phrases of Japanese and English blurring together kind of chaos. But I was an ignorant American, the tall, brown-haired white lady looking like a confused tourist, so of course I was funneled through with utter politeness and a tolerance I was grateful for, yet also resented. I didn't need their help.

I say that, but when I finally stepped out into the arrivals area and scanned the crowd for a sign or a screen or a hand-scrawled note featuring "Marissa Lennox," I found none. My heart leapt into my throat for a moment, but I swallowed it back down. No worries, the plane had landed a few minutes early.

Maybe my ride was running late. Maybe there was a miscommunication about the terminal. Maybe . . .

I scanned the line of men in suits and white gloves again, watching for a glimmer of recognition in their alert faces, but each one's eyes slid past me to the next arriving passenger. I didn't match their profiles. Of course I didn't.

I found a bench nearby where I could keep one eye on the sliding glass doors and the other on my oversized suitcase and assorted bags. But no drivers came rushing in, embarrassingly late to pick up the unfortunate foreign woman. I considered buying a coffee at the kiosk or indulging in my love of Japanese vending machines, but decided against it. I didn't relish shoving all my luggage into a tiny bathroom stall if I had to pee before I left.

And so, I waited.

A handful of older businessmen passed by, glanced surreptitiously my way, chattering amongst themselves with the self-assuredness of men who assume I can't understand them. One laughed and nodded. I caught a few of their words in passing: foreigner, tall, Chelsea Clinton. I chuckled and raised an eyebrow. Maybe Chelsea Clinton on her worst day—my frizzy brown hair with graying roots was already sneaking out of its scrunchie to spill across my oily face.

I tucked a strand of hair behind my ear and turned on my phone, careful to keep it in airplane mode. Damn it, I hadn't thought I'd need an international plan. I pulled up the email from Ogura Junko at the Yanagi Inn—no phone number, not even in the email signature. I leaned my head back against the hard wall, practiced the breathing technique Risa had taught me in the hospital months ago. *Breathe in, one-two-three, breathe out, one-two-three.*

I double-checked the email, noted the inn's street address. If no one came to pick me up, I could just step outside, find a cab, and give them Yanagi Inn's address (though the long ride from the airport to the remote inn would probably cost a fortune).

I wasn't helpless, after all.

But still, having no one to meet me . . . not a good omen.

Half an hour passed before I thought to check the printout of the grant paperwork Risa had sent me. I dug through my bags until I found it tucked in the pocket beside my laptop. I balanced the computer on my lap and smoothed the sheet of printer paper across its flat top.

I hadn't bothered printing the front page, only a few paragraphs from the middle, with highlighted parts I'd thought relevant. No contact info.

. . . for the purpose of documenting, via artistic photography and for the sake of posterity, the property known hereafter as YANAGI INN . . .

"Lennox-san?"

I glanced up sharply, nearly toppling the laptop. A sixty-something woman with graying, short-cropped hair stood over me. She wore a simple indigo kimono with a wide cream-colored obi belt, and a grandmotherly air of silent disapproval.

"Ogura-san?"

For a moment, she just towered over me, scrutinizing my face as if searching for something. Then she gave a barely discernable nod and turned toward the glass doors. I scrambled, shoving the printout and my laptop back into their bag. I didn't even have time to pull out my jacket.

"Wait!" I called after her, frustration creeping into my voice as I grabbed the handles of my various bags and rolling luggage.

It seemed like every one of the airport's many patrons turned and stared at me. I flushed and scrambled after Ogura, the only person in the building who hadn't bothered acknowledging my cry.

I tripped out of the automatic doors, following the old woman into the brisk night air. She was surprisingly quick in her traditional wooden sandals, weaving between travelers toward a slick black sedan waiting at the curb, its lights flashing. A driver in a black suit and white gloves hopped out of the car and started loading my bags into the spacious trunk. I thanked him, my cramped arms lightening with every bag removed from my care.

Ogura climbed into the passenger seat before the final bag was stored in the trunk, so the driver opened the door to the back and I slipped inside, grateful to sink into the soft leather interior.

It's dark, I thought vaguely, for both the car's tinted windows and the sky outside were inky, seductive, and as soon as I set down my camera bag, clicked my seatbelt, and rested my head against the cold window beside me, I was out.

Chapter Three

Someone was whispering. I opened my eyes, lifted my head off the window glass. Lights and large overhead signs flickered past at regular intervals, and the car purred like we were creeping down a freshly poured driveway. Must be on a highway.

Ogura was in the front seat, chatting with the driver in hushed tones. Though her voice was soft, I caught snippets—enough to get the gist of her one-sided conversation about the hassles of picking up ignorant *gaijin* women.

I sat up straighter, spoke up—in Japanese—just loud enough I was sure both parties could hear me: "It must have been troublesome to drive all the way out to the airport to get me. I apologize for the inconvenience."

Silence. Ogura didn't reply, but she inclined her head, very slightly, an acknowledgment of my statement. The driver remained silent.

Perhaps I should've held back the fact I speak Japanese. I stared out the window, processing the flashing of headlights, businesses, and homes as they blurred past. "How much longer is the drive?" I asked.

"Another forty minutes," Ogura answered, grudgingly, as if I had asked her to sew on a button the moment she was heading out the door for an important meeting.

"I see." I had no idea how long we'd been on the road already. I turned my attention to my camera bag, taking the opportunity to unzip each compartment and check the contents inside. The lenses I held up to passing flashes of light seemed whole, undamaged.

"Excuse me," I began again. "Do you know what I'll be asked to photograph at Yanagi Inn?"

Ogura twisted her body just enough she could stare silently at me in the intermittent flashes of light.

"For the grant? I'm supposed to be documenting Yanagi Inn, but the grant didn't provide many details."

Ogura and the driver exchanged a glance. Then she shifted back around in her seat. "No one tells me anything," she muttered so softly I wasn't sure I was meant to hear.

I leaned my head against the window again, silently counting the seconds between each flash of passing light until the gentle rocking of the car lulled me back to sleep.

I jolted awake when the car came to a stop after its long, silent drive. The two front doors closed with solid thuds, but I sat alone in the dark for a moment longer, groggy and disoriented. The car jostled as the driver unloaded my bags from the trunk, and Ogura's cold figure disappeared inside the inn. I grabbed my camera bag and scrambled out of the car.

The moment I stepped out into the night, the cold air hit me like a slap to the face. I'd been wrong to think that surviving Chicago winters would make everything else feel warm by comparison, but at least this cold came with an invigorating crispness found only in areas far from airports and population density; it reminded me of camping. I spun in a slow circle. No streetlights or storefronts or neighbors interrupted my view of the black night.

I breathed in deeply, until a shiver wracked my body.

The building in front of me was traditional, wooden, with a single-story, peaked roof. The structure itself was almost entirely obscured by overgrown, wayward bushes, as if nature itself was bent on swallowing the property whole. The only illumination, save for the pallid moonlight, came from a worn red paper lantern hanging from the covered entrance, shedding its feeble light on walls that were corroded and peeling, as if made of aging parchment.

I was reminded of an art exhibit I'd seen years ago. The gallery's walls had been covered with large, unsettling photographs of small-town haunted houses, the kind of properties that children mention only in whispers and that spawn urban legends. This façade was so forsaken, and so vastly different from the grand entranceway I had envisioned, that I began to wonder whether there'd been a mistake. But then I saw it—a battered wooden sign hanging by the front doors, carved with the name "Yanagi Inn," and my stomach sank. I was in the right place.

The driver was standing beside me, luggage in hand, waiting. I ducked my head in apology (what was I apologizing for?) and followed him down the short path to the inn's entrance. The granite walkway was lined with rounded black stones, the rock beds so infested by weeds I feared stepping off the path lest they reach out to trip me. There were no signs of life or movement, no other sounds besides our own hollow footsteps as we approached the inn.

Inside, all was silent and still. We walked through the sparse lobby, with its musty scent and smattering of chairs that looked to be from the 1970s. We passed an unmanned front desk with a worn leather guestbook on the counter and a wall of framed newspaper reviews behind it. We only paused to remove our shoes where the tiled floors of the lobby stepped up to a raised level of tatami matting.

The hallways were dimly lit, and the dry scent of dust and heating elements permeated the air. No one spoke. I followed the driver in socked feet, and he dragged my luggage through the narrow halls, following Ogura, although I couldn't see her. The silence was unnerving, accustomed as I was to the near constant commotion of living in a South Loop Chicago high-rise with thin walls and energetic neighbors.

But this silence wasn't the quiet found in relaxing vacation spots; it was more like being trapped in a jar with a lid dampening all outside noise. A muted, deadened soundlessness which made me tread lightly so I wouldn't be the monster to disrupt it.

I half expected to turn the corner and encounter the creepy twin girls from *The Shining*. I shuddered; why had I let Thad convince me to watch that movie?

After a few turns, we came to an abrupt stop and found Ogura standing in front of an open door. The driver placed my luggage inside, bowed, and disappeared down the hall before I had a chance to properly thank him.

I was loath to break the silence anyways.

A teenaged maid, dressed in a paler blue version of Ogura's kimono, was bustling about the room. She had pushed aside a low table laden with small, covered bowls and was laying out a futon and bedding on the tatami matting.

"Yuna-chan," Ogura broke the silence with a stern tone. "Lennox-san would like to retire now."

Yuna spun around, apparently unaware that she had company. Her long ponytail slipped over her shoulder as she bowed. "Good evening, Lennox-san," she said in heavily accented English.

I glanced over my shoulder; Ogura had already disappeared down the hall. "Oh, you can call me Mari," I replied softly in Japanese.

A smile of relief spread across Yuna's round, youthful face as she straightened. "You speak Japanese?" She spoke in a slight dialect, one I didn't recognize.

I returned her smile, though I'm sure it looked tired, strained. "I spent a lot of my childhood here. And then I went on to study Japanese in college."

Yuna's brow furrowed slightly as she took in my frizzy light brown hair and hazel eyes. "Forgive me for being blunt, but you're not half-Japanese, right?"

I chuckled and waved a hand in front of my face. "No. My family lived outside Yokohama because my father was an American expat working for Toshiba." I set my camera bag on the floor, rolled my shoulders to relieve the strain. "I went to an international school, but my parents refused to live in an expat haven, so we lived in a normal neighborhood, had Japanese friends."

"Oh. Why did you move back to America?"

I froze. Did I really want to get into all that right now, with a complete stranger, no less? I looked at my watch, hoping maybe the girl would take the hint. "Well, my parents separated and—"

"Yuna-chan." The dark specter of Ogura reappeared in the doorway. "I'm sure our guest would like to retire for the evening."

Good god, yes, thank you. I never thought I'd be relieved to see Ogura again.

"Of course." Yuna flushed, and she hurried to arrange the bedding. "What time would you like me to bring breakfast?"

"I don't even know what time it is now," I said with a sigh. "I'm sure my sleep schedule will be off. How about nine?"

I heard a quiet "*Tsk*" sound behind me. I turned, but Ogura was gone.

Yuna nodded, either ignoring or not noticing Ogura's disdain. She showed me the notecard with wifi information, then lifted the lids off the bowls on the table to reveal a variety of individually wrapped rice crackers and, I realized with a pang to my heart, mandarins. "I'm sorry we didn't have a meal ready for you. The kitchen was already shut down."

I walked Yuna to the door. "No worries, I certainly understand. My apologies for arriving so late. I hope I haven't disturbed any other guests." I was reminded of the eerie silence of the dark hallways I'd walked down. Were there any other guests?

"Oh, no need to worry about that." Yuna waved a hand in front of her face and chuckled. "Well, good night . . . Mari-san." She winked and left the room, sliding the door closed behind her.

I sank into the floor chair beside the table. She seemed like a nice girl, and it was good to have a friendly face here in this foreboding environment, but I had no more energy left to maintain a pleasant façade. I picked up a mandarin, but then replaced it in the bowl. Their presence was just a coincidence, but it still unnerved me. Instead, I unwrapped a large rice cracker and enjoyed a savory, if slightly stale, bite.

I let my gaze roam the room. Why did a teenager even work in a dilapidated place like this? A low table with a scuffed black top and two matching floor chairs, each with a threadbare red cushion. A single futon mattress with old-fashioned floral bedding laid out on the tatami floor, a standing paper lamp beside it. Several sliding doors leading to a private bathroom, a closet, and presumably out to a veranda. The room's only decorations were a scroll painted with stylized kanji and a vase of fresh pine branches, red winter berries, and bright white chrysanthemums. At least the flowers were fresh and new.

The space felt more like some forsaken grandmother's house than the esteemed ryokan I'd envisioned, but at least it was clean.

After a quick stop in the bathroom (with its disappointingly regular Western toilet), I stripped off the cardigan and jeans I'd been wearing for god knows how many hours and stared in the mirror. Bags under my eyes, my hair a stringy mess, my face greasy. Too angular, haggard. I looked like shit.

If only I could blame it all on international travel.

Too tired for a shower, I threw on pajamas and switched off the shoji paper lamp. When I flopped down on the futon, it emitted a faint floral scent, just as you'd expect at a grandmother's house. The mattress was firm, perfect really—the kind of bed I'd always wanted to sleep on when we lived in Japan, but Risa and I had both slept in frilly pink princess-themed canopy beds—which Risa loved.

But I didn't.

My body was heavy, sluggish, but my mind wouldn't stop whirling. I was in Japan again, after so many years. I would wake up tomorrow in a strange bed with new surroundings, new obligations, new people, and . . .

I needed my sleeping pills. But no, Risa had given me a hard look when she'd found the bottle in my luggage and handed me the bag of melatonin lozenges instead. But I've always hated having something in my mouth when I'm trying to sleep. It feels like an obvious choking hazard, like giving a grape to an active toddler.

Whatever. I closed my eyes, practiced my breathing exercises again. *Breathe in, one-two-three, breathe out, one-two-three.*

My heart rate slowed, my mind settled. I focused on the silence in the room. Somewhere, a clock tick, ticked away the seconds. I had started to drift off into a fuzzy realm filled with the steady hum of airplane engines and the quiet rustle of a hundred passengers shifting in uncomfortable seats when another sound invaded my mind.

A low, mournful keening.

It sounded like a far-off wounded animal, a whining dog. This was an isolated place—could there be coyotes? My eyes opened slowly. Were there even coyotes in Japan? I held my breath, listened with ears attuned to the eerie, distant sound.

No, it wasn't a howl. Was someone crying?

Mom.

I was a child again, lying in my princess canopy bed, pillow pressed against my ears to block out the sound. A whimper in the matching bed against the far wall; Risa must've heard it, too.

"Go to sleep, Risa," I whispered, and she fell silent. But the weeping from our mother's room continued . . .

It's not Mom, Mari. I squeezed my eyes shut.

My thoughts flew, perhaps rashly, to the young maid. As I strained to hear the whimpers filtering through the thin walls of my room, I clenched my jaw to keep my own emotions in check; I'd spent too many nights balanced on the brink of inconsolable tears not to relate. Yet what would a young girl like Yuna (for she couldn't be older than six-teen or seventeen) be doing in a place like this so late at night? Did she live here?

I opened my eyes again, stared at the dark ceiling somewhere above me. Maybe the cries really weren't human—a fox? Some kind of bird?

Or maybe they were just in my mind—childhood memories, emo-tional projections.

Or premonitions.

Damn it, where were my sleeping pills when I needed them?

I squeezed my eyes closed, tried to shut off my mind. But the words Risa whispered to me when she'd hugged me goodbye at the airport kept cycling through my brain.

It's what Mom would have wanted.

Oh, how I wished I knew if that was true.

Chapter Four

"You need to get out more, Mari." Mom set a cup of coffee in front of me on the kitchen table. She bustled around, closing cabinets and wiping off counters before joining me. I noticed her mug had a chamomile teabag instead of coffee.

"I get out plenty."

"I don't mean gallery events or client meetings. I mean get out there, see the world, live life."

Even though I drank it black, I stirred my coffee with a miniature spoon, clanking it against the sides of the mug. "Mom, if this is about me not wanting children . . ."

"No, honey, nothing like that." She sighed, wiped her hands on her apron. Mom looked tired. Her long, white-blond hair—usually perfectly styled—was now unkempt, like she'd just woken up. It was almost noon.

"Is everything ok, Mom? Are you feeling all right?"

"I'm fine, sweetie. I just worry about you. You live for your work, and I know you're passionate about it, but sometimes you need to have passion for other things."

"So this is a Thad thing." I frowned, my voice flat. She'd never taken to Thad, even after he'd come over every weekend to shovel her driveway.

"No, darling. I just want to see you happy, that's all." She reached for a mandarin from the bowl in the center of the table, mindlessly peeled it with her orange-tinged fingernails.

"Who says I'm not happy?" I dropped the spoon with a clink.

We stared at each other across the small table, the dishwasher humming and sloshing in the background. Why did she bother running the dishwasher? There'd only been a handful of dirty dishes; a fifty-eight-year-old woman living alone certainly doesn't eat much. Did Mom look thinner than usual?

"Mari, I won't be around forever. I just want to know you're on a good path." She twisted her silver ring around her finger, over and over again like she did when she was nervous about something. She hadn't eaten any of her mandarin.

I took a sip of my coffee, forcing myself not to wince at the temperature. "Mom," I said, setting the cup down on its saucer, "what is this really about?"

Mom sighed. "I just don't want you to have any regrets, my angel. Don't be like me."

When I awoke, the room was still dark, the air heavy and stifling. I lay motionless, only my eyes flicking around the room, seeking familiar shapes in the shadows. Only slowly did my memories of the previous day return. Japan, the inn.

At home I always slept with the fan on—even in the winter—and without it my own breathing made the room humid, suffocating. Each breath told me I was in a closed jar, slowly extracting the oxygen.

I crawled to the low table and found my phone. 4 a.m. Yuna and breakfast wouldn't come for hours.

Maybe I should go for a jog? Risa had somehow convinced me to bring my running shoes—though I hadn't used them in months—as if somehow the change of scenery would restore my former strength and stamina overnight.

I took a shower instead.

As I put on the inn's light blue yukata and tied the belt around my waist, I studied myself in the bathroom mirror. The yukata was made for a shorter woman, and the whole ensemble made me acutely aware of how the bones in my shoulders jutted out, how tight I had to cinch the belt. What would Risa say if she saw me like this, nothing but a scaffolding of bone wrapped in Japanese cloth? I'd gotten by with bulky sweaters back home, but winter clothes would only work for so long, even in Chicago. I twisted the ring on my middle finger, so loose it spun freely.

I leaned toward the mirror; at least my hair was clean, my face washed. I stared into my own tired eyes. *You can do this, Mari.*

Then I went back into the main room, switched off the lamp, and crawled back into bed.

Time passed. The room was pitch black, the air thick and warm—too warm. I kicked away the thick comforter, inhaled a heavy, oppressive breath.

"*Mari-chan . . .*"

My eyes opened to the darkness. Had someone called me? It'd been quiet, a distant whisper, but . . .

No, I'm just tired. Stressed. Jet-lagged.

Go to sleep! I screamed internally, squeezing my eyes shut.

But then, far off, echoing down the black hallways outside my door—the whimpering again, a plaintive, broken sound. My ears strained; was it animal, or human?

As if compelled, I rose to my feet. I slipped on the worn house slippers by the door and then, with a deep breath, slid open the door to the hall.

Silence. The corridor was deserted, the darkness weighty, with the stagnant stillness of last night. Hell, it was last night still. What on earth was I doing?

I placed one slippered foot out in the hall, slipped, and barely caught myself. A puddle? There hadn't been water in the corridor last night. Must be a vent leaking condensation, I told myself. I shifted my weight from foot to foot, my heart fluttering in my chest like a hummingbird. Before me lay two choices: retreat inside my room and go back to sleep like a sane person, or take another step out into the hall and follow the mysterious sound.

There was no way I'd be able to fall back asleep.

I stepped into the hall, slid the door closed behind me.

Yuna had said I didn't need to worry about waking other guests; was I the only person staying at Yanagi Inn? It was February, after all—it had to be the slow season.

Or maybe there were guests in another wing? I hadn't gotten a good look at the layout when I arrived; for all I knew, there were a myriad of wings spiraling like spokes from the main building, each with a Yuna to cater to them.

But no, something told me this ryokan's design was more helter-skelter, more like the Winchester Mansion—constructed without plan over the years by some mad architect to house the countless spirits of those murdered by the family's rifles.

I crept down the dark corridor, one hand brushing the wall. God, I hoped I wasn't the only one staying here. That'd be a bit too much like *The Shining* for comfort.

Something about this corridor didn't feel like the one I'd walked down last night. The air was musty and undisturbed, like a locked attic. Maybe I'd come from the other direction . . .

I stopped, closed my eyes to reorient.

Something hummed in the air. It wasn't electric, exactly, but it also wasn't murmurs, or running water, or any other normal sounds. Just an emanation reverberating in the hallway. Unseen waves: ultraviolet, gamma, some invisible radiation of life?

Or something akin to life.

The pulsing waves raised the hairs along my skin. I took a slow step backward, some animal instinct taking over my rational mind.

But then, up ahead down the hall, a door slid open, sending a sudden beam of light into the darkness. For a mad moment my body tensed to flee back from whence it came, all manner of irrational boogeymen flooding my imagination, but some vestige of rationality rooted my feet to the floor.

A dark figure stepped into the hall. My heart seized.

Then the figure turned toward me—Ogura-san. My tense shoulders sagged with relief, but she flinched when she caught sight of me, her hand flying to her chest. I must've scared the crap out of her, too—an unexpected *gaijin* materializing from an impossibly dark corridor.

"Lennox-san," she began in a stern voice. "It is too early for you to be roaming the halls, disturbing others. Return to your room."

I was transported to my childhood, to kneeling on the hard floor in front of the Japanese auntie my parents paid to watch over little Risa and me when they still went out on dates. I couldn't recall her face, but I remembered her voice. She wasn't ill-tempered, but she was stern, and when she asked a question ("Have you already eaten?" or "Did your mother say you could watch television?"), it always felt like an accusation, like she was judging rather than asking. I'd always felt compelled to lie even when I had nothing to hide. The memories stirred up old, disjointed emotions within me.

I opened my mouth, closed it, opened it again. Then I bobbed my head and spun on my heel, knocking off one of my slippers in the process. I scooped it off the ground and speed-walked back down the hall as fast as I could with one slipper on.

How dare that woman speak to me like I was a child! I smacked the slipper against the wall, making a satisfying *whap* in the stillness. And I let her do it! Why didn't I just tell her I was out for a walk but would certainly be respectful?

Now she'd never take me seriously.

I stopped, threw the slipper on the floor, and slid my foot back into it. No, the next time I saw her I'd just act cool and calm, in control of the situation. We would both chalk up my meek behavior to jet lag.

I slid open my own door and flopped down in the floor chair without bothering to turn on the lamp. The worn surface of the table was cool, and I laid my head upon it like I used to when I was a child and would come home upset from this-or-that at school.

Mom would be waiting for me in the kitchen, a plate of red bean mochi in hand. She'd listen, stroke my hair, and coax me into eating the chewy rice cakes, and before I knew it, we'd be laughing and joking and I'd have forgotten all about my problems for a few minutes.

I lifted my head. My gaze landed on the bowl of mandarins. Then I stared at the empty chair across the table, imagining, for a moment, the dark outline of my mother sitting there. My heart knotted inside my chest.

In that moment, I would've given anything to have Mom sit down across from me with a plate of store-bought sweets. Or Risa. Or hell, even Thad.

Ok, maybe not Thad. But a familiar face, a few gentle words? Anything but this—cornered and alone with a stern Ogura-san roaming the dark halls outside. I felt trapped, like a mouse in a cage with a hungry cat outside, ready to pounce.

My gaze roamed the near-complete darkness of the room, the unfamiliar lumps and shapes offering no comfort. I was in a strange place on the other side of the world, in a country I thought I'd never return to. Why had I accepted the grant so readily?

I laid my head back down on my arms, fought back the tears by scrunching my eyes as tight as I could. *Breathe, Mari, breathe.*

Sleep soon overtook me.

Chapter Five

Yuna arrived hours later, knocking quietly on my door. I sat upright, and grabbed my phone in a pretense of having been awake and waiting instead of having fallen asleep at the table.

"Come in," I called.

The aroma of hot coffee and buttered toast sent my stomach growling, and I flashed a weak grin at Yuna. She set down a large tray and arranged plates on the low table in front of me. Slices of thick white toast with jams and marmalade. A small bowl of fluffy scrambled eggs that still looked a bit runny. An incongruous green salad with a single red cherry tomato on top.

The western foods looked out of place on the traditional Japanese dishware. I fought to keep the frown off my face; I hadn't realized how much I'd been craving traditional Japanese food.

Were other guests getting steaming rice, miso soup, grilled local fish?

If there were any other guests.

Yuna finished off the table arrangement with a small vase containing a bright red poppy and poured me a cup of coffee from the carafe. "I hope you slept well?"

I inhaled long and deep before I answered.

"As well as expected." I ran a hand over my sleep-mussed hair. At least I'd taken a shower earlier. The events from the early morning rushed back to me; I didn't relish encountering Ogura-san again today. "Is it all right if I take a photo?" I gestured with my phone toward the breakfast dishes.

"Of course! Go right ahead." Yuna laughed and backed away from the table.

I adjusted the salad bowl and glass of orange juice to capture the light just so and snapped photos from different angles. Yuna looked over my shoulder.

"Those pictures are amazing! You're a great photographer."

I smiled, though the compliment grated my pride. These pics were barely Instagram-worthy. When was the last time I'd created my own art, instead of just displaying other people's work? "These photos are just to make my sister jealous. My real camera is over there." I gestured toward my black bag in the corner of the room.

"Oh! Are you a professional?" Yuna's face lit up. "I've always wanted to be a photographer—do you have Instagram? I have an account, but I'm sure it's nothing like yours."

I nodded and snapped one more shot, a close-up of the glistening red tomato. "Yeah, I'm here to photograph the inn." I paused, turned to look at her. "Actually, do you know who I should talk to about the grant? Ogura-san didn't seem to know any details last night."

"Grant?" Yuna frowned.

"The NASJ photography grant. You know, to document the inn?"

Yuna's brow furrowed. "Well, if it's business-related, probably the owner. She's not here, though." Yuna grabbed the carafe and topped off my coffee even though I hadn't taken a sip yet.

"Oh. Do you know when she'll be in?"

Yuna met my gaze for a moment, then glanced down, using a red cloth to wipe up a coffee drip. "I couldn't really say."

"I see."

Yuna shrugged. "My mother always says, 'When you're not sure what to do next, just sit back and don't break anything.'" She chuckled. "So why don't you just go explore the grounds?"

I was itching to get started on my work, but perhaps it would be nice to have a day to just settle in, scope things out.

"I heard the grounds are beautiful, but there weren't many photos online."

"Well, the gardens haven't been maintained, but you can tell how lovely everything used to be."

"Used to be?" I recalled the overgrown bushes by the entryway, the worn furniture. What had happened to this inn?

Yuna, ignoring my question, crossed the room to the sliding shoji panels along the outside wall and slid one open, revealing a shallow veranda. Two sun-faded rattan chairs and a table faced a wall of sliding glass panels overlooking a semi-fenced private garden. For a moment I saw a spectral vision of a young couple in their matching yukata lounging in these chairs back when they were new—sipping their tea and watching the birds hop along the edge of the bamboo fencing, distant furin chimes jingling in the summer breeze. But then the vision was gone, and only the old chairs in the cold, enclosed veranda remained. The sky was overcast and gray, threatening rain.

"You may not have the best weather today, I'm afraid," Yuna said, looking out the windows like a child hoping rain won't ruin her field trip.

"Indeed." It wasn't surprising, considering it was still winter. Why the hell did the inn, or the NASJ, or whoever dreamed up this grant, want a photographer to come in February, instead of early summer? Or at the peak of autumn foliage?

No, I wouldn't find brilliant colors for my photographs—only death and dormancy; it felt almost like a cruel joke.

"Yuna, I hope you don't mind me asking, but why do you work at this place? Are you even out of school yet?"

Yuna laughed, hugging the serving tray to her body. "Oh, this is just a part-time job—before school, some evenings and weekends. I'm just on-call, really." She smoothed a stray piece of hair that'd escaped from her ponytail behind her ear, lowered her eyes. "My favorite manga takes place in a ryokan, so I've always wanted to work in one."

She was so honest and open, it was hard not to find her endearing.

"Well, I should probably start eating before things get cold. Thank you, Yuna-chan." I put my hands together and whispered a quiet "*Itadakimasu.*"

"Of course." Yuna bowed. "Enjoy your day, Mari-san!" She slid the door closed behind her.

As I listened to her soft steps disappearing down the hall, I felt a pang of regret; why had I sent her away? I poked at the runny scrambled eggs with my fork, alone in the silent room. I took a sip of coffee. At least it was strong, much better than the airplane stuff.

Then, feeling pathetic, I pulled out my laptop to keep me company as I ate. Risa swore she could handle everything at the gallery, but she'd never had to oversee things by herself—I'd always been watching over her shoulder. What if something important had come up while I was on the plane? I scrolled down through a day's worth of emails. It didn't look like the gallery had caught fire just yet.

No emails from Thad—of course there weren't—but my heart still unexpectedly ached at their absence. There was an email from Risa. I opened it and smiled as I read my little sister's admonishments.

Relax! And enjoy the baths occasionally, for God's sake . . .
. . . Eat some good food (and send me pics—you know I'm jealous).
Please take care of yourself. Remember, it's what Mom would have wanted.

Risa, always the cheerleader. Tears welled in my eyes, and I swiped them away with the back of my hand. This was going to be a long four weeks. I clicked reply, but then stopped. What could I say to her? That everything had been a disappointment thus far? No, my response to Risa could wait—she wouldn't expect anything this morning. Or night. Or whatever the hell time it was in Chicago. I sighed and ate the tomato from the top of my breakfast salad.

I needed to leave the stuffy room, to breathe in some fresh air. Searching through the basket where I'd found the yukata and slippers, I found some split tabi socks so I could use the inn's wooden geta out into the garden.

I lifted my camera out of its travel case, shuddered, and set it back down. When was the last time I'd taken photos—real ones, with my Canon?

Not since before Mom's funeral.

It'd been over a decade since I'd set foot in a church for Grandpa Pete's funeral. That funeral had been upbeat, almost irreverently so, a true celebration of Grandpa's long life. Mom's funeral had been different.

Risa had held my hand, pulled me through the heavy front doors, prompted me to nod and smile politely at the murmured condolences before settling us into a pew in the front row. It wasn't Thad's fault he was out of town, that he couldn't cut the trip short to make it back for Mom's funeral, but it stung. Risa hadn't even asked where he was.

My Canon hung around my neck, dark sunglasses filtered my vision. While we waited for the service to begin, I tried to lift the camera, to capture the lilies and chrysanthemums adorning the pews, the dancing shadows of stained glass on the white stone floor. My mind had screamed, *This matters, Mari! Someday you will need this to remind you of today.* But I'd been numb, unable to lift the camera from around my neck, unwilling to remove the concealing sunglasses from my eyes.

In the end, I didn't take a single photo of Mom's funeral. I probably would remember the funeral more if I had. But maybe sometimes
forgetting is a kindness.

You can do this, Mari. It's just a garden.

Today could be about exploration, for discovering the best vistas.
No need to rush things; I could take a day or two to just discover the
space, formulate a plan. Four weeks was more than enough time to
gather material for a portfolio.

Through the glass I had a peek-a-boo view of the larger gardens beyond the bamboo fencing—shaggy pines, wild-looking bushes hovering
over craggy boulders. So haggard, forgotten. Melancholy.

In my yukata and jean jacket, and wearing my smaller camera bag
around my neck, I slipped through the sliding glass doors of my veranda
and outside into air so chill my breath came out in small puffs. I sat
down on the edge of the terrace that extended beyond the veranda and
slid on the geta sitting on the rock step. The sandals were tight over my
socks.

I'd visited Japanese gardens before, both in Japan and in various
cities around the world. Most of them had been compact, sometimes
even squeezed between city blocks, and they had all been meticulously
groomed—the bushes trimmed, the grasses snipped, the pathways regularly cleared of debris. So, despite Yuna's subtle warnings, I wasn't prepared when I stepped around the bamboo fencing of my private courtyard and stopped to take in my first glimpse of Yanagi Inn's gardens.

What must've once been a stunning view of intricately manicured
bushes, trees, and boulders was now a series of shaggy mounds, half-ob-
scured with vines and dead leaves, a testament to the entropy of nature. It didn't help that it was still winter, that no vestigial flowers were
blooming or fresh tendrils climbing. The dominant colors were gray-
green and murky brown, and the low, dark clouds overhead settled over
me like a shroud draped across my shoulders. How many gardeners
would have to be employed to keep such an estate maintained? And

how long had it been since that crew had been in service? This was not the beautiful, tranquil scenery I'd had in mind when Risa persuaded me to accept the grant.

But I was already here, and I had a job to do. I took a deep breath and followed the white gravel path snaking out in front of me.

Yet even with the unkempt, drooping trees, and the wild, uncut grass, something about the grounds captivated me. Hints of the garden's former glory were everywhere; in the subtle framing of the view from a granite bench, the perfectly spaced stepping-stones across the dry rock stream, the graceful fragility of an old pine tree propped up on a wooden crutch where its ancient, gnarled branches nearly brushed the ground.

Yes, there was beauty here. A somber, almost mournful, beauty.

I wandered on.

For all the overgrown remnants from yesteryear, I would occasionally see evidence of recent upkeep and repair; a juniper was skillfully trimmed, a granite water basin had been scooped of leaves and scrubbed clean. While these small spots of beauty were admirable, they were mere drops in a bucket, only serving to highlight the monumental task one would face in restoring the grounds.

Mom used to garden. Just scraggly flowers in pots on the front steps of her townhouse, and a smattering of plants in her postage-stamp back yard. She preferred herbs she could use in her kitchen or brightly colored pansies which she loved for their cheerfulness, rather than their practicality.

For the first few weeks of her hospitalization, I'd tried to keep up Mom's tiny garden, stopping by her townhouse every two or three days to water or pull out the weeds that inevitably grew. But during the lingering heat of autumn, with my schedule tightening and with me spending more and more time at the hospital, I didn't visit the plants as frequently, and when I did visit they looked worse and worse; the flowers were withered, the herbs gone to seed or nibbled away by birds or squirrels. Eventually I stopped coming all together. I asked Risa if she could be the one to pick up Mom's mail instead—just so I didn't have to see the physical manifestations of my negligence.

Thank god Mom didn't have any pets.

A cold breeze rippled through the shaggy pine trees around me, and they undulated like weary giants. I shivered, pulling my jacket tight across my chest. Every turn on the winding path delivered more and more vistas past their prime, the work of a clear master-gardener reduced to disheveled, gray-green plants and pools of water clouded with old leaves. I began to lose track of where I was and where I'd been; every direction of the snaking gravel paths appeared the same, and I had the sensation of being in the grip of a perpetual labyrinth, in which every turn, every path, was leading to the same, inevitable center.

I turned a corner and encountered the edge of a murky pond. I squatted down and stared into the water, dappled by light raindrops just beginning to fall. A single orange and white koi fish the length of my forearm rose out of the murk and opened his mouth, greedily gulping at the air. He was used to being fed. Or perhaps old enough to remember being fed by someone long ago.

I leaned forward—oh, how I wished I'd brought a rice cracker to share with this sad creature!—and saw my own reflection in the pond. A hole, deep inside my chest, widened with a wrenching ache.

Pond-Mari stared at me, judged me. Her face was drained, depleted—a pale shadow of her former self. She was wreckage I didn't have the energy to fix. I wasn't enough—I was never going to be enough.

The koi swam away, unsated.

At the pond's edge, I sank into the grass, which was too tall for a formal garden and now damp from the drizzle. The water seeped into my yukata, into my socks inside their sandals. My hair, coated by the fine mist, was already frizzy and tangling.

Why was I here? Was it to document the current, wild nature of the grounds or to bring out the hidden hints of the property's glorious past, perhaps in hope of bringing in investors to restore it? My mind returned to the grant printout still shoved in my laptop bag. Or was documenting the property "for the sake of posterity" the same as writing its obituary?

I was on the verge of dragging myself to my feet, slogging through the grass back to my lonely room to repack what little I'd removed from my bags, when a distant flash of movement caught my eye. A blur of white. I climbed to my feet, scanned the far edge of the pond—yes, there! A crane, pure white with flashes of black and red, all elegant and angular, had landed on the water's edge. He was taking slow, careful steps, lifting one impossibly thin leg out of the water at a time, his face ever vigilant.

I stood, transfixed, in the cold drizzle, wiping strands of wet hair out of my face. Such beauty. And what a stirring symbol for the ruins of this enchanting place—like a lotus flower rising out of muddy waters. My mind began formulating themes and imagery I could use for my eventual portfolio. But why was he here? Didn't those cranes only live up in Hokkaido?

The rain tapered off until it was little more than the occasional light drop on the surface of the pond, and the air was sharp and crisp, the lighting soft.

My camera.

I shifted the bag around to the front of my chest, fumbled with the zippers. My fingers trembled.

Then I closed my eyes, took a deep breath.

Relax, Mari—it's all right. This is only the first day. Photos can wait.

I let the camera bag fall to my side.

The crane took a few delicate steps along the water's edge then paused, one foot in the air. In that moment I could have sworn he stared me in the eyes, communing with me. Then he turned, flung out his wings, and after a few powerful steps thrust himself into the air.

I clenched my hands into fists, the moment lost. I tried to track his path across the horizon; he didn't fly very high, so he couldn't be flying far. The crane began floating downward into a landing position, but by that point he'd dropped behind the tree line, obscured by the pine trees specifically designed to control the vista.

"Beautiful, isn't she?"

A quiet voice struck up behind me, and I spun around.

A tiny old woman, not just short in stature but also fine-boned, stood behind me in the grass. She was dressed in a simple brown wrap top and trousers and outdoor sandals. In her hand she held a small trowel, a basket of sodden leaves in the other. Something about how her smile reflected in the deep wrinkles around her eyes struck a chord deep within me.

"Oh, the crane is a she?" I murmured as I took in the woman's sun-worn appearance. The groundskeeper?

"Yes, she has a nest not far from here. Or at least she used to." The old woman craned her neck as if to catch a view of where the bird had landed. "It is rather unusual to have a crane like her in these parts. But, then again, these gardens are rather special."

"I see."

We stood for a few moments in companionable silence.

Then I noticed the old woman was watching me closely. "What is your name?" She smiled again, but this time her eyes didn't reflect her smile, but rather narrowed as if inspecting my features.

"Marissa Lennox. But please, you can call me Mari. And you are . . . ?"

She laughed, as if it were a silly question. "I'm Honda Keiko. Tell me, Lennox-san—"

"Oh, please, just call me Mari." I understood the politeness, but this woman was older than my mother. Older than Mom would ever get to be. I swallowed, hard.

"Ok, Mari-san, why are you here?"

Ah, another great existential question.

But at least this woman wasn't like Ogura-san.

These words were not accusatory—they were more curious, probing. More like a priest asking me to search my heart and confess my sins.

"I'm not sure. I mean, I'm here to photograph Yanagi Inn for the sake of posterity, but I'm not sure . . ." I trailed off, gesturing with one useless hand. I couldn't finish that sentence without being rude. *I'm not sure if I'm supposed to be recording the sad state of this place or trying to capture the former, tragic beauty, now fully gone to seed?*

She looked me over, slowly, from my scraggly hair down to my wet tabi socks, then nodded. "I understand."

I'd never felt so seen.

Her tone hadn't been unkind or dismissive, but, rather, had a note of *I've seen all I need to see.* This must've been the case, for she followed this up with a short bow, looked up at the sky, and then walked away.

I watched Honda's departure, her strides unusually long for such a short person. I should've asked about the small improvements she'd been making to the gardens. I should've asked about the fish, and if anyone feeds them. A few minutes passed as I stood by the pond, watching the *plip-plops* of individual raindrops upon the water's surface, trying to summon enough energy to take out my camera and at least attempt a few shots of my surreal surroundings.

But I wasn't strong enough.

Instead, I turned from the pond to trudge back toward my room, just in time for the sky to open, unleashing a deluge of cold, cold rain.

I hugged my camera bag to my body, shielding it from the downpour. Why hadn't I brought an umbrella? My socked feet slid and slipped within the wooden sandals as I ran down the gravel paths in what I prayed was the direction of the inn. A crack of thunder sounded so loud it shook the very ground beneath my feet, and I stumbled, nearly fell, only just catching myself on a large boulder gray-green with slime.

I kept moving, my head bowed as I ran, allowing the icy rain to stream down my face and mix with my warm tears.

Chapter Six

Kira kira hikaru,
Osora no hoshi yo
Mabataki shite wa
Minna wo miteru
Kira kira hikaru,
Osora no hoshi yo

Mom was singing to me my favorite song—a Japanese "Twinkle Twinkle Little Star"—and she was wiping my brow with a cool, damp cloth. Her ministrations were soothing, reassuring, and I let myself simply be awash in the comfort of it. I opened my eyes to slits, not wanting to let her know I was awake, and watched her outline in the dimly lit room, the movement of her arms and shoulders as she tucked in the blankets around me, heard the gentle sound as she continued the song with a hum.

I smiled and opened my eyes a little wider, and Mom turned toward me.

But it wasn't Mom.

She had no face—just papery, peeling skin where my mother's hazel eyes and crooked nose and warm smile should be.

The not-Mom leaned over me. Clumps of her blond hair, loosed from her scalp, fell onto my blankets. Whimpering, weeping noises came from her not-mouth.

I tried to scream, but it came out a low moan, an animal noise of fear and aversion, and I scrambled out of my bed and backward across the tatami floor until my hand slipped and I fell down, down, down . . .

"Mari-san? How are you feeling?"

I opened my eyes to find Yuna leaning over me, brows crinkled.

Good question. My skin felt damp, clammy, and my heart had an erratic beat. I could remember a rough night of sweating, of tossing and turning. Of delirium. But now, as I looked around the room, the fog in my brain lifted a little.

And I was hungry—that was probably a good sign.

"Much better, thank you." I smiled up at her. The room seemed unusually bright and sunny. Yuna had opened up the sliding partitions to expose the veranda with its window-lined wall.

"I found you on the floor last night. You were delirious with fever, so I helped you into bed. Were you out in that storm?" Little mother hen Yuna frowned at me, full of disapproval.

I nodded. Memories of stumbling into my room and collapsing in a soggy pile rose in my mind. "What time is it?" The storm must have passed already.

Yuna sank back on her heels and gave me a bit of a smirk. "It's seven o'clock in the morning. You slept through the day and night."

I sat up. "You're kidding me."

"Nope! I was just coming to see if you were hungry."

What was wrong with me? I laid a hand on my growling stomach, my face flushing with warmth.

"Yeah, I think I'm starving."

"No problem! I'll bring your breakfast in right away." Yuna smiled and jumped to her feet. I marveled at how well she moved in her tight-fitting kimono. I certainly couldn't do that.

When she was gone, I sank back onto the bed. I must've caught something passing through airports or on the plane, but I'm sure to Yuna it looked like I got sick from the storm. I chuckled; I was a living trope.

I closed my eyes, tried to refocus, but fuzzy night memories were hiding just under the surface. Had I heard weeping again? I frowned, tried to reach out with a tendril of consciousness to dig deeper, but to no avail. Had it been Yuna?

I was at a loss for any other explanation. Should I ask her about it? Just say, "So, have you been crying in the middle of the night? Me, too! What's your trigger?"

No, I couldn't do that to the poor girl.

Yuna's soft knock sounded on the door, and she padded into the room carrying her customary tray. For a moment my heart soared, thinking she'd brought a resplendent display of the ryokan's finest Japanese breakfast items. But then she knelt and started unloading her dishes. White toast. Pats of butter. Slightly runny eggs.

I sighed inwardly but forced a smile. "Thanks, Yuna-chan."

After breakfast, I pulled out my grant printout, reread the few guidelines I did have:

> . . . for the purposes of documenting, via artistic photography and for the sake of posterity, the property known hereafter as YANAGI INN . . .
>
> . . . resulting in the aggregation of a completed portfolio, for the purposes of public display . . .

Via artistic photography. For the sake of posterity. Completed portfolio.
The grant paperwork was so vague I wanted to scream.

But that vagueness also left room for artistic interpretation. I could just capture beautiful images and sort everything out later when I had more information. At least it was a place to start. Besides, when in doubt, I could always follow the advice of Yuna's mother—"when you're not sure what to do next, just sit back and don't break anything." It was a plan, of sorts.

Though I was feeling better, I was still sweaty and gross and badly needed a shower—I did *not* want to be known as the smelly American.

But then I'd get down to work.

My fever was gone, my hair was washed, and my belly was reasonably satiated with a few bites of eggs and grapes. A smile twitched at the corner of my mouth. Maybe today could be a good day.

I adjusted the camera bag so it hung at my side, checked to make sure I had the right lens on my Canon. I wasn't going to approach this session with preconceived notions about what I should be photographing. I would let individual landscapes, nature itself, call to me.

I stepped out into the fresh morning of a new day and slid on the geta. They were clean; Yuna must've wiped off the mud and replaced them on the stone outside. I really needed to thank her for watching over me.

The weather was warmer than the day before, and the sun was shining through cottony wisps of clouds. The gardens felt so much more alive than they had yesterday in the dreary rain. I crunched along the gravel, startling the occasional rabbit or small sparrow out of the tall grass on the path's edge. It was early yet, and the air still had that crisp dampness which made me feel like I was breathing morning dew deep into my lungs. Yesterday's storm had left new puddles, filled granite basins with murky water, and formed ruts and channels in the gravel paths. I hopped over the small trenches as if playing hopscotch.

A light breeze swept over me, smelling of damp earth and teasing the last lingering drops of water off the overhanging pine branches to fall upon my head. I walked without conscious intent, letting my feet take me round winding turns, through tunnels of overgrown bushes which snatched at my yukata as I passed, knowing that somehow I would end up where I needed to be. I wasn't surprised when I found myself drawn to the lonely pond where I'd met the koi fish yesterday. Where I'd seen the crane.

I'd forgotten to bring a rice cracker for the fish. An image of the koi with his hungry lips sent a surprisingly strong pang through the hole deep in my chest. I shook my head, bit the inside of my cheek. It was just a fish; I'd been hoping for grilled fish for breakfast, for god's sake. Yet something about that fish stirred up such intense feelings of guilt it made me want to avoid the pond altogether.

Yet I couldn't keep away.

When I approached the water, I turned in a slow circle, taking in the view from all directions; the slight mist rising off the pond, the yellowed grass lining the gravel walkway, the old pine tree leaning on its mossy wooden crutch behind me. All was silent, all was still. Every view was like a watercolor painting left out in the rain, the colors running and blending into muddy browns and grays.

Nothing called to me. The camera at my side might as well have been a glass paperweight dragging me down, for nothing stirred me. Inside, I was nothing but deadened bones and sinews and organs going through the motions. This Mari was unable to summon enough of an artistic spark even for the minor task of framing a shot amidst such solemn, subdued beauty.

I sank down on a granite bench embraced by bushes, obviously designed to be a resting spot to take in the beauty of the pond and its environs. Beauty—what did I know about beauty? I hadn't made beautiful photography in years. Perhaps I didn't have an eye for sweetness and light anymore.

I slid the camera bag from my shoulder and set it beside me on the cold, hard bench. The dampness of the stone seeped through my yukata into my skin, and my body spasmed with an involuntary shiver.

What little energy I had left leeched out of my body, seeped out through my pores and down through the stone into the cold ground of this dilapidated estate with its scratchy bushes and foul waters and fish begging me—judging me—with their hungry maws.

I allowed my shoulders to sink. Entropy. It was swallowing me.

And it felt so natural.

But then a noise—a flutter of wings, perhaps—sounded beside me, and I lifted my head.

There, flying just a few inches above the still surface of the pond, was the white crane with its red and gray head. He—no, she!—was grace incarnate, with black beady eyes which saw everything, which took me in as well, sitting on my cold bench with my hair draggling in my face.

The crane flapped lazily, as if the grand skimming of the pond took little effort, but she kept her head forward, focused, as if she had somewhere to go. Somewhere she needed to be.

Without thinking, I jumped to my feet, grabbed my camera bag, and followed.

I ran along the gravel, though my feet slipped inside their geta and the camera bag banged against my chest. My breath came in painful, ragged gulps, and I scolded myself for my lack of conditioning; I used to be able to run for miles. The path kept meandering away from the pond, twisting deeper into the bushes and coniferous trees and rock gardens so covered with debris and moss only the sentinel stones were still visible, but I knew another water vista would eventually appear. I prayed I wouldn't run into Honda, though something told me she'd probably just laugh and point me in the right direction for my wild crane chase.

Running into Ogura-san would be another story.

There! A gap in the trees opened up, and I could see the crane still gliding over the water, almost impossibly slow. But then she rose higher into the air, swooping up to then curve down to land on a white stone pillar sticking up out of the water not far away. Maybe I could find a better vantage point and snap a picture.

After another curve around another pod of tall, scraggly bushes—there! The view opened before me—a beach of smooth gray stones disappearing into the water. And there, in the middle of the murky water, rose a line of stone pillars. The crane stood upon one, frozen, watching me like a statue on its pedestal.

For a moment the crane and I simply locked gazes. She was still some twenty feet away, but I could see into her beady black eyes, and I knew she could see deep into mine. Something inside me softened then, like a block of ice thawing in the sunshine, and I smiled.

I slowly reached down, unzipped my camera bag, and silently removed the lens cap from my Canon. I imperceptibly tilted my camera up until it was at the correct angle to take a shot of the crane without taking my eyes off her. I adjusted the angle again, held the shutter down for a series of shots. Tick-tick, tick-tick. I prayed the sound was quiet enough in the otherwise still air that it wouldn't startle the bird. I shifted my arms to the left slowly, tilted the camera again. Tick-tick, tick-tick.

Without warning, the crane spread her white wings and leapt off the pillar. With long, sweeping movements she flapped up high into the air away from me, legs straight out behind her like a graceful arrow my eyes couldn't help but follow.

The crane flew higher and higher until she landed across the pond on top of a weeping willow, its slender branches so long and drooping they dipped into the water. I took a few ginger steps out onto the gray beach to peer around the bushes. Oh—my heart began fluttering inside my chest—the tree wasn't on the far side of the pond.

It was on an island.

The pillars must be remnants of cylindrical piers from an old bridge. One that had been removed, but which clearly once led out to the island.

My breath caught in my throat. Distant vibrations of a cicada song tickled the edge of my consciousness, and my hands, still clutching my camera, began to tremble. Cicadas? I tore my gaze from the crane to glance around. It was February—there couldn't possibly be cicadas, could there? But then the sound faded, and all was silent once again.

I must've imagined it.

I slid my feet out of their sandals, pulled off my socks, and stared at the murky water, cluttered with the graying remains of duckweed. It couldn't be very deep here—could it?

My heart raced as I stepped into the cold (so cold!) shallow water, peering around the overgrown bushes to get a more complete view. The island seemed large—larger than entire urban Japanese gardens I'd visited—though it was difficult to discern its true size, and the edges were so wild with overgrown plants I could see nothing of its interior. The island clearly hadn't been touched in many, many years. I strained but couldn't see another access point.

Perhaps the old bridge was the only route leading to the crane's island. And it had been destroyed.

But I needed to get out to that island. I felt a sudden, wrenching compulsion pulling me from across the water. I was standing, feet immersed up to my freezing ankles, and gazing longingly out over the pond when I heard a rustling noise behind me.

I closed my eyes, dread rising inside my chest.

"*Lennox-san.*"

I let out a breath, smoothed down the front of my yukata in a vain attempt at dignity, and slowly turned in the shallow water toward Ogura.

She looked me over, starting at my bedraggled hair, moving down to my improperly fastened yukata, and finishing at my bare feet standing in the murky pond water. Her lips were a tight line with deep frown wrinkles on either side, her eyes narrow.

"What do you think you're doing?"

"I-I was just wondering about the island. Is there another way to get there? The bridge is . . . out." My voice came out quiet, excruciatingly meek.

"Perhaps the rules have not been adequately explained." Ogura spoke with a cold authority that shot straight through my skin. "You are not to stray from the authorized paths, and you are not to go anywhere near that island."

Under her stare I wanted to sink into myself, shrivel up inside my damp yukata until nothing was visible, nothing to judge or criticize. I stared at a moss-covered rock on the side of the path, silent, unmoving.

Then, with a quiet rustle, she was gone.

I gave the island one more long look then dragged my heavy feet out of the water and back, dripping, into their sandals.

The day had barely begun, and I was done—deflated like a pricked water balloon seeping out its last trickle of water. I began the long, plodding walk back to my room.

Chapter Seven

Once back in the inn and dressed in a fresh, seafoam green yukata, the world felt a bit more manageable. Yuna had explained that Yanagi Inn didn't serve lunch, and that guests generally went on outings during the day or into the village for a midday meal, but if I didn't feel like leaving the property, I could request some onigiri to stave off hunger. I told her that suited me fine. I didn't even know how far it was to the nearest town. So now, left out on my low table, was a large rice ball wrapped in clear plastic and three packets of soy sauce.

Three? Who on earth would use three packets for a single onigiri? It seemed a bit much, even for an ignorant American.

I was hungry, so I unwrapped the onigiri. The scent of sour plum filled my senses and I inhaled deeply. Though I'd never used soy sauce on onigiri in my life, I craved the familiar flavor and picked up one of the sauce packets. After an unsuccessful attempt with my fingernails, I bit the edge with my teeth and tugged, ripping the packet open and spilling its contents on the floor in one terrifically smooth motion. The deep brown liquid seeped into the fibers of the tatami mat.

Shit. Shit. SHIT. I scrambled around, searching for a napkin or cloth to soak up the dark liquid. What I wouldn't pay for a single paper towel!

Finding nothing of use in the austere room, I groaned and used the sleeve of my seafoam yukata to dab at the sauce, hoping it would magically suck up all the liquid, leaving the flooring unmarred. It didn't work. Of course it didn't. A deep brownish splotch the size of a quarter was clearly visible on the otherwise pristine mat. I was doing a bang-up job of being the stupid American.

After hiding the incriminating soy sauce packet in the bathroom trash, I returned to my onigiri. As I savored the familiar flavors from my childhood, I thought again about Risa, about how I still hadn't responded to her email. But what could I say? Risa didn't need to know how terribly everything was going, how run-down and forsaken the glorious Yanagi Inn really was.

I opened my laptop, pulled up Risa's email, and hit reply.

She at least needed to know I was still alive.

With my hunger satiated and sanity somewhat restored, I unzipped my bag and pulled out my camera, a fierce determination punctuating each movement. Why did I let Ogura-san get to me so?

The grant paperwork had said something about a portfolio and a public display of the images. What if I got permission to have an exhibition back home at the gallery, in addition to whatever was done here in Japan? Would that be allowed? A slow smile spread across my face as I pictured a blown-up image of the crane on the gallery's north wall, ikebana vases filled with fresh flowers sitting on the white pedestals I typically used for displaying pottery. I could ask Hamamura-san with the Chicago Ikebana Club to help and . . .

I was getting ahead of myself.

But the idea of my own photography hanging in the gallery warmed my soul, set my body in motion. I could still salvage today, take beautiful photographs wherever I found inspiration. Yanagi Inn was more than just its gardens, after all; it made sense for me to capture interior photos, too.

I lifted the camera with trembling hands, took a deep breath. *You can do this, Mari.*

I snapped a close shot of the blood-red poppy in its tiny vase, then tilted the camera back to check the image. There, I did it. I was taking photos again, and that alone was a big step.

Moving slowly around the room, I took shots of the mundane pieces of beauty I found; the wintry ikebana flower display, the sunlight spilling through partially opened shoji screens and across the tatami mats, the worn calligraphy scroll on the wall. I dug through the dark recesses of my brain to recall the stylized symbol. Harmony? Peace?

For a brief, perverse moment I considered photographing the soy sauce stain on the tatami mat, a Rorschach blot on an otherwise unmarred surface.

I decided against it.

Buoyed by the pockets of beauty I discovered in my own room, I poked my head out into the hallway. Empty, silent. I slipped out of the room, camera in hand.

Even at midday the hallways were dark, the doors to adjoining rooms all closed. After a few arbitrary twists and turns, I was surprised to find myself in the front lobby with its 1970s decor. No one was behind the reception desk, so I lifted my camera and began snapping photos. The rattan chairs, the stack of glossy brochures for local restaurants, the framed black and white newspaper reviews of the inn from decades past.

I snapped a close-up of the brown leather guestbook on the counter with its stylized willow tree logo on the front. Then curiosity got the better of me and I opened the book. Page after page of signatures and dates and comments and, incongruously, some childish drawings.

I stared at the drawing of a single Japanese maple leaf, traced the lines of red ink with the tip of my finger. Something about the little sketches felt oddly familiar. I pulled back the pages and let them flip through my fingers. The Japanese maple leaf floated down the side of the page like in a flipbook. I smiled. On the final page of the sequence a little cicada, sketched in green, was sitting on the leaf. I marveled at the insect; someone was quite the little artist. Then a humming, buzzing, the sound of an enormous tree populated with trilling cicadas filled my head. And laughter—children's joyous laughter. I could almost feel the warm sun on my skin, smell the distant woodfire smoke. I closed my eyes to savor the sensations, but the sounds faded away, the memory disappearing as quickly as it'd surfaced. At least it'd felt like a memory.

With trembling hands, I lifted my camera and snapped a photo of the tiny maple leaf and its cicada friend, capturing the image the only way I knew how.

As I continued turning the pages, I couldn't help but read snippets of guest comments:

"The most relaxing stay I've had in years . . ."
". . . couldn't have asked for better service from Yanagi Inn's okami and her staff."
"The gardens were superb, as always."

I glanced at the dates. Nearly thirty years ago.

My throat tightened, and I closed the book, gently. What had happened all those years ago? Why had the owner let everything fall apart when Yanagi Inn was clearly once such a special place, its gardens such an extraordinary feature? The questions gnawed at the back of my brain.

I took one last look around the dated lobby, then stepped back up onto the tatami floors and into the dark hallways to continue my expedition. If only I'd had a chance to see the estate in its prime. How beautiful it must've been. I sighed.

After a few moments of tiptoeing in silence, the sound of whistling struck up in the distance. I cocked my head—the song was familiar, in a tickling-the-edges-of-my-mind kind of way. It was a sad tune, not at all the kind of song one would generally whistle while working (for I assumed it was one of the staff going about her daily duties). I finally approached an open doorway, a small "Closed for Cleaning" wooden sign hanging beside it, leading to the baths.

I pushed my way through the hanging cloth noren with the symbol for "hot water," through the changing room and, still following the sounds of whistling, stepped through the doorway into the steamy bath area. Then I froze.

Mom.

Wearing a navy blue kimono, sleeves tied back, mopping.

Mom.

Whistling her favorite song, her unmistakable blond hair pulled back in a loose ponytail. Pushing a mop through the strands of wet hair slicking the tile floor.

Ice water trickled down the back of my yukata and goosebumps erupted down my arms.

No, no, no. Not again.

I bit back a sob and pressed the heels of my palms into my eyes, taking deep breaths and inhaling the inexplicable aroma of freshly peeled mandarins. *Calm down, Mari, calm down. It can't be Mom, it can't be.*

I reopened my eyes.

The woman was Yuna.

Of course it was Yuna, in plastic sandals, scrubbing the tile floors around the baths with a wet mop. I let out a long, slow breath. *What the hell is wrong with me?* I couldn't blame lack of sleep or jet lag or sleeping pills this time.

I practiced my breathing techniques, brought my heart back under control, one hand braced on the doorframe. Thank god Yuna hadn't seen me yet.

Yuna's dark hair was tied back and covered with a bright red tenu-gui, and her cheeks were rosy from her exertion in the warm room. The water droplets on the tiles glistened, and for a moment it was as if time stood still, and in slow motion I lifted my camera to capture this perfect moment.

I don't know if she heard the flutter of the camera or if she just sensed my presence, but Yuna turned and looked up at me, her surprise warming into a smile. She leaned against the propped-up mop and wiped her forehead with the back of her hand, posing as the stereotypical hard-working housekeeper. I laughed, my anxiety evaporating, and I snapped a few photos before she relaxed into laughter herself.

"I hope it's ok if I take a few photos? I guess I'll have to get signed releases from the staff at some point . . ."

"Of course! But I thought you'd be out photographing the grounds again today?"

The laughter died on my lips, but I forced a smile. "I was, but I thought I'd take some interior photos, too. It's ok if I scout around inside, right?"

"Well, I'm not sure there's much to photograph inside. Besides me, of course." Yuna posed again with the mop, throwing up a peace sign and winking.

I smiled, and obligingly took another flurry of photos.

"I better get back to work—Ogura-san will kill me if she thinks I'm playing around instead of cleaning."

I leaned against the doorframe and watched her scrubbing tiles awhile longer. Memories of scrubbing the floors in the international school I attended as a child floated to mind. Funny, how the teachers decided that making the kids clean the school was one of the Japanese traditions they wanted to maintain.

"Want some help?" I pulled off my camera and hung it from a wooden towel hook on the wall, then began rolling up the sleeves of my yukata.

Yuna turned back toward me, eyes wide. "You're joking, right?" A vague frown appeared on her face. "I-I have a lot I need to get done."

"Not at all! I enjoy cleaning. It's therapeutic to give something a good scrub." I kicked off my slippers and held out a hand for her mop.

"But Ogura-san . . ." She looked toward the doorway, brow furrowed, as if her boss might appear at any moment.

A twinge of anxiety shot through me, but I forced a smile and patted Yuna on her mop hand. "Oh, who cares what Ogura-san thinks!" I said with more confidence than I felt.

She relinquished her mop with a chuckle and a shake of her head. I set to work mopping the tiles with a vigor I hadn't felt in a long while, soon building up a fine sweat in the moist heat of the room. The movements felt energizing, satisfying like scratching an itch; I wasn't lying when I told Yuna I found cleaning therapeutic. I just rarely did it.

Yuna had been watching me from inside the empty bath as she wrung out some cleaning rags. "You're an interesting woman, Mari-san. Not at all what I was expecting."

"Oh?" I paused in my vigorous mopping, wiped my soy sauce-stained sleeve across my forehead. "And what kind of woman were you expecting?"

"I'm not sure. Ogura-san said—" Yuna broke off, turned away for a moment like she was too occupied with a stubborn stain on the edge of the bath. "Well, I wasn't expecting a guest to help me with my chores. But I do appreciate it." She lowered her voice, leaned toward me. "Ogura-san does tend to overload me with tasks sometimes."

"It does seem odd to have you scrubbing this whole place—has anyone even used the baths recently?"

"Well it's the off-season now, but usually we have a couple regulars who come in and bathe a few times a week." Yuna waved her wash rag dismissively, as if a few patrons a week were normal for a ryokan of this size.

I stopped mopping, turned my full attention back to Yuna.

"But what has happened to this place? Why are the gardens so overgrown? I saw an island, and there used to be a bridge but it's gone, and the grass is so high . . ." I gestured with exasperation toward the high overhead window looking out to the gardens.

Yuna sighed, dropped her rag in the bucket, but didn't look up to meet my gaze. "I did hear the inn used to be very popular, bustling with guests. But that was before my time." She reached into the bucket, squeezed out the soapy rag. "I've heard the owner has bad memories of that island, but I've never pried into her reasons."

What kind of bad memories would make a businesswoman turn a bustling vacation destination into the vacant shadow of a resort it was today?

"Do you know when the owner will be back?"

"Back?" Yuna cocked her head.

"When she'll come here to the inn? So I can talk to her?"

Yuna turned away again, idly rubbed her rag against the wall of the tub. "I really couldn't say."

I felt my heart begin to sink, but then I gripped my mop tighter. No, this was good—maybe without the owner around I'd have more freedom.

"Are there any other routes out to the island? I'd love to visit it."

Yuna shook her head. "I wouldn't know. Since the owner prefers it left alone, we leave it alone." Her tone carried a finality quite at odds with her usual happy-go-lucky nature.

I nodded, though I was hardly satisfied with that answer. Something about that island called to me, drew me in like a flame drew in moths.

Or cicadas.

Yuna was watching me, and I realized I must've been staring into space, the buzzing cicadas dancing on the edge of my consciousness.

I shot an embarrassed smile at her and started mopping again.

The wooden handle was rough in my hands, and I wondered if Yuna's palms were blistered from her work here. But I kept mopping, feeling the muscles in my arms and shoulders warming up. If I needed a Band-Aid later, it'd just be a reminder of scrubbing the bath together with Yuna, of sweating through the thin fabric of my yukata, of my body feeling more alive than it had in a long, long time.

That night I woke up shivering, grasping for the blanket I must've kicked off in my restless sleep. I sat up in the dark, unable to reconcile any of the vague shapes in the room around me.

After a moment, the fog cleared. *Oh, the inn.* I fumbled at the foot of the bed until I found the thick comforter, pulled it up over my shoulders, and closed my eyes again.

But sleep wouldn't return.

Events from the day played through my mind, from the good (scrubbing the baths with Yuna) to the bad (encountering Ogura while ankle-deep in cold pond water). Remembering Yuna's cheerful expression as she posed for my pictures brought a smile to my face, even as I lay sleepless in the night. Not all the inn's charms rested in its forgotten gardens.

As I sifted through the day's images, and the old guestbook's achingly obsolete reviews flipped through my mind, a sound of soft whimpering arose in the distance. The whimpering was quiet, but in an unsettling way, as if the source of the sound was being muffled, smothered by some large, unseen hand.

My ears strained for more, my eyes now wide open and staring into the darkness.

Could it be Yuna? I propped myself up on my elbows, my heart racing. I tilted my head, allowing the rise and fall of the whimpers to roll over me. No—after being with Yuna so much that day, I began to doubt it was her. Not only did it lack the cheerful energy Yuna exuded, but the very tone and timbre were not Yuna's.

But if it wasn't Yuna, then who?

Or what? I shivered. Dark, winged shadows flitted through my brain.

But then an image of the graceful white crane, gliding over the water of the pond and settling into the nest on her desolate island rose to my mind and I wondered; could those sounds be the lamentations of the lonely crane?

This thought melted my fear into a much gentler poignant ache, and I settled back under the comforter, flexing my icy feet under the blanket until they began to feel warm again. Soon the crying faded, or else I fell back asleep, for the next thing I knew it was five a.m. and I was wide awake once again.

Chapter Eight

"Yuna," I said quietly as she laid out the plain toast, runny scrambled eggs, and green salad arrangement I'd become so accustomed to, "do you . . ."

I stopped, uncertain how to delicately ask about the crying. The subtle idiosyncrasies of the Japanese language had never been my strong suit. It was hard enough to keep from constantly swearing.

"Do-you-think-you-could-bring-me-a-Japanese-breakfast-tomorrow-please?" I spluttered out in a rush.

Shit. I hadn't meant to say that. I looked down at the floor, at the soy sauce stain on the tatami. The edges of the stain were hazier than before, as if morphing into something different. Almost like the shape of a tiny skull.

No, it was just my imagination. I tugged my comforter to cover up the incriminating stain.

Yuna looked up at me and for a moment my heart sank. Why had I asked her that? Now I must look like the ungrateful, demanding American woman who must have her dishes served just so. I might as well have asked for a silver spoon and a tureen of shark fin soup.

But then a smile broke across Yuna's face. "Of course! Oh, I'm so glad you asked. Ogura-san said you wouldn't like Japanese food because—well, you know," Yuna faltered, turned her gaze downward, "but I had a feeling you'd prefer a Japanese breakfast." She started stacking the plates of untouched food back onto her lacquered tray. "Oh no, please—I didn't mean right now! I'm happy to eat the breakfast you brought."

"It's no problem at all, Mari-san! Our motto at Yanagi Inn is '*It is always our pleasure to please our guests.*' We are more than happy to make you a breakfast better suited to your tastes."

The line felt canned, practiced, but Yuna looked so happy to be clearing the dishes of the uninspired meal that I didn't have the heart to object any further. Plus, the mental image of steaming rice and hot miso soup made my stomach growl.

Yuna rushed out the door and slid it closed behind her with a single, socked foot. I smiled at her boundless energy.

I remained in bed, luxuriating in the idea of a maid bringing me a warm, delectable breakfast while I relaxed. Normally, I hated being waited on, actively disliked eating at fine restaurants where the waiters tried to put cloth napkins in ladies' laps, or even going to a friend's house who insisted on cooking everything herself while I had to stand back, helpless, and watch her cook and plate everything for me. But today I felt like a rajah of old, waited on by my many servants who hovered in the sultry wings of my palace, anticipating my every need.

Then I immediately felt guilty and scooted over to the table.

Yuna returned so quickly that I wondered if the chef had had a spare breakfast waiting for just such a request. She brandished a lacquered tray laden with the heavenly scents of a true ryokan breakfast, a satisfied smile upon her face.

I inhaled deeply, savoring the scent of warm rice and grilled fish. Now *this* felt like Japan.

As Yuna set out the many dishes—a rounded mound of white rice, miso soup with cubes of tofu floating on top, an elegant plate with grilled fish, tiny dishes of pickled daikon and eggplant—I summoned the courage to ask the question I'd meant to ask her before. "Yuna-chan," I began again slowly, "do you go home at night when you're on duty? Or do you sleep here at the ryokan?"

Yuna let out a laugh, loud and jarring, almost knocking over the tiny vase with its single red poppy she had just placed on my table. "Of course I go home! Did you think I live here? I have a life outside this job, you know."

"I didn't mean it like that. I just . . ." I trailed off, idly repositioning a piece of fish with my chopsticks.

Yuna, still kneeling beside me, cocked her head.

I chewed the inside of my lip. In the light of day, my question sounded silly even to me. I picked up my phone, snapped pictures of my breakfast dishes from various angles, readjusted the flower in its vase and slid it closer to my teacup. Click. Finally, a breakfast to make Risa jealous. But then again, my little sister didn't have the same nostalgia for Japan that I did, since she was only six when we moved away. I didn't even have photos to help remind her, since Mom "accidentally" left all our photo albums behind. No wonder she remembered next to nothing about our life here. I barely remembered, and I was ten when we left.

Yuna was still watching me closely, hugging the serving tray to her chest. "What is it, Mari-san?"

I took a deep breath. "Do you know anything about the nighttime crying?" I continued nonchalantly taking photos, tweaking the angle of the ceramic bowls and plates here or there, though I snuck a quick glance at Yuna's face.

She hesitated for a telling moment. "Crying? I'm sure it's just the wind. This ryokan is over a hundred years old—it is very drafty."

I set my phone down on the table with a click. We both remained silent, unmoving. I stared at the rounded bowl of rice, artfully sprinkled with a few black sesame seeds, trying to decide how to respond. "It's not the wind."

"Oh Mari-san!" Yuna leaned forward, dropping her tray to the tatami floor. "Do you want to know what I really think it is?" She paused dramatically, eyebrows raised. "A spirit—or a ghost!"

A thin trickle of ice dripped down my spine. "Yuna-chan," I said, trying to control the quaver in my voice, "you read too much manga."

"No, I mean it—I heard it once, the crying, very late at night before I even started working here. It wasn't natural."

"It could just be the crane."

"The crane? What crane?"

We stared at each other for a few heart beats, at an impasse.

"Never mind." I picked up my chopsticks, snapped up a piece of pickled daikon.

Yuna nodded, picked up her tray. Her lips were tight, and her eyes had lost their sparkle. I wanted to say something to her but was at a loss. For some reason I didn't want to talk about the crane—as if it were my own private discovery, and I wasn't ready to bring in anyone else yet. Besides Honda-san, of course.

Yuna bowed silently in the doorway, then left the room.

I set down my chopsticks, stared out the glass windows to the rocks and shaggy bushes beyond.

I'd never believed in ghosts.

Years ago, Risa convinced me to go on a ghost tour of Chicago and I just found it boring—besides the genuine history of the old buildings, of course. It didn't make sense for a human being to die and then leave behind some part of itself in an old hotel or a graveyard as if it were a discarded scarf or worn hat. Death was permanent, immutable. I clenched my jaw, fighting back the sudden wave of emotion I knew would, if unchecked, devolve into tears.

Yet . . . I couldn't explain the sounds any more than Yuna could. Maybe there really was something out of the ordinary at work, even if it wasn't ghostly.

Or maybe Yuna really did just read too much manga.

After my first true ryokan breakfast, I set out into the gardens again—armed with my easy-access camera bag and travel umbrella—intent on finding the crane.

My feet led me down the gravel paths, the air around me cool but not cold, the sky gray but unthreatening. My belly was full, yet I had a lightness in my step. The twists and turns of the garden's paths were slowly becoming familiar—here, the intersection with the gnarled old pine resting on his ancient crutch, there the mossy rock garden with a cracked granite bench. I smiled at these landmarks, warming to their seasoned personalities, but didn't linger to appreciate them. I had somewhere I needed to be.

Soon I found myself at the spot where the old bridge had been, where I'd seen the crane resting on the broken column, but no one was there. Just an old toad croaking on the edge of the water. I squatted down, snapped a few photos of him, though his gray-brown skin blended so thoroughly with the mud and leaves I wasn't sure how well he'd show up.

I stood, then turned in a slow circle, assessing my surroundings. The weather was surprisingly warm for late winter, the sun just now peeking out of the clouds. I closed my eyes, savored the sensation of warm light on my eyelids. Sometimes it was the little things—a friendly smile, the feel of sunlight on skin—that made life feel worth living.

When I opened my eyes, a scrubby path—more deer trail than cultivated walking path—appeared before me, winding its way through the bushes. The hairs stood up along my arms as I took a step toward it. I could've sworn it wasn't there before. The trail didn't have the characteristic gravel of the "approved" paths, but something about it called to me, pulled me forward.

I stepped through the tall grass onto the trail, ducking under the low-hanging branches of a Japanese maple in need of trimming. Yes, this felt right. I pushed on, farther and farther, winding in and out of trees and around bushes, occasionally crossing over the normal gravel paths, only to plunge again onto their wild cousin, all the while praying Ogura-san wouldn't appear out of nowhere with her ice queen gaze and remind me to stay on the paths. But I was on a path. Wasn't I?

I paused beside a small pool of stagnant water with an inert bamboo deer chaser beside it. The thick bamboo tube was poised, stationary, over its rock, no longer filling itself with the running water from some hidden hose. I took a step back, envisioning the scene with fresh eyes. This must have once been quite beautiful. And for a moment I did see it—the pool of water, cleaned of its debris and sparkling clear, with the underground pump forcing water into the bamboo, the *crack* as the bamboo tube filled with water and pivoted down to hit the rock and unload its water back into the pool.

I pulled out my camera, popped off the lens cap, but the vision was gone. The sun disappeared behind the clouds again, and before me stood a murky pond and a broken water feature overshadowed by shaggy, overgrown greenery.

Nothing more.

But there was still beauty here, in the worn, abandoned state. The green haze in the water, the dark stain of moss on the pale bamboo, the clusters of duckweed spreading across the surface. I snapped photos from a few angles, a smile growing across my face. Yes, there was beauty here.

Letting my camera fall back against my chest, I stepped over knee-high weeds to reach the deer chaser itself. I tilted back the bamboo like a seesaw, then let it fall back into place. *Crack.* The sound of bamboo hitting stone was louder than expected, and I winced in the otherwise silent air. A cluster of distant ravens startled at the sound and rose into the sky with a flurry of wings and disgruntled caws. I raised my head to watch them depart, and gasped.

My crane.

Perhaps she had been startled by the sound as well; she was flying overhead, gliding with minimal effort just above me in the cloudy sky.

I was rooted to the spot, watching her every movement, when she opened her mouth and let out a loud, mournful call.

The sound rang out through the clear sky, silencing everything else, from the croaking toad to the distant, angry ravens.

A chill ran down the back of my neck; the crane's woeful cry was nothing like the sound I'd heard in the night.

Chapter Nine

I lifted my camera to capture the crane in motion, her beautiful, black-tipped feathers fluttering in the air like a courtesan's fan.

But a photograph wasn't enough. I let the camera drop back into its case and took off running down the deer path, an urgency burning in my veins, though the logical part of my brain was bewildered by the rush. I only knew I had to follow.

I dodged between overgrown evergreen hedges, and the needles stung my face, my arms, the scratches making me itchy and red. I stumbled over a misplaced rock, twisting my ankle, and I winced but kept going, unable to stop.

Finally, I stumbled out into a clearing, falling to my knees in the tall grass fringing the water's edge. Somehow, I'd ended up on the far side of the estate, for there was the island's opposite bank—and it was surprisingly near, just thirty feet or so across a cold expanse of pond.

As I took a moment to catch my breath, a sound rose all around me—the trilling of a myriad cicadas, so loud this time my hands flew up to cover my ears.

But as I looked around, I saw only bare trees and cold, murky water. Not the time or place for summer bugs. This shouldn't be happening. I squeezed my eyes closed, took deep breaths, the ache in my chest reverberating with the sound surrounding me. *It's all in your head, Mari. It isn't real.*

The sounds faded away. I let out a long, slow breath and opened my eyes.

More features were visible on this side of the island—the remains of a small tea house building, an artificial hill—although most of the island's interior was still shrouded by the tall stalks of bamboo growing up to the water's edge. I couldn't see the crane anywhere, but some uncanny, innate sense told me she was there, somewhere on the island. Calling to me.

Instinctively, I stepped forward and found myself standing in the murky shallows of the pond, my sandals and socks still on, soaking the hem of my yukata in the cold, cold water.

Oh, what if Ogura-san could see me now? I shivered and shot a nervous glance over my shoulder.

I stared down at my feet in the icy water, at the tiny flecks of old gray-green duckweed bobbing in clusters. Floating together in the greenish pool, the clumps looked almost like lily pads hovering over my shadowy feet. The lighting was perfect, the overcast sky concealing shadows. Such beauty.

I bent down, though my feet were now all pins and needles, taking care to keep the damp hem of my yukata out of the water. I reached for my camera, but then stopped. There, just a few inches below the surface of the water, was a flat, white stone. I sucked in air through my teeth. Was it a submerged stepping-stone?

I kicked my wet sandals back to shore and pushed away the duckweed with my socked toes to reveal the whole stone. It was at least a foot in diameter, flat on top, nearly a proper circle. Though now slimy with green moss, it might have once been a lovely, white marble stepping-stone. But how was that possible? Had some giant come along and hammered it into the soft ground under the water?

I took a deep breath and pressed my weight down upon it.

It held.

I stepped my second foot out onto the marble stone, trembling as I realized I was standing in the pond now. On a slick and slimy stone. *Focus, Mari, focus. You're ok.*

But would I be ok if I fell in?

I'd never learned to swim. Mom had been vehemently against it, insisting it was safer to just avoid the water. Risa had stubbornly sought out adult swimming lessons when she went away to college—seemingly became proficient—but not me. Maybe it was Mom's fears that colored my own views on swimming, but sometimes it felt like more than that. My aversion was primal, visceral. An animalistic response to danger.

I took a deep breath. I'd just have to be careful not to fall in.

I found a thick stick on the bank and used it to wave through the water in front of me, to clear away the duckweed and feel about for another stone.

There. A glimmer of white under the surface, and my stick hit something solid. My heart expanded in my chest; one stone could be a coincidence, but two stones were a path. I pushed heavily on the stone with my stick, testing its resistance, then stepped out onto it. This one was submerged lower than the first, so I was standing in six inches of icy water, but my yukata was beyond worrying about anyways, and I was too exhilarated to worry about the numbness of my toes.

You're ok, Mari. You're ok.

I made my way toward the island in this manner, sweeping with my stick, taking ginger steps forward, one at a time. When I was about halfway between the island and the mainland, I made the mistake of turning my head, gauging my progress.

I was standing in the middle of a pond.

My body began trembling, my palms going nearly as numb as my cold, submerged feet. I felt vulnerable, naked, as exposed as if I were standing on an open stage in the middle of an auditorium, spotlights focused on me. I froze, my eyes darting in all directions.

My ankle wobbled on the slick stone, and I dropped to a crouch, hugging my knees to make myself smaller, less noticeable in the middle of this body of water.

What the hell was wrong with me? I squeezed my eyes shut against the glimmering green water surrounding me.

I couldn't move. Couldn't even open my eyes.

Breathe, Mari, breathe. I could hear Risa's voice murmuring quietly in my ear, her warm hand on my shoulder.

A minute later, I opened my eyes, the panic slowly leeching out of my pores. An orange and white koi fish was swimming lazily in between the stepping-stones, his round O of a mouth opening and closing near the surface, pushing his way through the green duckweed. Again, the ache in my chest, a yawning hole as I gazed at the fish. Yet there was such beauty, like someone had spilled gallons of edamame across the surface of the pond. I scrambled to unzip my camera bag, eyes glued to the beautiful fish.

But the zipper was already open.

My camera bag was empty.

Chapter Ten

"**M**om, you didn't have to give me a present."

"I know I didn't *need* to, silly girl. I wanted to get you something because I'm proud of you. You don't take enough time to celebrate your accomplishments, sweetheart."

I moved my plate of half-eaten matcha cheesecake aside to make room for the wrapped box. I peeled the tape off one corner—the floral paper was thick, handmade, the expensive kind Mom always insisted on buying and which always made me nervous to tear. Mom leaned across the table in her striped apron, eyes glued to the box as if she were the one dying to find out what was inside. I unfolded the last edge of paper, exposing the slick white box underneath. My gaze bounced across the surface, taking in the picture, words, logo as my mouth slowly opened.

"Wait, is this the—"

"Do you like it? I wasn't sure what kind of camera to get, so I swore Patricia and Ryan to secrecy and got them to share some expert knowledge." I could feel her searching my face, but I honestly didn't know how I should respond.

"Of course I do! But this . . . it's too much! I can't accept this." I started folding the fancy paper up over the edges of the box, even though I knew it was ridiculous.

"Sweetie pie," Mom laid her hand on mine, stopping me from my futile attempt to rewrap the gift. I stared at her hand, at the familiar orange stain of her fingernails from the peeling of innumerable citrus fruits. "Just accept that someone wants to do something nice for you. For once."

I let out a deep breath, lifted my hand off the paper. It fluttered back down, exposing the Canon 6D Mark II box.

I fought down a girlish giggle, torn between texting Tricia and Ryan to chew them out or buying them a drink for advising my mother to pick this outrageously expensive camera.

I turned back toward Mom, a hesitant smile on my face. "Thanks. I mean it, thank you so much—you don't know what this means to me. But you can't afford this!"

"You deserve this, darling. Don't let anyone tell you otherwise." She patted my hand again. "I mean it."

How did Mom know what I needed to hear?

I don't know how long I spent retracing my steps, diving through bushes, trying to reconstruct the wild path I'd taken in pursuit of the crane. Now with some distance between me and the island, my attempt to cross the pond felt foolish—not to mention inappropriate. How could I have been so careless, chasing after the crane like she was the White Rabbit to my Alice? And how could I have lost that camera, of all things?

My fingertips were raw and my forearms covered in tiny cuts, but I pressed on, unwilling to leave a single inch of path unexamined. But the deer trail I'd followed before seemed even less cohesive in the other direction, and I found myself losing track of it all together. Nothing looked familiar. The overhanging trees were menacing, grasping for me with greedy fingers; the vines snagged my feet, trying to drag me to the ground. Where was the pool with the deer chaser? I spun in a circle, frustration burning up what little patience I had left for the great outdoors. The tiny scratches up and down my arms stung with evergreen sap, and it was all I could do to avoid scratching them till they bled.

I had to admit it to myself—I'd lost the trail.

I'd lost my camera.

The trudge to my room was a blur of tears, but somehow I made it back and slipped off my wet sandals on the veranda. If my futon had still been laid out, I would've fallen onto it, soiling the comforter with pond water.

Instead, I laid my head down on the table like I had as a little girl. Why did it have to be that camera? My hands tightened into fists on the tabletop. I couldn't photograph the inn "for the sake of posterity" using only my damned phone. They could've just asked Yuna to take the pictures if it were that simple.

Calm down, Mari. The camera had to be out there somewhere—there was still hope.

Unless it fell into the pond.

A dark image formed in my mind—my camera, clogged with weeds and mud, being dragged into the murky depths of the pond's dark water by a gray and water-logged hand . . .

I shook my head to clear it, but a misty fog remained behind.

My gaze roamed somberly around the room, focusing on the black skull-shaped stain I'd made on the tatami mat, on the wet footprints I'd trailed in from outside. In my absence Yuna had tidied up, put away my bedding, opened the screens to let in the brisk air. And I'd come in and messed it all up again.

I crept down the lightless hallway in the direction of the baths, hoping beyond hope that Yuna would be there cleaning again. I didn't have the strength to handle this alone, but maybe if I found Yuna she could help me. It must be nearing noon—would Yuna even still be here? What the hell day was it? I frowned, unease clouding my reasoning.

The halls were silent, musty, and every one of my senses was tingling on high alert. But the only sounds were the scuffling of my slippers on the wood floors and my fingers trailing the wall beside me, orienting me in the near darkness. My breath came quick and sharp in my lungs. But then . . . a noise. I stopped, held my breath. A thump, *scrraape*, a thump, *scrraape*.

I pressed my trembling hand against the wall, unable to take another step.

Dark, irrational images filled my mind. Horror film killers wielding kitchen knives, gangsters dragging a bloody body they'd chopped up and thrown into a laundry bag. The eerie sounds filled my brain with humanity's worst depravities, and I squeezed my eyes shut like a child closing her eyes on the boogie man hiding in her closet.

But the sounds were drawing closer. The prey animal inside me awoke, instantly light on my feet, with *Flight!* screaming in my veins. I spun and fled down the hall, seeking nothing but a place to hide in that long, featureless corridor.

My hand, still trailing along the wall, hit a doorframe. In my mad flight I didn't pause to think if anyone might be inside, but instead just flung open the door. Thankfully, it was dark. I stepped inside, slid the door closed behind me, and crumpled to the floor.

I held my breath and tried to listen for the thumping in the hallway over my own beating heart. Thump, *scrraape*—coming nearer. The thin door behind me no longer felt sufficient—I needed to hide, put something hard and solid between me and whatever was making that sound out there in the dark hallway. I stumbled through the room, my eyes adjusting to the low light filtering through the edges of the screens.

I wasn't in a guestroom, as I had assumed. The layout seemed identical to my own room, down to the sliding closet doors, but the furniture was all wrong.

I scrambled on hands and knees away from the door, away from the ominous sounds I found so much more terrifying than the unidentified crying in the night, though I couldn't begin to explain why. I scrambled to the closet door, slid it open. It was full of extra comforters and covers, but I shoved aside a stack to squeeze my body into the lower level, the shelf low and protective over my head. I slid the door closed behind me.

I'd hidden in closets like this as a child, sometimes with Risa, sometimes alone, sometimes as part of a game, but sometimes because I was hiding from the world. From my mother. From ghosts.

True darkness. And the faint scent of jasmine—some kind of soap or detergent. I allowed myself to unclench my muscles, to relax against the hard wall and cover myself with the plush bedding. I was safe.

Seconds ticked by. With the comforters and the door between me and the outside world, everything was muffled, distant. My ragged breaths were filling the small space with moist air, making it harder and harder to breathe, but I couldn't tell whether the *thing* was still making its way down the hallway, so I resolved to stay put for a while longer to make damn sure.

A minute passed. My heart rate slowed. I became calmer, saner. For a moment I almost laughed—what was I doing in this closet?

But then I heard the quiet *swish* of the door to the hallway opening and I froze, fingers biting into the comforter hiding me, all the hairs on my arms rising and tingling in unison.

The door slid closed, and then light flooded the room beyond the closet, seeping in under the door beside me. I'd closed the closet door too well, hadn't left even a gap, and I didn't dare open it even a fraction to spy on what had just entered the room. I closed my eyes, attuning my ears, clenching the comforter even tighter to keep my entire body from shaking.

One more *scrraape* and then silence. Whatever it was had dragged its load inside and dropped it. My mind contrived myriad shapes for that object—but all were dark and heavy and covered in some kind of black, wet covering.

A few footsteps, something settling into a chair. How long would I have to hide in this closet? I was sure the pounding of my heart was audible, my damp, rapid breath filling the cramped space. Part of my mind wanted to run, to just fling the door open and make for the hall-way and back to the safety of my room, but I calmed that madness, reminded myself that I was likely being foolish, a grown woman hiding in a closet at the first ambiguous noise.

I brought my breathing, my heart, under control and listened as best I could through the closed closet door. The fluttering of papers. A desk drawer opening and closing. Nice, mundane sounds. Was this an office?

At that thought my face burned, and my heart caved deeper into my chest. I couldn't let anyone see me huddled under a pile of comfort-ers like a child playing hide-and-seek. What was it about Yanagi Inn that set my imagination down such a dark, terrifying rabbit hole that I had ended up like this?

A telephone rang, the sound at odds with my surreal situation, as well as unusually outdated—was that a real landline? Then the ringing stopped, replaced by the muffled sounds of talking. I slid open the clos-et door a fraction of an inch, hoping to pick up the words.

"Yes, she arrived. Though I don't understand why she—"

Ogura's voice. A double-edged sword of relief and anxiety soundly replaced any lingering terror.

"Yes, of course. I understand." Her voice lacked its usual iciness, held a deferential tone I wouldn't have expected Ogura-san to be capa-ble of. Was she talking to the owner? I tried to shift my body so I could peer through the crack, but my knee bumped the door just enough that I froze, lest I draw attention to myself.

"On Wednesday? No, not at all. Of course, we look forward to re-ceiving you." Silence, then the click of a receiver returning to its cradle.

Wednesday—just a few days away. Did that mean I'd finally get a chance to meet the owner?

Minutes passed as Ogura sat at her desk, performing unknown clerical tasks. My contorted muscles ached, my lungs labored in the hot, dense air. I needed to get out. I needed to talk to Yuna.

Yuna—my camera! In my closet-hiding drama I'd managed to forget how I'd lost my most treasured possession. I balled my hands into fists. *Get out, Mari!*

Mad, convoluted plans of how to distract Ogura-san and escape formed in my mind (throwing my voice, setting fires, telepathy) when she abruptly stood, switched off the light, and left the room, sliding the door closed behind her.

I remained still. Would she return momentarily, and I'd slam into her as I dashed out the door? Or was this my only chance to escape unnoticed? Perhaps it didn't matter anymore—I needed out.

I took a final, deep breath of stale tatami and jasmine soap. *Now.* I slid open the closet door and stumbled out on cramped legs. I caught myself on a desk and rushed to the door, slid it open, and fled outside.

Out in the hall I should have calmed down—I was in neutral territory, nowhere forbidden—yet my nerves were tight, my adrenaline running hard and fast, and I knew I couldn't stop until I was in the safety of my own room.

I stumbled back down the dark hallways, and when I finally made it through my door, my whole body shuddered with relief. I sank to my hands and knees and crawled to the spot where my bed usually was, adrenaline seeping out of my body like a fine mist, replaced by an acidic burn in my muscles and stomach. I lay on my belly, sprawled flat on the tatami. I fought to keep my eyes open, but why was I fighting? I let them close. In the final moments before I drifted off to sleep, I realized with a distant kind of alarm that I never figured out what heavy object Ogura-san had been dragging.

And I hadn't closed the office door behind me.

Chapter Eleven

The corridors were an endless series of twists and turns, the walls dark and dripping with foul water. But the little girl wouldn't stop running, her sobs reverberating in my ears. I ran and ran, chasing after her but never closing the distance between us. "Wait, I want to help you!" I cried, but the words were drowned out by the deafening trill of cicadas . . .

I awoke to the soothing sound of Yuna moving around my room in her white-socked feet, and the comforting scents of ryokan breakfast. Warm rice. Grilled fish.

My mind was hazy, still filled with last night's dream. I scrunched my eyes closed tighter. At least it'd felt like a dream. Someone was crying—or had I been the one crying? I think I'd gone to investigate . . .

Yuna was chuckling. "Good morning, sleeping beauty!"

I opened my eyes.

Then I bolted upright, my face flushed. I raised a hand to my cheek, feeling the sweaty imprint of tatami weave on my skin. I'd spent the whole night sleeping on the floor?

"How long did I sleep?" I muttered, smoothing my bedraggled hair.

"That depends on when you fell asleep." Yuna knelt and began laying out the individual ceramic dishes on my table. "I can't believe the evening maid didn't at least wake you for dinner."

I inhaled deeply, savoring the aroma of roasted green tea and the citrusy scent of ponzu sauce. My stomach growled, loudly. I covered my belly with a hand and flashed a grin at Yuna.

She chuckled again. "Well, you must be starving. What made you fall asleep so early?" She paused in her table arranging, looked me over slowly. "Are you unwell?"

Damn those existential questions.

Memories from yesterday surged over me: my mad dash pursuing the crane, losing my camera, terror-filled minutes hiding in a closet. The maybe-or-maybe-not-dream. I glanced down at my yukata, splattered with mud and half untied. I must look crazy.

No wonder she thought me unwell.

Yuna discreetly turned away as I flushed deeper and scrambled to readjust my clothes to an acceptable level of modesty.

But at least Yuna was here—my one friendly face in this foreboding inn. Maybe she could help me recover my camera. Maybe she could help me make sense of everything.

"I'm fine, but Yuna . . . I hate to ask this, but I don't know who else to—"

"Oh!" Yuna interrupted me. "Hold that thought." She jumped to her feet and skittered out of the room like an excited child.

I chuckled at her youthful energy and crawled to the table, flopped into the floor chair.

The white teacup Yuna had just filled was warm in my hands, and I closed my eyes, inhaled the roasted, slightly bitter aroma. *This.* This scent. I needed more of it in my life.

Yuna returned, holding something behind her back like a surprise birthday present, a mischievous grin on her face. "This was left on your veranda." She unveiled the parcel with a "ta-da!" expression on her face and set it down with a clunk beside my bowl of rice. It was wrapped in a navy blue furoshiki, a white wave pattern decorating the fabric.

"It was left for me?" I stared at the beautiful cloth, not comprehending.

"Go on, open it!" Yuna knelt beside me, bouncing up and down.

"Who is it from? Was there a note?"

Yuna sucked in her breath. "Oooo . . . maybe a secret admirer?"

I snorted. A snapshot of Thad handing me an unwrapped Chicago Bears sweatshirt on my last birthday flashed to mind. Yuna definitely read too much manga. "Unlikely. Are there even any eligible men staying at Yanagi Inn?"

"More than you can handle!" Yuna laughed and patted my shoulder, but the mirth wasn't reflected in her eyes.

I gave her a wry smile, then untied the loose knot. The dark blue wrapping fell away, and I gasped.

My camera.

"Wait, isn't that your camera? The one you were using in the baths?" Yuna harrumphed.

I stroked the camera through blurry eyes, ignoring Yuna's words. My fingertips traced the strap—it was wet. Then I picked up the camera, my fingers flying over the body, checking its integrity. It seemed fine, thank god.

"Well," Yuna climbed to her feet, clearly disappointed by the turn of events. "I'll leave you to it."

My eyes shifted from the camera back to the meal she'd arranged for me. "Sorry, yeah, thanks!" I said, but Yuna was already performing her perfunctory bow and sliding the door closed behind her.

I took a deep breath, praying silently to whatever gods might be listening that my camera was still functional, that the precious photographs it contained were still intact and not irretrievably lost.

When the camera switched on with its familiar clicks, relief spread through my body. The red light above the memory card flashed for what seemed like ages before the screen came to life, but then there they were—my photos of the crane. Not perfectly framed, which I hadn't expected anyway, but I had captured her elegance, her beauty in the sleek line of her body, the sharp contrast of her white to her red to her black. A fine start.

After I satisfied my concerns, I switched off the camera and set it down, gently, on the table. Only then did I notice the flash of color in the bottom of the furoshiki—a tiny, red origami crane. It must have been wrapped up with the camera.

I plucked the delicate, paper bird off the table, held it on the flat of my palm. So small. At this scale it must have taken great skill to fold it. I raised my palm, peered into the tiny crane's absent eyes. Was this little fellow a calling card? My camera must've been returned by someone who knew about the crane. Someone who knew *I* knew about the crane.

Honda-san.

I pinched the crane's wings between my fingers, made it rise into the air as if flying. I brought it down to rest on my mound of rice, as if it had flown to the top of a miniature snow-topped mountain.

The tiny, blood-red crane sitting atop the snowy rice struck a chord within me, like the reverberation of the perfect note within my bones. I picked up my camera, snapped a flurry of photos from different angles, then checked the viewfinder. Now *that* was a picture to send to Risa. I really should take more food pictures on this vacation.

Vacation? Wasn't this supposed to be work? I was forgetting my purpose.

I lifted my camera again for a moment, then set it back down. I needed to thank Honda-san for finding and returning my camera—I had to let her know how much that meant to me. But Yanagi Inn seemed so isolated, so remote; I was in no position to buy a thank you gift. I didn't even know the distance to the nearest village, didn't know if I could walk it or if I needed to hire a car. How long had it been since I'd stepped outside the inn's boundaries? Time seemed to pass differently here, as if the inn and its gardens were running at a different speed than the outside world, and if I stepped outside I'd find myself jarringly out of sync.

I shook my head. First was breakfast. I pressed my hands together, whispered *itadakimasu* as had been ingrained in me since childhood, and ate.

Eating seemed to have cleared my head. Satiated, though not uncomfortably full, the way only a solid Japanese-style meal could leave me. I snapped a photo of my nearly empty dishes, though I couldn't have explained why.

Perhaps it was proof. Proof that I existed, that I'd occupied this surreal space and eaten these meals. That all of this wasn't some bizarre dream and I'd wake up in my apartment in Chicago with some pressing deadline and an emotionally difficult text from Thad to answer.

Perhaps it was because, this time, I wanted to remember my days in Japan.

Reviewing the after-photos sent a surge of warmth through my body. I was a messy eater—grains of rice floated in the dregs of soup, dotted the tabletop—but that just made the consumed meal look all the more satisfying, authentic.

I should take more "after" pictures. The world is messy after all; at least my life sure as hell was. Grains of rice on the table. Dirty socks. Unbrushed hair. The word "authenticity" rang in my ears as I pressed my hands together again and whispered *gochisosama* to an unseen chef somewhere in the estate.

Chapter Twelve

I took a quick shower and changed into a clean yukata (this one an unusual shade of orangey-melon), then sank to my knees beside my largely still-packed luggage and began rummaging. What could I give to Honda-san? And what about Yuna? Mom had instructed me on gift-giving back when we lived in Japan. Whenever we would visit someone's house or travel to a hot springs resort or seaside town, we would always bring some local citrus fruit or crackers or sweets back with us for my father's coworkers and our neighbors.

During my flurry of packing for Japan, I'd had the foresight to run to the store and grab a few Chicago-specific items: small boxes of Cracker Jacks, a tin of Brach's candies, and my favorite—bars of Vosges chocolate. At the last minute, in a flash of inspiration, I'd also thrown in a copy of *Flora and Fauna of Illinois*—a gorgeous little book showcasing the plants and animals of the state. I wasn't sure at the time why I'd bothered to bring it, but now it came full-circle in my mind. Honda-san, with her love of gardening and nature and animals, would be just the person to receive the book.

I found the plastic sack, pulled out the decorative box of mini Vosges chocolate bars. A good choice for a girl like Yuna. I set the box on my low table, making a mental note to give it to her when I next saw her.

The book was harder to find—it wasn't with the other gifts. But I'd already unpacked my reading books (a few favorite Murakami novels) and it wasn't among them. I sighed, slumped back onto my heels. Was it time to admit I needed to unpack all my luggage?

I stared at the pile of luggage in the corner. It was probably good that this gift-search had come up, else I might never have unpacked. Yet there was something unsettling about unloading my personal effects into this room, even though it had started to feel, if not quite homey, at least like my home base. Like a safe spawn point in an unsettling video game.

I finally found the photography book in the bottom of my carry-on (no wonder that thing was so heavy), underneath the newest issue of *Popular Photography*. I flipped through the book's glossy pages; still in good shape. Yes, it would make a good gift.

It took longer to find appropriate packaging, as I hadn't had the foresight to pack any tissue paper or a folded gift bag. I eyeballed the furoshiki Honda had used for wrapping my camera, but decided it might be cheesy to reuse the same wrapping for a thank you gift. Then I remembered I'd brought a few scarfs with me—some of the many accessories I'd plucked from Mom's closet when Risa and I were going through her things. They weren't items I recognized as Mom's favorites or anything, so I didn't have to feel bad giving them away. Still, though . . . I held a scarf, patterned with black and yellow sunflowers, up to my face and breathed in its scent. Mandarins. I closed my eyes, exhaled a deep breath. Then I carefully wrapped the book in the scarf, trying my best to mimic how Honda had wrapped my camera, as I fought back the tears.

Stop it, Mari. I blinked rapidly.

But someday they'd all be gone—all the little reminders, the mementos I'd taken home. They'd break or get worn out or lost or I'd give up and take them to Goodwill and one day I'd look around and realize I didn't have a single thing left to remember Mom by.

Stop it, Mari!

I dropped the partially wrapped book on the table and closed my eyes.

Breathe, Mari, breathe. I spun the ring on my finger around and around as I practiced my breathing exercises. This would pass.

I opened my eyes, ready to focus again. The wrapping didn't have to be perfect—it just had to cover the damned book.

I pulled the scarf off the book, wrapped it around like I would a sheet of wrapping paper except I tied off the ends with a simple twist-handle. There—I smiled.

Not perfect, but good enough.

The sun was high in the sky when I stepped outside. It shed little warmth, but I appreciated the friendly rays. I tilted my head upward and closed my eyes just to feel the sun on my eyelids.

Vitamin D. A pang of annoyance shot through me. I'd left my vitamin D supplements at home. Well, all the more reason to go outside, to feel the sun on my skin.

With every glint of sunlight on the surface of the water, and every flicker of movement as some animal startled at my approach, my hands grabbed for the phantom camera around my neck, itching to capture the transient beauty around me. But I'd left my camera back in the room in a fit of paranoia, so I had to keep reminding myself to just enjoy my surroundings, that I needed to be present *now* and not assume that everything was there for me to slip into a back pocket for later enjoyment. Not that there was anything wrong with capturing that perfect moment in a permanent, fixed state. I was a visual person, after all, and photography was my way of preserving memories.

My way of preventing loss.

But now was not that time. I grasped the scarf package tight in my hand and pressed on, swallowing my regret at leaving my camera behind with every iridescent dragonfly and just-budding tree branch I encountered on my search for Honda.

I began with the pond. Dragonflies flitted and swerved in a hypnotizing dance along the water's surface, but I wrinkled my nose at the smell. Some new algae or other slimy reddish-brown growth was spreading in the water, and an unpleasant scent of murk and rot was rising off the surface. My eyes searched the edges—for Honda, for the crane—but nothing new availed itself. I rushed away from the water, eager to rid myself of the foul stench.

But where to next? I'd started to construct a mental map of the grounds, fleshed out over time as I'd explored further and further. Perhaps Honda would be by the old tea house?

Mom had taken tea ceremony lessons when I was a child. One of our neighbors used to teach the classes and invited my mother out of the blue one morning when Mom was taking our trash out to the collection site. Was it so obvious that Mom needed friends that complete strangers would approach her and invite her to social events? She did stand out with her peroxide-blond hair and nearly six-foot frame. I paused on the path, letting the memories course over me. She'd gone to the lessons for weeks, leaving me at home to cook dinner (usually just Cup Noodles) for me and Risa while she was at her class.

What had she done for dinner on those nights?

I shook my head of its non sequiturs and continued down the path toward the tea house.

The tea house was little more than a raised two-room structure with sliding doors and a narrow veranda. Its wooden planks were green with age, but a few had been replaced over time—possibly Honda's handiwork.

Even before I spotted her sitting on the front veranda, I sensed she would be there. I approached on silent feet up the slight hill, hesitant to disturb her, for she appeared to be meditating or perhaps just listening intently. I stopped, cocked my head, but I didn't hear anything of note. When I walked closer, she opened her eyes.

"Mari-san, how are you?" She smiled warmly, beginning to stand up.

"Oh, don't stand for me, Honda-san. I'm sorry to have bothered you." As I said the words, a tiny, petulant voice inside me cried out, *Why aren't you working on the gardens? They need so much help!* The surge of anger surprised me, and I tamped it down as quickly as it came. God knows I wasn't in a position to criticize another person's work ethic lately.

"No, it's time I got up. What brings you out here?" She straightened her back, slowly, like a cat stretching.

"Oh!" How could I have forgotten my whole purpose so quickly? I held out my awkwardly wrapped book. In the daylight, the sunflower scarf looked bright and garish, not at all like the elegant furoshiki it was mimicking. Was it too late to pretend this wasn't a gift? Why hadn't I just brought the book unwrapped?

Honda was studying me, a mild smile on her face. "Is that for me?"

I nodded. "I wanted to thank you for returning my camera. You have no idea how much that meant to me." I held out the bundle, and she accepted it with both hands and a bow of her head.

"You do not have to give me a present, Mari-san. It was nothing."

"It wasn't nothing. I thought I'd dropped the camera in the pond or lost it forever."

Honda allowed a warm smile to grace her face. "I found it in a rather odd location—did you hang it on that maple branch and forget where you'd left it?"

"I-I didn't hang it anywhere, I was . . ." I couldn't think of a way to finish that sentence without sounding even more crazy. The camera must've fallen out of its bag and someone picked it up, but that someone apparently hadn't been Honda.

Thankfully, Honda was too occupied with the gift to notice the confusion passing over my face. She unwrapped the scarf as if it were a precious offering, laying each corner out to reveal the book underneath. Such care only exposed the paltriness of my gift compared to what she'd returned to me, and I cringed inwardly.

"How nice," she murmured, running her calloused fingers over the cover. I wondered if she could read the words, but perhaps that didn't matter; art and photography transcend language. She flipped through the pages of goldenrods and sunflowers, prairies and canyons and lakes, a look of quiet interest on her face.

I breathed a sigh of relief.

"It's where I'm from . . . the photos, that is. It's a photography book of the flora and fauna from my home state."

"How lovely." She turned the book over, seemed to be reading the back cover.

Honda-san gave off the unhurried vibe of someone who allots time in direct proportion to its worth. I couldn't help but feel I was disrupting her allocations, throwing an unknown variable into her carefully examined calculations.

"I-I should get going."

"Thank you, Mari-san. I appreciate the gift." She bowed, and I returned the gesture, though it felt clumsy.

I turned to leave, but Honda spoke up behind me. "Would you like this scarf back?"

I froze, my eyes fixed on the worn wooden bench in front of me, a tight lump lodging inside my throat. "Oh, it's all right. You may have it." I kept the waver out of my voice through sheer will.

"It's ok, Mari-san. I can tell it belongs with you."

I stood motionless, unable to turn around for fear she'd notice the tears burning in my eyes. But I nodded, and a moment later Honda's plastic garden shoes crunched across the gravel toward me. I knew I should turn around, smile graciously, but it was all I could do to remain standing. It didn't matter—a moment later I felt the silky fabric of Mom's scarf draped over my shoulders. I bowed my head in silent thanks, not trusting myself to speak, and walked briskly down the path back toward the inn. The sensation of Honda watching my retreating form restrained me from running, but my fingernails bit deep into my palms as I blinked back hot tears.

Chapter Thirteen

"Oh Mari-san, you didn't have to." Yuna grinned at me, eyes shining.

"Do you like it?"

"Of course! It's chocolate, right?" Yuna turned the box of chocolate bars over as if inspecting the ingredients.

"Yeah, it's a famous brand from Chicago. You've been so nice to me—I just wanted to show my appreciation." I smiled up at her from my low table, with its gorgeous spread of pickled dishes, fresh tofu, and obligatory miso soup. "Actually, Yuna-chan, could I take a picture of you? Next to my breakfast?"

"Me?" Yuna flushed and adjusted the neckline of her kimono, though she couldn't hide the wide smile sneaking across her face.

"Oh, just kneel down." I stepped back a few steps, and Yuna knelt beside the table, hands clasped in her lap.

I grabbed my camera off the floor, popped off the lens cover and snapped a flurry of pictures. "Great, now pretend you're setting out the dishes."

Yuna, laughing, held back one sleeve and began picking up and replacing each of the dishes on the table with a dramatic flourish. She glanced at me with a coquettish smile and winked at the camera and I burst out laughing, imagining how the photos would turn out.

"Perfect! Now all my friends back home will know what ryokan maids are like."

"No, you can't show those to your friends!"

"Oh come on, why not? You look adorable." I laughed, but put the lens cover back on the camera.

"I wish I did." Yuna stood up, straightened out her kimono. "I can never seem to pull off the look as well as the girls in the manga."

I opened my mouth to tell her that, seriously, she looked great when she blurted out, "Mari-san, do you have a boyfriend? Back home in the U.S.?"

My mind flashed to images of Thad: lying naked in my bed, eating take-out Chinese on my couch, staring at his phone as I screamed at him to get out for the umpteenth time.

"It's complicated."

I expected her to stop there, to take a polite metaphorical step back from the topic, but not Yuna.

"Complicated like you don't know how he feels about you, or complicated like you're not sure how you feel about him?"

Yuna cocked her head and looked at me with such sincerity, as if she were talking to one of her teenage friends instead of a thirty-five-year-old foreigner, that I had to restrain a laugh.

"Both. Or maybe neither. I had a boyfriend, but then we fought, and I left the country." I shrugged.

"Don't you want to get married?"

Ah, the naiveté of youth.

"I don't know. It's not really that simple." I set my camera down on the table with a click. "To be honest, I don't really know what I want."

"I'll bet your boyfriend gave you that crazy scarf." Yuna's tone was teasing, and even though I knew it was said in fun, I had to bite back a harsh reply.

My hand flew to my neck.

"It was my mother's. She died."

I turned away from the table then, pretended to look out the veranda windows as I blinked back tears yet again. She didn't mean anything by it. Yuna was just a kid; I had to keep reminding myself of the decades between us. But the rawness of my emotions seemed to make every off-hand comment feel like salt when it should've rolled off my back like water.

Silence. I imagined Yuna's pained expression, but I couldn't bring myself to face her.

"Oh Mari-san, I'm so sorry. I had no idea."

"I know you didn't. Don't worry about it."

Moments passed in silence. I reeled myself back from the brink of tears, but at my core I was tender, sensitive, as if a single touch or wrong word would throw me into sobs. I tightened my jaw and turned back to look at Yuna, managing a small smile to show I was fine. My jaw ached, as if I'd been clenching it all night in my sleep.

Yuna nodded back at me. "I know what you need. Come with me."

She stood and turned to leave the room, clearly expecting me to follow.

"Wait, now? Where are we going?" I scrambled to my feet. After a moment's hesitation I untied the scarf from my neck and laid it on the table next to my untouched breakfast.

Yuna didn't answer, just skipped out the door and beckoned to me with a mischievous smile on her face.

"There's something I want to show you," Yuna whispered behind her hand as we walked side by side down the hallway.

I just nodded and went along with her. Having Yuna with me made the dark corridors far less unnerving, but I still tried to map where we were going, a fear tickling the edge of my mind that I wouldn't be able to find my way back to my room alone.

After a few twists and turns, I began to see light up ahead, as if a spotlight were hitting the wall ahead of us.

I slowed my pace. "What is it?" I whispered to Yuna, a tremor in my voice. She just smiled and grabbed me by the hand, pulling me onward.

As we approached, it dawned on me that the light was daylight. One section of wall, perhaps 15 feet long, was made of floor-to-ceiling glass, looking out into an open-air courtyard.

Yuna turned to watch my awed expression as I took in the postage-stamp Japanese garden growing in the center of the inn. All the garden elements (the stone benches, granite lanterns, even trees and bushes) were miniaturized versions of reality, nothing taller than my knee. The effect was striking, but also unsettling.

On three sides were solid walls of frosted glass (although I detected the outline of a door in one of them), leaving only the close wall transparent, and it felt for all the world like looking into an alien aquarium housing a miniature microcosm only 15-foot square. In the tiny white gravel paths and evergreen hedges I could see the shadowy sister of the gardens outside, and even as my eyes feasted on the otherworldly beauty of these perfectly manicured bonsai trees, my heart ached at the bittersweet realization that the ryokan's gardens had once been this magnificent. This was how they should be.

If only Yuna had told me where we were going, I could have brought my camera.

Perhaps Yuna misinterpreted the tears brimming in my eyes; she decided to fill the air with chatter as if to distract me.

"Do you see the tiny tea house? When I first came here, I used to sit in front of the glass and gaze at the garden every chance I got."

I nodded absently at her words. "Does Honda-san take care of this garden?"

Yuna took her eyes off the garden to stare at me. "You know Honda-san? Why would—"

"Yuna-chan."

We both froze and turned slowly toward the sound of Ogura's voice, as if we were children caught with our hands in the cookie jar.

Yuna must have sensed my unease, for she jumped into action. Performing a quick bow, she replied cheerfully, "Ogura-san! I was just showing our guest the jewel of Yanagi Inn, as I know she appreciates beauty. I believe Mar . . . Lennox-san may want to photograph the court-yard garden."

At this, Ogura stood up a little straighter (if that were even possi-ble), and I could swear the hint of a smile graced her lips. "Very well, Yuna-chan. Please attend to the linens as soon as you are done here."

"Yes, Ogura-san." Yuna bowed again.

As Ogura passed, I bobbed my head, although she didn't acknowl-edge me, just kept her head held high and gracefully disappeared into the shadows of the corridor in her white-socked feet.

After a few moments, Yuna turned to me and whispered, "Ogu-ra-san herself tends to the courtyard garden. She takes great pride in it."

Ah. I nodded and took in the small space with fresh eyes. Ogu-ra-san was a talented gardener. She had to be passionate about the art to maintain this space, small as it was. It was hard to imagine her kneeling to trim the grass with pinking shears, yet something about the overall effect fit in nicely with Ogura's demeanor—classically beautiful, refined, everything in its proper place.

After a few more moments of appreciative silence, Yuna spoke up again. "I should probably go now. If Ogura-san notices I haven't gath-ered the linens, she'll be upset."

I nodded. "Thanks for sharing this with me, Yuna. It truly is spe-cial." A warm smile spread across my face. "I think I'll stay here a little while longer, if you think that's all right."

"Of course, Mari-san! You are a guest here, and the garden is for everyone."

She took such pleasure in small things, like showing off a lovely view to a new friend. When had I lost that gift?

Yuna disappeared down the hallway, and I sat down in front of the wall of glass. As my gaze roamed over the tiny features, a feeling of déjà vu stole over me. A few of the bonsai appeared to be tiny weeping willows. I thought, rather belatedly, "Oh, like the name of the inn!" and then a memory sprang to my mind so viscerally I felt I was watching it in real-time. My mother, sitting on a wooden stool in our small backyard in Japan, wearing a white sundress and apron, trimming her weeping willow bonsai.

Since Mom didn't have many friends in Japan, she took up hobbies she could practice in the house or our small garden. One day she'd declared she wanted to take up the art of bonsai. A week later, she brought home a small tree, a kit of tools, and a glossy photobook on the art.

Mom poured her heart and soul into that tree, trimming it regularly (sometimes to the poor thing's detriment), her passion bordering on obsession. When we moved to Chicago a few years later, Mom was devastated to learn she couldn't bring the bonsai with her.

She must've known it wouldn't travel overseas very well, but she put off addressing it for so long that we had already packed and the moving company had arrived to pick up the boxes when she finally talked to the movers about the tree. They said the company wouldn't transport anything alive, plant or animal, and she'd have to leave it behind. There was no way she'd leave it with Dad (who was staying behind in Japan), so she ended up gifting it to our neighbor, an elderly woman who lived alone.

Mom was so paranoid the old woman would forget to water and care for it, as the woman was more than a little forgetful, and I remember Mom nearly in tears, begging the poor woman to write down on her calendar when the tree should be trimmed.

Maybe that's why Mom always had a garden wherever we lived after that. Even in her townhouse she kept that little collection of potted plants and garden herbs.

I should've gotten her another bonsai tree.

Now, gazing at the tiny willow, I felt a sudden desire to garden, to cultivate new life with my own hands. Photography had always been my creative outlet, but it did not breathe new life into the world the way working with plants did. Yet I didn't have a single flowerpot in my apartment back home. That would have to change.

A lot of things were going to change when I got back home to Chicago.

Chapter Fourteen

After breakfast, I told myself it was time to get down to business. With my camera bag heavy around my neck and Mom's garish scarf tucked into my yukata pocket, I set out to take some photographs.

It occurred to me that I hadn't taken any photos of the inn's exterior, so I wound my way through the halls, through the empty lobby, and out to the front of the building.

In the light of day, the inn's disheveled exterior was more depressing than eerie. The overgrown bushes, the peeling paint—they felt like mere symptoms of a greater disease affecting the entire property. I popped off the lens cap and framed my shots: the worn wooden sign, the red paper lantern, the black stones lining the path infested with weeds. Then I stood back, far down the gravel drive, to get an expansive shot of the building's front, the camera's quiet shutter clicks the only noise in the otherwise silent air. I shivered and started to walk back inside.

But no, I told myself, there was more of the building than its entryway—I should walk the perimeter, capture the exterior from multiple sides. I skirted the edge of the building, feeling like a burglar, though it was late morning and I was a guest, but soon encountered a rustic wooden fence blocking my way. I sighed, snapped a few photos, but they were uninspired. Maybe I could try the other side.

But then I saw movement where the fencing met the wall of bushes lining the building. A bird? I crept closer, camera at the ready. No—two shining eyes stared out at me from inside the shaggy bush. Cat eyes. I squatted down, called gently, "Here kitty-kitty." I raised my camera, hoping for a cool shot if the cat emerged.

Then a rustling, and the eyes were gone. Crap. I dropped the camera to my chest.

But where had the cat gone? Surely it didn't live inside the bush. I crept closer, following the line of the fence, and pushed the bushes away. There—a panel missing from the fence where it abutted the building. Big enough for a cat. Maybe big enough for me.

I chuckled to myself. Why should I squeeze through broken down fences? I could just go around the other way. But then I heard talking behind me, coming from the front of the building. Ogura. Giving directions to an employee, perhaps. There wasn't anything wrong with me being out here, I scolded myself, but still my heart rumbled inside my chest. I had to make a choice: go back the way I came and possibly face Ogura, or act like a child and squeeze through a cat hole.

I chose the cat hole.

This time, however, I paused long enough to ensure the zipper on my camera bag was firmly closed before I plunged forward and edged through the opening, trying not to snag my yukata on the rough wood or the greedy bushes. I popped out on the other side, forced through another snarly evergreen bush, and then I was free.

I was in some side yard, on an unglamorous side of the building, just a narrow passageway of gravel along a featureless edge of the inn. There was an occasional sliding door, but no verandas. I took a moment to gather myself, smooth down my clothes and hair.

At least I was in the gardens again.

How quickly I had abandoned my plans to photograph the building and given in to the temptation of wandering. I told myself it was the way Ogura-san had startled me, that I was just wanting to put distance between myself and the inn, but it was more than that. It was as if my feet carried me of their own accord, directing me onto the paths which would take me to the pond.

This time, as I stood on the water's edge, I could feel the pull of two differing possibilities—one path turned me around, back to the inn and away from the island. I could still take my photographs, discuss options with the owner, and do my job while minding my own business. But the second path led forward across the submerged stones onto the island. This second path was exciting, but also terrifying. Something about the island unsettled me. It was risky, too, for I was straying not just from the known but also from the permitted. I knew the island was a forbidden space, and I would be breaking the trust of Yanagi Inn's owner and staff if I trespassed there.

Yet something had drawn me here—to the pond, to the island. I couldn't ignore this pull I was feeling, or the strange things I thought I'd been hearing—the cicada songs or the crying at night. I was starting to believe these things were all connected.

And that the connection might somehow involve me.

I kicked off my sandals and peeled off my socks.

When I took a tentative step onto the stepping-stone, submerged a few inches under the pond's murky surface, the water was a shock of cold to the ball of my foot that sent a shiver through my body. Standing on that first stone (and looking like I was magically floating on the surface of the water, I'm sure), I scanned the sky and the treetops on the island, searching for my friend the crane.

When I didn't spot her, when I didn't see any life at all in the trees or sky—no ravens or sparrows or even any insects—my heart clenched inside my chest, doubt creeping in. I hadn't realized I needed her blessing, that magnificent crane, sole master over the now-desolate island, but now that she didn't appear to me when I was finally making my entrance, I was left with a heavy foreboding.

I shouldn't be doing this.

Yet I couldn't turn back, couldn't resist the lure of the island—not when I was so very close.

I took another step out into the water, using a stick to tap-tap-tap and smooth away the duckweed until I found the exact center of each stone. I progressed a few more steps in the same fashion, sweat beading on the back of my neck, though the air was cool and my feet were submerged almost up to my ankles in cold pond water. Though a little voice in my head told me to stride forward boldly and not even pause lest I lose my nerve, I stopped to catch my breath when I reached the center stone and looked around me as I'd done before.

And there it was, that sense of being exposed out in the middle of the water where I was not allowed, where if I slipped I would be instantly submerged in the cold darkness, unable to swim. Unable to breathe. I closed my eyes and pressed my toes against the smooth surface of the stepping-stone, pushing down the sensation of a hot spotlight framing my face.

Breathe, Mari, breathe.

I was back on stage. My first violin recital performed in a large auditorium in front of hundreds of people—parents and grandparents and students and instructors. My violin was in the rest position, tucked under my arm, and I squinted against the spotlight, scanning for my mother.

She wasn't there.

I was sweating, the streams trickling down under my crisp white dress, and I blinked and blinked against the light. *She said she'd be here!* I couldn't do it with all these strangers, the challenging stares of Japanese mothers and grandmothers, all wondering what this *gaijin* girl was doing up on stage, looking bewildered and so alone.

My instructor, Yamada-san, stood in the wings, hidden by the curtain from the audience, but I could see her gesturing for me to lift the violin to my shoulder, to begin. She must've thought I had stage fright, but that wasn't it at all.

I just needed Mom there. I needed to see her smile, to know she, among all these other audience members, wanted me to succeed. But she wasn't there. My bow hand tightened into a fist.

I lifted the violin to my shoulder and Yamada-san relaxed, drooping a little with relief, but I didn't start playing. I craned my neck, still scanning the audience for Mom's platinum blond hair amongst the sea of dark heads.

Nothing. I waited another breath. Then another. Murmurs rose from the audience, someone coughed, a child laughed and his mother shushed him.

Still I didn't start, and Yamada-san mimicked frantic bowings in the corner of my vision. Sweat dribbled down the back of my neck from the hot spotlight, and I wiped my forehead with the back of my bow hand.

Then—*bam!* The auditorium door slammed open and the entire audience turned with an audible creak toward the back to see the newcomer and my heart soared—Mom, towing little Risa behind her.

I wanted to clap (someone in the audience, clearly connecting the blond woman to the struggling little white girl on stage, did start a round of applause), but instead I waited patiently for Mom and Risa to slide into the nearest empty seats, and then I placed my bow on the strings, inhaled a quick breath, and began to play, my eyes never leaving Mom's.

I opened my eyes and gazed down at my feet, lightly submerged in the water, duckweed encroaching as it quivered in the slight current. A smile warmed my face, and the spotlight disappeared. No one was watching me. At least no one in this world.

My grip tightened on my stick, and I poked in the water for the next stepping-stone. For a few moments I couldn't find it, and alarm shot through my body, but then *knock*, I hit a hard surface, and with a few taps and swipes I had found my next step. I shifted my weight, placed my foot on the next stone (this one deeper, submerging my ankle), a profound sense of accomplishment washing over me.

Everything worth accomplishing can be accomplished one small step at a time. Baby steps, Mari.

And with my stick-swishing and small steps from stone to stone, I finally made my way to the island.

Chapter Fifteen

T he moment I set foot onto the island, I collapsed to my knees on
    the wet shore, overcome with nervous exhaustion. I didn't relish
the return trip, but that would come later. For now, I was safe.

I glanced over my shoulder at the other side of the pond. No Ogura-san rushing to the water's edge, shouting and waving a broom at
me for my transgressions. From the mainland, the island's interior
wouldn't be visible thanks to the overgrowth of boundary bushes and
trees, the groves of bamboo that had long been left unchecked. So I
quickly pushed through the fuzzy branches of junipers and pines to find
myself, finally, in the island's core. Away from judgmental eyes.

I stood amid entropy incarnate. My gaze slid from one vision of
decay and disorder to another: the ruins of an old tea house, little more
than a moss-covered roof and three bowed walls besieged by vines. Gravel trails, reminiscent of the paths on the mainland, so overtaken by grass
and debris that they were almost indiscernible. Cracked granite basins
filled with decomposing leaves. Stone benches nearly obscured by the
bushes embracing them.

My heart ached, and I wondered if I had been wrong—was this island nothing more than a mirror of the main gardens, further distorted
due to longer neglect?

But then I heard the cicadas.

A quiet buzz at first, their song rose louder and louder until they were a crashing crescendo of deafening trills. I could focus on nothing else. I clapped my hands over my ears and squeezed my eyes shut, fighting off the sensory overload.

But then, as if someone had pushed the mute button on a TV remote, the cicada song stopped.

I slowly removed my hands from my ears and opened my eyes.

Summer.

Tree branches, heavy with vibrant green leaves, swayed overhead, the breeze scented with a bouquet of innumerable flowers. But it wasn't just that—the garden was healed: the tea house was restored, the white gravel paths pristine, and the azalea bushes carefully shaped.

Time slowed. My heart thudded loudly and painfully in my chest. A single fat bumblebee drifted silently past my nose.

Then the cicada song returned. The sound sirened in my ears, but this time it felt natural in the summer day, and down the path I could hear the distant laughter of children. I spun toward the sound and—

It was all gone. The summer, the sounds, even the breeze.

I blinked. I was surrounded by the somber grays of an abandoned garden in late winter.

Was I going mad? Something about this place (the inn, the gardens, the island) was infecting me. It wasn't just the cicadas and the laughter. I'd heard ghostly crying at night, felt inescapable compulsions to go where I wasn't supposed to go. And Mom—why was I seeing my dead mother?

I took a deep breath in, held it, then let it go. After my hallucination (for what else could it be?) of the garden in full summer glory, the overgrown chaos around me shaded everything with a heavy milieu of sorrow, and I walked in a guilt-tinged reverential silence along the paths, treading upon the withered leaves and petals of long-ago seasons. An eddy of icy air stirred up the dregs nature had left behind, compelled me to wrap my arms around myself for warmth as I walked on.

An image of my mother's forsaken potted plants rose before my mind—the sweet basil, oregano, and spearmint plants now drooping and dried, turned that unique color of dusty gray-brown found only on beloved plants left to ruin.

I stood in the center of it all, turning in a full circle to take everything in, a slow fire burning up through my sternum. Why had this magical place been forsaken? My mind ticked through a catalog of tasks to be done, my annoyance growing—how many years had this garden been abandoned and allowed to go to seed? Ten? Twenty?

As I took my mental inventory (debris removal, pruning, planting), a tickling started up in the back of my brain. The shape of a stone lantern here, the cluster of willows there. Why did they look so familiar? It certainly looked like the perfect backdrop for a movie—was it something I'd watched as a child? I followed the winding gravel trail, ducking under the branches of an overgrown holly tree. Yes, I had known there would be a bench there, under a comically large crepe myrtle. But how . . .

Then I laughed. The courtyard garden inside the inn. It was a tiny, perfect mirror of this island garden, a microcosm contained within the walls of Yanagi Inn. My eyes opened anew, I strolled the paths, noting each landmark—some more overgrown or ill-proportioned than others— verifying my theory.

It was as if I'd eaten one of Alice's cakes and now found myself wandering through the tiny paths inside the miniature courtyard garden. I looked up, half expecting to see Ogura-san's enormous head gazing at me from behind an immense panel of glass. But no, this was real, this overgrown garden of Eden. The courtyard might be the jewel of the inn, but this garden must've once been the crown of the entire estate.

Thankfully, the stone features of the garden were largely ageless—it seemed only the living, breathing elements had suffered. I stumbled across what had once been a serene rock garden, its sands raked with utmost care and precision, but was now so invaded by moss and weeds that little sand was visible. Only the large sentinel rocks in the center of an otherwise featureless landscape showed that the area had once been a focal point.

I settled onto a bench under the shade of an overhanging maple tree, though the chilly, overcast day hardly required a shelter—and the bare branches could hardly be said to provide it. Gray, I thought, as my gaze roved the scenery in front of me—everything had a pallor over it, as if it had been dusted with the sleeping powder from *Sleeping Beauty*.

Beside my bench was a raised granite basin, the size of a bathroom sink and filled with murky water. I idly picked up a thick stick from the ground, stirred up the dark bottom of the basin, turning the water into a gray sludge. The activity felt familiar, setting off long-unused synapses in my brain as if I'd done it before. I kept swirling, a witch stirring her cauldron, staring into its depths to revive the sensation again. But the image was gone, the moment lost.

I stood and started walking down the path.

But the itching on the edge of my memory followed me. *Of course the island is familiar, Mari, you studied its miniature for almost an hour!*

But it was more than that. I turned a corner and knew I would find a stone lantern before I even peeked under the obscuring branches. I whispered, "white pebbles," and then turned another corner to see a faux stream of tiny rocks trickling past. I walked inside the white stream, though I knew it was forbidden (all of this was forbidden!), and understood subconsciously where I was headed, though on the surface I had no clue. "A bridge," I whispered, my feet crunching the tiny stones, and around the bend I found it—a striking half-moon bridge crowning the white rock river, just as I'd seen it in my mind.

A child's laugh. I spun around, but of course I was alone, no children were anywhere near this forsaken place. I frowned at my mind's tricks and kept walking, the unease settling upon me like layers of incense dust. I was drawn to the bridge, which must've once been painted a brilliant red and was now worn and peeling, but some hidden memory kept me from climbing its steep sides. *Under the bridge*, I thought, and though it was tight, I bent and duck-walked underneath it, my camera bag bouncing against my knees.

On impulse, I began digging in the white stones with a stick, like a child playing on a sandy beach. I hit something. Something hard and solid. I drew in a slow breath and then unearthed a small wooden box in the exact spot I'd chosen to dig. A chill ran down my spine.

I'd known it would be there. And there was no way this buried box would've been visible in the microcosm garden inside the inn. My hands trembled as I lifted the dusty box out from the stones.

I turned the box over in my hands, searching for a latch or lock, but found none. Mystified, I ran my fingers over the inlaid wood patterns. Ah, a puzzle box! I poked and prodded the different colored segments of wood, some budging, some sliding, but none opening. I shifted in my squatted stance, thighs straining from the unaccustomed position.

Then I sighed, and set the box back in the hole I'd dug in the rocks, fully intending to cover it back up and walk away, but . . .

I couldn't. I couldn't even take my eyes off it.

I pulled out my camera, took a few shots of the box from different angles. But it wasn't enough.

Well, I found myself reasoning, I could just take the box back to my room, discover its secrets at my leisure. I'd bring it back, of course—I'd just be borrowing it.

I knew these were justifications, that the box wasn't mine to take, yet I couldn't fight the urge to take it with me. I pulled Mom's scarf from my pocket, tied it into a cloth bag with handles, and secreted the small box inside, even as a lump of guilt formed in my throat.

I turned to leave, but then spotted something on the underside of the bridge. Something was carved on one of the worn wooden planks. I squinted. Numbers? I grabbed my camera, snapped a photo with flash, and inspected the viewfinder. 080890. A code? For a moment I was struck by a sense of déjà vu, and as I ran my fingers along the hard edge of the numbers, my conscious mind struggled to see whatever was playing out behind the curtains of my subconscious.

It didn't work.

I sighed and duck-walked out from under the bridge, carrying the scarf bag with its illicit cargo with me.

After stretching my cramped muscles, I pulled out my camera again—slowly, apologetically, as if I were a tourist in a solemn Catholic cathedral. There was something sacred about this place, about the wayward trees, the dead vines shrouding the stone features. Like an ancient burial ground rediscovered after being left undisturbed for centuries.

I felt like an intruder.

And I suppose I was; even though I was a guest at the inn, I was not allowed here on the island. Perhaps this was too much, this trespassing, and someone would find out about my activities, perhaps even call the police.

But, I thought, I was only taking photographs—that couldn't hurt, right? Just a few, here or there. And no one had to know; the pictures I took on the island didn't have to be part of the portfolio I would ultimately put together "for the purposes of public display" after I left Yanagi Inn and returned to my apartment in Chicago, to my microwaved single-serving meals instead of the elaborate Japanese breakfasts, to my plush American bed instead of the firm futon mattress upon the tatami.

An ache radiated through my heart and out through my body, but I tamped it down. My old life, with its complications and stress and grief, felt very far away.

I decided to focus on the minutiae of the island, the tiny pockets of beauty rather than the tangled mess of its totality. Fortunately, these pockets were everywhere; in the mossy sentinel rocks, in the surprisingly white marble bench shrouded by deep evergreen branches. The uncovering of each new scene was deliciously illicit; maybe I would make a photobook of nothing but the pictures from this island and keep it just for myself—never let anyone else see them. Art for art's sake.

A cluster of towering bamboo, click-click. The remnants of uneven stepping-stones emerging from a sea of moss, click-click.

That's enough, Mari. You should head back.

Yet I kept wandering.

I entered a small clearing at the edge of the pond and spotted a waist-high stone figure perched on a raised mound. I brushed aside the clinging vines and sucked in a breath as I realized what it was: a Jizō statue—bodhisattva, guardian of travelers and children's souls. I'd seen plenty of Jizō statues around Japan, of course, but usually off to the side of well-traveled paths or in cemeteries. Not in the middle of a ryokan's gardens. His rounded, bald head, the tattered remains of a red bib around his neck, a broken, sun-bleached, red and yellow pinwheel lying on the ground beside him—what was he doing here?

Time froze, the air around me grew dense and difficult to breathe. I ached to touch the rounded head of the Jizō statue, to retie his bib, to repair the negligence, but no. I was an intruder. I shouldn't be here, taking pictures of this sad, hallowed garden where I was forbidden to set foot. My photos felt tainted, invasive, like contraband from a poacher.

And yet . . . the statue was striking, a profoundly moving image in this lonely, wild space. Like the old baby doll I'd once seen in a photograph of Chernobyl, poking up out of the tall weeds in what had once been an amusement park. How much time *had* passed since anyone touched this garden? My fingers twitched; I wanted, needed, to capture this powerful image.

I lifted my camera.

In a flurry, I snapped photos, slowly rotating around the statue to try different angles. Then I dropped my camera back to my chest with a frown. This felt sacrilegious, even to my heathen self.

The statue needed to be shown respect. Maybe I could come back, clean it up, give it a new bib, restore some of its dignity so it radiated like a beautiful lotus in the middle of a murky pond instead of being just one more muddy rock.

With effort, I made myself turn away, although the image of the speckled gray statue remained seared in my mind. It was time I returned to my room.

I braced myself for the walk back across the slippery stones, though I found the anxiety lessened this time. Perhaps it was because I knew I'd braved the treacherous path once and survived; I knew I could reach my destination this time.

But as I dipped each foot into the cold water, legs trembling, I couldn't get the island's images out of my mind. After experiencing the woeful, neglected state of the garden, I needed to know more. When my feet once again touched solid ground, I released a deep breath, shook out my arms and nerves. Where would Honda-san be this time of day? I glanced up at the sun, gauging the time.

I'd stopped wearing my Fitbit watch since coming to Yanagi Inn. Shedding that wristband had been like removing a yoke from my neck and stepping into a simpler existence. A world with rounded bowls of white rice for breakfast, strolls through aging Japanese gardens, and luxuriating in hot spring baths.

I really should go take a bath one of these days.

It was probably around noon. Where would she eat lunch? Inside the inn? Even thinking of lunch brought a low rumbling to my stomach.

Then, somewhere distant, I could hear the low, hollow ringing of a bell. Faint at first, it grew louder as I attuned my ears, and I turned myself, slowly, orienting my body toward the mysterious sound.

Away, I thought. The ringing was coming from the opposite direction of Yanagi Inn.

Chapter Sixteen

I followed the bewitching sound of the bell down winding trails into unknown territory. Past the far edge of the pond, past an artificial hill covered with the remains of sago palms, until a wall came into view—the boundary of Yanagi Inn's grounds.

The white plaster wall was some eight feet tall and quite thick, with mossy wood shingles along the top. A plain bamboo gate stood where the gravel path met the wall, separating the inn's gardens from whatever strange lands lay beyond. A single fist-sized stone tied with a black hemp rope sat on the gravel path in front of the gate.

Anxiety crept through some back door of my mind, bringing with it an image of Ogura's disapproving grimace. I couldn't leave the grounds, could I?

The idea of passing through the gate into the unknown space beyond disturbed me so much that I nearly turned and quick-walked all the way back to the safety of my room.

But no—the ringing of the bell sounded again, this time much closer—it wasn't fear of reprisal holding me back now. A vision of myself opening the gate and finding nothing but a black blanket of nothingness spanning out for eternity rose in my mind, sending my heartbeat throbbing through my veins.

I shook my head to clear it. I would have to leave eventually. Even invited guests must depart once their time was finished. How long *did* I have here at the inn? I knew I had four weeks off work, but I couldn't remember the grant paperwork giving any time stipulations. How many days had already passed with me barely noticing? Four? Five?

But I'd already come this far, so I pushed open the gate. It had no latch or bar and swung open with ease—so much so that my rough push smacked the gate against the other side of the wall with a loud thud, startling a handful of crows into the sky with angry caws and a fluttering of loose, black feathers.

The gravel path continued, but the change of scenery was striking; I faced a grove of tall pines surrounding what looked to be a simple Buddhist temple not much larger than the tea house on Yanagi Inn's main grounds. The bell sounded again, louder this time, clearly emanating from inside the temple.

On quiet feet, I crept through the grove of pines. I climbed the few steps and peered into the temple's dim interior, spotting a dark figure knocking the bell with a mallet.

A gasp escaped my lips. Honda-san.

She still wore her plain brown wrap top and pants, and she looked like the same old Honda, but this time it all came together clearly into one cohesive image. I cursed my own presumptuousness. Honda wasn't the groundskeeper at Yanagi Inn; she was a Buddhist nun.

No wonder I'd confused Yuna when I'd asked if Honda-san maintained the courtyard garden.

Honda's back was toward me, so I slipped down the steps as quietly as I could, sneaking away like a child who'd just witnessed her parents having sex.

I clenched my fist around the handle of my scarf bag and picked up speed when I hit the path, wanting nothing more than to slip back into Yanagi Inn's grounds and fall onto a bench, face hidden behind my hands. But sometimes fate has different plans.

"Mari-san!"

I froze at Honda's cheerful call at my back. I was close—so close!—to the gate, but I couldn't pretend I hadn't heard such an obvious, friendly greeting.

I turned back toward the temple, back toward Honda, and forced a smile. I could think of nothing to say that wouldn't be idiotic, so I just bowed.

Honda returned the bow, standing at the top of the temple's stairs. "Won't you come in?" She gestured to the temple behind her, as if inviting me into her home.

Perhaps she was.

But I shook my head. "Oh, I-I have to be getting back. I have to check on my photos." *Lame, Mari, lame!*

Honda nodded slowly, still smiling. "I understand. Wait just a moment, however. I have something for you."

She disappeared into the temple. I walked back slowly, hoping to only meet her halfway, but she still hadn't returned by the time I reached the bottom steps.

Moments later she reappeared, with a green omamori talisman cradled in her palms. She stood one step above me—making us oddly the same height—and offered it to me. I bobbed my head in appreciation and accepted it.

It was a green brocade talisman with a bodhisattva on the front. Puzzled, I looked up at her kind face.

"This is a special healing talisman. Something tells me you could use a little help recovering from loss."

Mom had always had charms like this dangling off her purse, her luggage, even her keys. She'd made wishes on a succession of daruma dolls and, when we moved back to the U.S., the first thing she did was hang a horseshoe over our front door. She was superstitious through and through. Maybe it was just her way of fighting off the darkness, for maintaining hope even through her depressive bouts.

Was Honda-san remarkably perceptive, or was I just that transparent?

Tears welled in my eyes, and I bowed my head in thanks, unable for the moment to speak. I closed my hand around the talisman, gently, and cleared my throat. "Thank you, Honda-san."

She laughed, patted me on the shoulder. "You are very welcome. But I've kept you long enough, you can be on your way."

I flushed, remembering my flimsy excuse for rushing away. "Actually, I was hoping to ask you a question."

Her thin eyebrows raised.

"What do you know about the island?" I gestured behind me vaguely. "Why was it abandoned?"

"The island?" Honda looked at me for a moment, evaluating something in my expression. "You don't—" she began, but then broke off. Her gaze drifted to the thick white wall separating her domain from that of Yanagi Inn.

I raised my eyebrows in return.

"You are drawn there, aren't you? Perhaps it is your lingering grief, just like the crane . . ." Honda trailed off, her eyes lost in the distance. I waited, as patiently as I could, for her silence had a depth to it, a promise of more to come.

After a few measured moments she continued. "The island was declared off-limits after . . . an accident occurred there." Her gaze met mine momentarily, gauging my reaction, before she continued. "Yanagi Inn's owner also suffers from grief, you see."

I nodded slowly. An accident, grief, the Jizō statue—they were connected somehow. And Honda—not Honda the groundskeeper, but Honda the Buddhist nun—seemed part of this, too. I would wager a month's salary she knew more than she was willing to share.

I longed to confess to her, to tell her that I'd walked through the island's somber gardens, had been compelled to steal a buried puzzle box, had witnessed the forsaken statue. I longed to tell her I wanted to make things right somehow. But my guilty conscience—and the fear that I'd be forbidden to ever return if the truth came out—kept me silent. For Honda-san was right; something was drawing me there, and the idea of never visiting that captivating garden so overgrown with vines that it was like an ancient ruin returned to nature only made the pull stronger. So I kept my mouth shut.

I bowed, thanked her for the talisman again, and turned to leave—grateful she didn't ask about the contraband in the scarf I carried, though I could tell she'd been gazing at it.

As I passed through the bamboo gate and returned to the familiarity of Yanagi Inn's grounds, a seed which had been germinating in the back of my brain all day finally burst through to the surface; the Jizō statue—it hadn't been mirrored in the courtyard garden. I was sure of it.

Did that mean it was a more recent addition, or simply that it wasn't a feature the owner wanted on display? Perhaps Ogura-san had decided to omit it.

The isolated island, the Jizō statue, the owner's grief. Yes, these threads were all connected somehow—I could feel it.

I tied the talisman to the strap of my camera bag as I headed back to my room, my mind churning with questions.

Chapter Seventeen

When I got back to my room, I sank into the floor chair and nibbled on the onigiri waiting for me on the table. I pulled out my camera and began scrolling through the photos I'd taken on the island: the mossy rocks, the vine-covered tea house, the yellowed stalks of towering bamboo. I was right; the photographs were eerie, yet beautiful—powerful even. I flipped through the images, one after another after another, the browns and grays blurring together.

I paused when I came to the first photo of Jizō, his tattered red bib fraying along the edges. The image gripped me. If I were at home, I would've printed out a hard copy so I could pin it to my wall or carry it around with me in my purse. I stared at it awhile longer, at the solemn face of the bodhisattva in his wild surroundings. I clicked to the next image, then the next. Each a new angle, showing off the statue in a slightly different light, literally and figuratively.

On the final image, I froze.

My eyes narrowed at the space just behind Jizō's head, at the barely visible, shadowy outline of—

I needed to see a bigger image.

I grabbed my laptop. My fingers fumbled for the memory card and shoved it in the port as I typed in my computer's PIN with my left hand.

Sinking against the back of my floor chair, I watched the system search for new photos. I tapped my finger on the table, resisting the urge to click reload, reload, reload. Now it was downloading—when was the last time I'd downloaded my pictures? How were there 458 new images?

I groaned, stood up from the low table lest I go mad. I stomped to the bathroom, closed the door behind me, and sat on the lid of the toilet, which buckled alarmingly under my weight. My head fell into my hands, elbows resting on my knees.

Surely I was seeing things. It was a trick of the light, a lens flare, memory card corruption.

Or maybe I just had death and ghosts on my brain.

I washed my hands and splashed cold water on my face. Then I looked at myself, hard, in the mirror. Sane enough. Tired, too thin, but sane. I ran a hand through my frizzy hair.

Let's try this again.

I took a deep breath, went and sat down in the floor chair, and tapped the touchpad to wake up the screen.

Download complete.

I clicked and scrolled, pulled up my most recent images. Not that one, not that one . . .

There it was, filling the screen of my small laptop. An image of the Jizō statue, taken from straight on, the sun overhead shedding only a faint shadow beneath him.

And behind, just over his left shoulder, was the translucent specter of a child's face.

I never told Thad.

I convinced myself the issue was mine and mine alone, that it was just a roadblock—a lamentable roadblock, but one nonetheless—and something I would tackle myself. I even went so far as to book a clinic appointment, never letting on what I was doing. In my mind it fell under the heading of Things Thad Doesn't Need to Know About.

In retrospect, maybe that was the moment—more than two years ago now, back before Mom got sick—when things began to go wrong. I didn't let him in. I made the decision to exclude his input (rather than even consider the possibility of raising a child together). I didn't confide in him, even when—two days before the impending appointment—I was doubled over with pain during the miscarriage and took a taxi to the hospital rather than call him.

I never even asked him if he wanted to be a father. That's not how one should treat the love of their life. Hell, that's not even how one should treat Mr.-Right-Now (though I've always abhorred that title). I didn't even call him after I made it home, a prescription stashed in my purse and a heavy-duty pad between my legs. I hid in the bathroom, determined to face it alone.

What did he do to deserve such distance? Why was it only with the clarity of hindsight and separation that I was able to see who was the apathetic party in our relationship?

I should've told him. I *would* tell him. Someday.

Chapter Eighteen

The small wooden stool wobbled under me, and I sprawled my legs to keep from tipping over, my bare feet slipping on the soapy floor.

It'd been too long since I'd washed in a public bath. Every time I heard a tiny creak I spun to look toward the doorway, self-conscious and irrationally terrified that one of Yanagi Inn's "regulars" would come walking in. I dumped a final bucket of water over my head, rinsing away the remaining shampoo. I wrapped my hair in a small towel and curled it on top of my head. I was ready to enter the bath.

I scuttled across the tiles like a crab scrambling for the sea, overtly naked in such a large, open space. *Calm down*, I could almost hear Mom say. *Only gaijin* are uncomfortable at the baths—you'll stick out even more if you try to cover up. Everyone will wonder what you're trying to hide.

I made it to the edge of the water and slipped in up to my shoulders, my pale skin flushing pink with the intense heat. Steam rose off the water like a fine mist, and I closed my eyes, allowing the muscles in my back and shoulders to relax in the warmth. How decadent to be bathing in a hot springs bath in the middle of the day on a, what, Tuesday? Risa, at least, would approve of this self-care.

I squeezed my eyes shut, sank down further into the exquisitely hot water, allowing the heat to infuse my skin, sting my eyelids. The Jizō statue with the ghostly visage watching over his shoulder rose again in my mind. I exhaled through my nose, sending bubbles up to the surface of the bath.

Then I burst up, like a cresting whale, rivulets dripping down my face, into my eyes. The water smelled of citrus—lemon? Yuzu? I hadn't seen anything strange by the statue when I snapped the photo, had I? The scene had been striking, of course, but not fantastic. Not horrific. I wasn't the kind of person to believe in ghosts or spirits, damn it. I shivered, but it may have been from overheating.

It was a trick of the light, a lens flare, corruption of the memory card. Repeat, repeat, repeat. For what else could it be?

I kicked my feet gently in the water, enjoying the tickling of bubbles along my skin. What was it Honda had said? That the inn's owner "suffers from grief"? And she'd implied it had something to do with the island, with its being abandoned. But even Honda hadn't said anything about ghosts. I cocked my head, wiped the water off my brow with the back of one hand. Did Buddhists believe in ghosts?

Mom had believed in ghosts. She'd perpetually thought our house outside Yokohama was haunted because of the creaking, settling sounds, the whines we heard during storms, the way insignificant objects (mostly papers—receipts, grocery lists) would disappear, only to reappear in the most unlikely places the next day. I'd laughed it off, chalked it up to Mom's superstitious nature, her loneliness, and, later, her depression. The elderly woman next door convinced her to have a Shinto priest visit to purify the space, to wave his stick with strips of paper on it, and sprinkle salt. He declared the space purified, accepted the envelope of payment from my mother, and we went back to our normal lives.

The creaking and whining noises continued, of course. As did the lost scraps of paper. But Mom didn't mention them anymore, just wandered around the house looking for her lost grocery list, a strained smile on her face, because the house had been cured. No need to worry anymore. Everything would be fine.

I took a deep breath, plunged my face back under the water, and forced my body to remain submerged. *Everything will be fine, Mari.* But I knew it was a lie. I was luxuriating in a hot springs bath instead of documenting Yanagi Inn. I was exploiting a cultural grant on the other side of the world, instead of facing reality back in Chicago. I was running away, again.

A subtle movement stirred the water beside me. Something soft, like a strand of wet hair, caressed my shoulder.

I burst up out of the water, eyes wide and searching, gasping for air. Nothing, nobody. I was still alone. I twisted the silver ring around and around my middle finger, so loose I wondered how it hadn't fallen off and gotten lost. I took deep breaths, trying desperately to keep my heart under control.

You're fine, Mari. Calm down, damn it.

I rose, slowly, to my feet and walked carefully back to the changing area, too distracted to be self-conscious anymore in the cavernous room.

After my bath, I felt ready to tackle the puzzle box. I laid the scarf package on my low table and unwrapped it, reverently, revealing its hidden contraband. The outside of the box was still covered with a fine white dust, so I wiped it gently with the scarf.

Then, a noise out in the hall. Quiet footsteps, a whisper.

I scooped up the box and fled to my bathroom; I didn't relish having to explain the box's presence to a member of Yanagi Inn's staff.

I sat on the lid of the toilet fiddling with the puzzle box for an embarrassingly long time. The box didn't rattle or jingle when I shook it, so it probably didn't hold coins or rocks or anything hard. But there had to be something inside; it was a puzzle box, meant to keep things secret. What else could it be hiding—a scrawled message?

A tingling started up my back. What if it *was* a message?

Slow down, Mari. I held the box up to the light, scrutinized it from every angle. It was beautiful, a true piece of craftsmanship. The mosaics of light and dark browns in intricate patterns—there was something familiar about it. Had I owned a puzzle box like this as a child?

I closed my eyes and let my hands glide across the box, sliding bits and pieces of wood as if by instinct until finally I slid a panel off the back, revealing a small void in its center.

But the box was empty.

I turned it upside down and shook it, but only a gritty powder of dust escaped onto the tabletop. Something had been inside this box, once long ago.

A flash of incomplete memory jolted me—a perfect leaf. Once, inside this box, there had been a single, perfect Japanese maple leaf. A red leaf. Why did I know this with such certainty?

Returning to the main room, I found my camera and clicked through the gallery of images I'd taken since arriving at Yanagi Inn, searching back, back in time. There was Yuna, posing with her mop, and—yes! A close-up shot of the flipbook drawings I'd seen in the inn's guestbook. Of a tiny red maple leaf and a cicada.

I stared at the photo. These did not feel like coincidences.

I stirred up the leaf dust with one finger, my brain tick-tick-ticking like a gas stove that couldn't seem to light.

Wind woke me in the night. The inn's beams and boards creaked and groaned, like a giant was shaking the framework with his enormous hands. I was vividly reminded of my childhood home in Japan, of hiding under my covers during storms, the creaking so loud I was afraid the roof would fly off or the walls would collapse upon me. No wonder Mom thought that house was haunted. I lay on my back, staring at the dark ceiling, listening to the howling and the creaking and the rain pattering on the roof. I hadn't even realized it was going to rain, let alone that a storm of this magnitude was on its way. Then again, when was the last time I'd checked the weather on my phone? I'd been so isolated here at the inn, the wider world felt distant, unreal.

Maybe I should check my email again. What if Risa was trying to contact me? What if the gallery had an urgent client question? What if Thad—

No, Mari. I closed my eyes, resisting the urge to sit up and reach for my phone, charging against the wall. Everyone knows you're out of the country. If something comes up, it'll be dealt with without you.

I checked the time on my Fitbit by the bed. 2:07 a.m. I sighed. I'd thought I didn't need the melatonin, but I hadn't factored in unexpected thunderstorms and anxieties about email and now my mind was dredging up images of that ghostly face behind the Jizō statue and . . .

I scrambled for the plastic bag of melatonin lozenges and then lay back down. My eyes squeezed closed and I forced myself to relax, rolling the lozenge around in my mouth. A deep rumble of thunder shook the ground beneath me, and I shuddered under my covers.

A flash of lightning lit the room for an instant, and my gaze fell upon the puzzle box on the low table, wrapped again in the sunflower scarf. I thought of the dust I'd inadvertently dumped out of it—the remains of the perfect leaf. I closed my eyes and envisioned it—a tiny Japanese maple leaf, the size of a quarter and the color of pomegranate.

I remembered seeing it, the perfect leaf, sitting in my hand. I remembered . . .

Chapter Nineteen

I must've fallen back asleep, for the next thing I knew the lozenge was gone and I was sitting upright in bed.

The storm was still raging, the wind howling and the inn's ancient beams creaking. But now another sound was layered over the wind and driving rain.

Weeping.

And as I sat there, my breath coming fast, the crying grew louder and louder, amplified as if competing with the storm raging outside.

I crawled to the door. As quietly as I could, though nature was providing enough cover for three Maris, I slid the door open a crack. Yes, the weeping was coming from down the hall. Goosebumps prickled my skin; I had to go find the source.

If the hallways of Yanagi Inn were dark during the day, they were black holes at night. The inky darkness was so complete I felt I could touch it and come away with my fingertips blackened. I kept one palm on the right wall and my bare feet shuffling along the cold wooden floor to keep from tripping over unseen objects.

I shouldn't have allowed that thought into my mind, for now with each tentative step I expected to encounter something uncanny or repulsive; my toes twitched as if anticipating the brush of a hairless rat tail.

The wind picked up even more, and the beams over my head creaked and moaned. Then I heard it again—the low keening akin to a wounded animal. Yet it almost certainly wasn't. How could I have thought that might be a crane? It had to be the mournful cries of a human.

Of a child.

I forced my feet to keep inching down the impossibly long hallway, despite the images of disembodied hands and tangles of matted hair I irrationally imagined awaiting my every step. The wind howled and buffeted the walls again, the creaking and groaning so like a horror film's soundtrack that my addled brain half-wished I'd brought a camcorder to document my clichéd trip down the halls of this haunted house in all its shaky-cam glory.

My passage felt like a perpetual time loop in an unending series of twisting and turning corridors. Yet still I continued, one foot sliding in front of the other, fingertips pressed against the rough wall. And there, there! The cries again, louder this time, and infinitely human; certainly no crane, no misattributed wind. The source was close, maybe even behind the next door.

But then my face brushed against something—cloth?—and I stumbled backwards, barely keeping my footing in my shock. I fumbled with my hands and discovered there was indeed a noren two-panel curtain, hanging halfway to the floor, blocking the hallway. I swallowed a few times, pressed a hand to my chest. *Breathe, Mari, breathe.*

If there was writing on the curtain, I couldn't tell because of the darkness, but its presence came with a sense of foreboding; I was entering an unknown section of the inn. With a shaking hand I pushed aside the curtain, a musty smell emanating from the old cloth, and stepped into the corridor beyond.

The air here was cold, very cold. I continued my creeping, and a short distance later encountered a door at the end of the corridor, a dead-end after a long series of tunnels. I leaned in to press my ear against it, and was struck again by the musty, murky scent—like a stagnant bird bath full of decomposing leaves. I waited, my breath coming out in puffs, for the cries to emanate from behind the door.

I didn't hear the crying again, but something else—there, a quiet whimper, like a child might make when she realizes her cries are going unanswered and all her mournful energy has been spent in vain. Whoever was crying was indeed behind this very door.

At that moment, my head began to throb. Mild at first, it soon felt like an excruciating headache that pulsed with each surge of blood through my veins. I laid a steadying hand against the wall, pressed the heel of my other palm into my forehead. The moment soon passed, leaving a dull ache behind.

I focused again on the door. This was a point of no return, surely, for once I opened this door I couldn't unknow what was beyond it. But I'd spent too many nights listening to these cries, spent too many hours pondering the mysteries of this inn and its gardens. I was ready for some answers. With a deep breath, I slid the door open a mere inch, as quietly as I could, praying the rumbling storm outside would cover any rattling.

Light blinded me for an instant and I had to avert my eyes; I'd become a sightless mole creature in my long sojourn down the dark corridors, and now even the dimmest light was offensive. When I'd blinked my way back to normalcy I tried again, leaning in close to the gap.

I sucked in a sharp breath—there was a girl.

A little girl, kneeling on a worn futon, weeping into her hands. A flickering lantern on the tatami beside her provided the only light, and the flame sputtered like it was caught in a perpetual draft.

The girl was dressed in a dirty, gray-green yukata. Her dark hair was wet, long, and dripping foul water onto the bed beneath her. A fetid stench wafted off her, the scent of decomposition and stagnant water.

At that moment, as if choreographed by some unseen sadistic god, a crash of thunder shook the entire inn, sending tremors through my body. The girl snapped her head up, her dark hair cascading in front of her face. She slowly turned in my direction. I panicked. I slammed the door closed, fell back a step, then another, backing away from whatever it was I'd just seen.

I flew down the hall, my bare feet slapping the wood floor. Blind to my progress, my face smacked into the foul curtain and I flailed my arms until I was past it. Then I sprinted down the dark corridor, arms waving in front of me like antennae, far too panicked to attempt any silence.

The farther I got from that room, however, the slower I ran, and the frenzied energy burned out of my body. Eventually, I slowed to a stop. What was wrong with me? I pressed a palm to my chest, gasping for air.

What did I just see?

Finally, I fell into my room and slumped against the door. My emotions swarmed inside me, unidentifiable and fierce.

Breathe, Mari, breathe.

I was as tense as a strung bow, and I found myself pacing back and forth across the length of my room, clenching and unclenching my fists.

Maybe Yanagi Inn wasn't good for me after all. Something about this place was pulling me in dangerous directions, taking me places I wasn't at all sure I wanted to go.

Maybe I should just leave. I could sense two diverging paths in front of me: one in which I fled the inn and left all the mysteries behind, and one in which I stayed and saw both my duties and my curiosity through to the very end, no matter how unsettling the results.

I let my head fall into my hands, but instantly regretted it; my fingers still smelled of that musty curtain. I rushed to the bathroom, turned on the sink's faucet to wash my hands and splash cold water on my face. When the water hit my nose and mouth, however, I noticed the smell was even worse. I stumbled back a step, spitting and wiping my mouth on my yukata's sleeve. Foul water, swampy water—it was the same stench as was in *that room*.

I realized all was eerily quiet—the storm had stopped, and the only sounds were the water gushing in the sink and the pounding of my heart in my ears. I pressed a hand to my chest, closed my eyes. *Breathe, Mari, breathe.*

When I reopened my eyes, water was pouring out over the edge of the sink. I reached to turn off the faucet, but quavered as I saw the basin was clogged with hair. Clumps of sodden, blond hair floated in the water, spilling out onto the tiled floor, pooling toward me, the stench of dank and rot growing more and more pronounced. I let out a garbled cry and stumbled backward into my room, scrambling for the door—I had to tell someone, I had to—

I froze halfway into the hall when I realized all was dead silent—the water had stopped. My breathing came in ragged gasps as I walked, slowly, to peer back into the bathroom.

There was no water on the tiled floor. No water in the sink, save for a few drops as evidence of recent use. The air held nothing of that awful stench.

There was no hair.

I collapsed to my knees on the perfectly dry bathroom floor.

Five minutes later, I was shoving clothes inside my blue luggage with no rhyme or reason, and a sheet of paper fluttered to the floor. I picked it up and unfolded it—the grant printout.

I sank to my knees and let my eyes slide over the words I'd read and reread so many times since I'd arrived. But the words didn't mean anything. So much ambiguity, so much left up to interpretation. What did "for the sake of posterity" even mean? What the hell was an "aggregated portfolio"? The words that I had been clinging to now felt woefully insufficient. Why hadn't I asked more questions before I accepted this damned assignment?

I crumpled the paper into a ball and tossed it into the corner. I kept packing until I had everything thrown into my bags and I was so exhausted I felt my arms dragging me to the floor. In the morning I could talk to Yuna, ask her to apologize to the owner for me, tell her I wouldn't be able to fulfill my obligations for the grant. Not getting reimbursed for my plane ticket would hurt, and it'd probably cost a fortune to fly back to Chicago on such short notice, but I had some savings. It could be done.

Part of me wondered if I could get a car to pick me up right then, in the middle of the night, but a saner part of me knew this was madness, so I pushed my bags aside and collapsed onto my bed. In a matter of minutes, I fell asleep.

Chapter Twenty

In my dream, I was a girl again—young, but also tiny, the size of a sparrow, and I was walking through a forest of grass, each blade the size of a tall topiary bush. I was laughing and running with my hands out to my sides, hitting the blades of grass as I went. And there was someone with me, a girl following some distance behind, and though I couldn't see her I knew she was there, could hear her laughter, too.

We were looking for something, and though too tiny to see where we were within the totality of the garden, we were having such fun the importance dwindled away. Then, like a helicopter over a landing pad, an enormous magnifying glass hovered over me, bringing the sound of trilling cicadas instead of rotating blades. And behind it glared the immense eye of Ogura, magnified to horrifying proportions. I wanted to scream a warning to my companion, to run away, but I was frozen to the spot like my feet were caught in tacky mud. I could do nothing but stare up at Ogura's gigantic, watchful eye growing ever closer.

I dragged myself up out of sleep, a sense of urgency tickling at the back of my mind.

Slowly, my eyes opened. Was I supposed to look for something? For someone? I sat up in bed, cast my eyes around the room, and spotted the blue luggage poking out of the closet.

I lay back down and closed my eyes, the line between dreams and wakefulness still hazy and indistinct. There was a storm last night. And the crying sound, and an overflowing sink, and something about a little girl? And she was following me?

No, something wasn't right.

I crawled over to check my luggage. Well, I certainly had been planning to leave. The sense of impotence and fear that had so fueled me last night still lingered. Maybe it really was best if I left the inn, left Japan.

It's not like—

Yuna's light knock sounded on my door. I dropped my carry-on bag and kicked it back inside the closet. "Come in!"

Yuna slid open the door with her usual sunny smile, carrying the tray laden with my familiar breakfast foods, but she must have either noticed my packed bags or the guilt stamped on my face, for her smile faded and she averted her eyes. All-business Yuna surfaced, and she bowed her head and began laying out my little ceramic dishes.

I sank into my floor chair and cleared my throat. "So, that was quite the storm last night, wasn't it?" Part of me just wanted an innocuous topic to break the ice, but another part longed for confirmation that not everything I'd experienced in the night was a dream.

At this obvious bid for conversation, Yuna's face lit up, though she didn't stop repositioning my dishes of pickles into pleasing arrangements. "It was! Did you hear all that thunder? I wouldn't be surprised if there was storm damage around the grounds. I saw some branches down along the road when I came in."

I nodded, and took a tiny sip of my scalding green tea. "Can I ask you a question, Yuna-chan?"

Yuna sank back on her heels, giving me her full attention.

"Why does Honda-san come work in the gardens if she's not the groundskeeper?"

A sudden realization dawned across Yuna's face, and I allowed myself a self-deprecating smile in response.

"I'm not sure why, to be honest. I think she just loves to garden. Or maybe she just loves Yanagi Inn." Yuna shrugged. "There is something about the gardens that draws you in, isn't there?"

I nodded vaguely and let my gaze wander to the windows beyond the veranda. Perhaps there was some truth to this—the gardens had an emotional pull, a provocative appeal in their chaotic state which made them irresistible. Yes, I could see why Honda-san would be drawn back to the gardens time and again.

Yuna had finished laying out my breakfast and was now staring out the windows, lost in her own thoughts, her chin resting in her palms. Perhaps the gardens had worked their magic on Yuna, too.

"Yuna," I began slowly, not wishing to knock her out of her thoughtful reverie. "Is there a child staying here at the inn?"

A frown formed on Yuna's dreamy face. She shook her head and jumped to her feet without making eye contact. "Of course not." Her response was clipped, vexed, and I wished I could take back my upsetting question, even as her answer shook me to my core.

There was no child at Yanagi Inn.

My thoughts swirled as Yuna gave a stiff bow and carried her tray out of the room. Belatedly I called out a "thank you for the food!" but she was already in the hall, and I don't think she heard me.

Was the crying girl I remembered just another dream? Or had I seen a girl who didn't exist? My heart raced, but I couldn't pinpoint whether I was terrified or exhilarated.

Perhaps both.

My mind returned to the shadowy image in the Jizō photo. I shoveled a mouthful of rice and rolled omelet into my mouth and then crawled over to pull my laptop out of its sleeve.

I chewed thoughtfully as the computer powered up. I'd taken a dozen photos of the Jizō statue, but only one had captured anything that looked like a shadowy face.

I wasn't prepared to use the term "ghost" for the shadowy image, not even after my memories of last night, but I had trouble denying the possibility of a presence. I'd seen a lot of sensor dust and the myriad other issues that can come up within photography, but this didn't fit any of those irregularities. I gulped down big mouthfuls of miso soup and leaned in closer to my screen. And I knew it hadn't been photo-shopped; no one had seen the photos except me, and no one had had access to my computer except me, and—

I gasped. I couldn't breathe—panicky fireworks exploded in my brain. I was choking—oh god, how could this be happening? Chunks of tofu and seaweed floating in the soup—I shouldn't have been gulping it. *Cough, Mari, cough!* I tried to, but air wasn't coming through. My head was a balloon rapidly overinflating, strands of seaweed were growing and spreading inside my throat, peeking out of my mouth, and my mind screamed *get help!* But I didn't know how to raise an alarm. I needed someone—Ogura, Yuna, anyone at all. I tried to climb to my feet but my legs were wobbly noodles, and I crashed back down, one hand clutching my throat, my vision going fuzzy.

And there, sitting in the chair across from me, was Mom. Mom in her pale blue hospital gown, thin and gaunt, her eyes closed as if sleeping.

No, it can't end this way. Risa—I can't leave her all alone!

I fumbled around on the table, grabbed the tiny vase with its single blood-red poppy and hurled it as hard as I could toward my closed door, and it smashed against the wood and shattered into a thousand sparkling pieces.

Footsteps, running. Someone must've heard. I turned toward the door, the edges of my vision tunneling into black, but then Yuna was in the doorway! Staring at the broken glass, then looking up at me with my hand at my throat and she was running to me, shards of glass be damned, and she fell to her knees behind me. "Mari-san!" she said in an urgent, but amazingly controlled voice, "I'm going to perform the Heimlich Maneuver on you now."

I nodded dumbly, thinking in some dark recess of my mind what an oddly formal announcement that had been, and the next thing I knew Yuna's strong arms were around me and she forced her fist into my abdomen and I felt a rush of air and then I coughed up a seaweedy glob of food onto the table.

I inhaled hard and the air hurt my aching esophagus—but I could breathe! I gulped air for several breaths, and turned to face Yuna, her sweet round face as pale as cream, her eyes wide, and she placed both hands on my shoulders, looked me in the eyes and said, "ARE YOU ALL RIGHT?"

I nodded, cleared my throat, cleared it a second time, then croaked, "Yes. Thanks to you."

Yuna broke out into the biggest smile I've ever seen, but when I leaned in to give her a hug, I noticed her whole body was trembling. We sat for a minute in each other's arms, full of relief. Adrenaline seeped out of my pores, and I just leaned into my friend, soaking in the comfort of human contact. "Thank you," I whispered.

We separated, and I leaned back to look at the mess I'd made of the table and the floor. At least I hadn't chosen to throw my laptop at the door. "I'm so sorry about the mess, Yuna. I don't know what I would've done if you hadn't—"

"Let's not even think about that, Mari-san." Yuna replied briskly, standing and brushing off the front of her kimono. "Clever to throw the vase, by the way. I heard the crash clear down the hallway." She smiled at me and stepped gingerly around the broken glass to the door. "I'll be right back—don't try to walk yet."

Yuna returned with a plastic bucket and some gloves to retrieve the shards of glass, though she told me to sit tight because she'd need to vacuum the area, too, to suction up any remaining pieces. She offered to bring me more food, but I told her I'd lost my appetite.

I sat staring at my laptop's black screen, waiting for Yuna to return with the vacuum.

It was probably just my imagination, but something about what had just happened didn't feel right. Who chokes on *soup*, for god's sake? But it was more than that. I could almost feel the tangle of seaweed, the sensation of the strands growing and stretching in my throat. Of being unable to breathe.

It'd felt like drowning.

I shook my head. No, it was just a bizarre accident, just me being careless as I ate.

But somehow it didn't feel like an accident.

I could've died. Right there, right then, could've been the end of my life. And what would I be leaving behind to show for it? Some art from years past, a damaged relationship, a messy apartment. Some legacy.

And Risa. Risa would be completely alone in this world. Well, at least she had Diego. My heart warmed, picturing them snuggling on my sofa together. One of these days he'll work up the courage to propose.

Risa. I felt a twinge of guilt. I should check in on her, see how she's doing. After all, I wasn't the only one who lost Mom a few short weeks ago.

I used a cloth napkin to wipe the soup-splatter off my laptop (thankfully it hadn't gotten into any of the keys) and pulled up my emails.

There were already two emails from Risa, and a smattering from friends and associates in the art world. I only opened Risa's.

She sounded well. A poetry class . . . Ginkgo was fine . . . Diego had taken her to a new pizza place with crazy toppings. All things that made me smile. I hit reply to Risa's most recent email, let my fingers hover over the keyboard. I wasn't sure how to put my experiences, my state of mind, into words. My time here at the inn had been some of the most bizarre and inexplicable days of my life. Not something I could easily put into an email.

Maybe I should send her a photo of the crane?

I hovered over the "attach" button, but something stayed my hand. I wasn't sure how to explain it, but I wasn't ready to share the crane with anyone yet.

I'm glad to hear you're doing well. The inn isn't quite what I expected, but it's certainly interesting. I miss you. Maybe we can Skype sometime?

Love, Mari

It was short, succinct, but Risa would understand.

I shoved my laptop aside, not tempted at all to pull up social media or the weather or any of the myriad other online distractions I used to succumb to.

I found myself pitying the Mari who had her phone constantly in her hand, who flicked from one app to the next in an endless search for stimulation or validation or whatever it was she perpetually sought but could never seem to secure. That Mari felt very far away indeed.

And her world felt very far away, too; the world of emails and appointment alerts—somehow none of that felt real. Even Thad, handsome Thad with his hipster glasses and flannel shirts, felt like someone I used to know a long time ago, a man from a dream, perhaps. A surprising pang shot through my heart at that revelation.

But this, I thought, looking around my ryokan room with its creepy soy sauce-stained tatami mat floors and sliding screens. *This* felt real.

I closed my laptop and stretched my arms up to the ceiling. I would have a bruise tomorrow where Yuna had graciously shoved her fist in my abdomen. But I could also sense every muscle in my neck and arms, and some were delightfully sore. I rotated my shoulders one at a time and smiled. My body was feeling stronger than it had in a long while. Perhaps it was the time I'd spent out in the gardens, the fresh air I'd been breathing in. Or the fantastic, healthy food I'd been eating.

No, I couldn't leave yet. Not while these mysteries remained unsolved, not while breath was still left in my body. It would take more than a brush with death to keep me away from the island.

Yuna returned, lugging an old vacuum, her sleeves tied back.

"Thanks again, Yuna. You saved my life," I said quietly.

She looked up from unwinding the vacuum's cord and smiled.

"Well, I'm really glad you're still here, Mari-san."

Yes, I'm still here. I turned to look out to my tiny private garden beyond the veranda.

And I'm not going anywhere.

Chapter Twenty-One

After my shower, I changed into the fresh yukata Yuna had set out for me—perhaps her polite way of pointing out I'd spilled miso soup all down my front. This yukata was a cheery yellow with a sprinkled pattern of what might've been abstract lemons. Where did Yanagi Inn buy these things?

Yuna had cleared away my largely uneaten breakfast and wiped off the spills and crumbs. She already did so much for me, and now she'd saved my life. How could I ever repay her?

I glanced at my open laptop. A reply from Risa.

Already?

Hey Mari, I just got home. Want to Skype?
Love, Risa

My fingers trembled on the keyboard. I hadn't expected her to reply so quickly. I could ignore her email for the time being, pretend I hadn't seen it yet, wait a few hours and "accidentally" reply after she'd gone to bed . . .

No. *Stop running, Mari.*

I pulled up Skype, sent Risa a quick message:

Mari: I can call in just a sec. Voice only. I just got out of the shower.
Risa: No way! I want to see your smiling face.
Mari: All right. But don't make fun of me.

Risa replied with a thumbs-up emoji. My heart fluttered like a hummingbird's inside my chest. *Well, I guess this is happening.* I smoothed back my wet hair and rearranged the front of my yukata, then clicked the call button before I had time to reconsider.

"Hi Mari!" Risa's cheerful voice piped in, and the sight of my little sister with her curly blond hair and bright red glasses sent a wave of homesickness over me.

I took a deep breath and turned on my smile. "Hi Risa, how's it going?" I was dying to ask whether Diego had given her the ring yet, but knew I'd have to wait for her to bring it up, or else I could ruin the surprise.

"Great! But tell me about you—how are you doing? How's the inn?"

"It's . . . even better than I expected. The food is amazing and the staff is super fun and quirky. And, before you ask, yes—I've tried out the bath. It was glorious."

Risa squealed. "I'm so jealous! Tell me more!"

The corner of my smile twitched. I didn't want to outright lie to my sister, but something told me this really wasn't the time to break out the "everything here is wasting away, there's probably a ghost, and I literally almost died five minutes ago" honesty. I didn't want Risa to feel guilty for sending me here when all she'd wanted was to give me a chance to flex my artistic muscles again.

"I actually can't talk for long right now. But listen, I was wondering—what do you remember about living in Japan?"

"What do I remember? Honestly . . . not a ton. Only bits and pieces. What our house looked like, that park we used to walk to, stuff like that. Why do you ask?"

Why *was* I asking her?

It was unfair to expect my sister to fill in the blanks for me, make the connections I wasn't yet able to make myself. For the umpteenth time, I wished we had photo albums from our years in Japan, visual cues to trigger our memories. Something told me the answers did indeed lie in my own past—I just couldn't figure out the right questions.

Risa must have sensed my distraction. "You look good, Mari," she said, gently, pulling me from my reverie.

I smiled back at her. "Thanks, you too." I paused for a moment. "Hey, do you know if the grant stipulated a completion date? Everything was such a whirlwind, I didn't pay close enough attention to the details. Could you email me that contract?"

Risa's nostrils flared for a split second, and I wondered if I'd landed on a sensitive spot, but then she smiled. "I'm not sure, but yeah—I can try to find it and send it to you."

"Thanks."

For a moment, neither of us spoke; we just bathed in each other's presence. But then I told Risa I should probably go, I had things to do, and thankfully she didn't press the issue.

Chapter Twenty-Two

My luggage, haphazardly packed in the night, still loomed in the corner. While the doubts and fears of yesterday lingered, my sense of powerlessness had been replaced by a fierce determination. I had to finish photographing Yanagi Inn. And something told me I wasn't done with the island, even if I wanted to be. The pull was too strong for me to just walk away; it was as if there were a thread tied inside my navel connecting me to the island, and every moment I wasn't there I could feel the taut string straining.

I dumped all the spare clothes, books, and toiletries out of each bag and slowly put things away. Not in arbitrary piles like before, but in correct locations—folded up in the closet, put in the chest of drawers, on the bathroom counter, etc. There. I felt well and truly moved in for the first time. It felt . . . right.

I grabbed my camera and slipped out of my room into the hallways. My first instinct was to tiptoe down the halls as I had every time before, but this time I didn't. Perhaps it was the energy in the air I always felt after a good storm, or perhaps it was my near-death experience and newfound resolve to throw myself into investigating the mysteries of the inn, but I didn't feel small this time when I walked the corridors. I felt strong, tall. Powerful. Let Ogura-san see me, strolling the halls with my camera. Let her ask, in that condescending tone of hers, where I think I'm going and I'll tell her—*I'm going to photograph the courtyard garden, Ogura-san.* And then maybe I'd snap a photo of her shocked face before I breezed past her.

I found the courtyard garden, and was once again staggered by its perfection, even more so knowing it was an exact replica of the gardens on my beloved island. No, perhaps "coveted" was the better word. The uncanny connection I felt with the abandoned island had made me feel like it was mine, and mine alone. I frowned, the thought unnerving me.

But how did I know which one was the replica? I let my gaze wander across the tiny garden's features. Was this some miniature blueprint? Or was it the opposite, and the island's garden was created first, and this tiny plot of land was an homage to the original, a pocket-sized version that could be enjoyed without leaving the comfort of the inn?

With these chicken-and-egg thoughts tumbling through my mind, I pulled my camera out of its bag, screwed on a polarizing filter to eliminate reflections, and started taking photos.

I stood back as far as the narrow hallway would allow, to try to capture the small garden in its entirety. Any documentary work on Yanagi Inn wouldn't be complete without the detailed inclusion of this jewel. So I photographed the seams, where the glass met the walls, and rotated the front of the polarizer to match all the angles of light to show off the amazing craftsmanship of this small space within the inn's interior.

But beyond mere documentation, I wanted to detail the garden in its ideal form, capture exactly what the island's gardens *should* look like. How fortunate I was to have this perfect blueprint; I held my camera high above my head and stood on my toes to get the best overview I could. Perhaps later in my room I could sketch out a detailed map from these photos.

I crept in closer and focused on the minutiae, on the shapes of the bonsai trees and the relative heights of boundary hedges and the colors of flowers. The dry garden's sand was raked into lovely waves and swirls, and I wondered at how tiny a rake Ogura-san must use. How did she manage to keep this garden so beautiful in the cold weather? I put a palm to the glass enclosure—it was surprisingly warm.

I marveled at the neatness of it all, how tidy and trimmed and perfect the entire scene was. Except . . . I lowered my camera. A single maple leaf lay in the center of the garden, presumably blown in from last night's storm, in the precise spot where, in the island's garden, the Jizō statue stood. I pressed my face to the glass and looked up into the sky; Ogura-san must tidy the courtyard quite regularly. My eyes scanned the perimeter of the garden; whoever constructed this space must have done an excellent job with the drainage, too.

As I was squatted down by the glass, examining the edges of the carefully trimmed grass, I sensed someone behind me. I spun on my heels and found Ogura hovering in the hallway.

I stood and smoothed down the front of my yukata, eyes cast down. *No, Mari. Be strong.*

I met Ogura's gaze. Her expression was not unfriendly—more curious than anything. I opened my mouth to speak politely about the loveliness of the garden, to appeal to her sense of pride, or even simply to make some inane comment about the weather we were having, but instead I opened my big mouth and blurted, "There's a leaf in there."

Ogura raised one finely plucked eyebrow, but remained silent. I gestured behind me to the courtyard garden, my heart pounding. "I-In the garden. A leaf blew in. Probably from the storm." *Way to go, Mari. Now it sounds like you're criticizing her garden maintenance.*

"Ah," she said, turning her gaze to the glass behind me. "Well, I shall just have to pick it up, shan't I?" And she smiled at me.

Not a big warm smile, but it wasn't mocking or sarcastic, either. Just a smile.

I'd take it.

She turned and walked down the hall, and I wondered whether she was off to gather gardening supplies, but after just a few moments

I saw movement on the far side of the courtyard. Part of the back wall opened, and Ogura stepped into the garden from the hidden door. I couldn't help but laugh. Suddenly the stern Ogura-san was tiptoeing through this miniature garden like a giant trying not to wake the inhabitants of a village. She glanced up at me, saw my laughter, and smiled back.

She eased across the scene, obviously well-versed in where to place each foot so as not to damage the plants or tiny fixtures. Then she reached down and plucked the maple leaf between two fingers and held it proudly aloft for me to see, her chuckling unmistakable, though muffled by the thick pane of glass between us.

For a moment the scene struck an absurd chord of déjà vu for me, this giant Ogura-san in the tiny gardens, but then I laughed and applauded with childish enthusiasm. Ogura bowed and then turned and tiptoed back to the hidden door in the far side of the courtyard. I watched her progress, admiring the poise of this giantess as she traversed the delicate terrain.

When she had almost reached the door, I was struck by a burst of inspiration and raised my camera. A flutter of clicks and I'd captured the moment perfectly. Ogura-san, the elegant giant, tiptoeing through her glorious gardens.

Chapter Twenty-Three

Honda knelt on the white gravel path, a large wicker basket filled with twigs and wet leaves on the ground beside her. She lifted a hand in greeting at my approach.

"Good morning!" I called out. "May I help?"

Honda nodded, so I settled down on the ground beside her and began plucking leaves out of the gravel to add to her basket. "What do you do with all the debris you collect?"

"There is a compost pile in a corner of the estate." Honda gestured vaguely toward the north. "All the clippings and leaves end up there, and eventually they will be used as compost to help breathe life into the new plants and trees. Anything too large gets burned."

I nodded. How long had it been since new plants were added to these gardens? Even the better-maintained areas here on the mainland looked like they'd been abandoned for a decade. Honda-san, apparently out of the goodness of her heart, had been trying to fight off the worst of the deterioration, but fresh new plants were another matter altogether.

Still, something about taking the wreckage from the storm, the old leaves and sticks, and letting it mellow with time until it could be used to breathe new life into the gardens was beautiful. And poignant.

We worked in silence, every few minutes shuffling to a new section of the path (for it looked like Honda-san wasn't ready to tackle anything beyond the pristine walking trails), plucking up remnants of the storm piece by piece.

What would we do if a large branch were down? I envisioned an entire dead tree uprooted, its gnarled roots exposed. I remembered walking through Mom's neighborhood back home after a storm and finding the ground littered with sticks. Occasionally, entire branches twice as long as I was tall would have fallen across a road and neighbors would band together to drag them out of the path of traffic or call upon the one guy with the gas-powered chainsaw.

I realized I hadn't seen a man since the driver brought me and Ogura back from the airport. This was an enterprise run entirely by women, it seemed. While I was mentally calculating how much weight the tiny Honda-san and I could drag, my musings were interrupted by a snuffling sound from the nearby bushes. I froze, instantly alert. That was too loud to be a squirrel or bird.

I was scrambling backwards, a yelp on my lips, when a black nose and cream-colored snout emerged from under the bushes, just a few feet from me. My eyes widened. That certainly wasn't a squirrel. Did Japan have raccoons? And why was this one so brazen—weren't raccoons nocturnal? Did it have rabies?

A fuzzy head emerged from the bushes and I realized what I was looking at.

"A tanuki!" I whispered, pointing at the fuzzy creature poking out of the bushes. Honda turned around and smiled, casually, as if this weren't unusual in the slightest. I'd never seen a tanuki in the wild before, even with the years I'd spent in Japan. Ironically, the only tanuki I'd seen in person was at a zoo in Atlanta just a few years ago.

"Oh, that's just Goro." Honda waved a dismissive hand.

I stared at the fat, fuzzy creature now shuffling toward Honda as if I didn't exist.

"Good morning, Goro-san," she said in a sing-song voice, fumbling in a little pouch hanging from her waist. She pulled a few blueberries out of the pouch and tossed them to the tanuki, who nimbly caught them in mid-air.

I gaped. Was this her pet?

Honda must have seen the look of incredulity on my face, for she laughed and reached out a slow hand to pat the tanuki on his fuzzy head. "Goro-san has been coming to visit me for years."

"And . . . he just lets you feed him? And pet him?"

"Her, actually—I didn't realize that when I named her. But yes, she and I get along well. Care to give her a pat? She won't bite. She's quite civilized."

I leaned forward and used two fingers to stroke down the black ridge of her back. Her fur was soft, but bristly in the way only wild animals seem to be. Her scent was musky, but not unpleasant, and I could feel her muscles twitching as she scarfed down the blueberries Honda kept feeding her.

"Blueberries are her favorite," Honda said, by way of explanation. I nodded, as if we were discussing a spoiled grandchild rather than what felt to me like a near-mythical creature.

Honda gave Goro a final pat on the head, showed her the pouch was empty of blueberries, and the tanuki went wandering back under the bushes from whence she came.

I exhaled a deep breath, shaking my head. "Honda-san, you really have a way with the natural world, don't you?"

She chuckled and duck-walked a few steps to pick up more leaves from the path. "I suppose you could say that, Mari-chan."

A smile warmed my face. Mari-chan. It'd been a while since someone had called me by that childish name. But hearing it from an elderly, nature-loving Buddhist nun didn't bother me at all. I watched Honda's slow, practiced movements, loath to disrupt the peaceful, companionable silence we had cultivated, but also itching to press her for information.

"Honda-san," I said slowly. "Do you know anything about a child inside Yanagi Inn?"

Her hand froze in mid-air, but she didn't turn to look at me. "A child?" She began picking up leaves again.

"Well, sometimes at night," I began, leaning forward, "I hear crying. A child crying." I didn't want to tell Honda-san I'd actually seen the girl, sobbing, on her bed. I still wasn't convinced that'd been real, although it felt as real as the tanuki-petting I'd just experienced.

Honda still didn't turn around, but I could see she was staring off into space now, the storm's debris forgotten. "You certainly are attuned to grief, aren't you, Mari-chan?"

There it was again, that knowing voice, as if Honda-san saw everything about my past. I had never told her about my time in Japan, or about my mother's death, had I?

I nodded.

Honda nodded to herself. Then she turned and stared off into the distance again, looking in the direction of the pond and its island.

"The owner's daughter would be about the same age you are now, had she not died." Honda let the word *died* hover in the damp air for a few moments before continuing. "And sometimes that grief can linger."

She shot a glance in my direction, scrutinizing my expression, though I wasn't sure what kind of response she expected from me.

"I see."

Lingering grief. Did that mean the little girl was an unsettled ghost?

A cold breeze swept over us then, and I hugged my jacket tight to my chest. Memories of the foul, swampy miasma surrounding the sobbing child rose in my mind.

I shivered, then cleared my throat.

"Have you seen the crane around recently?"

Honda nodded. "I thought I saw her this morning, heading to her nest. Though of course it is empty."

"Where is her nest?"

She gestured vaguely. "On the island."

"Oh." It made sense; the crane had led me to the island—first when she revealed the destroyed bridge and then later when she showed me the submerged stones. She must have wanted me to find the island, her home.

"The crane used to have a mate, a lovely male, and together they had eggs. But then he disappeared, and she's been alone ever since." Honda sighed. "She still returns to her nest, though."

No wonder the crane had such an aura of mournful beauty. She was alone, missing her mate, probably looking at their nest and wishing he were with her.

Was every living creature capable of grief?

We didn't speak again until after a full hour had passed tidying up leaves and sticks. Then Honda stood and stretched out her back. "Thank you for your help, Mari-san. It is nice to have company. Well, company that isn't covered with fur or feathers."

I laughed, picturing again the tanuki munching on her blueberries. "Thank *you* for your hard work, Honda-san."

I paused again, knowing I'd be kicking myself later if I didn't ask at least one more question, though my heart was thudding in my chest. "D-did the owner's daughter die on the island?" I blurted out, and instantly wished I'd chosen my words with more care.

A pained expression passed over Honda's face as she scrutinized my expression again, and I feared I'd brought up some bad memories for her. She turned in the direction of the island, as if the view weren't blocked by the trees and hedges in between. "Yes," she said softly, almost as if it were to herself. "She did."

"Mom," I said, grabbing a plate of inari sushi off the conveyor belt in front of me. "Why haven't you ever remarried?"

It was a heavy question to drop on someone during a quick "let's meet at the kaiten sushi place to catch up" lunch, but it was a question that had been gnawing at me lately.

Maybe it was all the crap going on with Thad and his mention of marriage that got me thinking about my parents, of their failed marriage.

At least I didn't ask her, *So Mom, why did you never take us back to visit Dad? or Why do we only have one photo of him?*

Mom shoved a piece of tekkamaki in her mouth and began chewing, holding up one finger in a "give me a second" motion I've used more than once when buying myself time. I waited patiently, one eyebrow raised.

She cleared her throat, took a sip of the complimentary green tea. "Well, I think I got so used to being alone that I didn't really think about remarrying. I was basically a single mom even when we were still married, since your father worked so much. Sometimes weeks would go by without me even seeing him."

I nodded, although it didn't feel like a complete answer. Before I could open my mouth, she started talking again. "When you girls and I came home to Chicago, I thought about trying to date, but found I'd lost interest. I'm better at being alone, you know." She looked wistfully at the sushi chefs in the center of the conveyor belt track, rolling the maki rolls with such practiced precision it looked easy.

"But aren't you lonely?"

It took Mom a long time to reply, and when she did her voice sounded faint and far away. "You know, when you were little, your father used to call you his 'little sunflower.'"

"I remember," I said quietly, stirring some wasabi into my little dish of soy sauce. "I guess my hair was more like Risa's back then."

"True," she said. "But it was more than that. He said you reminded him of a sunflower, cheerful and sunny and always following him around, like he was your sun god." She tightened her lips into a smile bordering on grimace. "Do you remember that old song he used to sing? 'Those Endearing Young Charms?' It had that bit about the sunflower:

No, the heart that has truly loved never forgets,
But as truly loves on to the close;
As the sunflower turns on her god, when he sets
The same look which she turned when he rose."

We sat in silence for a few minutes, both staring at our half-eaten plates of sushi. I shot a glance at Mom's face. Were those happy memories for her? I had few memories of my parents together, though I could remember how they argued. Mom was a yeller, I knew that.

She had a small smile on her face as she swirled her dish of soy sauce. Did she regret how things had ended between her and Dad? Regret that they never reconciled before the accident killed him a few years after we left Japan?

"Cocky bastard," she muttered.

Well, there went that theory.

Chapter Twenty-Four

After Honda and I parted ways, I wandered through the gardens for a time. The air was fresh and brisk, with a hint of woodfire smoke on the light breeze. Cleaning up the storm's debris with Honda had been cathartic, though our conversation about the little girl had only served to raise my anxiety.

But I was ready now to revisit the island. There were answers on the island—this I felt deep in my bones.

If only I knew what questions to ask.

I scrounged in the bushes abutting the water until I found a good branch for swishing away the leaves and duckweed. Then I slipped off my sandals and tabi socks and cleared the pond's surface enough that I could see the first, submerged stepping-stone.

I took a deep breath.

The water was cold, but not entirely unpleasant. I made my way slowly across the submerged stones, and after each step the duckweed would reform around my foot until it looked like I was standing ankle-deep in edamame. Surreal.

Soon I was stepping onto the solid ground of the island, leaving no sign of my passing after I lifted my final dripping foot out of the water. I realized, after a moment, that I hadn't been afraid. Perhaps because the surface of the water looked so solid, so much like land, it hadn't even seemed like water to me. Or perhaps I'd just become bolder, braver during my time at Yanagi Inn.

I explored the island more slowly this time, stopped to smell the proverbial roses. Oh, how I wished there were roses! I looked around me at the bare branches overhead, the muddy debris of seasons and seasons of leaves left untouched upon the ground. I recalled the flash of summer I'd experienced—the vibrancy of the flowers, the scent of honeysuckle and blossoming azaleas—and my heart ached. But, I reminded myself, not every day was going to be a perfect summer day. And that was ok.

The storm had indeed taken its toll here, though there was beauty in the destruction. I pulled out my camera and began snapping photos. An evergreen branch still covered with deep green needles laying across my path. Click-click. A brown oak leaf stuck to the side of a granite lantern, as if découpaged there just to contrast the stone's stark white surface. Click-click. A puddle reflecting the skeletal branches of the overhanging Japanese maple. Click-click. I captured each of these moments on my camera, my heart swelling with each shot I committed to the semi-permanency of digital photography. There was just something about capturing these moments in time, freezing these shots of perfectly imperfect ephemerality that made me feel alive. I swore to make more time to bask in the changing seasons when I got home.

I made my way to the far edge of the island, to the Jizō statue, and inhaled, savoring the smoke-tinged, damp air deep in my lungs. The distant sound of the temple bell rang out and I smiled. After cleaning up, Honda-san must've made it back to her happy place, too.

The Jizō statue had a few wet, golden leaves plastered to his bald head, so I peeled them off and tossed them into nearby bushes. The statue's presence made more sense now that I knew the owner's daughter had died somewhere on this island. Jizō was said to accompany the souls of dead children to the afterlife, carrying them in his capacious pockets. In a way, this solemn spot was a memorial to the owner's daughter. I bowed my head and pressed my hands together before the statue, whispering a few words of vague prayer.

My silent moment was interrupted, however, by a quiet calling, the sound of a bird. The crane? I cocked my head; it didn't sound too far away. Perhaps she was rebuilding her nest after the storm. The idea of the poor lonely creature's home being damaged sent a sharp pang into my chest.

I crept on soft feet toward the sound, hoping not to disturb or scare her; this was supposed to be her private sanctuary. I was loath to be the obnoxious American barreling in and disturbing the peace once again.

When I'd snuck closer to the cluster of weeping willows along the pond's edge, I could hear rustling sounds, and the quiet snapping of twigs. There, under the sheltering branches of a heavily weeping tree, the crane was standing beside a nest of sticks some two or three feet across, busying herself with twig adjustments. Up close she was so much larger than I'd anticipated (almost as tall as Honda-san!) that for a moment I trembled, uneasy standing so near such a sharp, magnificent creature—particularly when she was protecting her nest. But soon the fear passed; the crane had no reason to hurt me. After all, she had led me to this island.

Hadn't she?

I watched her for a few minutes, following her beak's sharp, precise movements, admiring how hard and single-mindedly she worked on the rebuilding, alone.

Rebuilding. I turned to survey this unused corner of the island, surrounded by the weeping willows. How beautiful it must have looked once upon a time. But everything can be rebuilt, everything can heal, given the proper time. Isn't that the beauty of nature, and of life?

I pulled out my camera, snapped a flurry of shots of the crane busying about her nest. Such poise, such dedication. What I wouldn't give to have her clarity of vision, her sense of purpose.

A brisk gust of wind coming off the pond sent a chill through me, and I hugged my arms around my body. Though spring was on the horizon, the icy chill of winter was still an ever-present possibility. I really should've brought my coat.

"Mom? Is everything all right?"

Mom had a knack for calling at the wrong moment—when I was just about to walk out the door or step into the shower—but she never, ever, called me at work. I glanced over my shoulder at Risa talking to the caterer. Only two days before Mr. Liao's show opening. I didn't have time for personal calls.

"I'm sorry, sweetness, I know you're busy. I just wanted to—"

"Look, can I call you back? I have the caterer here right now, and I need to check on when the courier is going to—"

"Mari." Mom's voice was suddenly sharp, tinged with anger. "Can't you just let Risa take care of those little details? Isn't that why you hired her? So she could take some of the admin stuff off your plate? You can trust her."

I sighed. "I know that Mom, but there are some things Risa can't handle and I—"

"Give her a chance, Mari! Shouldn't you be spending your time doing photography yourself, instead of just selling other people's work?"

I stood, stunned, mouth slightly open. Where had this tirade come from? Since when did Mom care about these things?

"I-I'm sorry, Mari. I'll call you back later." Mom's voice was suddenly quiet, subdued. She hung up before I had a chance to respond.

I set my phone down on the table, took a deep breath, and went to apologize to the caterer for the interruption even as a dark sense of foreboding filled my body.

I could deny it no longer—something was wrong with Mom.

My eyes opened in the dark. Outside my room, the corridor reverber-ated with the sounds of sorrow, the heart-wrenching sobs I had come to know. And tonight they were louder, drawing me like a moth to a flame. I slipped out into the hallway in bare feet.

Darkness, inky and complete. I shuffled, palm dragging on the wall beside me. This time there were no sounds besides the girl's cries, no moaning winds or creaking beams, yet somehow that made it worse, the crying more overt. How was no one else in the inn hearing this? Or perhaps they heard it, too, but had learned to cover their ears with pillows, refusing to acknowledge what it might be.

Or perhaps I was the only one there.

After what felt like only a few moments of walking, I passed through the musty curtain leading to her room. Then I was at her door, sliding it open a crack. And there in the flickering lantern light was the girl, lying on her futon, sobbing into her hands.

Her long hair hung in a cascade in front of her face, still dripping foul water onto her bedding and clothes. The filthy yukata she wore might've once been a lovely sage color but was now a muddy gray-green like the dormant duckweed outside.

I teetered on the edge of fleeing, the foul, swampy odor invading my nose, my head pounding, but something held me there, a nocturnal voyeur of this young girl's suffering. She didn't seem to have noticed me. I remained in the hallway, content to marvel at this impossible child, until she let out another cry—this one as keening and tormented as I'd ever heard: *Mari-chan.*

Mari-chan. She was calling for me.

As if in a trance, I slid open the door.

Despite the aching waves pulsing anew into my brain, I crept across the cold tatami floor on bare feet and then fell to my knees beside her. The scent made me gag—a rank, wet odor of decay—and I covered my nose and mouth with the long sleeve of my yukata. Something deep inside me stirred, however, and in that moment all I knew was that there was a child before me, hurting, deeply, and I did the only humane thing I could think of—I spoke to her.

"Are you all right?"

The words tumbled from my mouth before I could restrain the absurd question. Of course she didn't answer, just lay on her stained comforter, hands still obscuring her face. She rolled away from me toward the wall, intensifying her mournful wail.

Waves of emotion buffeted me, like the crashing of angry waves on a beach, and I had to grit my teeth against the strain. But still I reached out and laid a hand gently on the sobbing girl's shoulder. It felt solid, real.

For a moment her crying quieted, like I'd turned down the volume with a knob, and she slowly dropped her hands from her face.

Oh, I thought, for her face struck a familiar chord deep within me.

The girl looked at me, blinked, but then resumed her crying, though with less intensity—just the quiet seeping of tears from her eyes. She didn't cover her face again.

I leaned in close, gathered her thin frame in my arms, and held her as she cried.

Chapter Twenty-Five

"So Mom, how did it go at your appointment?"

I unwrapped the scarf from around my neck and laid it on Mom's table. She was bustling around the kitchen as usual, but as my eyes tracked her, I noticed subtle differences. Her movements were slower, and she kept one hand pressed against the countertop as she shuffled around the small space, as if uncertain of her balance.

Her response was so delayed I wondered if she'd heard me, but after a long pause she said, "Fine, pumpkin. Just fine."

I frowned. Her hand shook as she pulled the heavy mugs out of the cabinet over the stove.

"Mom, are you all right?"

She set the mugs on the counter and wiped her hands on her striped apron. "Oh, before I forget—I have something for you, honey."

I opened my mouth to protest, but she disappeared out the doorway. She was hiding something; her nervous energy would give that away even if her odd behavior didn't.

When she reappeared in the kitchen, she seemed out of breath even though I hadn't heard her go up the stairs. She was carrying a small white box in hands that trembled slightly.

"Mom, I—"

"I've always wanted you to have this, darling. I want you to know that." She interrupted me by shoving the small box in front of my nose, and I couldn't help but take it from her. The box was so light it seemed impossible that anything was inside, but when I took off the tiny lid it uncovered a ring.

My heart clenched inside my chest. This wasn't just any ring—it was silver with an engraved floral pattern. Mom's favorite. I glanced at Mom's right hand, at her orange-stained fingernails, at her naked ring finger. She never took off that ring.

"I-I don't understand, Mom. Why aren't you wearing it?" I plucked the ring out of the box's soft cushion and held it up to her like a petulant child disturbed by a deviation in her comfortable routine.

"I think it's time for you to have it, honey. Don't you like it?" Mom was leaning on the table, watching me closely.

"Of course I like it—that's not the point." I turned my gaze to the empty white box. "I'm not ready for you to give it to me, though."

Mom sighed, and finally took the ring from me. She inspected it for a moment, and as she turned it in the air, I noticed how thin her fingers were. When had my mother become so frail? She was only fifty-eight—she wasn't even old yet.

"Mom, y-you're ok, right?"

But Mom just smiled. She stuck the ring back into the formed cushion of the box and closed it. "I understand, Mari. Maybe I'm not quite ready to give it to you, either."

A trickle of relief sank into my body.

Mom nodded, reading the expression on my face. "So how about that coffee?"

Our eyes met and unspoken words passed between us.

"Thanks, Mom, that'd be great."

I have no memory of how I made it back to my room that night after visiting the little girl. I only know I awoke the next morning to Yuna's familiar knock sounding on my door.

"I'm glad you're up! I was afraid you might be sick." Yuna knelt beside my table, began laying out my breakfast dishes.

"Sick?" I glanced down at my rumpled yukata—damp in spots and emitting a faint swampy odor.

"Oh! I have news." Yuna paused in her arranging to beam a smile at me. "We will have a special visitor to the inn today." A mischievous glint shone in Yuna's eye like she had a secret she was dying to share. Or like when she teased me about my boyfriend.

"How mysterious. Is it a new guest?"

Yuna shook her head. "No, not exactly . . ."

I raised an eyebrow.

"It's Yanagi Inn's owner! She'll be arriving sometime this after-noon. And . . ." Yuna leaned forward, "she specifically asked to meet with you!"

"Great! I've been wanting a chance to talk to her."

Even as the words left my mouth, I realized they were half-empty. I kept telling myself I needed to talk to the owner, but once I did, I might be given hard guidelines. My instinct-driven photography might become more regimented.

But maybe that would be good for me. How many days had already passed? A week, or more. I kept reminding myself I had four weeks, but it must be less than three by now.

Honda had told me snippets about the owner, about her loss and grief, but I realized I knew very little about her personally. How did experiences like that change a woman?

"Yuna-chan, what is the owner like?"

"Oh, I think you'll like her. She's so elegant."

Not much of a description. Elegant could describe Ogura-san. And most of the other older Japanese women I'd met.

"Great, but do you know—"

"Well, I'd better be off." Yuna stood up with her tray. "Have a good day, Mari-san!" Yuna bobbed her head and was out the door before I could thank her.

What an impossibly upbeat girl, I thought, as I finally crawled to the table.

It was only later, when I was walking down the hall to the baths, that a thought occurred to me; since everyone simply called her "the owner," I didn't even know the woman's name.

I closed my eyes and sank deeper into the bath, letting my eyelids steep in the hot water. I never took baths at home in Chicago; if I managed a five-minute shower in the morning, I considered myself fortunate. Luxuriating in a bath like this was the height of opulence, yet nothing was really stopping me from filling the tub at home, lighting some aromatherapy candles, maybe even pouring a glass of wine, and having a good soak. Maybe I'd buy some of those bath bombs when I got home.

I reopened my eyes and let out a startled yip, like a tiny dog who just had his tail stepped on.

I wasn't alone.

Yuna stood by the doorway leading to the changing area, a small round tray in her hands and an amused grin on her face.

"You scared me!" I slid one hand to cover my chest and the other my lap, but immediately felt silly. It shouldn't be a big deal for another woman to see me in the baths.

"I'm sorry, Mari-san." Yuna's chuckling betrayed how she really felt. "I wanted to surprise you with something."

She knelt beside the bath and set her wooden tray on the floor. On the tray was a square wooden cup and a large ceramic saké bottle nestled in a bowl of ice.

"You brought me alcohol? Isn't it like nine in the morning?"

"But it's the perfect thing when you're soaking in the hot baths! Go on, give it a try. You can thank me later." With that, Yuna stood, bowed, and left the saké set behind.

Well, I shouldn't let it go to waste.

I filled the cup with the cloudy white liquid and took a tentative sip. Yuna was right—it was the perfect drink for the baths: cool, refreshing, and such a smooth flavor. I leaned back against the wall of the bath and savored the drink sip by sip. No harm in just enjoying a little, right?

Time passed, and I refilled the cup once, twice, three times, and my head was light and floaty, as if bobbing along the surface of the water—a beach ball in the waves. I closed my eyes, set aside all the bizarre occurrences I'd experienced at the inn, and imagined I was lying on a hot sand beach, letting the waves lick my feet.

But then I heard something—a quiet splash—and a sweet tang of citrus tickled my nose. It had to be Yuna, sneaking up on me again, tossing some yuzu into the water for ambiance. It had to—

I opened my eyes.

No, no, no.

Mom.

She sat on the other side of the bath, some eight feet away, her blond hair pinned on top of her head, though strands of it dusted her shoulders, floated in the hot water around her. Her head was turned, staring off over her shoulder, so I couldn't see her face.

But it was her.

I flailed, tried to stand, one foot slipped on the bottom of the bath and I fell, plunging under the water. And then I was submerged—impossibly deep—and I opened my eyes underwater though it was cloudy and so hot it stung my eyes like a million needles. And there was my mother's blurry, naked body across the bath from me, unmoving.

I opened my mouth to scream—the hot, stinging water rushed inside. I choked and my arms flailed, yet I couldn't seem to reach the surface.

A reel of indistinct images flashed in front of my mind. Mom passed out in her bed, an empty bottle of saké and a blister pack of sleeping pills lying next to her. Holding Risa's tiny hand as we walked the few blocks to the konbini to buy food for dinner. Counting out 5-yen coins to cover the ice cream I let Risa pick out so she'd think it was a fun outing.

No! But more memories spilled out of me. A little girl, laughing, knee deep in water. A scream—my scream—and it was cold, so cold . . .

No! Breathe, Mari, breathe!

Then I was sitting up, panting, wet hair spilling over my face. I pushed it away, gulping for air.

I was alone.

I hurled the wooden saké cup across the room and let it crack against the wall. *What the hell is wrong with me?*

Five minutes later, I lurched out into the corridor, hair dripping wet, and so desperately needing a glass of water that I could hardly see straight.

I should've known better than to drink so much saké.

Head still spinning from the drink, from the overheating, from the horrifying visions, I wobbled down the corridor. When I turned a corner I, of course, plowed straight into Ogura.

When we collided, the stack of towels she'd been carrying tumbled to the ground, their perfect folds coming undone and spilling across the hallway.

"Oh, I'm so sorry! Here, let me help." I knelt, began scooping up the towels.

Ogura's hard stare burned into me, and I'm sure I turned a bright crimson. My hair was a mess, my yukata hastily tied. I tugged the loosened fabric further across my chest.

"Just leave it, Lennox-san. The towels will have to be rewashed anyways." Her voice was icy. "Besides," her mouth twitched, "the owner has arrived, and she would like to see you."

My stomach dropped. Already? I swallowed, swallowed again, fighting off the very real fear that I would vomit all over Ogura and her tumbled towels.

"R-right now? I need to go back to my room. I-I need a glass of water."

"There will be tea in the banquet room."

"Please, Ogura-san, just five minutes. I can't face her like this." I despised the pleading in my voice, like I was a young child begging to stay up after bedtime.

Ogura's eyes narrowed, but she made an assenting grunt and headed back in the direction of my room, leaving me kneeling in a sea of unfolded towels.

I jumped to my feet and hurried after her.

Chapter Twenty-Six

I rushed around my room, combing my wet hair and searching for the travel-sized bottle of mouthwash I could've sworn I'd packed while Ogura stood guard outside my door. In the mirror my reflection looked wild-eyed and pale. *Keep it together, Mari, keep it together.*

Ogura's impatience breathed on my door like dragon's smoke, but I paused before leaving my room. My laptop. Would the owner expect to see the photos I'd taken? Damn, I should've put together a preliminary slideshow, should've been more prepared.

I grabbed my laptop and stepped out into the hall.

Ogura led me down a narrow corridor I hadn't yet explored, as I'd thought it for staff only. She pushed through a short noren curtain, and it flapped in my face. I flinched and pushed my way through it, heart pounding.

We entered a surprisingly large room, which I surmised had once been the dining hall in the inn's heyday. I envisioned spectral figures of guests in matching yukata seated at the long tables, steaming dishes laid out in front of them, boisterous laughter. Now the long, low dining tables were draped with dust cloths and covered with boxes. All except one. A woman sat at the far end of the room, occupying the one un-covered table, bare save for a stack of record books. I felt like a lowly peasant come to petition the emperor as I crossed the length of the room, Ogura leading the way. I tried to keep my gait steady despite feeling a bit woozy and awkwardly hiding the laptop behind my back.

"This is Yanagi Inn's owner, Kishi Hitomi," Ogura said softly, and with a deference I wouldn't have thought her capable of. Then she turned to Kishi-san and bowed deeply before the seated woman. "I've brought the photographer to see you."

Kishi-san.

The name kindled a faint spark of memory in the recesses of my brain. Kishi. Why was it so familiar?

Kishi glanced up from her ledger at our approach. She looked at me, and for a moment her eyes widened and she opened her mouth as if to speak, but then closed it into a firm line.

Ogura must have registered her reaction, as well, for she murmured a polite apology for disturbing her and shot me a fierce, reproachful look as if all of this had been my own ill-advised plan. Kishi simply waved her hand in a dismissive gesture, but she continued to stare at me.

She was a small woman, clearly slight of build even in her heavy seafoam and silver kimono. Her face was creased, but in a pleasant way that implied a lifetime of smiles. At odds with her otherwise fastidious and conventional appearance, her black hair was loose about her shoulders and spilled down her back like the mane of a messy child. Kishi-san must've been about the same age as Mom. This thought sent a sharp pain through my heart.

At first it looked as though she had a fuzzy blanket on her lap, but when the blanket jumped up on the table, I realized it was a gray and white cat. I caught myself before a frown spread across my face.

It's not that I didn't like cats—I did. But I was also allergic to them.

I realized Kishi and I had been staring at each other for several long moments without performing any kind of greeting, so I bowed formally, cringing slightly as my wet hair slipped out of its hastily constructed bun and into my face. The bow threw off my already tenuous equilibrium, and I stumbled forward. Gritting my teeth, I straightened, smoothed back my hair with one hand and said, "Good morning, Kishi-san. Thank you for this opportunity."

Kishi smiled warmly and reached a thin, elegant hand up to stroke the cat. It arched against her palm, its backbone sticking up visibly through its fur.

"You are very welcome, Lennox-san. I hope your stay has been comfortable. I apologize that the inn is not like it was before."

I froze. It would be blatantly disingenuous to disagree about the inn's state, but I didn't want to disparage anything about the property, which, I realized with sudden clarity, I had come to love.

I chose my words carefully, resisting the temptation to rub my itching nose. "My stay has been most comfortable. Your staff does credit to the grand reputation of Yanagi Inn."

Kishi bowed her head, deeper this time, and I took this as confirmation I hadn't completely embarrassed myself.

"I'll get right to the point." She continued stroking the cat, each movement sending a dusting of gray fur floating through the air to settle on the table. I clenched my jaw to fight off a sneeze. "I don't often come back to Yanagi Inn, and my time here is short."

Kishi hesitated, as if uncertain how much she should say. She paused in her petting, too, and the cat turned toward her and bumped its bony head against her palm until she continued.

"I wanted to see you, Lennox-san, and check how you are doing. I was sorry to hear about your mother."

My mother? Before I could reply, she spoke up again.

"Where are my manners? Please, won't you have a seat? Would you like some tea?"

I nodded, though I was wary of getting closer to that dander-covered table and the mangy cat, and knelt on a cushion opposite of Kishi. She gestured toward the door, and a maid who wasn't Yuna brought in a tray with tea service. I accepted a cup with a dip of my head. Kishi was closely watching my hands during this transaction, and I wondered if I'd forgotten some subtle piece of etiquette, or if she'd noticed that I'd bitten my fingernails down to embarrassing stubs over the past few months.

"Your ring . . . it is lovely."

Oh.

I only wore one ring. "Thank you. My mother passed it on to me."

I laid my hand flat on the table and we both gazed at my middle finger. The engraved floral pattern did tend to catch the light. After a minute of heavy silence, the cat threatened to rub against my wrist and I snatched up my cup to take a sip of tea, my eyes itching.

"Oh!" Kishi said, pulling the bony creature back onto her lap. "Of course, the fur is bothering you. My apologies."

"No, no, it's no problem," I said, though my protestations were weak. Were my allergies that obvious? I shifted on my ankles, my feet going numb from the unaccustomed position, and took another sip of tea.

While I sipped, I shot a glance at Kishi over the rim of my cup. She was idly petting the cat on her lap and staring at her untouched tea, obviously deep in some thought or memory. This wasn't going how I expected at all. It felt more like an awkward visit with a relative I hadn't seen in years than a business meeting.

"I-I'm progressing well with my photography. I'm really enjoying exploring and documenting the grounds." I took another sip of the scalding tea, wishing it were a tall glass of ice water with an allergy pill instead, then set the cup aside and pulled out my laptop.

I turned the screen so it would be visible for both of us and pulled up my photos.

As I flipped through images, I rattled on about my ideas, though I wasn't sure Kishi-san was really listening. "I'd like to take some more photos of the baths in different lighting, and more of the exterior of the building itself . . ." Click, click, click.

I should've been paying more attention. I should've thought about the fact I hadn't curated this file in any way before showing it to the owner, because as I was scrolling through photo after photo of the inn and its grounds it was inevitable that I'd hit some photos I'd regret.

I gasped audibly when a photo of the peeling red bridge popped up on my screen.

Shit, shit, shit. I couldn't bring myself to look at Kishi. I just closed the laptop with a quiet click and we sat in silence for a moment.

Maybe she hadn't recognized the bridge. Maybe she'd forgotten it was on the island, not the mainland.

I cleared my throat and turned toward her. "Kishi-san, I—"

"Thank you, Lennox-san. Your photographs are lovely."

I opened my mouth to reply. She didn't look mad, just . . . pained? Mournful? Maybe disappointed? She gave me a tight smile.

I clenched a fist under the table, took a deep breath. "Is it all right if I take photos everywhere in the estate?"

Kishi's eyes bored into me, as if she could read my real thoughts and intentions engraved in the soft lining of my soul. I stared down at my tea, spinning the cup in my hands, before continuing. "I want my portfolio to be as thorough as possible. F-for the sake of posterity." I could feel my face flushing. "That's what I'm here for, right?"

A quizzical expression passed over Kishi's face for a moment, but then she looked down at the cat and resumed petting. "Yes, of course. Yes, you have my permission to document anything on the premises, excluding the staff-only offices."

I bowed my head and thanked her quietly, a small thrill running through my body. Wait, was she making fun of me? Did she know about my inadvertent closet adventure a few days ago?

Her face was inscrutable.

No, maybe I was reading too much into her statements. I didn't understand this woman, and not just because I was still a bit tipsy. She was elegant, yes—I surreptitiously inspected her fine pale kimono and silver accessories, her incongruously loose hair—but there was a hint of coldness to her manner, like she'd put up a wall between us, that made it hard to feel any connection.

"Well, I shouldn't detain you any longer. Thank you for taking the time to meet with me. I hope you enjoy the remainder of your stay." Kishi smiled at me, although it had little warmth.

My cue to leave.

"Thank you, Kishi-san—I'm sure you are a busy woman." I returned her smile and inclined my head in a slight bow. I grabbed my laptop and rose to leave, sneezing as delicately as I could into my sleeve.

I had almost reached the door, when she called out to me one last time.

"How long do you plan on staying here at Yanagi Inn?"

I stopped, and turned to look at Kishi's face. Still inscrutable. Had I overstayed my welcome already? My anxiety rose like a noxious gas inside my brain.

"I-I'm not sure. The grant didn't really say . . ."

She smiled, and this time it felt a shade closer to warm. "Take your time, Mari-chan. You are welcome to stay as long as you need."

Uncertain how to respond, I simply bowed, more deeply than before, and then turned on my heel and walked quickly out of the room.

As I headed down the dimly lit corridor and pushed my way through the short curtain, my footsteps lightened, as if a dark weight had lifted from my body. I hadn't realized how heavy the emotions were in that room, or perhaps I was just elated now that I had official, if somewhat tacit, approval to do what I'd already been doing—exploring and photographing the forsaken island's gardens. I sped up, eager to tell Honda, eager to visit the island again.

And then, for the second time that day, I ran head-on into Ogura.

At least this time she wasn't carrying dozens of towels.

I yelped, then murmured a string of obsequious apologies, while Ogura remained silent, blocking the corridor with her body.

"Let me be clear, Lennox-san," she said, her nose in the air, nostrils wide. "You have disturbed the owner enough already. It would be best if you didn't stay any longer than absolutely required. And you are not to bother the owner again."

My mouth hung open for a long moment before I bobbed my head and muttered, "I understand." Then I skirted around her rigid form and speed-walked the rest of the way back to my room, cheeks blazing, eyes itching, and a foul taste lingering in my mouth.

Chapter Twenty-Seven

I sat next to Mom's bed, trying to pretend we were just having a normal kitchen table chat surrounded by the comforting scent of coffee, instead of sitting in a hospital room infused with artificial cherry cleaner. I surreptitiously sought other scents (the Bulgarian rose perfume on my wrist, even the baby powder deodorant of my shirt) just to avoid the odor.

Perhaps my nerves were making me oversensitive, for no one else seemed bothered. Certainly not the nurses, so desensitized they probably didn't even realize they carried the scent on their bodies and hair when they left this godforsaken place.

Mom had been taking a nap when I came in, so I'd sat down in the plastic bedside chair and pulled out the small paperback I keep stashed in my bag. *Kitchen* by Banana Yoshimoto.

Though the subject matter hit a bit close to home, it was my go-to "stuck in a boring situation" book. Its pages were dog-earned, its cover torn and re-taped.

After a few minutes, though, Mom had opened her eyes and smiled at me. Her blond hair was thinning and her skin sagged—she had aged so much in recent weeks I almost wouldn't have recognized her. "Mari, you should've woken me."

"I know this'll sound super clichéd, but you looked so peaceful I didn't want to wake you up." We both chuckled, but Mom ended up in a coughing fit.

"Yeah, well, cliché or not, there's plenty of time for me to lie here peacefully after I'm dead. I'd rather spend my remaining time awake and talking to you, pumpkin." She reached out and patted my hand. Her fingers were sticks, and I found myself envisioning the part of Hansel and Gretel where Hansel fools the evil, nearly blind witch by sticking chicken bones through the bars of his cage to prove he isn't plump enough to eat yet.

"What? You've got plenty of time, Mom. You've got this." I smiled warmly, though my heart was pounding, and I squeezed her hand between both of mine. Skin and bones, nothing but cold skin and bones.

"Oh, Mari. One of these days you'll have to wake up, child."

She sounded so weary, so exasperated, a frown spread across my face. This wasn't like her.

Mom gently detached her hands from mine and slid a ring off her skeletal middle finger, the only ring she ever wore after she and Dad divorced and she moved Risa and me back to the United States. She held the silver band between her forefinger and thumb for long moments, turning it slightly from side to side so it would catch the light.

Oh god, she's trying to give me her ring again.

My own hands trembled, and I clasped them together in my lap.

"Mari, I'd like you to have my ring."

I remained silent, eyes glued to the shining band, jaws clenched tight.

"It was given to me by a dear friend, many years ago, and it's always reminded me to stop and appreciate the beauty and wonder of life." She turned one of my hands over and set the ring in the center of my palm. "I've always known I wanted you to have it one day. You're too much like me, darling girl. You need reminders to stop and breathe sometimes, too."

"You need the ring, Mom, not me." I pushed the ring back into her hands and for a moment we were a tangle of fingers and fists pressing against each other and I wasn't sure who had the ring anymore.

"No, Mari, I don't need it any longer." Her voice was soft, and her eyes were wet, filled with empathy for a daughter so incapable of facing the truth.

"You're not dying, Mom!"

A moment of silence, interrupted only by the whirring and beeping of machines.

"Mari—I'm ready to give the ring to you. Please don't make this any harder for me than it needs to be." Her voice had a sharp finality to it. I wanted to argue, to insist that she was talking nonsense, overacting like she always did. I wanted to take the ring and force it onto her finger— not this weird skeletal bone that her finger had turned into, but her real finger of flesh.

But I couldn't do that to my mother, not when she was . . . like this.

I accepted it, placed it on the ring finger of my right hand, the same finger Mom used to wear it on before she'd become so skeletal.

"It suits you, Mari." Mom was smiling, her head leaning back against her propped-up pillows.

I held up my hand for both of us to see, but I only saw a blur through my tears. I pressed my lips together tightly and nodded.

That evening, I sat at my low table, nibbling on the wrapped rice crackers that seemed to keep magically reappearing in my room. I clicked through the photos I'd shown Kishi earlier, ending on the incriminating photo of the bridge.

Maybe it wasn't as obvious as I'd thought. Kishi-san hadn't really been paying close attention; maybe she'd missed the fact that it was a photo from the island.

I sighed and closed the file.

On a whim, I clicked on another file of photos, an older one from back when Mom was still alive and healthy.

Though I only had one photo of my dad, I had tons of pictures of Mom. Thank god for that. The idea of ever forgetting her face, forgetting the way her big smile lit up a room, would be too much to bear.

Dad, however, was frozen in time for me—just a single snapshot of him and Risa and me standing in front of a temple during some kind of festival. He would always be in his early thirties in my mind because of it. At least he'd been smiling.

I clicked on the first image. A photo from two Christmases ago with Mom and Risa sitting beside the small artificial tree Mom decorated every year. Mom, healthy and full of life. My heart ached so much to hear her voice, to hear her sing an out-of-tune rendition of "Jingle Bells," I had to move on to the next photo.

Thad wearing swim trunks on a pier with our cruise ship behind him in the distance. Thad in a pinstripe suit at some gallery event.

Thad. His name provoked a bittersweet smile.

He had surprised me with that cruise trip, even though he was terrible at planning things and usually left scheduling up to me. And he came to every gallery event that he was in town for regardless of what kind of art it was. Why had I not noticed these little gestures at the time, back when they still mattered?

I kept clicking.

I found photos of home, of Ginkgo lying upside on the couch with his belly exposed, of Risa in my kitchen making a special stir-fry she'd learned in a cooking class, holding up the wok with a wide grin on her face. I smiled.

Then came a series of photos I'd snapped on a walk in my Chicago neighborhood—reflections of buildings on the lake, sunlight filtering through the trees lining the walking path, a single dandelion growing up through a crack in the sidewalk.

I remembered showing these photos to Risa, and how she'd loved the dandelion photo the best. She'd convinced me to share it on my Instagram and use the hashtag #BeautyFromAshes. Beauty from ashes. New growth rising from the old, so poignantly beautiful, so filled with hope. Like the beautiful orange koi fish rising to the surface of the murky pond.

I looked back at the photo of the dandelion growing out of the sidewalk and grinned. My little sister always did see the beauty in ordinary things, the sublime growing out of the ashes that most people overlooked.

I sighed; I had been a terrible big sister lately. Glancing at the clock on my laptop, I did a few quick mental calculations. Risa would be at work right now—I could send her a text. I'd never really been the kind of person who sent random, cheerful, "thinking of you" kind of texts before, but maybe I could become one.

I tapped my finger on the tabletop, running through options of what to say to her, but they all felt trite. Then, with a burst of inspiration, I opened my photos and flipped to the pics I'd taken that morning at breakfast. I selected my favorite photo of the rounded bowl of rice, my perfectly grilled fish, the miso soup with its bright green wakame, and texted it to Risa with "Bet you're not eating as well as me!" and a wink emoji.

I imagined the grin on her face when she saw the beautiful spread, and a few seconds later she replied:

No fair! I knew you'd make me jealous! ☺

A faint, distant sound of weeping in the night. The little girl—she needed me.

I slipped on quiet feet down the hall, moving quickly, my anxiety rushing me forward despite the darkness. Left, left, then right, then left again—within moments I was pushing aside the musty curtain leading to the girl's room and sliding open her door.

Darkness. The lantern wasn't lit.

Silence. Her crying had stopped.

I was robbed of all sensations, save for the murky, swampy miasma invading my nose.

"Hello?" I called, softly, my voice trembling.

Nothing.

I held my breath, listening for the tell-tale sound of breathing or quiet rustling in the room, but heard none. Dead silence. My heart stuttered, an erratic arrhythmia inside my chest.

On wobbling legs, I lowered myself to the ground and crawled on hands and knees to where I remembered the lantern, praying to any gods listening that I didn't place my hand on anything wet and unspeakable.

I bumped into the lantern with my outstretched hand, and the tiny flame ignited.

Light flooded the room. I shielded my eyes with a sleeve, but only for a moment; then I located the bed, the little girl in her dirty yukata. Relief.

She was sitting up, alert, and staring at me. She was pretty, though her button nose was red from crying and her hair was still wet, dripping, in her face.

"Hello," I said, gently, hoping to put her at ease. "What is your name?" I spoke softly, half afraid that by breaking the silence I would shatter whatever uneasy balance existed in this space. But pieces of the larger puzzle were slowly beginning to form in my mind, and I had to find out if I could slide them into place.

"I'm Suzu," she said at long last.

Oh, how that name struck a chord deep inside me, like hearing the opening notes of a favorite childhood melody long into adulthood. I nodded, goosebumps erupting down my arms.

Suzu . . . was that the name of Kishi-san's long-dead daughter? Yes, I thought, even as I realized with some unease that no one had ever mentioned her name.

I was surprised that this epiphany didn't throw me into a panic. Perhaps the dreamlike nature of my night leant such an air of unreality that the concept of ghosts was distant and vague.

"I'm Mari," I said, moving to kneel beside the little girl. The murky, swampy smell was much fainter than before. "Do you mind if I ask why you are crying?"

Suzu sniffed, and I wished I had a tissue to hand her, even as a voice in the back of my mind insisted that ghosts shouldn't need tissues—yet here we were. She looked away from me then, turning her head to look toward the blank wall. "Because Mama is . . . very sad."

With those words, a wave of emotion struck me, like a tsunami coming ashore. It knocked me with the force of a physical blow, and I fell back onto my hands, eyes wide.

She was crying because her mother was so overcome with grief? It had to be Kishi-san. I thought of the older woman I'd seen that morning (had it really been the same day?), her long, loose hair, the cold demeanor, the elderly cat. Yes, I could see how a person drowning in grief could manifest in that way. But I was also certain the last thing Kishi-san wanted was for her daughter's ghost to forever be caught up in the maelstrom of her own grief.

Regaining my composure, I smoothed out the wrinkles in my yukata, tucked a crazed strand of hair behind my ear. Deep breath. "Suzu-chan, are you saying you are sad because your mama is sad?"

Suzu nodded. "I was playing near the water, and I fell in. I-I didn't come back up." Her eyes scrunched up so much I feared she would start crying again, but instead she made her hands into fists and fought back the tears with visible effort. "Now Mama hates this whole place. She doesn't want to come back."

She didn't come back up.

I forced down the sick turmoil in my stomach. Suzu was speaking of her own death—did she realize that? And did she know her mother was here at Yanagi Inn?

"H-have you tried telling your mama how you feel?" The question sounded so inane—so painfully hypocritical—but I wasn't sure how else to broach the subject.

Now Suzu turned to look at me. She cocked her head as if I'd just asked the most nonsensical question. "Mama can't see me."

Oh. Well, that did complicate matters.

"Do you want me to tell your mama that you're here? Can I relay a message?"

Suzu shook her head, looked down at her wringing hands.

I frowned. "Are you . . . stuck in this room?" I remembered the stories I'd heard as a child about ghosts that were bound to a specific place, unable to leave. But why would that place be this room if she had drowned in the pond? An image of the ghostly face in my Jizō photo rose in my mind.

Suzu frowned, still staring down at her hands. Anxiety was wisping off her in visible waves, and her eyes were filling with tears.

I spoke up quickly.

"Do you want to come with me? We could go for a walk." The idea of roaming the dark corridors with a child's ghost at my side made me shudder. "W-we could walk through the pretty gardens together."

Her lower lip quivered. "The gardens aren't pretty. They're broken and covered with death."

I pictured the Jizō statue splattered with mud and wet leaves, the tea house collapsing with rot, the murky ponds with their gray-green duckweed. The images click-click-clicked through my mind until a burst of light lit up the back of my brain, like a vintage camera flash.

What did Honda tell me rises out of death? New life.

And what did Risa say grows out of ashes?

Beauty.

The ideas came full circle in my mind. What if, out of the death and ashes of the island, I could bring new life? What if that beauty could help Suzu-chan?

My mind raced through the possibilities; images of a renewed Jizō statue, fresh flowers and tidied paths flashing through my brain like I was scrolling through images on my camera. The desire to restore and cultivate life surged up inside of me, the compulsion so strong it took my breath away. Maybe that's why I was here. Maybe something wanted me to come restore the island's gardens, bring new life out of the death that permeated the grounds.

The path in front of me seemed clearer than it had in a long, long time, and my whole body felt airy, light. Yes, I knew what I needed to do now—for the sake of the gardens, for the sake of Suzu.

And for myself.

"Suzu-chan, would you like it if I made the gardens beautiful again? Would you come see them with me?"

I caught a sparkle in Suzu's eye at those words. Her face broke into a cautious smile, like the sun peeking through a cloudy sky, and I wanted nothing more than to see this sad little girl happy. "Yes," she said quietly, shyly. "I would like that very much."

That smile. I stared for a moment at her lips. Her smile was lopsided, but not like she was half laughing or smirking. She was born that way, I realized, and this realization stirred up vague memories inside me.

I knew a girl with a mouth like that once.

I blinked. Suzu was watching me, expectantly.

"Well, if it's ok with you . . . that solves it, then. I'll fix the gardens, and then you can come see just how beautiful they are." I paused, piecing together my thoughts. "Were the gardens on the island your favorite?"

"The island was my favorite spot in the whole world." Her words were soft, wistful.

At her words, a pang shot through my body and the trill of cicadas rose in my ears—this time faint, distant. But the sounds disappeared as quickly as they came. My head ached, but I managed to keep up my smile.

"Perfect. When I've finished with the island, you and I will go there, ok?"

I held out my pinky finger and she smiled, grabbing it with her own. For a moment I marveled at how solid and warm her finger felt against mine. Not at all like I would expect from a ghost. "It's a deal," we vowed in unison, and smiled.

Memories struggled to surface, near-firings in my brain, but I shoved them aside.

Yes, I knew a girl like that once.

Chapter Twenty-Eight

The air sensor in Mom's nose quivered with each breath. I stared at it, willing it to flutter, its movement a reassurance that my mother was still breathing, still alive.

Her eyes were closed, but I could tell she wasn't sleeping. The sympathetic nurses described it as "taking a rest" so she could build up her energy—which the rapidly spreading cancer was stealing from her—for talking. That was fine with me.

There was still so much to say.

Mom's eyes flickered open and I grasped her thin hand between both of mine and squeezed gently.

"Mari," she whispered.

"Yes, Mom. And Risa is here too." I gestured to the other side of the bed where my little sister had nodded off, her curly, blond head slumped against the back of her chair.

"Risa—" I started to call, but Mom cut me off.

"Oh, let her rest. I know it's exhausting to care for the dying. Besides, I want to talk to you alone for a moment."

Dying. I tried out the word in my head. My mother is dying. Mom is dying. I expected a surge of anger, a pang of fear, but . . . nothing.

I nodded.

"Mari, I want you to listen. There are some things I need you to do for me. Promise me."

Her dying wish. My breath caught in my throat. Oh my god, this was her dying wish like in a god-damned movie. I wasn't prepared for this. I needed a pencil and paper. I should wake up Risa—she was much better at crap like this—I should . . .

Mom squeezed my hand slightly, and I had the unsettling impression that was the most strength she had, that she was giving that squeeze every ounce of energy she had gathered up when resting.

"I-I promise."

She nodded, with effort, and I could hear the slight scrape of her bald scalp against the hospital pillow, making me realize I couldn't remember the last time she'd moved her head.

"First, I want you to find my engagement ring. It's in a jewelry box hidden under my master bathroom sink. Take it and give it to Diego. Tell him to get it cleaned. Heck, he can have it reset if he wants to clear it of bad luck. And when he's ready, he should give it to Risa." She paused a moment to catch her breath. "That ring was my mother's, and she gave it to your father to propose with. I want Diego to do the same when he's ready. I know he will be."

I nodded through blurred vision. "Ok, Mom. I promise."

Mom took a few shallow breaths and started again. "My second request is important, too." She broke off with a cough, cleared her throat. "You are more sensitive than Risa. You always have been. But I want you to be happy. Don't grieve for me. Sad is fine, missing me is fine, but don't let it consume you. I know how you are, Mari." She paused, took a few deeper breaths. "Always remember, you were the one who survived, and you need to live like it."

The one who survived—what an odd way to put it.

"Promise me, Mari."

Although her request was not at all what I'd expected, although it was decidedly unfair, I nodded.

I looked Mom in her watery eyes and said, "I promise." Words I knew I couldn't keep.

But I could try. For her sake.

She smiled weakly, and I knew she didn't believe me either, but the words had been said and that was all we could do between us. Then she turned away. Her gaze fell on a vase of flowers on the bedside table, next to the bowl of mandarins Risa kept well-stocked, the scene looking all the world like a staged still-life painting.

"Oh!" Mom raised a trembling hand toward the large snowballs of pale purple flowers in full bloom. "Who brought the hydrangeas?"

"Oh, I'm not sure. I think they were delivered, but I never saw a card."

"Ah . . ." Her voice trailed off as she reached her trembling finger to touch a delicate petal. Then she was silent, lost in some reverie.

Minutes passed where the only sound was the quiet beeping of some life-monitoring machine and the hum of countless others. I watched the faint rising and falling of Mom's thin chest inside its blue hospital gown to ensure she was still breathing. Then, without looking away from the flowers, she spoke up, so quietly I had to lean forward to ensure I didn't miss a single word: "I would like to speak to your sister now."

"*Risa!*" The name came out of my mouth with more ire than I'd intended, but it felt impertinent of Risa to sleep at a time like this. How like Risa to pass, untroubled, into sleep while I had to keep watch and count the flutterings of our mother's limited breaths.

Risa awoke with a snort and a start, and the empty styrofoam cup she'd been holding tumbled to the floor. Well, almost empty. "Risa!" I snapped again and came around the side of the bed with a tissue to mop up the small spill.

"Sorry, I must've fallen asleep." Risa's grin was sheepish, like a child who'd been caught with her hand in the cookie jar but hoped to be cute enough to escape punishment.

Mom just smiled indulgently at her youngest child. I'd never felt our birth order so keenly.

"Mari, could you give me a few minutes with your sister?" She spoke to me, but she never took her eyes off Risa, with her honey-blond curls and over-sized trendy red glasses—a look I could never pull off. I muttered something vague about needing fresh coffee anyway, and stood to leave.

I'm embarrassed to admit it now, but when I stepped outside the door I hovered, telling myself I just needed to retie my shoe, just long enough to hear Mom say, "Clarissa, there are two things I need you to do for me."

I ate my breakfast so quickly Yuna laughed and commented on my healthy appetite. In the past, such a remark might've upset me, turned my critical eye inward upon myself, but I was in a different place now. Besides, I knew Yuna didn't mean it as an insult.

It felt satisfying to eat with relish again, and I knew a healthy caloric intake would do me good; I would need the extra energy for all the physical labor I intended to put into the island's gardens.

I went to look in the bathroom mirror. Pressing both hands to the counter, I leaned in close, inspecting my face at different angles. Then I stood back, stripped off my clothes to get a fuller view of myself. Yes, I did look healthier. My skin had a soft pink color, my hair had a nice sheen, and my face had a softness to it I'd lost after Mom got sick and I'd nearly stopped eating altogether.

I found myself spinning the silver ring on my finger as I smiled at myself in the mirror. The ring was getting harder to spin.

Even though the morning's air was quiet and still, without even a breeze to stir the dew from the grass, something told me Honda would be at her temple rather than in the gardens. I strolled down the twisting gravel paths toward the boundary wall. The cool air was invigorating and I inhaled deeply, feeling the moisture absorb into my lungs. But then a wave of anxiety passed over me; what if Honda-san wasn't exactly pleased that I'd received permission to visit the island? Well, close to permission, I thought with a twinge of shame. Why hadn't I just asked Kishi-san directly? Even as I asked the question, though, I knew the answer; because I could've been told *no*. And somehow not visiting the island was no longer an option for me.

When I reached the gate between the inn and the temple grounds, I hesitated only a moment before opening it and stepping through; the border between Yanagi Inn and the temple was blurring more and more in my mind. Maybe it was because Honda-san seemed like such a part of the gardens. My optimism that she'd be willing to help was buoyed by this thought.

Honda wasn't sitting on the steps, and for a moment I doubted my intuition. But I couldn't leave until I'd checked, so I climbed slowly up the first few steps.

"Um . . . hello? Honda-san?" I called softly from the middle step, hesitant to invade any further into this sacred space uninvited. The interior of the temple was dark, foreboding, and for a moment I wished I hadn't come.

I'd never felt shy about entering Buddhist temples as a child, probably due to both the childhood lack of inhibitions and the fact the temples I tended to visit—on New Year's Day or during Mom's somewhat random bouts of experimental yet devout religiosity—were more urban, more popular than this out-of-the-way, clearly rarely visited temple. The temples I'd been familiar with were accustomed to the playful footsteps of young children. If this temple had a personality, however, it would be the cross, crotchety old grandmother-type who scolded the neighbor-hood children for making too much noise.

But you are not a child, Mari! I had to remind myself yet again. Some-thing about returning to the country of my youth left me feeling eternal-ly infantilized, as if time had frozen for me and I was still the same girl who'd spent her childhood here, regardless of how my body had grown.

I exhaled, then sank to the steps. Why had I been so certain Hon-da-san would be here? She could be anywhere on the inn's grounds. Hell, she could be anywhere at all; it's not like Honda-san was tethered to the temple and the inn. She was a free woman and could go wherever she wanted.

I assumed she had to go into town from time to time. Come to think of it, where did Honda-san live? Inside the temple? My mind whirled with all the questions I'd never bothered to ask, and I berated myself for ever thinking her such a simple person.

Mom used to scold me for being "self-centered" in the most liter-al sense—for being so focused on my own concerns that everyone else appeared to be flat, two-dimensional, a mere caricature of a person. Perhaps Mom hadn't been so far off in her assessment of me. I'm sure Thad would agree.

I was ruminating on these thoughts, sitting in a crumpled mess on the temple's stairs, when I heard footsteps crunching on the gravel path. Honda-san.

I jumped to my feet, suddenly self-conscious.

"Mari-san! What a nice surprise. What are you doing here?" Honda smiled warmly as she approached. She wore a slightly different outfit this time—a navy blue wrap top and matching pants, a floppy straw hat—but she still had her bamboo basket tucked into the crook of her elbow.

"Good morning, Honda-san. I-I wanted to tell you about my meet-ing with the owner." As I spoke the words, however, they suddenly felt insubstantial and trifling—a silly reason to be trespassing on temple grounds in their caretaker's absence.

But Honda raised her thin eyebrows and her face lit up at my piece of gossip. She was such an interesting woman. I made a mental note to take her portrait before I left Yanagi Inn. Perhaps standing by the temple's bell? No, as much as Honda-san was clearly a Buddhist nun, it seemed more appropriate to take her portrait in the gardens, amongst the plants and animals she cared for so much. Yes, I would take her portrait on the island. After it was revived.

"Kishi-san is visiting? How . . . unusual. Please, tell me."

Honda joined me on the temple steps and listened attentively to my every word, muttering the occasional *ah* or *mmmm* to show she was following me. I told her of my discussion with Kishi-san, about the cat, and finally (triumphantly!) about how I had asked permission to photograph every part of Yanagi Inn and its grounds.

"Don't you see? I have permission now!" I wanted her enthusiasm to match my own, for her to experience the same elation I felt for not just exploring the island, but also reviving it.

"Kishi-san gave you permission to visit the island?" Honda raised a single eyebrow.

"Kind of," I said, then bit my lip. I swore to myself that I'd be more honest with Kishi-san the next time I saw her.

She eyed me critically for a moment and then nodded. "So, what is your plan?"

I paused, taken aback. My plan? I'd convinced myself that Honda-san was interconnected with the estate's mysteries, and that she would want to help me. Hell, I'd hoped she'd even spearhead the garden renewal process. My only experience was watering Mom's houseplants, and I'd even failed at that.

But this was my idea, and I needed to take action. I needed to take control if I wanted to see change. Maybe I was finally learning that lesson.

"I-I have to restore the island, of course. I want to make it beautiful again, bring it back to its former glory." I recalled Ogura's abrupt admonishment in the hallway. "If it's even possible to do that before I have to leave."

I'd debated whether to tell Honda-san about meeting Suzu. If I were being honest with myself, I still wasn't convinced our nighttime interactions weren't just dreams, or hallucinations. The rational part of my brain, which had served me just fine so far in life, still denied that I'd met a ghost. Perhaps she was a real, living girl who enjoyed toying with me?

But then I pictured Suzu's dripping black hair, the eerie emotions coming off the girl like waves, and shuddered. At any rate, I wasn't about to embarrass myself by letting someone else in on my experiences. At least not yet.

Honda stared off into the distance, nodding slowly as if she were attending to some internal conversation. Then she turned to face me (how small she was! More than a head shorter than me, even when sitting) and said, in a highly formal, grave voice, "I would be honored if you would allow me to assist you, Mari-san." She followed this grand statement with an incline of her head.

Tears welled in my eyes. "Oh, thank you, Honda-san." I laughed, and then turned away, blinking back tears. "I really need your help."

Then Honda laughed with me, and the wrinkles around her eyes grew even deeper.

"Wonderful, I am happy to offer it. I cannot compete with the full team of gardeners once employed at Yanagi Inn, but I'd be honored to lend my assistance. I, too, would like to see that island revived." She paused, looking thoughtfully into the distance. "How shall we begin?"

I stared off into the forest of dark pines surrounding us, at the sunlight streaming through the many textured branches. My fingers twitched, wishing for my absent camera.

How on earth *should* we begin?

We would need supplies, tools. It was so early in the year we probably couldn't do a great deal of planting yet. Would the ground still be hard in early March? But we could still start with pulling weeds and trimming back trees and designing our future plantings . . .

Designing! My blood surged in my veins and I jumped to my feet. Honda rose to her feet, too, and I laughed. "Sorry, I just got excited. I remembered something—do you know the courtyard garden inside Yanagi Inn?"

"Inside the inn? I've never seen it; I have only rarely ventured inside." Something about Honda's tone discouraged further questioning.

I considered for a moment. "Could you meet me there, at my room, tomorrow morning? Say, at 8:30? There's something I want to show you."

Honda searched my face, her own brow slightly furrowed, hinting at apprehension. "I'm not . . . Well, I will meet you."

"You know which room is mine?" Oh—I immediately felt foolish— she'd left the camera on my veranda. But Honda-san just nodded.

"Thank you, Honda-san," I whispered, even as I wondered at her concern.

Chapter Twenty-Nine

When Yuna came in to gather my breakfast dishes the next morning, she took one look at me, already dressed and looking far more awake than normal, and said, "Big plans today?"

She had that twinkle in her eye that told me she was half-jesting, so I just smirked back at her.

"Yuna-chan, do you think I could meet with the owner again today? I want to apologize for my behavior yesterday—I can't believe I drank so much."

Yuna paused, empty rice bowl frozen in mid-air. "Oh, sorry, I think the owner has left already."

"What? She just arrived yesterday!"

"S-She doesn't normally stay the night." Yuna hurriedly began loading my empty dishes onto her tray.

Yuna's hastened movements, her avoidance of my gaze; did Kishi-san know about the ghost girl after all? Did she avoid spending nights here at Yanagi Inn because she, too, heard the nighttime crying of her daughter?

Yuna flicked a glance at me, but I was too lost in thought to fully register it. She slipped out of the room before I could ask any more questions.

Moments later, a quiet knock sounded on my veranda door. 8:30 on the dot. I rose and slid open the panels to find Honda standing on the rock step outside.

I shouldn't have been surprised she chose this point of entry. All the same, it felt oddly avoidant, as if she were sneaking in the back door of a movie theater to avoid buying a ticket. Maybe taking her out into the halls to show off the courtyard garden wasn't such a good idea after all.

I realized I must've been standing there, staring at her, for quite a while. "Oh!" I said, belatedly. "Sorry, please come in."

Honda didn't reply, but simply smiled and carefully slid off her worn sandals on the rock to leave beside my geta, as if it were a normal entryway. When she stepped inside, she glanced briefly around the room and then turned her gaze on me. "Good morning, Mari-san."

"Good morning! Thank you for coming." I bobbed my head. She smiled and then fixed her gaze on me again, expectantly.

Oh, right. I hadn't even told her why I wanted her to come. I took a deep breath, my mind racing. I could just show her the photos—that would be good enough.

"Please, come in, come in. Have a seat by the table." I gestured with both hands, feeling unusually flustered in Honda's presence.

She knelt on her ankles beside the low table, a look of mild amusement on her face as she watched me. No, it wasn't her presence that unsettled me—it was the incongruity of seeing Honda indoors. Like finding a deer in the middle of one's kitchen.

"I wanted to show you some pictures I took—I think they can work as a visual blueprint for how to restore the gardens on the island." I settled down at the table, jiggled the mouse to wake up my laptop.

When I opened the first panorama view of the courtyard garden, I heard the quick intake of breath beside me.

I smiled, my insides warming.

"This," I said, clicking slowly through the photos, "is the replica garden found in Yanagi Inn's courtyard. I don't know its full history, but I know Ogura-san maintains it now, and I think it represents the way the island's gardens once were."

I pointed my finger at the screen. "See the bridge here? And the tiny tea house there? All of the pieces are represented, but in miniature." I paused. "Except for the Jizō statue."

Honda was absorbed in the photos on the screen, and I wasn't sure she was even listening to me. The faint glimmer of tears shone in her eyes. Was it like a window into the past for her? Did she, too, suffer from seeing the island, clearly once so extraordinarily beautiful and serene, in such a state of disarray?

"I think we can rebuild the island's gardens using these photos as our guide. We can restore everything to how it was before . . . before it was abandoned." I watched Honda's face closely. "What do you think?"

She turned to look at me, although it was clear she was still lost in some corner of her mind. But then she smiled and said, "Yes, I think we should try."

That afternoon, Honda and I met at a stone bench overlooking the pond, and she began writing out a list of tools we would need to get us started: refuse bins (as Honda's small basket was insufficient for the scale we had in mind!), shovels, loppers. I'd suggested a wheelbarrow, picturing the landscapers I'd seen back home in the U.S., but Honda pointed out we'd be working on an island without a bridge. No, we would have to carry everything in and out by hand, across the treacherous sunken stones—though she explained that my "stepping-stones" were actually just pillars themselves, once covered with large stone planks to form a footbridge. She looked thoughtful, then added "rubber boots" to the list.

"Fine, no wheelbarrow then. Good thing we're both strong!" I pushed back my sleeve and flexed a bicep, and Honda did the same, her arm small but wiry, and we laughed. We were both giddy with nervous energy (or at least I was, and Honda-san was kind enough to humor me) and I felt more like we were compiling a list of toys we wanted for Christmas than a list of trowels and tree trimmers.

Honda had her own small truck she used for traveling into town for supplies, and she invited me to accompany her on her expedition. I declined and forced my credit card on her instead. At that moment it felt like the outside world had ceased to exist beyond the gates of Yanagi Inn, and if I were to peer beyond the walls, all would be darkness. Or maybe it was the pull of the island, that taut string connecting me to it, unwilling to let me go. In any case, I wasn't prepared to leave. Not even if it were for only one day.

Chapter Thirty

In the days that followed, Honda and I visited the island every day, from morning until dusk. Only the lengthening hours of sunlight made me aware of the passage of time, and some days disappeared in a blink of an eye.

I'm sure Yuna wondered where I went, though she never said a word—just wished me a good day and poked fun at me when she increased the size of my breakfasts yet again to accommodate the extra calories I was burning. Yuna also only smiled and nodded when I asked if she could start sending two onigiri for my midday meal. I'm not sure if she thought I was addicted to the rice balls, or if I was just that hungry, or if she knew I was meeting someone out in the gardens (perhaps she thought I had a lover!), but she was kind and discreet, and I appreciated her supportive friendship during those weeks.

During our initial ripping and tearing and clearing out of the old, dead, and rotten vegetation, Honda and I had crept near the crane's nest, but not so close as to disturb the bird or make her feel we were intruding into her space; we wanted her to feel welcome and secure in her home.

Honda assured me the crane would take care of her own zone, particularly if everything around her was neat and tidy and she had fresh twigs to use. So we gave her and the weeping willows a wide berth and concentrated on the other parts of the island.

We would see the crane flying in from time to time, and I'd taken to waving to her as if she were a neighbor coming home from work. Honda laughed at first, but then she took to waving, too, and she would call out, "Welcome back, Tsuru-san!" and sometimes the crane would call out an "I'm home!" in her squawking bird's call, completing the sense of community.

Honda and I mostly worked in silence, though we always worked near each other, weeding the same section of gravel path or pruning the same thick, evergreen bushes. Sometimes we would chat, quite pleasantly, and I think we grew to be friends, or at least companions who had grown comfortable with each other. I learned more about Honda's past, how she was the youngest of four sisters and had been sent to study with an aunt at a Buddhist temple near Kyoto when she was fifteen because she was such a troublemaker.

Honda-san, a young troublemaker? It made me laugh to think about it, to picture this kindly, calm, grandmotherly woman as a wild teen, drinking and staying out late, hanging out with dangerous boys. I teased her, asked if she still had a few of those dangerous boyfriends, and she laughed, but then she winked and said, "You never know," and I was left to wonder if she might indeed have a beau in the nearby town.

During one of our brief breaks, when Honda pulled out a thermos of hot green tea and two small cups, and I pulled out the two onigiri, I built up the courage to ask another personal question. "Honda-san," I said, carefully unwrapping the plastic wrap from my rice ball, "may I ask how old you are?"

She laughed and set down her cup of tea on the bench beside her, turning to me. "How old do you think I am?" Her eyes smiled, and I admired the fine network of spiderwebs that appeared beside them, her sun-weathered skin. I took a moment to eye her silver-streaked hair pulled back into a bun, her tiny but strong hands, her short but straight stature.

"Not a day over sixty-five," I said, hoping I was close enough to not be falsely flattering, but young enough not to insult.

Honda threw back her head and laughed again, nearly knocking over her tea. Her eyes filled with tears, and she pushed back the sleeve of her brown work shirt to show her wiry bicep, an echo of our earlier display. "Not bad for an old woman of seventy-nine!"

"No, I don't believe it. Seventy-nine? You look amazing, Honda-san! If I'm half as strong as you at your age, I'll consider myself lucky." I shook my head in disbelief.

"Eat well, work outdoors, lead a clean life," she said simply, with a shrug, and we went back to our snacks. Today's onigiri was filled with umeboshi, and I savored the sour-salty flavor of the pickled plums that lit up my tongue and puckered my lips.

I washed it down with a sip of strong green tea and closed my eyes, preserving the moment.

Each time we entered a new part of the island, I pulled out my camera so we could examine the photos from the courtyard garden to get our bearings and make our plans. When we made our way to a corner of the island, lined by unruly boundary hedges on three sides, I pulled up its photos and we both leaned in close to check the layout. Honda laughed.

"What's funny?" I asked, scanning the small image.

Honda used her little finger to point at the cluster of carefully groomed mounds of rosemary, some two feet tall, in the photo. "Where do you think this is?"

It took me a moment to grasp her meaning. I lowered the camera and scanned the space until my eyes landed on the six-foot-tall, eight-foot-across mound of shaggy green stems in the center of the garden. "Did they turn into *that* monstrosity?"

Perhaps it shouldn't have surprised me that the real-life bushes and trees on the island—which hadn't been touched in decades—would no longer resemble the tiny, picturesque plantings mimicked in the court-yard garden. But face-to-face with the true nature of entropy, the effect was absurd.

"How on earth are we going to make this bushy monster look like the cute little mounds again?"

The size difference alone was daunting, but even the idea of rep-licating such elegant shapes felt nearly impossible. Particularly for two relatively inexperienced arborists.

"We don't."

I turned to Honda, surprised by her resolute tone. "What do you mean? We're just going to leave it like, like *that*?" I gestured toward the overgrown, unkempt bush-thing.

"No, we don't need to leave it as is. We just shouldn't let the per-fect become the enemy of the good." Honda's tone was forceful, and I turned to look at her in surprise. "This garden is not about perfection, Mari-san. It never has been."

I stared at her, blankly.

Honda furrowed her brow, searching for the right words. "We don't need the island to return to its former state. Aging is both natural and beautiful—garden designers know this. We just need to find it a new appearance that is pleasing, that fits." She waved at the rosemary bush or at the garden or the island in general. "None of this is ever going to be the same as it was back then. That's not what we should be striving for. The island just needs a new normal."

A new normal.

The words resonated with me on a deep level.

Of course, Honda-san was right. We weren't obligated to match the island to its miniature version in the courtyard. I'd used the term "blueprint" like it was a design we had to follow, but there were no rules for what we were doing. A rush of excitement surged through my veins at this freeing thought.

I wanted the garden to be beautiful, tranquil, a healthy space—not just for Suzu and Kishi, but for Honda and Yuna, and anyone else who might find comfort walking through nature's splendor.

We could make the island's garden reminiscent of what it was before, but not the same. The garden had aged, and its new appearance should reflect this maturation. Just like a clothing designer wouldn't design the same dress for a woman of fifty that she wore when she was twenty.

And how I couldn't expect my life to look the same as it did before Mom died. Things would have to change. Things *were* changing.

A *new normal.* Yes, I liked that idea.

"You're right, Honda-san. We can make the gardens a new kind of beautiful."

She patted me on the arm, picked up the hedge trimmers, and marched toward the woody monstrosity. "I could use some dried rosemary anyways," she said with a chuckle.

C h a p t e r   T h i r t y - O n e

H onda drove into town every few days to gather more supplies for
our projects, but I never accompanied her. The gardens still felt
like their own tiny, untethered microcosm unconnected to the outer
world, and I was loath to break that spell.

Along the path between the crane's willow trees and the herbal
garden with its woody monstrosity, we encountered a stone basin with
a deep crack running down its side. Clearly, it was no longer watertight.
Honda pulled out her small notebook, began taking notes for her next
shopping trip.

I spoke of caulking, of mixing a small batch of concrete, of something to fill the gaps. Honda spoke of flowers.

"What is your favorite flower, Mari-san?"

I paused for a moment, taken aback.

"Well," I ran a finger along the smooth top of the basin, "maybe . . .
sunflowers?" I looked away, blinking back the sudden pressure of tears.

"Ah, like in the book you gave me!"

It took me a moment to realize she must be talking about the *Flora
and Fauna of Illinois*. I nodded, glad she'd at least thumbed through it.

Honda eyed the waist-high basin critically. "I think sunflowers
would be too big, don't you?"

I pictured huge, towering golden flowers with thick stalks and heavy heads rising up out of the basin and chuckled. "You're thinking we should fill the basin with soil and plant flowers in it?"

"Sure, why not? The crack will provide good drainage for the soil."

Why not indeed? While Honda rattled off a list of possible flower options—poppies, pink or purple phlox, blue nemophila—I ran my finger along the crack.

I smiled. Perhaps cracked didn't always mean broken.

Every day, I brought my camera and documented our progress. I snapped photos from multiple angles before we began, then took more photos at the end of each day to show how far we'd come. I'd laugh sometimes, saying it felt like we were on a landscaping challenge TV show, but I don't know if Honda-san got the reference.

Some days the before- and after-photos were disheartening, and it felt like we'd only knocked the smallest dent in a huge block of marble. Those days I would slump back to my room, worn out and discouraged, questioning why we were even bothering. But other days I would share the photos with Honda and we would marvel at how far we'd come, and my heart would swell with pride when I flipped back and forth between the *before* and the *after*. If only we had more days like that, we'd be done in no time.

But time didn't pass the same in the gardens of Yanagi Inn; the individual moments could last for an eternity or blur together into a kaleidoscope of colors and scents. Sometimes I had the unnerving sense that some goddess was watching our progress, pressing the pause or fast-forward buttons at will.

It wasn't that we were rushing to finish our projects. I did worry about my remaining time at the inn—and avoided running into Ogura at all costs—but I was more anxious to alleviate Suzu's sorrow. At times it felt like the weight of a young girl's eternal soul rested in my hands, and I would lie awake in bed at night, tormented by this heavy responsibility.

I still visited Suzu some nights. Though most evenings I fell onto my futon, exhausted, and didn't awake until the sun rose the next morning, on the nights I woke to her cries I went to Suzu's room, where I held her and stroked her wet hair. Though it made my chest tighten to repeat such promises, I told her again and again that I would bring her to the island just as soon as we were done, when the early spring flowers were blooming, and it was a happy, healthy place again. This seemed to soothe her for a time, but nothing would keep her from weeping again another night.

And each time I returned to my own bed, a tight fear clenched my insides. What if my plan didn't work? What if I'd been wrong, and these pieces were all disparate problems, unable to resolve into a final, cohesive puzzle? But then I would remind myself that all of life was a gamble, and all I could do was take things one step at a time.

Though the days were steadily getting warmer, we were still occasionally surprised by an icy breeze. "Honda-san," I said, wrapping my arms around myself, "do you believe in ghosts?"

We were planting poppy seeds in the fresh soil of the cracked basin. Honda was silent for a minute before answering, sprinkling the seed-and-sand mixture on the loosened soil. "I believe in many types of spirits. Do you believe in ghosts, Mari-san?"

I set down my trowel and stared into the distance. "If you'd asked me six months ago, I would have said no. But now . . ."

I trailed off, uncertain whether I should continue. Should I tell Honda-san about the ghost girl? Would Suzu mind if I did? Honda-san was a Buddhist nun, after all—kind of a specialist in the domain of death. Did that extend to ghosts, as well? I didn't think Suzu needed to be kept secret—her loud sobbing in the night suggested she didn't mind being heard—but rather she just wasn't perceptible to everyone. At least not on the level I perceived her.

"There's a ghost, a spirit, who I see sometimes. In the inn." I watched Honda's face closely, but she just nodded and kept sprinkling the seed mixture.

"The crying I hear at night—it's a little girl, and . . ." I took a deep breath. "Her name is Suzu. I think she's the ghost of Kishi-san's daughter."

Honda set down her plastic bag, wiped her forehead with the flowered tenugui cloth she kept tucked inside her shirt.

"You could be right, Mari-san."

I waited in silence for several heartbeats, expecting her to continue, but as the seconds ticked by, I realized she was waiting for me to speak.

"Do you know much about ghosts, Honda-san? Do you know why no one else at the inn seems to notice her?" I hated the desperation that was leaking into my voice, and the pinch in the bridge of my nose which told me I was close to tears.

But I had to know more—this mystery was too much for me to keep bottled up any longer.

"You have suffered great sorrow recently, lost someone very dear to you, no?"

I nodded, clenching my jaw. "My mother."

"Perhaps you are able to perceive this spirit because you are sensitive to grief. You are attuned to it. I believe that strong emotions are like wavelengths that travel through the air, and some are too high or low for the average person to pick up. It takes a person already familiar with that wavelength to perceive it."

I nodded slowly, letting the words sink in. "I understand what you're saying. I do think her emotions affect me, like I can feel them—even from a distance."

Honda nodded.

"She told me she was sad because her mother was sad. And that the island looking so forlorn made her sad. So I promised her I'd fix it up and then I would bring her here." I paused, looked down at my hands, clasped tightly in front of me. "I'm sorry, I know I should've mentioned this earlier. But I also just truly wanted to restore the island. I really want it to be lovely again."

"So do I," Honda said wistfully. "I think it will be good to bring Suzu-chan here. Perhaps seeing the restored garden will help ease her suffering. Help restore her, as well."

Another icy breeze blew over us, ruffling my hair. "Do you know if the Jizō statue was erected after Suzu-chan died?" I gestured vaguely in the direction of the statue. "I didn't see it in the courtyard garden, so I wondered if it were a newer addition."

"Yes," Honda said so quietly it was almost a whisper. "It was erected there to memorialize Suzu-chan after her death."

I nodded. "To be honest, I've been afraid to refurbish the Jizō myself. It feels . . . sacrilegious somehow." A vision of the ghostly face beside the Jizō statue rose in my mind. "I would be more comfortable with you restoring it. Is that all right?"

"Why, because I am a Buddhist nun?" The words snapped like a crab's pincers, and I was taken aback for a moment, unsure what had caused her to speak harshly to me for the first time.

"W-well, yes. But I'm sorry, it's ok, I can—"

"No, it's fine. I know what needs to be done." She let a tight smile slide across her face, as if to reassure me there were no hard feelings, but the tension remained palpable.

"Thank you, Honda-san. I—"

I was going to tell her how much I appreciated her help, even though it wasn't her job, even though she didn't really have anything to do with Yanagi Inn, and yet she was here with me every day, all day, performing strenuous labor to restore the gardens with me. I was *going* to tell her how much I enjoyed her company and how glad I was to have met her, but I was interrupted when a bird pooped on my head.

"Ah!" I cried, glancing up and gingerly raising a hand to touch the top of my head. The crane, with her elegant glider-shaped wings and long legs, passed by overhead.

Honda was laughing so hard she had tears streaming down her face, and even though I was disgusted and mortified, her mirth was contagious. I had to join in.

When she'd calmed enough to talk, Honda held up a hand. "Mari-san, this is such good luck!"

"Good luck?" I groaned and dabbed at the top of my head with a dry leaf. Honda held out her floral tenugui, but I waved away her offer, not wanting to soil her nice cloth.

"Getting pooped on by a bird, particularly such a special crane, is good luck!"

I paused in my leaf-dabbing. "Are you sure you're not just trying to make me feel better?"

"No, I am completely serious. This is a very good omen." She patted my arm and pushed herself to her feet.

A good omen. It did feel like my luck had turned around lately. My energy had increased—maybe I'd even go on an early-morning jog one of these days?—my appetite was back, and I was immersed in the moment so much more than I had been in past months.

Or years. Perhaps it was all the outdoor exercise, the fresh air, and the pleasant company.

Or perhaps it was because I had a goal. And not a selfish one, either, for I knew on some level that I would have to leave Yanagi Inn once my project was completed, that I wouldn't be able to enjoy the fruits of my labor. No, I was doing this for others: for Suzu, for the owner, for the livelihood of Yanagi Inn. Perhaps once Kishi-san saw how lovely the island's long-neglected gardens could be, she would hire some groundskeepers to revive the rest of the gardens Honda-san had been struggling with for so long. Maybe once the gardens were in good order, guests would come back and Yanagi Inn would be a thriving business once more.

I snapped out of my musings to see Honda watching me, a gentle smile on her face.

"All the same, Mari-san, you should probably go wash your hair."

Chapter Thirty-Two

One day I confessed to Honda-san that I'd always admired how gardeners created crutches for old trees whose tired limbs had extended so far from their base that they strained to keep them up. Honda suggested we give it a try, saying she had the perfect patient in mind. She led me to an ancient pine with a horizontal limb jutting out so far from the trunk that the limb brushed the tall grass beside it. We tested the limb, both of us lifting with all our strength, to see if it were possible to lift it higher off the ground. It was.

"See, we are very strong!" Honda had declared, and I agreed, feeling my own arms, amazed at how my own body had firmed and strengthened since I'd come to the inn. We fashioned a T-shaped crutch out of worn beams from the old tea house (we'd determined it was best to disassemble the old structure, rather than attempt to rebuild it) and managed to maneuver it beneath the limb, wrapped with a strip of rough jute cloth between the bark and the crutch to protect it from rubbing. When everything was in place, we secured the crutch to its branch with twine. We stood back, admiring our handiwork, and when I took my after-photos that day the image brought tears to my eyes.

I learned so much during those long days on the island—and not just about the specific trees and shrubs and how to prune them, but how to set stepping-stones flat into the ground, how to add oil to a gas-powered chainsaw. Sometimes I wondered how Ogura-san and the few other employees at the inn could possibly remain oblivious to what we were doing, though Honda-san and I had purposefully left the obscuring hedges and bamboo around the island's edges to protect the privacy of the interior. But we were far from quiet, far from subtle in our movements. Part of me wondered whether they just turned a blind eye to our activities, just as I wondered whether they turned a blind eye to the ghostly nocturnal crying.

I learned a great deal about wildlife, too, for the animals were curious about our work and came to visit from time to time. Honda brought seeds to scatter for the friendly birds that landed near us, and nuts for the squirrels and chipmunks who inevitably found their way to sniffing at our feet. I asked Honda-san once whether her tanuki friend Goro was likely to show up, and she laughed and remarked that he only entered the water to fish, not to swim long distance.

"Honda-san," I said, holding a shelled peanut in my hand to coax a squirrel closer. "Do you think we should build a better path to get out to the island? I don't think we're equipped to rebuild bridges, but maybe there's something we can do?" The squirrel stretched out her neck as far as it would go and nimbly snatched the nut from my fingers. She then sat down and spun it in her hands to remove the skin.

"Ah, perhaps if we'd been smarter, we would've done that in the first place! Then maybe we could have used your wheelbarrow to carry in the gravel and big stones." She laughed, and I joined in. But the concept stuck with me. Maybe a new path could be the finishing touch to our island restoration.

It felt inaccurate calling it a restoration, although I knew that's what we were doing. I wanted to call it healing, but it felt odd to use that word for a space, even if it were a living space. But the island, and its gardens, felt more alive every day, as if it were a single living, breathing organism that was coming to life more and more, with every new stone we laid and every new seed we planted. New birds, new fish were showing up, as if the island's newfound vitality was inviting them in, welcoming them with open arms to add to the ecosystem's livelihood.

Chicago, and everything in my previous existence, felt very far away, like things that had happened to someone else. That life belonged to a different Mari—not this new person slowly unfurling inside my old skin, waiting to burst forth.

"Look, Mari-san, isn't it lovely?"

Honda pointed at the blooms just beginning to explode on the tree beside our path. The tiny flowers looked almost like puffed popcorn that someone had dusted with a pink strawberry flavoring.

"They're gorgeous! What are those? Not cherry blossoms, right?"

Honda shook her head as we stopped to appreciate the tree. "This is a blossoming plum tree—its blooms are usually the first sign of spring."

What day was this? I reviewed my faulty internal calendar. It must be late March by now—had we really been working on the island that long? My four weeks were surely almost over; I needed to check my flight details.

Time was getting away from me.

We admired the blooms for long minutes, a cool breeze gently caressing the branches.

"Back home, my favorite first sign of spring was daffodils. My mother liked to grow them in her yard, just so she could wait for them to appear and announce to the world that spring had arrived."

Tears welled in my eyes, fast and with such pressure it alarmed me. I blinked them away, wiped at my eyes with the sleeve of my yukata. Honda patted my shoulder but said nothing, allowing me time to recover in companionable silence.

As the weather grew warmer, fresher, I felt compelled to run.

Though I hadn't gone running in months, one morning I awoke early, with itchy feet. So before I met Honda on the island, even before breakfast, I threw on my sweats, tied on my running shoes, and slipped off my veranda and out onto the crunchy gravel paths.

The early morning air was crisp, and the gardens were alive with the soft hum of insects and the morning calls of birds. Round drops of dew hanging on the tips of overgrown grass shone with tiny rainbows, and everything felt new and fresh. I had to restrain my speed, thanks to the curving trails and loose rocks, and it felt somewhat sacrilegious to run on such paths, designed as they were for contemplative strolls. But as I jogged, as my muscles loosened and warmed and the old sense of well-being diffused through me, I found myself lost in thought.

We were almost done with the island—only a few more small jobs here or there, tasks that shouldn't take more than a few days, assuming fair weather. But did I even have a few days? I still needed to check my tickets, email the gallery, see if I could stay just a little while longer . . .

And then—and then!—when we finished our restoration these care-free days would come to an end, and I would have to confront my old life again. Before I knew it, I had traveled a full circuit around the gardens and found myself back at my veranda. How small the gardens felt when jogging! But my face was flushed, my lungs were stinging with the chilly March air, and I felt more *alive* than I had in a very long time. I smiled, slid off my shoes, and was met with the scent of warm, steaming rice as soon as I slid open the doors.

It was late afternoon, on what turned out to be our final day of restoration, when Honda handed me the small fabric sachet she'd made from various trimmings from around the island. It smelt of rosemary ("The rosemary monstrosity!" I said, laughing) and spearmint and cypress and other green, herby things.

I vowed to treasure it, to keep it in a drawer with my clothes so they would always smell like the island.

She smiled. "I believe now it is time for you to see the Jizō statue."

"Wait, he's done? When did you have time to work on him?"

"A woman can have her secrets," she said, a cryptic smile on her face.

I followed her through the winding path of stepping-stones, past neatly trimmed holly trees, past the sentinel rocks now fully encircled by soft moss—the sands completely abandoned in a wise executive decision by Honda-san—until we reached the protected cove where the Jizō statue resided. We approached in respectful silence, keeping even our footsteps as muted as possible.

My breath caught in my throat. The Jizō statue was perfect. Though Honda had left him dappled with moss (he, too, should be allowed to age, after all), his gentle smile seemed more peaceful now that his surroundings had been cleared, a new red bib had been tied around his neck, and Honda had left a few mandarin oranges as an offering on his stone base.

The area around his feet, which had been several inches deep in rotting leaves and other debris, was now swept clean, and fresh gray river rocks surrounded him like water.

"It's like he's standing on an island!" I said, delighted by the symmetry and symbolism.

Honda nodded. "I think he is much happier now."

"Definitely." My fingers tightened around my camera case. "Is it all right if I take pictures?"

"Of course." Honda stepped back to give me room.

I snapped photos at various angles to capture different lighting, the backdrop of just-budding purple flowers adding a lovely depth. But memories of the ghostly face from when I first visited this spot rose to my mind and I lowered my camera, uneasy.

Had that face been Suzu's?

Perhaps Honda noticed my disquiet, for I could sense her gaze upon me. She pulled a string of brown beads out from her pocket and held them up, sliding her fingers along the beads as her gaze roamed the area around the statue.

She noticed my attention and chuckled, sticking the beads back inside her pocket. "They help me to see things more clearly," she said simply, and patted her pocket.

I wasn't sure what to make of her cryptic statement, so I just smiled.

Finally, I put my camera away, and we stood in silence, observing the statue in his new environment. The scent of sweet plum blossoms lingered in the breeze.

"We're done, aren't we." I spoke softly, my words not so much a question as a statement.

"Yes, I suppose we are."

I had expected to feel excitement or even a wave of relief when we finished the monumental task we'd set out to complete. I'd even thought about inviting Honda-san back to my room, where we could have a celebratory cup of tea, perhaps, or maybe even some saké. But now that we were done, my body was awash with a sense of nostalgia.

But it was more than that.

My nerves were tingling with anxiety. I knew I'd have to confront the fact that I'd offered to bring a ghost out to this island, but now that the time was near and there were no more tasks—no more flowers to plant, no more rocks to replace, no more bushy monstrosities to tame—I couldn't push back the inevitable any longer.

"I'm scared, Honda-san," I whispered.

Honda didn't reply, but she must have heard me, for she reached out and held my hand as we stood side-by-side. Her hand was rough and warm in mine, so very strong despite its tiny size. Tears rose in my eyes, but I didn't cry. I gave her hand a gentle squeeze, and she squeezed mine in return.

The sun sank down toward the horizon, spreading a warm orange and pink glow across the sky as Honda and I stood side-by-side watching the shadow of Jizō-san grow longer and longer across the bed of newly budding hydrangeas.

Chapter Thirty-Three

That night after dinner, I called Risa. She didn't object to my idea of staying at the inn a bit longer. In fact, she encouraged it, saying all was fine at my apartment, all was fine at the gallery. *Relax!* she'd said. *Enjoy more baths!*

At the thought of my last bath, a sick lump formed in my stomach, but of course I didn't tell Risa that. She didn't need to know about those disturbing experiences—not yet, at least.

The airline was more reticent, but thankfully, after paying an exorbitant fee, I was allowed to change to an open-ended return ticket. Relief flooded through my body; I knew I was where I needed to be right now, knew I had to finish what I had started. And now I could leave on my own terms.

Unless, of course, Ogura-san had any say in the matter.

I lay on my futon, eyes closed and body as relaxed as breathing exercises could get it, but sleep never came. My mind was chaos, scrolling through all the changes we'd made to the island, all the minor cuts and bruises and bird poops I'd experienced over the past few weeks. My brain was a movie reel I couldn't shut off.

I had to admit that I was scared of what would happen when I tried to get Suzu to leave her room. What if she refused when push came to shove? What if she really was bound to the inn, unable to leave, and all our hard work was for nothing?

No, I shouldn't think that way. Even if I couldn't help Suzu, reviving the island was still a move in the right direction. I had enjoyed it, enjoyed Honda-san's company and the feel of the fresh air in my lungs and the sun on my face and the new strength in my arms and legs. No, I would never say it'd been for nothing—it had meant too much to me.

I sat up in bed. What if I just went to her now? Why had I always waited for her cries to invite me?

But even as I asked the question, I realized I knew the answer—because the many faces of failure were too terrifying. What if I got lost in the dark, winding corridors? I'd never been brave enough to seek out her room in the daylight, for fear the room wouldn't exist, or that I would find something unspeakable there.

What if I found her room tonight and it was empty? What would that even mean? Some part of me knew I was only able to keep my fear in check, compartmentalized into a rational corner, because Suzu didn't *feel* like a ghost to me. She felt alive and real; my hands didn't pass through her when I reached out to touch her, she didn't flicker or turn translucent. But if I entered her room unexpectedly, she might have to materialize somehow. She might show up out of a wispy nothingness or appear, suddenly, at my back when I was kneeling by her futon, and then her hand would grab my shoulder, and—

Stop this, Mari!

I was breathing hard, my fingers trembling where they gripped my comforter.

I lay back down, brought my breathing under control. No, I would just wait for her to call me. No need to rush things. Maybe neither of us were ready for this next step.

I awoke to the faraway sounds of Suzu's crying and bolted upright in bed. A glance at my phone told me it was 2:02 a.m.

With a deep, steadying breath, I rose to my feet, slid on my house slippers, and steeled myself before opening the door. *This is no different than before, Mari.* I followed her cries like I'd done so many other nights, taking turns in the hallways without thinking, not even pausing to get my bearings. And soon I was brushing past the musty curtain and then standing in front of Suzu's door, ready to slide it open.

My hand on the handle shook, and I bit the inside of my lip. *Come on, Mari. This is why you did all that hard work. This is what it's all led up to.* My head began to throb, and I pressed my fingertips to my temples. *Deep breaths, Mari, deep breaths.*

Then, before I could change my mind, I slid open the door.

Suzu was lying on her bed, as usual, facing away and sobbing into her hands. I stood for the length of several heartbeats just watching her, summoning courage around me like a shroud, before I whispered, "Suzu-chan?"

She rolled over. Suzu didn't stop crying, but she lowered her hands and in the dim lighting I could tell she was watching me in return. Her crying grew softer; she recognized me as a friendly figure.

I knelt beside her, ignoring the foul scent of rot and swamps, and smoothed her dripping hair back from her forehead. *She's so warm,* I thought as I had so many times before. Almost feverish.

"It's ok, you don't have to cry. I have good news!" I put on my most cheerful expression, though my heart was fluttering inside my chest. "Honda-san and I have restored the island."

"Honda-san?" The girl whispered, her petite mouth turning into a tight frown.

"Yes," I replied swiftly, "we both worked on the island, and it is so beautiful. I can't wait for you to see it!" I kept stroking her hair as I spoke, and her crying subsided down to the occasional sniff. Hope sparked in my chest.

"Are there flowers?" Suzu spoke so softly I had to lean in to hear her.

"Yes, beautiful flowers."

"Is the tall bridge still there?"

I smiled at her hopeful tone. Then came a flash of summer again; the red bridge, the cacophony of cicadas, a child's laughter. But, just as suddenly, the image and sounds faded away, leaving a bittersweet ache in my heart.

"Yes, Suzu-chan. With a fresh coat of red paint and everything."

Suzu was staring at my face so intently it was as if she were trying to read a tiny font written on my forehead, and I couldn't help but feel she, too, was seeing the images in my mind.

"Will you take me there, Mari-chan?"

Mari-chan. I smiled. What a thing for an eight-year-old to call a woman in her thirties.

"Of course I will."

"Will you take me there *right now?*" Her eyes were wide.

"That's why I'm here!" Thank goodness she was willing to go with me, to leave this depressing room. Yet the unease still clung to me like a cold sweat. Being willing didn't guarantee she was able.

I held out my hand and pulled her to her feet. She was so tiny—she barely came up to my ribcage.

"Ready?" I scanned the room for a jacket or slippers or shoes, more out of habit than rational thought, but the room was as bare as the first time I'd entered it.

Suzu nodded, her eyes shining.

She was so real, it was too easy for me to forget that she was . . . not human. It still didn't feel quite right to think of her as a ghost, at least not the kind of ghost portrayed in media. I held her little hand in mine, and her skin was still so warm it felt like a mug fresh from the dishwasher.

Of course she didn't require shoes, but I felt like an irresponsible adult taking a little girl outside, barefoot, in the middle of a chilly spring night. *She's not a little girl*, I reminded myself over and over again, even as I squeezed her warm little hand in mine and headed for the door.

"C'mon, Risa. You have to eat it." I held the spoon of rice porridge in front of my little sister's lips, but she pressed them together even more firmly.

"Stop being such a baby! You like okayu. Remember when Mom made it a few weeks ago and you gobbled it up?"

Risa held a chubby hand in front of her mouth to ward off my spoon before answering. "Well yours doesn't taste like Mom's. Your okayu tastes like salty gray yuck."

I looked down at the bowl of rice porridge. Ok, so maybe I had put a bit too much soy sauce in it.

"Well, this is all we have. Mom's not here, but if she were I'm sure she'd make you eat porridge, too." I held the spoon back up, raised my eyebrows.

"I want Mama!" Risa wailed, balling up her four-year-old fists.

I sighed, set the bowl down on her side table. "I know, Risa, I know. I'm sure she'll be back soon." It was lies—Mom probably wouldn't come home until super late again—but Risa didn't need to know that.

I pulled my little sister into a tight hug, her skin damp and hot to the touch. "Want me to bring you a cool towel?" I murmured.

"Uh-huh." Risa sniffed and nodded, settling back down in her fluffy blankets.

I rushed to the bathroom, fighting back tears.

Where was Mom when I needed her?

I couldn't do this alone.

When we stepped outside, the chill hit me like a spritz to the face. There was an energy in the air, a tang of ozone like before a thunderstorm, and I looked up at the dark, cloudy sky. The hairs on my arms stood up, tingling. Perhaps a storm was coming.

Or perhaps something otherworldly was about to happen.

I quickened my stride.

With little moonlight, the paths were impossibly dark. I should have brought a light. An image of myself, passing through the dark, twisted gardens, a tiny ghost holding one hand, and a paper lantern lit by a flickering flame in the other—yes, that would've been the finishing touch to this surreal expedition.

Thankfully I knew the route to the island well by now, and Suzu didn't have any trouble traversing the uneven path. I steeled myself to sneak a glance at her feet, just in case she was gliding over the ground without touching it, but she just marched along beside me, her quick, tiny steps trying to keep up with my longer stride.

"How will we get to the island?" Suzu's voice sliced through the silence, and I jumped. I hadn't noticed how eerily quiet the dark night had been until she spoke. Not an insect, not a rustling of trees in the slight breeze, not a croaking frog. Just dead silence and the sound of my own beating heart. Suzu was staring at me, waiting for me to answer. I swallowed, took a deep breath.

"Well, we can't use the old bridge. I-It's gone. But there is another path, a secret path, that I'll show you."

Suzu nodded, as if I'd confirmed her suspicions—though I wondered how she would've known the bridge was gone. She remained silent, plunging us once again into the utter stillness of the night.

As we approached the water's edge, I broke the silence myself and began pointing out features barely visible on the other bank. "Can you see that cypress tree? I trimmed that one. And the . . ."

Suzu was slowing down, a weight pulling on my hand.

No, no, no.

I kept talking, kept pulling, trying to keep up our pace as if momentum alone could carry us over the water. I prattled on, saying anything that could distract her. "Honda-san and I did so much work to the island—it looks so different! We even brought in new rocks and gravel . . ."

Without slowing, I slipped off my sandals and awkwardly tucked them under my arm.

Suzu froze, letting go of my hand.

"What's wrong, Suzu-chan?" I fought to keep the quaver from my voice.

"Why did you take your shoes off, Mari-chan?" Her voice was small, but held a hint of anger—a hint of threat—behind it.

I stopped walking. "Don't worry, there are stepping-stones. I just don't want to get my shoes wet."

"Wet?" Her voice grew louder, her entire body quaking.

"It's fine, Suzu-chan." I faked a smile, made soothing movements with my hands, as if taming a wild horse. "Look, I can even carry you across if you'd like. I was nervous at first, too, but now I hardly notice it at all."

"No!" The little girl screamed, and this time her voice was loud, piercing, like a tornado siren, terror and anger rolling off her in waves.

I flinched at the sound and shot a glance back toward the inn. Oh god, what if Ogura-san came rushing outside and confronted me? How on earth could I explain what I was doing, let alone explain Suzu-chan?

But it didn't matter. When I turned back around, Suzu was gone.

Chapter Thirty-Four

"Suzu-chan?"

My body began trembling, then shivering. I wrapped my arms around myself, my gaze darting in all directions, hoping beyond hope that Suzu-chan would pop out of the bushes, laughing—the whole thing a prank.

But no, she had disappeared. Just winked out like she'd never existed.

I stopped calling, stopping searching, stopped trying to convince myself that Suzu wasn't really the ghost of a child who had drowned in that same pond, but somehow a real, live little girl who was solid and warm and charmingly called me Mari-chan.

Keep it together, Mari, keep it together!

But I couldn't. I took off running back toward the inn.

My sandals were still tucked under my arm, and the stones and sticks were sharp on my bare feet, but I didn't stop. I just ran, blindly, stumbling over dark objects, oblivious to the cuts on my feet. The crisp energy I'd felt earlier had evaporated, leaving only a dreary dampness, like I was running through a fog. The only sounds in the otherwise silent night were my feet slapping the hard ground or crunching on gravel and the breath coming fast and heavy in my mad dash to . . .

safety? Normalcy? Sanity? All I could do was run. When I finally made it back to my room, I dropped my sandals on the floor and fell face-first onto my futon. I was trembling, shivering, so I wrapped myself up in the comforter like a Mari-caterpillar in her cocoon.

Breathe, Mari, breathe.

I buried my face in the comforter, breathing in the jasmine scent, fighting to slow my heart and keep from hyperventilating.

Suzu-chan was gone. Suzu-chan was gone. My mind hitched like a skipping record. She's gone . . .

The aching hole in my chest widened, widened, the sense of guilt ripping it open until a dam within me burst and the tears streamed down my cheeks. I snuffled into my blankets like a little child. I hadn't saved Suzu-chan. I'd failed her. Failed Yanagi Inn, failed myself.

All of it was my fault.

I clasped Honda's rough hand in my own, fighting off tears. "What if that was my only chance to fix things?"

When I'd woken up that next morning, Yuna had already set out my breakfast and let me sleep in. I'd forsaken the inviting aromas and immediately rushed out to the temple, hoping to find Honda there.

She had taken one look at my wild state and sat me down on the temple steps. Then she'd listened to my story of last night's events, silent but attentive through my rambling, half-mad account. Then she'd stared off into the distance, nodding as if to herself.

"It seems to me," Honda said slowly, "that the child is afraid of water."

I wanted to scream. "Yes, I get that! But what if I messed everything up and now she'll never appear to me again? What if she's just *gone*?"

"You overthink things, Mari-san. If the child is afraid of water, we just need a different way of getting her to the island."

"But we don't have *time* to rebuild the bridge!"

There, I'd said it. The dreaded *T*-word. I knew that I couldn't stay at Yanagi Inn forever, couldn't keep begging extensions for time off from the gallery. And despite Kishi-san's assurance that I could have all the time I needed, Ogura-san was waiting for the smallest excuse to kick me out.

I knew I would wear out my welcome soon.

And the grant. Risa had sent in the application, paid the fees. She'd taken care of everything, waved her hand dismissively when I'd asked for details and told me not to worry so much. The whole thing was starting to feel like some practical joke—at my expense.

"Mari-san!" Honda's sharp tone snapped me out of my worry cycle. "You are overthinking again. I'm sure there are other options. A bridge would be perfect—but we don't need perfect." She cocked her head, looked off into the distant trees.

I sorted through ideas in my head. What if we found something to add to the top of the stepping-stones to make them taller? Or maybe we could—

"A boat." Honda nodded solemnly. "We could use a boat to travel from shore to shore."

"But where would we get a boat? I certainly don't know how to build one."

"I don't have those skills either, but I have a friend who does. He normally builds fishing boats, but he has built small leisure craft, as well."

I'd done some pontooning with Thad once or twice during camping trips, but other than that I'd only ever gone out in paddle boats, like the ones on the moat around the Emperor's Palace in Tokyo. It wasn't far to the island—I'm sure I could manage—but the idea still made me queasy.

"Do you think you could ask? Maybe we can just borrow one from him?" I didn't know how much boats cost, but I suspected it would be a great deal more than the seeds and gravel we'd been purchasing. "Hold on, this 'friend'—is he your boyfriend?" I raised an eyebrow, gave her a knowing smile.

"Perhaps." She chuckled and pushed off the steps to stand. "I shall take my truck and go see him." She shot a glance back at me, still sitting on the steps. "Would you like to come?"

"No, unless you think you'll need my help, I'd rather stay here." I smiled up at her. "Plus, I'm sure you two lovebirds don't want me in the way."

She chuckled, shaking her head. "All right—if I am successful, I'll bring the boat here to the temple. Shall we meet back here this evening? Either I will have the boat, or . . ." She shrugged. "We will have to discuss another plan."

I rose and stood beside her. "Thank you. I always feel better after we've talked. I don't know how to repay you for your kindness."

Honda-san waved a hand in front of her face. "I'm not helping you, Mari-san. I'm helping everyone. Including myself." She smiled, a little wistfully. "It has made me sad to see the grounds so disordered. It lifts my mood to make improvements, see the garden reviving. So you see, I am just being selfish." Her smile widened until the lines around her eyes crinkled like craft paper.

I laughed.

"I'll meet you back here around 4 p.m.?"

She nodded and held up a hand in farewell as she headed toward her truck, parked somewhere behind the temple.

"Mari," Risa said, looking me up and down, "you don't look so good."

I sighed, slumped down onto my couch. Ginkgo was nudging my foot with his snoot, begging to be fed. Everyone wanted something from me today.

"Well, how should I look after Mom's funeral, huh? Bright and chipper?"

Seeing Risa's fallen face, I regretted my peevishness instantly. It's not like she hadn't just attended her mother's funeral, too. But I was sick of people commenting on how pale I looked, or the bags under my eyes. I just wanted to be left alone.

Risa sat down next to me on the couch, picked one of Ginkgo's long hairs off her black skirt. "Look, Mari, I know this may seem like an awkward time to bring this up, but I've been researching this grant . . ."

The maid-who-was-not-Yuna, who was older and grumpier and who never even tried to speak to me, had already cleared my untouched breakfast dishes by the time I made it back. At least she'd left behind a bowl of mandarins, a few rice crackers, and my customary pair of onigiri.

My stomach growled, loudly. I'd gotten so used to my regular routine of meals that skipping breakfast was kind of a problem. Back home in Chicago, I'd often skipped breakfast on my rush to work. On the nights Thad stayed over, I usually left before his alarm had gone off, slipping out of bed and closing the doors gently so as not to wake him.

What must that've been like for him? To wake and find me gone, without even having said goodbye or kissed his forehead?

I could really be an insensitive ass sometimes.

Frowning, I sat down at the low table.

I unwrapped the first onigiri. Perfection. This one was filled with salted salmon roe, and it was savory and salty and made my stomach growl all the more. Why had I stopped making onigiri at home? Even if I only cooked for myself, I could at least make onigiri once in a while. Or a simple yakisoba or bowl of udon. At least the cook had stopped sending packets of soy sauce along with the onigiri. My gaze wandered to the spot where I'd spilled on the tatami mats awhile back, leaving that creepy skull-like stain. My eyes went wide. The stain was gone. I ran my fingertips over the spot, but couldn't tell whether the fibers had been so thoroughly cleaned it didn't leave any evidence of the stain, or whether an entire new mat had been put down. Or if the morbid stain had all been in my imagination.

I'd been so oblivious lately, so caught up in my own activities on the island, I hadn't even noticed my own surroundings. Then a pang of guilt stabbed my chest; when was the last time I'd even had a real conversation with Yuna?

I made a mental note to remedy that and opened my laptop. While it woke up, I unwrapped the second onigiri and finished it off in just a few bites. I definitely needed to make onigiri at home.

Three emails from Risa. I opened them in order from oldest to newest, hoping she didn't get increasingly annoyed, but she didn't seem bothered by my lack of response. Her emails were peppered with cheerful comments like "I'm sure you're super busy!" juxtaposed with "Hope you are having a relaxing time!"

I scanned through her updates about outings with Diego (no proposal yet, it seemed), anecdotes about Ginkgo and what he'd chewed up in the apartment. Nothing urgent at the gallery, nothing about the grant.

I chewed my lip. Maybe it was time for me to do my own research. I opened Google and typed "NASJ photography grant" into the search field. I scrolled through the results, but nothing seemed to fit. I tried "NASJ grant" and finally just "NASJ"—what did that stand for, anyways?—but I couldn't find any hits that made sense to me.

What the hell was going on? I chewed on my thumbnail nub, unease settling over me.

Maybe I had the name wrong. I scanned through all of Risa's emails over the past three months; I couldn't find anywhere that she mentioned the name of the grant.

Where was that print-off? I scrambled through my laptop bag, but came up with nothing. Then a sinking sensation settled in the bottom of my stomach. I'd balled it up, tossed it aside. Yuna or not-Yuna must've thrown it away.

I hesitated, then hit reply on Risa's most recent email.

Hi Risa,

Glad things are going well. Hey, could you email me a copy of that grant contract? Everything's fine—I just have a few questions.

Hug Ginkgo for me.

Love,

Mari

The rest of the world could survive a little longer without me, I mused, closing my computer with a quiet click. Then I peeled a mandarin, popped a slice in my mouth and chewed slowly.

But how had Risa found out about the grant if it wasn't even Google-able? Word of mouth, perhaps. Risa always had been good at networking.

But still, something wasn't sitting right with me.

Thad was sitting cross-legged on my couch while I paced back and forth in front of the wall of windows overlooking Lake Michigan.

"Four weeks is a long time, Mari." Thad's voice was low, subdued, but I could tell he was mad by the way he slammed back his Heineken.

"Don't you think I deserve a break, damn it?" I threw the photography magazine I'd been pretending to read on the coffee table.

"That's not what I'm saying—I just meant you could've told me more than two days before you left!"

"I've been busy."

"So busy you couldn't send me a 'hey, I'm going to Japan for a month' text?"

"I *thought* it would be better to tell you in person." I sighed, flopped into the chair across from him. "Besides, I've had a lot on my mind."

"Yeah, your gallery. Your mother, your sister." Thad finished his beer, set the bottle on the coffee table with a click. "There's no room for me."

"That's not fair. You know I've been through hell lately and—"

"Yeah, and maybe if you'd let me in, just a little, I could help you."

I opened my mouth to reply, but he was already on his feet, grabbing his flannel overshirt.

"Goodbye, Mari. Thanks for the beer."

And then he was gone.

Chapter Thirty-Five

I knew I didn't have to rush—I still had fifteen minutes until it was time to meet Honda—but I couldn't help speed-walking all the way to the temple.

My heart was pounding; would she have a boat with her? Would we be able to transport it to the pond, just the two of us? I imagined tiny Honda with her sleeve pushed back, showing me her bicep, and smiled. We could do it—one way or another, we'd make it work. We'd managed everything by ourselves this far.

But what would we do if she couldn't get a boat? I'd been ruminating all afternoon, but short of turning the submerged stepping-stones into a flat, walkable platform, magically finding a hot air balloon, or creating some kind of floating platform with milk jugs and plywood, I was at a complete loss. All our hopes seemed to be riding on the boat idea, and I wasn't the kind of person who liked keeping all her eggs in one basket.

I closed my eyes, envisioning Honda by the temple's steps, standing proudly next to a small, lightweight boat. An extremely safe and un-tippable boat. With a deep breath, I pushed open the gate to leave the inn's grounds.

Honda was sitting on the temple steps. Alone. Boatless.

Better start looking for a hot air balloon.

Honda must have spotted me, for she stood up. I raised a hand in greeting.

"No luck? With the boat?" I tried to keep my tone light-hearted, though I felt anything but. I wouldn't have admitted it at the time, but a tiny part of me also let out a sigh of relief. The thought of coaxing Suzu-chan into a boat so soon after my last failure was terrifying, to say the least.

"Oh, I had luck. Come, I'll show you." Honda gestured, and I followed her around the side of the temple, my interest piqued, my hopes rising, albeit nervously.

We rounded the temple, skirting the grove of pine trees so dense little light filtered through, and I realized I'd never even been this far onto the temple's grounds before. The temple itself seemed to be surrounded by dark forest, with only a gravel road cutting a path through the trees out toward civilization. And there, parked on a gravel pad, was Honda-san's red flat-front mini pickup truck.

And also there, resting on a two-wheel trailer towed behind the tiny truck, was a wooden boat.

"Your boyfriend actually gave us a boat?"

"Of course!" Honda marched over to the truck and began unhooking the trailer. "But we have to be very careful with it. This is a project he is working on for a client."

"Is it, uh, unfinished?" I circled around Honda, taking in the entire craft. I scanned for missing planks—damn, I knew nothing about boats.

"Just missing a few decorative details. Don't worry, it is ready for the water."

I still eyed the "in-progress" craft warily. The boat was as long as a canoe, but wider—enough for maybe three people to sit across in the center bench, and only tapering slightly at the ends. It was made of a light-colored yellow wood and a long oar was lying inside down the length of it. I would just have to accept Honda's assessment. We had hoped for a boat, and we were given one. I should be grateful. I *was* grateful.

But I also couldn't swim.

"And look," Honda said, sliding a metal attachment with rubber grips on either end onto the front of the trailer, "we even have handles."

"Impressive—I like it!"

"We can take it as far as the gate now, but we should wait until dark to wheel it to the pond. I have flashlights in the temple we can use, no problem."

I nodded, ready to accept her wisdom. "Sure, sounds good."

Lugging the boat required a little elbow grease, but with both of us pulling, it was certainly doable. Within a few minutes we'd maneuvered the boat down the gravel path until it rested by the bamboo gate. Honda and I brandished our biceps at each other and laughed.

Now we were ready for tonight.

I promised to return soon after dark so we could pull the boat to the pond and hide it out of sight. I asked Honda-san if she wanted to come with me this time when I tried to retrieve Suzu, but she demurred.

"I think this is something you need to do alone, Mari-san. I may not even be able to see her."

"But what if she's really, truly gone? Or what if I can't convince her to try again?"

"Then I don't think having me around will help. Don't worry." She patted my arm. "You can do this. I believe that she still trusts you."

That evening, back in my room, I inhaled my dinner and then sat on my veranda with a cup of hot green tea, watching the sun set. My plan was surreal; ferrying a ghost in an unfamiliar, unfinished boat across a cold pond in the middle of the night? Had anyone told me about this absurd idea a few months ago, I would have scoffed, would never have believed I was capable of such irrational behaviors and beliefs. *Yet here we are.* I smiled wryly.

As soon as the sky could conceivably be considered dark, I slipped out of my room and headed to Honda's temple.

Traversing the gravel paths in the dark was a completely different experience than during the day. The night was alive with sounds, different sounds than came out in the light; the quiet rustling of small animals in the bushes as I passed, the deep, throaty reverberations of toads croaking along the edge of the pond. I paused, turning a full circle in the darkness, taking a minute to fully experience the sensations, the cool breeze bringing the scents of distant blooms and cut evergreens.

I wanted to fix that moment forever in my mind, for I could feel the end of my days at Yanagi Inn approaching. How many more times would I be able to walk these paths? Breathe this air? Trail my fingers along the azalea bushes or listen to the sounds of the wind whispering through the crane's willow trees?

I knew that I had captured many of my experiences on camera, in frozen images of transient beauty. But physically experiencing those things was very different. I was finally beginning to understand that.

The sky was fully darkened by the time I reached the gate, and Honda was already waiting for me on the temple steps when I passed between the boundaries of the two estates.

She wore a jacket, and carried two flashlights, as well as a small shovel. "You never know," she said, seeing me eyeing her gear.

We each grabbed a handle on either side of the trailer, and the boat rolled behind us, bouncing and jolting with every uneven bump or rock it hit. We walked slowly, mindful that the boat was a temporary blessing and would have to be returned in good shape to Honda's boat-building boyfriend.

As we approached the dark edge of the pond, doubts began creeping into my mind. Piloting this boat without Honda-san was madness. And what would we do with the trailer?

As if reading my mind, Honda said, "I should be able to tow the trailer back to the temple and store it there. Empty, it should be light enough." We stopped and set the front end of the trailer on the path and examined the boat for any damage.

"But what about the boat itself? Do you really think we can hide it here?" I eyed the bushes.

"I don't believe anyone will pass by. Besides, if all goes well tonight, maybe something like a boat on the water won't be a concern."

I considered her words. I'd been so obsessed with the individual steps (of finishing the garden projects, of convincing Suzu to visit the island) that I hadn't taken the time to consider what success might look like. Would bringing Suzu to the island somehow change everything at Yanagi Inn? Yet things already were changing—I could feel it in my bones, sense an undefinable, yet undeniable, transformation in the air around me.

We pulled out the long wooden oar, and Honda demonstrated how to use it from the rear of the boat. My hands were shaking as I mimicked her motions, but I nodded, listening and memorizing her motions with the oar. I tried to tamp down my fears (fears of tipping the boat, fears of crashing the boat, fears of losing the oar) but they were roiling just under the surface.

Once we unlatched the trailer and lowered the boat into the water, we tied it off around the sturdy base of a bush, close enough to shore it was mostly obscured behind the bushes.

"Are you sure you don't want to come with me? To convince Suzu?" My voice came out wistful, needy.

Honda laid her hand on my arm. "Mari-san, you will be fine."

We said goodnight. Honda wished me good luck, and made me promise to tell her everything the next morning. I took one final look at the boat's rope to make sure it was secure, then headed back to my room, nerves tight as bow strings and dread rising like steam in my brain.

Chapter Thirty-Six

M*ari-chan.* I clawed my way up through sleep. "Yeah?" I murmured, before I'd even opened my eyes.

Silence.

I sat up, glanced around the dark room, but I was alone.

My phone read 2:21 a.m. Was Suzu crying? I cocked my head, straining my ears. Still silence.

What had awakened me?

The events from earlier in the evening flooded back: Honda, the boat. I needed to talk to Suzu tonight.

I rose and went to the door, pressed my ear against it. Why wasn't she crying? My heart rattled inside my chest. What if I really had scared her off last night so she'd never appear to me again? What if she had truly disappeared forever?

The rational part of my brain told me to lie back down and wait, to see what would happen. But I was tired of sitting around, letting opportunities pass me by while I did nothing; I wasn't going to miss this chance. I slid open my door and stepped out into the hall.

Silence. I took a deep breath, and then turned left. How many times had I walked these halls at night, yet somehow I couldn't remember the way . . . left, then right, then—no, something was wrong. I retraced my steps.

Something was wrong. Something was wrong. I couldn't do it without the cries to follow, I couldn't remember the way, I—

Stop it, Mari!

I froze in the middle of the dark hallway, a cold breeze rustling my hair. I forced my eyes to close.

Breathe, Mari, breathe.

I tried to focus my ears on any possible sounds. The faraway dripping of water. The hum of an electric heater.

Then . . . whispers? I took a few steps forward, silent on my feet. Yes, definitely quiet whispering. And it sounded like the voice was saying, "*Mari-chan.*"

I kept my eyes closed and walked slowly, my fingertips trailing the wall, my ears attuned to the faint little whispers. Yes, those I could follow.

For the first few moments I was so happy to have direction, a sound to follow, it didn't occur to me that the quiet whispering of my childhood name should be ominous, disturbing. But as I stole slowly through the corridors, as I had on my very first night at the inn, my fears rose around me like toadstools from the dark earth. What if I was naively walking into the arms of a now-vengeful spirit? Or what if I didn't even make it that far? Losing my tenuous grip on the siren's voice would strand me, lost and helpless and alone in some nebulous hallway within this surreal version of the inn. But then my face pressed against that foul curtain, and I breathed in the stale scent with relief; I'd found my way to Suzu's corridor.

I crept forward, pressed my ear to her door.

Mari-chan. Mari-chan.

She was whispering my name.

I slid open the door, slowly.

There was Suzu—and she wasn't crying. She knelt on her futon, still dressed in her dingy green yukata, and her lips were forming my name over and over again, chanting it like an incantation and for a moment I thought it like a reverse séance, with the spirit calling for the living. She looked up at me and our eyes met.

I froze.

Was she mad? Did she think I had coaxed her out to the pond for sinister purposes, and now she'd lured me here out of spite? My skin turned cold, clammy, and I stumbled back a step. I shouldn't have come. I shouldn't be trying to force her into anything. What if she was some vengeful spirit and—

But then her crooked little smile spread across her face.

"You came!"

I let out a deep breath, beamed a relieved smile at her.

"I thought you wouldn't come back ever again. I thought you were mad at me." Her voice was quiet, so much like a child who thought she'd been scolded.

I knelt beside her, brushed the wet hair out of her eyes. She looked so different when her face wasn't distorted with tears. Her eyes were a deep brown, her eyebrows like tiny, soft caterpillars. Her skin was pale, and her small nose reminded me of the button mushrooms I loved in salads. Though her hair was still dripping, the swampy odor she'd exuded in the past was now faint.

"Mari-chan? You aren't mad at me, are you?" Again, her peculiarly familiar smile. I'd been worried she wouldn't trust me anymore, while she'd been scared I'd be mad at her. It was as if we were schoolyard playmates, both afraid we'd irreparably broken our friendship over some small misunderstanding.

"No, Suzu-chan, I'm not mad. I would never be mad at someone just for being afraid. You are afraid of the water, right?"

Suzu nodded.

I paused for a moment, unsure how much I should reveal.

"I was afraid of water at your age, too. But you know what? I have a surprise for you tonight. A brand new, very safe way to reach the island." I spoke slowly, gauging her response. Her smile was still there, her eyes still attentive, curious. So far so good. "It's a wonderful boat, and I can ride with you the whole way." I swallowed, took a deep breath. "Will you come with me?"

Her tiny eyebrows scrunched together slightly, and I could almost hear the wheels turning in her head, the anxiety starting to burn in her stomach. The swampy, rotten odor I knew from my earlier visits rose from her, assaulting my nostrils. I kept my face neutral.

"It will be safe, I promise. Do you trust me?"

At those words, her face relaxed. "Of course I trust you, Mari-chan." Her words were so matter-of-fact, like her faith in me was implicit.

What had I ever done to deserve such trust?

"Then let's go! I can't wait to show you the island." I held out my hand and, after only a moment's hesitation, she grasped it.

Chapter Thirty-Seven

The moon was nearly full, shedding a cold light on the garden paths as Suzu and I walked along them, holding hands once again. Her tiny hand was still warm in mine, feverishly so, and so solid and real I found myself doubting my memories of her disappearance the night before. Did our physical contact reassure her as much as it reassured me? No, of course not, I thought. This was a ghost I was talking about.

Wasn't it?

We walked in silence, each lost in our own thoughts or wishing our own wishes, and the night around us was silent as well. The rustling and croaking and signs of nocturnal life I'd experienced alone had all stilled, as if Suzu's presence dampened the living world around her. I shook this thought from my mind, focused on the task ahead of me, and before long we were nearing the edge of the pond. Suzu slowed down, dragged on my arm more and more with every step. I gave her hand a squeeze.

"Trust me, Suzu-chan. Should I bring out the boat?"

She nodded and let go of my hand.

I held my breath as our contact was broken, terrified she would wink out like an extinguished candle the moment our bodies separated. But she remained. I sighed with relief, though I kept one eye on her while I bent down and untied the rope from the bushes. *Please don't disappear, Suzu-chan. Please.*

I pulled on the rope, tugging the boat further up onto the shore until I was confident it wouldn't sink back into the water—and far enough Suzu could easily step inside without getting her feet wet.

Then I gestured grandly toward the boat. "See? A fine boat to float us to the island."

She didn't come closer, but she also didn't move farther away. I felt as if I was coaxing a wild squirrel to eat out of my hand, fearful of scaring it off forever if I made the slightest wrong move.

"You said you trusted me, right? Then please trust me now. Take my hand, Suzu-chan." I reached out my hand, sensing that if she made the decision to come to me, she would be committed.

I was right.

She came forward, grabbed my hand, and allowed me to help her into the boat. I positioned her on the center bench, where she held onto the wooden seat with a two-handed death grip, and then I pushed the boat, gently scraping along the gravel, until it finally floated.

Now it was my turn. I took a deep breath and then eased into the back of the boat myself, careful not to rock the small vessel any more than necessary. Then I used the oar to push off from the shore, and we were floating on the dark waters, moonlight shimmering on the surface. I swallowed hard, twice.

With the oar in both hands, I mimicked the slow motions Honda had shown me, guiding the oar back and forth like a fish's tail. It took a minute to get the rhythm down and the boat to move in a straight line, but I spoke soothingly to Suzu all the while, anything to keep her mind—and mine—off the dark waters below us.

"You will love the island, Suzu-chan, I just know you will. I can't wait for you to see how we've trimmed the trees—they've grown, you know, but I think they look even better as they are now. And some of the flowers are just beginning to bloom, and . . ."

I couldn't tell if she was listening, or just focusing intently on the seat in front of her because she didn't want to see the water, but it didn't matter. We were making it.

Suzu would visit the island again.

But then we jutted against something under the surface—a branch, a submerged rock?—and the front end of the boat lifted up out of the water a few inches.

Oh god, why had we been so confident the water would be unobstructed and deep enough for a boat?

I took a deep breath, then continued talking, though my voice quavered. "You should've seen all the brush we pulled out of the gardens, and all the old leaves!"

I swished the oar like mad—hoping the boat would come unstuck with coercion—but luck was not with me.

If I didn't fix this, Suzu would scream, would disappear. Her knuckles were white on the bench. Waves of emotion hit me, the sick dread and terror flowing off Suzu's small body.

Breathe, Mari, breathe.

"Just a sec," I said brightly.

Holding the edge of the boat with one hand and the oar with the other, I crept toward the front, keeping my steps slow and steady, balanced from left to right. I eased past Suzu on the center bench, murmuring inane comments about trees and flowers and any other soothing things I could think of, using the oar to balance me out. Then I made it to the front and I knelt, plunging the oar into the dark water and fumbling around with it in a wild attempt to get unstuck.

Thud. I hit something hard with the oar, and I pushed against it, pushed again harder, pushed with all my strength (praying I didn't break the oar, or damage the poor boat—oh, what would Honda's boyfriend say?) but also wanting nothing more than to be done with this damned boat ride. I was willing to smash the thing to pieces if it meant standing on the island, on solid ground, with Suzu still by my side.

I maneuvered the oar and pulled, pulled, pulled on it like a le-
ver. Then a scraping sound and whoosh—we were shoved backward, off
whatever submerged obstacle had snagged us. I stumbled, unbalanced,
dropping the oar. It clattered in the bottom of the boat and I flung out
my hands; one caught the edge of the boat, but the other caught nothing but water, and terror seized me as I saw myself, as if I were a specter
floating above, top-heavy and toppling over the edge into the dark, dark
water with its large, sharp stones on which to hit my head and never
rise again.

But then a tug on the back of my jacket, and it was enough—*just*
enough—to pull me up and back into the boat, trembling, dripping.

I turned around, and Suzu sat back down, also trembling, her face
even paler, if that were possible. But she was still there. She'd stuck with
me, had even saved me.

"Thanks," I whispered.

She just nodded and went back to her stock-still position, though
she gave me more room as I passed by this time. I took a deep, steadying
breath, and navigated around whatever underwater obstacle had almost
been my undoing.

The entire journey, even with my painful fumblings, took only a
few minutes, though maneuvering the boat onto the island's shore was
more difficult than I'd anticipated. But finally—*finally*—I managed to
splash ashore, pull the boat higher onto the gravelly beach. I helped
Suzu out of the boat, eyeing her closely as her bare foot touched solid
ground. But nothing happened; just reaching the island itself was not
the objective, it would seem.

Suzu even helped me tie off the rope around some thick bamboo,
though she still hadn't spoken since we'd left her room. But that was all
right. She was understandably nervous—terrified, even. She was a ghost
being coaxed back to the place of her death, after all.

I took Suzu's hand in mine and it was so hot I nearly dropped it,
but I knew I couldn't do that to the poor girl, so I held on, ignoring

the discomfort. As we walked up the slight slope, away from the water, I shot a glance at her, at the tiny wisps rising off her body like steam. Her anxiety was palpable, a physical substance seeping into my pores. "This way," I said, simply, gesturing up ahead.

When we left the water behind and entered the gardens, Suzu's heat dissipated, the anxiety reduced to a low simmer. And her face! At the sight of the moonlit flowers and trees, exuding new life and energy, Suzu's face broke out into that lopsided smile I'd seen back in her room, and she released my hand to turn in circles just to take in the beauty around her. Illuminated only by moonlight, the freshly trimmed bushes, the scrubbed stone lanterns, the stepping-stones and moss—they were all enchanting, magical, and my heart swelled inside my chest.

"Oh, Mari-chan. It's even better than I remembered!" Suzu bent to smell a freshly cut azalea bush, ran a finger along the edge of a granite water basin. She rushed from one scene to the next, pausing at each to stare at its vista for a moment or two.

I just followed her, a few paces behind, letting her explore at her own pace, in her own way, feeling like a parent watching her child at the zoo. When we turned a corner around an oversized—but neatly trimmed—holly bush, the white pebble river and red half-moon bridge came into view, perfectly lit by the moonlight. Suzu let out a gasp and began running to the bridge.

And time slowed down.

Suzu's feet moved, but in slow motion, and the roar of late-summer cicadas filled my ears. The glare of sudden midday sun made my eyes squint, and the scent of dry grass and dust filled my senses. It felt like I was in the middle of a long-forgotten movie sequence. Or a dream.

I stopped, closed my eyes against the searing light.

"Mari-chan?"

My eyes flew open, and I was back in the moonlight in early spring, back with the ghost girl in the here and now. Beads of sweat formed on my forehead. I inhaled a deep breath, but couldn't shake the feeling I was teetering on the edge of something. A point of no return. I wiped my forehead with the back of my hand, jogged over to the bridge to catch up.

Suzu was trailing a forefinger along the bridge's curved railing and I smiled, remembering how Honda and I had sanded and painted the bridge just a short week ago.

But Suzu's smile had faded, her face darkening. "I'm glad you brought me here, Mari-chan. But Mama would be so upset. She feels so guilty about what happened."

I opened my mouth to respond, but didn't know what to say. Her change of mood was sudden, and her words struck a chord deep within me. "How do you know that your mother feels guilty?"

Do any of us ever know how our parents feel?

She seemed to ignore my question, just trailed her fingers along the bridge.

"I remember playing here, on this bridge." She spoke quietly, perhaps more to herself than me. "I had a little car, and I'd start at the top and let it roll all the way down. Sometimes I'd let it roll off the bridge and into the river." She stretched up on her tiptoes and looked over the railing into the pebble stream below.

A flash of memory rushed back to me again. I could see a little car, bouncing along the red railing, hear the laugh of a little girl.

"Blue. It was a blue car," I whispered.

Suzu glanced up at me with a smile and nodded. "It was a Power Rangers car—Papa bought it for me in Tokyo. Before he moved away."

An icy dullness spread throughout my body. My limbs couldn't move, my lungs struggled to bring in air. How could I remember that little blue car?

"Suzu-chan," I said slowly, enunciating each syllable carefully. "Have I been here before?"

The ghost girl cocked her head, her lopsided smile slowly warming up her face. "Of course you have, Mari-chan. Don't you remember?"

Chapter Thirty-Eight

"H-How do you know that?" My words came out a whisper. She laughed and shook her head. "We used to play here! You and me, here on the island."

Suzu's lopsided smile. Her little blue car. The bridge with its rocks and summer cicadas. These memories—they were all real.

The memories must've always been there, but they'd had the fuzzy boundaries of half-remembered stories or a movie I'd watched once long ago. Now that I faced the real, physical space, those memories from my childhood clicked in my brain. But, I reminded myself, there were a lot of memories from those years I never wanted to relive.

"I do remember . . . I used to come here sometimes. And there was a little girl." A flash of a lopsided smile, the cypresses in the background. A child's laughter. "That was you?" I turned to face Suzu.

Mom's dying words rose in my mind: *Always remember, you were the one who survived.* She hadn't been talking about the fact I was going to outlive her—she'd been talking about me surviving, while Suzu had died. More and more puzzle pieces were sliding into place, yet a tingle of unease and doubt tickled the back of my brain. Had this whole thing been part of an elaborate, insidious plan to bring me and Suzu back together, back to the island? But to what end?

"Of course it was me!" Suzu laughed. "I used to love it when you came over to play."

I nodded slowly, let my eyes wander over the white pebble river snaking away from us. I still felt like I was missing something, like details were hovering just on the edge of my memory. "Oh, the puzzle box! I found it here a few weeks ago, just where we'd buried it."

Suzu's brow furrowed. "Puzzle box?"

A sudden stab of guilt; would Suzu be mad that I'd taken it? "You know, the little wooden box, with the mosaic patterns? It took forever to remember how to open it again." I looked down at my feet. "It's in my room. I-I meant to bring it back. I will, though, I promise."

Suzu frowned deeper, and waves of energy started pulsing off her again—this time angry, malevolent. "We didn't play with a puzzle box, Mari."

Something didn't feel right. I swallowed back a lump in my throat. How could she forget the puzzle box, when she remembered everything else so much better than me?

"It's ok, Suzu-chan. Here, I'll show you where we buried it. Maybe that'll help." I gestured for her to follow me under the bridge. After a moment's hesitation, she did.

I duck-walked to the spot where I'd uncovered the buried puzzle box. It was too dark to see them, but I ran my fingers across the cuts in the underside of the wood: 080890. If it wasn't a code, maybe it was . . . a date?

08/08/90.

August 8th, 1990. I would've been eight. Living in Japan. Did Suzu and I carve that date as a remembrance of our time together? We played here under the bridge a lot—it really felt like it'd been a special place to us. Like our own hidden hideaway, secret even from our moms. Yet Suzu remembered none of it.

The puzzle box, too. Vague memories of the box hidden in my little backpack when we travelled here, like I didn't want Mom to know

I'd brought it. I only pulled it out when I knew she wouldn't see. Like under the bridge with Suzu.

Suzu only needed to stoop a little to fit under the bridge. She squatted down next to me when I poked at the rocks.

"Right here. This is where we buried the box. It used to have our perfect leaf in it, remember? A tiny, red maple leaf." I looked up at her dark face, a hesitant smile on my face.

"That. Didn't. Happen." Suzu's voice was petulant, angry. She didn't meet my gaze, but rather just stared at the spot I'd poked, frowning.

It shouldn't have been a big deal (lord knows I'd forgotten so much from those days), but Suzu's unease was making all of this worse, making me more and more concerned that something was not what it seemed. "It's all right if you don't remember, Suzu-chan. I'm sorry I took it. I'll bring the puzzle box next time, ok?"

Suzu didn't answer. But the anger seemed to have shifted to anxiety, now tinged with the sorrow I used to feel in her room. She stood, suddenly, and ran out from under the bridge, hunched so she didn't smash her head.

Please god, don't let her disappear!

I scrambled out from under the bridge, searched in a desperate circle. But there was Suzu, suddenly standing on top of the bridge again.

I smiled up at her, relieved. "Do you want to see the rest of the island now?"

"Of course, Mari-chan!" She was smiling again, and as my own mood lightened in response, I wondered for a moment how Suzu's emotions affected me so.

I let out a little chuckle. *Mari-chan.* Of course she still called me that childish nickname. Frozen in time at age eight, she was still the little girl I had come to see on her special island—and she still thought of me the same way.

As childhood friends.

Eight. No wonder I didn't have more recent memories of her; Suzu must've died not long after we'd carved that date into the bridge.

We took our time exploring the rest of the island. I say "we," but it was really Suzu exploring and me tagging along after her like an indulgent parent. I smiled with an almost maternal pride (not for the girl, but for the gardens I had nurtured) each time Suzu squealed with delight at a new discovery or admired the long, weeping arms of the crane's willow trees. I wondered if Suzu remembered the crane, if the crane had even been around almost thirty years ago when Suzu and I had played here. How long did cranes live?

When we entered the cove where the Jizō statue stood proudly in his pond of rocks, protected by the horseshoe of purple hydrangeas just beginning to bloom, Suzu stopped.

Her eyes traveled from the statue to the vibrant purple petals, so bright they glowed in the moonlight. But she didn't say anything about the Jizō's presence, just stared for several minutes, and I watched her face closely. It remained oddly passive. I wanted to grab her shoulders, force her to look at me, ask her if she understood its significance. Why was she so bothered by the puzzle box, yet this statue didn't faze her?

I sighed.

Soon it would get light, and I think we both sensed it—the subtle changes in the still-dark sky that heralded morning. I had brought Suzu to the island, had shown her the fruits of our hard labor, even brought her to the Jizō statue, yet nothing had happened. Something still wasn't quite right, something was missing . . .

Suzu turned toward the horizon where the sun would rise, though it was obscured by holly trees. "I think Mama would be happier if she knew the island looked like this." Suzu smiled, though it was a sad little smile, made all the more melancholy by the twist of her little lip.

"I hope so, Suzu-chan."

A plan began unfolding in my mind. "Do you think we should invite your mother next time?"

She nodded silently, her gaze still focused on some spot in the distance. Then she closed her eyes and, as the first hint of light warmed the sky, she dissipated into nothingness so peacefully that I wasn't even afraid.

Chapter Thirty-Nine

I awoke to the familiar sounds of Yuna setting out my breakfast dishes, though she was clearly trying to make as little noise as possible. I felt a pang of guilt as I watched her through slit eyelids, moving about her morning routine with such care. I had been so absorbed in the island I hadn't taken the time to talk with Yuna in a long time.

"Yuna-chan."

She jumped, nearly spilled the pot of hot tea on the table. Her hand flew to her chest, and she set the teapot down gently.

"Mari-san! You startled me. I had no idea you were awake."

I chuckled and sat up. "Sorry, I just woke up."

Yuna finished laying out the bowl of soup, the rice, the pickles, and then arranged the two wrapped onigiri by the teapot.

A pang of nostalgia struck my heart. I would never sit on a cool granite bench and share an onigiri with Honda-san again, would I? That stage of my life had already passed, and the realization of how fleeting it had been only made the memories more poignant.

"Would you like one of the onigiri?"

She laughed, and picked up one of the plastic-wrapped rice balls, turning it over in her hands. "You're sure you don't need two?" Yuna raised an eyebrow at me.

"No, not today." I paused, not wholly sure how to frame my strange requests. "Do you have a minute? Can you sit and eat with me?"

"If it's about where you've been going and what you've been doing, I'm dying to know." She flopped down by the low table, already unwrapping the onigiri. "I'm all ears."

I smiled, picked up the other rice ball, and started talking.

I told Yuna all about the crane, the island, how Honda-san and I had been working so hard to restore it.

And then I told her about the ghost girl (oh, how Yuna's eyes widened!) and the boat, and finally about how I wanted to invite Kishi-san to visit the island.

"Do you think you could help me? I need to contact Kishi-san, but I don't know where to start."

"Wow. Just wow." Yuna was still staring at her empty wrapper.

"Yeah," I sighed and slumped onto my elbows on the table. "I know, it's a lot."

"It's all crazy. You know that, right?"

"Oh, I'm aware."

Our gazes met and we both laughed.

"Well, I like crazy. Let's do this."

We snuck out of my room and sprinted down the dark hall, giggling like schoolgirls skipping class. I didn't give a damn if Ogura came along and scolded us; it felt too good to feel young and alive.

When we reached Ogura's office and Yuna had knocked and stuck her head in to make sure it was empty, we slipped inside and closed the door behind us. In the spirit of camaraderie, I told Yuna the story of my traumatic (and now embarrassing) time in the closet, and she stifled her laughter behind her hands for a full minute.

"It's not funny! I was terrified." My hurt tone was only half-joking.

"You were so scared of an old lady with a bag of gardening supplies that you hid in a closet?" Yuna kept giggling.

"Anyways," I said, with a pointed glare at Yuna, "I heard Ogura-san using a landline. We just need to find the owner's phone number, right?" We circled around the desk to look at the office-style desk phone. It had a line of buttons, with various hand-written labels. Thankfully one label read *Kishi*.

"Ok great. Listen—I just need you to call her and convince her to come back to Yanagi Inn. Like, tonight." I gestured to the phone. Then I realized how rude that must've sounded. "I-I think it would be so much more natural coming from you." I performed a deep bow, only half in jest.

"Yeah, yeah, I get it. But what should I say? I can't just call up the owner and say 'please come to the inn immediately' without giving any kind of reason."

I frowned. Yuna was right. I guess I'd assumed that an employee could just call up her employer and say she was needed, but Kishi-san wasn't an ordinary employer. Yuna would indeed need a compelling reason.

"Could you say something happened to Ogura-san? Like she's out sick?"

Yuna shook her head. "No, I don't think that would work." Her brow furrowed. "Can't we try something that isn't a lie?"

There was such a pleading look in Yuna's eyes that a pang of guilt shot through me.

"I'm sorry, Yuna. I know I'm asking a lot of you—I shouldn't add to that by pressuring you to lie."

"Thank you." Yuna's relief was palpable.

"Maybe you could say something about there being an emergency on the island only she can deal with? Is that too cryptic?"

She considered this for a moment. "That's not bad."

"And it's the truth. If you need to, you can say that I'm the one asking, like you're just the messenger."

Yuna let out a quiet laugh. "Mari-san, why am I the one making this call again?"

I took a moment to consider. It'd made so much sense before, but now that we were getting into the truth, maybe it didn't make as much sense. "I-I'm not sure," I admitted.

Was I afraid to talk to Kishi-san again? I pictured the elegant but severe woman, with that bony cat crawling all over her, and for a moment that image overlapped with a much older image. A fuzzy scene of Mom and a younger Kishi-san, together, picnicking on a flowered blanket on the grass while I played hide-and-seek behind bushes with Suzu. No, I was afraid she wouldn't believe me if I told her this crazy story over the phone, and I wouldn't be able to convince her to come to the island. But if she were here and I could show her in person . . .

I placed my hands on my thighs and performed an earnest bow this time. "I would be very grateful if you made the call. You are so much better at explaining things than I am."

"I can give it a try. The worst she can do is say no, right?" Yuna's response was so casual and unconcerned I had to bite back a harsh protest. What if Kishi-san wouldn't come? I couldn't leave Suzu's situation the way it was now and go home to Chicago. I could already imagine the haunting what-ifs, the aching sense of incompletion if I abandoned the inn and ran away. No, Kishi-san had to come back to the inn so everything could be put to rest before I had to leave.

Yuna had her hand on the receiver and was watching me expectantly. I nodded. "Let's do it."

She brought the receiver to her ear and pressed the button, her free hand balling into a tight fist on the desktop. I waited for what felt like an eternity, watching Yuna's expression, waiting for the telling moment when either Kishi-san answered, a stranger answered, or the call went to a voicemail or answering system.

There it was—a slight intake of breath, the flicker of a smile— success! "Hello, this is Chisaka Yuna. I am very sorry to trouble you."

Yuna bobbed her head apologetically, even though Kishi-san obviously couldn't see her.

A pause, while the owner responded.

"I hate to trouble you, Kishi-san, but I was wondering if you could possibly come back to the inn?"

Pause.

"As soon as possible."

Pause. Yuna's brow furrowed. I leaned in, hoping to hear clips of Kishi's side of the conversation, but it was too muffled.

"It is very important." Yuna scrunched her eyes tightly closed, and blurted out the rest of the message, "Something has come up regarding the island, which only you can help with."

Another pause. I held my breath.

Yuna swiveled to look at me while she spoke. "Is Lennox-san involved?" She raised her eyebrows. I nodded.

"Yes, she is."

So Kishi-san had already guessed about my involvement. Were we really that transparent?

Wait. Of course Kishi-san would connect me to the island—she knows I used to play there with her daughter. Kishi-san knew me as a child. Kishi-san knew Mom. Did Dad ever come here with us? I recalled the flash of memory about the picnic, the way Mom was smiling. No, something told me our visits were Mom's little secret—two lonely women with workaholic husbands bonding over tea.

"Yes . . . she is here with me."

Pause.

My heart thudded, sick and heavy in my chest.

"Can you speak to her?" Yuna raised her eyebrows at me again, and I froze, unable to speak.

I nodded, swallowing hard.

"Yes, here she is." Yuna gave me a nervous smile and handed the receiver to me.

I cleared my throat.

"Hello Kishi-san."

"Good morning, Lennox-san. Please tell me what this is really about."

Kishi-san was so direct. I weighed my options; if I didn't reveal enough information, she'd think I was wasting her time. But if I gave away too many unusual details—those best provided in person, along-side physical evidence—she'd just think me crazy.

"It has come to my attention that you are needed at the inn. As soon as possible." I paused, trying to remember the polite, vague terms that had been used on me in the past. I'd never been good at dancing around topics, yet still making my intentions clear. "I'm sure you will understand that it is difficult to explain at this time."

Silence. I clutched the phone receiver so tight to my ear it hurt.

She's going to say no, she's going to say she's too busy, she's going to tell me to never call her again and stop wasting her time. I can't let her say no!

I blurted out the first thing that came into my head. "It involves my ring."

In retrospect, I must have known that the ring Mom gave me had something to do with Yanagi Inn, with the island, with Kishi-san, with *everything*. But it was only at that moment—when seized with the crush-ing desire to get Kishi-san to come back, to make her realize that my return and the island and her daughter were all interconnected in some profound way—that I synthesized the information enough to put it into words. I prayed I was hitting close enough to the truth that Kishi-san would agree to hear me out, even if I didn't know what significance the ring held for her. Or for me.

"You recall, Lennox-san, that I prefer not to visit the inn."

I scrunched my eyes closed so tight they hurt. "Yes."

"Yet you still request that I return, so soon after my last visit."

"Yes," I said, though my heart ached inside my chest. I couldn't begin to imagine how Kishi-san must be feeling, but I had to believe that this was all for the better. That what I was asking would help her, not make everything worse. "I'm sorry to have to ask you, truly, but I—"

"All right, I'll come."

My heart sang, and my whole body flooded with relief. "Thank you," I whispered.

Chapter Forty

It was nearly noon when I finally made it out to Honda's temple. I found her waiting on the front steps, and I waved as I approached. She jumped to her feet.

"Mari-san! I've been waiting for you."

I felt a flush of guilt for being so late, and it must have shown on my face, for she sat back down and patted the steps next to her with a smile. "I'm sure you have your reasons, no? Tell me what has happened."

I sank down on the steps beside Honda and told her everything—from taking the boat out to the island, to involving Yuna in this whole fiasco, to convincing the owner to return. Honda listened to the chaotic, jumbled story spilling out of my mouth, occasionally nodding or muttering her quiet acknowledgments to show she was following me. At the end she patted me on the arm and said, "Now what?"

I paused to consider the deeper implications of that question. I would talk to Kishi when she arrived, of course, and since she was already making the trip to Yanagi Inn, I'd assumed I could convince her to visit the island. But what would I do once she was there, just give her a tour? Wouldn't she demand more satisfaction than that? I would have to get Suzu to visit the island again, too—somehow bring the two of them together. Was that even possible? What if—

Honda disrupted my thoughts, probably sensing my inner turmoil. "Would you like me to come this time? I am not Kishi-san's favorite person, but perhaps I can help with the reunion."

I relaxed into a smile. "I would be very grateful for your assistance." I paused, wondering how much I should pry. "May I ask what happened to make things uncomfortable between you and the owner?"

Honda squinted at me for a moment, as if looking for an ulterior motive behind my question. But then she sighed and looked off into the distant trees. "I was the one who found Suzu-chan's body."

It took me a second to register Honda's comment. Accustomed as I was to walking hand-in-hand with the girl, the idea of someone discovering Suzu's dead body was jarring. "I-I'm sorry. That must have been awful."

She nodded, a simple acknowledgment of my sympathy.

"Even though she was . . . already gone, I think there are those who blame me for not doing more."

Blaming the messenger. We are all so illogical when mired in grief. I wanted to ask if she had been involved with Suzu's funeral, but the pained expression on her face stopped me from pursuing the matter further. I looked away.

"Well, thank you for offering to help—I'm sure I'll need it." I paused, turned back toward her. "What are we even trying to do, Honda-san?"

I'd meant this as a serious question, an earnest appeal for enlightenment, but it came out wistful, vague.

"I think," Honda said, climbing slowly to her feet, "we are trying to help Kishi-san."

"And bringing her to the island and reuniting her with her daughter's ghost will do that?"

Honda shrugged. "We will find out."

I wanted to let it go at that, but there was an itching suspicion in the back of my mind. Part of me wanted to push down my doubts, pretend like they didn't exist—as I realized I'd done in my relationship with

Thad. And with Mom. But another part, the part that had ventured out of my room to find the source of the nocturnal crying, who had braved the submerged stepping-stones to explore the island—*that* Mari told me I needed to see this ordeal through to the end, and that meant facing every dark corner of it.

And asking for help when I needed it.

"There's something that's been bothering me," I said, standing up slowly. "About the ghost girl. About Suzu-chan."

Honda had been staring off into the distant trees, but now she turned toward me, her deep brown eyes searching mine.

"I'm not sure how to put this, but I'm not 100 percent convinced the ghost girl is really Suzu-chan." I paused, expecting Honda to agree with me and remind me that, of course, ghosts are not real, but her expression remained neutral. "Maybe this is completely normal for ghosts, and I'm just woefully ignorant but . . ." I trailed off, uncertain how to put my doubts into words.

"But . . ." Honda prodded gently.

"But there are, well, holes. I don't mean that literally," I said quickly, not wanting to suggest she was some gruesome, transparent specter, "but more like she doesn't feel quite complete. Maybe that's normal, though."

"Something about it bothers you?"

I considered her question. "Yes. Something about Suzu doesn't feel right. She told me we were friends when we were little, and while I believe her and have some vague memories of that time, she didn't seem to have the same memories as me."

How do you determine whether or not a ghost is who she says she is? The more I thought about it, the more unsettled I became. How had she even recognized me after all these years? Why had she snapped at me when I brought up something she didn't remember? And why wasn't she surprised by the Jizō statue? I replayed our conversations in my mind and shook my head.

"She seems to know things about the island that she shouldn't know, and she got upset when I pointed out discrepancies. It's almost like she's an A.I. reproduction of the real Suzu. Or a clone."

Honda's face was calm, unaffected, but I could tell she was digesting everything I'd said.

I laughed. "Or maybe I just watch too much anime."

This made her smile.

"I guess what I'm trying to say is that something about Suzu-chan makes me uneasy. I know it's probably not fair of me to ask this, but do you think I could be doing wrong, doing something *bad*, by bringing her together with Kishi-san?"

Now Honda's brow furrowed. "What kind of wrong?"

"Well," I pursed my lips for a second. "What if the ghost girl isn't really Suzu but a fake Suzu, like an evil spirit trying to lure Kishi-san out to the island, and I'm the unwitting accomplice?"

Honda nodded slowly and turned to stare at the trees. She pulled her rosary of brown beads out of her pocket and began shifting them through her fingers.

"I think you may indeed watch too much anime, Mari-san." She let out a laugh, then turned to me, smiling. "But then again there are a lot of things we don't understand in this world, so perhaps you are right. It is best to have your walking stick before you tumble, so I will be prepared, just in case." She put the beads back in her pocket and patted it.

I nodded. Just knowing that Honda would be there during the fateful meeting between mother and daughter certainly made my heart feel lighter.

"I don't know what time Kishi-san is arriving, but can you meet me by the boat tonight?"

Honda nodded. "I will come at sundown and wait for you."

A rush of gratitude surged through my body. Honda-san was a true friend. Just like Yuna. Somehow, I had managed to forge two friendships—with two very different women—in such a short period of time, when I hadn't made a new friend back home in years. Even the friends I had were mostly work acquaintances or Thad's friends. It felt good to make real human connections. I bowed, deeply, and held it for a moment.

"Thank you, Honda-san. For everything."

Honda must've noticed the quaver in my voice, because she looked me up and down, then leaned in and scrutinized my face. I glanced away.

"Mari-san, do you have a few minutes? I could use help with something." She'd turned on her cheerful voice and her face held a warm smile, though I knew she was up to something.

But so far, Honda-san's "somethings" hadn't steered me wrong.

"Sure . . ."

She gestured for me to follow her.

We walked around the back of the temple, past Honda's little truck parked on the gravel pad, and down the driveway. I'd never been to this part of the property. It was lovely and thick with evergreen trees, and though no creatures were visible, the sounds of life—the breaking of twigs, the chitters of squirrels and chirps of birds—were all around us. We came to a clearing amidst the pines, with a large brush pile in the center. Sticks and branches, hunks of logs, twisted vines all in a chaotic pile as tall as me and twice that in width.

"I've been collecting the larger debris, the parts that won't compost well. Eventually I burn it all here." She wiped her hands on her brown pants, looked up at the sky. "I think it should be dry enough now. Want to help?"

Five minutes later, Honda returned from the temple carrying a cloth bag and two long-reach lighters. She handed me one, and then demonstrated the finer points of starting a brush fire. Within a few minutes we had a roaring blaze reaching into the sky, and we stood back, broad smiles on our faces.

The shimmering air above the fire was hypnotic. An occasional flake of ash or a scrap of burning embers would float up into the sky, hover, then extinguish.

Too bad I don't have my camera.

The fire's energy was raw, wild, and contagious; I began whooping and dancing around the fire like some fairytale witch. Honda joined in, and soon we were running circles around the fire, arms waving over our heads, catching glimpses of each other across the flames burning the evidence of our hard work on the island.

The fire reached its peak of frenzy and then relaxed, burning steady and bright and hot. We slowed our mania, breathing hard, and came to rest beside one another, gazing at the inferno, sweating through our shirts.

"Now," I panted, as soon as I could catch my breath, "I can picture wild-teenager Honda-san."

She laughed. "And *you* didn't set any fires when you were young?"

My smile faded. The smoky scent of burning wild brush invaded my nostrils, my mouth, infusing my clothes, my hair. Sand between my toes . . .

A beach bonfire. Risa and I running around like lunatics in our summery yukata. Turning around and realizing Mom was curled in a ball on her blanket, crying. *I don't know what to do. I don't want to scare Risa, I—*

A few tears managed to escape my stinging eyes, and I wiped them with the back of my grubby wrist. Honda laid a hand on my arm. "Your mother?"

I nodded, blinking furiously.

"Did you not get to say goodbye?"

Oh, if only it were that simple.

"No, I—there was time enough for goodbyes and all that. It's just—"

Honda nodded, made small, encouraging hand gestures for me to continue.

"I-I'm sure this will make me sound like a terrible person, but I never got to tell her how I really felt. How much she hurt me. To be honest, my time in Japan . . . I don't even want to remember a lot of it." I looked at my feet, shook my head. "I loved my mother, of course, but sometimes I hated her, too. Hated the times she wasn't there for me and my sister, hated the selfish decisions she made, hated . . ." I gestured vaguely around me, unable to speak any more.

Honda stood beside me, companionably, and we listened to the fire in silence for a few moments. Then she nodded, as if to herself. "I have something for that, too."

She rummaged in her cloth bag and pulled out a small pad of paper and stubby pencil like the kind she'd used to write down our supply lists and renovation ideas. She thrust these into my hands saying, "Write your mother a letter."

A letter.

I stared at the blank white paper, letting her words sink into my brain. Honda had turned back toward the fire, giving me a modicum of privacy.

I sat down in the dirt, used my leg as a platform.

A letter. To my mother.

I began writing.

Mom,

I hate that you never got help, never admitted you had a problem.

I hate that you left me and Risa alone at night when you went out.

I hate that you didn't trust me enough to ever tell me the truth.

I hate that you destroyed all our photos so I can barely remember my childhood.

I hate that you left Dad and never told us why.

I hate that I never got to have a relationship with Dad because you never brought us back to Japan.

I hate . . .

Once I started writing, I couldn't stop. I was scribbling, scribbling like mad, covering the front of the first sheet, and then starting on the back. *I hate . . . I hate . . . I hate . . .*

I could almost feel myself releasing angry-Mari piece by piece like she was one of those burning logs losing parts of itself into the ether.

And then, after a few minutes, I ran out of steam.

I stood and approached Honda, who had taken out another pad and pencil and was writing her own letter of some kind, although less maniacally. I couldn't help but sneak a glance at her paper, at Honda's surprisingly neat kanji and hiragana writing.

I only caught two words: *Suzu* and *gomen*—"I'm sorry."

Honda finished writing and began folding her paper, gently, expertly, until it was a delightful white paper cube. She held it up on her palm for me to see and then tossed the cube into the hungry fire.

Nice.

Could I remember how to fold any origami? I stared at my own letter, searching my mind for childhood memories of brightly colored papers folded into cranes, frogs, goldfish. I used to be good at flowers, but I wasn't sure . . .

No. I smiled and began folding my small paper into a tiny paper airplane. No need to worry about perfection. This would take the letter to Mom just as well.

Honda smiled and nodded, and I drew my arm back and threw the tiny paper airplane letter as hard as I could, sending it nearly straight up, and then lazily flopping down into the inferno.

I watched for the two seconds it took the flames to devour the paper beyond recognition. "Goodbye, Mom," I whispered into the fire, eyes filling with tears.

Honda was muttering quietly to herself beside me, and I swear I saw her wipe a tear away with her sleeve, too.

Chapter Forty-One

For the first time in weeks, I didn't finish the dinner that the not-Yuna maid brought me; my stomach was so sour and anxious I only picked at the mountain vegetables and local tofu.

As soon as a knock sounded on my door, I was on my feet and ready to rush to the old banquet hall. But then the door slid open, and Ogura stood in my doorway.

"What did you say to make Kishi-san come here?" She spoke quietly, but it was a commanding tone, and I could feel my internal eight-year-old Mari quaking in her boots.

No, Mari, you are not a child.

I met her gaze, my chin held high. I hadn't noticed during our previous encounters, but I was several inches taller than Ogura.

"I told her the truth. That she was needed on the island."

Ogura blanched visibly. "You want to take her *there*? How could you be so cruel?"

"No, you don't understand. I need to—"

"I understand well enough, and I will not let you take the owner to that horrific place." Ogura's entire body was trembling, fists now clenched at her sides.

My head spun, desperately searching for words to make Ogura-san change her mind. Telling her the truth would get me nowhere, yet vague suggestions weren't going to be enough.

"Ogura-san, I—"

"No, you listen to me. You've come here, traipsing all over the grounds like you own the place, not caring whose lives you upend. And I have tried to respect the fact you are a guest here. But now you have gone too far." Ogura's voice grew louder and louder as she spoke, her eyes flaring. "I won't let you hurt her, Lennox-san. Not again. And that is final." With that declaration, Ogura turned and left my room. She slid the door closed behind her with a solid thud.

I stood, bewildered, in the middle of my room.

She won't let me hurt Kishi-san *again*? What did Ogura even mean by that? I had the unsettling impression that she knew things about me that I didn't.

The anger on her face had been so raw, so pained, a new realization dawned on me. Ogura's number one goal had always been to protect Kishi-san. Even her agitation at my arrival—she must've recognized me as the little girl who used to play with Suzu and been worried how my presence would affect the owner.

I let out a sigh, pressed the heels of my palms against my eyes. Sympathetic intentions or not, I couldn't let Ogura stand in my way. Kishi must be here in the inn already, and I had come too far to not push forward, no matter the obstacles.

Besides, this was almost guaranteed to be my last chance to talk with Kishi. Ogura would likely throw me out in the morning, even if it meant she had to pack my luggage herself.

With a determined step, I strode to the door and tried to throw it open. The door stuck. I frowned, tugged again. Still, it wouldn't budge.

No, no, no.

I leaned all my weight against the inset handle and it only budged a fraction of an inch. I fell back, gasping.

Had Ogura locked me in my own room?

I didn't even know if that was possible. She must've wedged some-thing on the other side to keep the door from moving.

Now I was trapped, a mouse locked in a cage with an angry cat prowling outside.

But, no—and here I let out a laugh—there was more than one way out of this room.

I shoved aside the shoji panel and stepped out onto the veranda. Ogura was not going to keep me from Kishi-san.

I slid my feet into garden sandals and crept out into the night. But where to go? I sized up my options. I could sneak around to the entrance, but surely it would be locked. Did the dining hall have a veranda?

Creeping around the exterior of the building, I marveled at how dark—how devoid of life—it looked at night. I pictured for a moment Ogura pacing the hallways inside, keeping watch to ensure I didn't emerge from my room to stir up more trouble.

I approached a guestroom's veranda at random, tried the door, and thankfully it slid open. I kicked off my sandals and slipped inside.

The air was so musty I held my breath as I moved through the dark space, anticipating where the table would be if it were my own room. I pressed an ear to the hall door before I slid it open.

The hall was empty, silent, dark.

I took a deep breath and stepped out into the hallway.

With every tiny sound, I shot a glance over my shoulder, half-ex-pecting Ogura to come storming down the hall after me, eyes blazing red. I wound my way through Yanagi Inn's twisted pathways, strug-gling to remember where the dining hall had been. When a footstep sounded behind me, I panicked. I found the nearest door, slid it open, and jumped inside. Yet another musty guestroom. Were there truly no other guests here at the inn? The footsteps passed by out in the hall, along with the slight rattle of a tea service on a tray. Probably just the evening maid, I reasoned, and, after a few moments to catch my breath, I stepped back into the hallway.

I picked up my speed. What if Ogura-san was already in with the owner, whispering dark lies about me in Kishi-san's ear? Or, worse, what if Ogura-san was guarding the dining hall's door, and I wouldn't even be able to get inside? I took one final turn and found myself in the narrow corridor I remembered from before, so I rushed forward, gave one final glance over my shoulder, and pushed through the short noren curtain.

Kishi was sitting at her table in the former banquet hall. Thankfully, alone. But this time, instead of accounting ledgers, she had a partially eaten dinner spread before her, identical to the one I'd left behind in my room.

Before I could say a word, she looked up at me with surprise. "Lennox-san. I wasn't expecting to see you. Ogura-san just told me . . ."

She trailed off as I rushed across the room toward her. I shot a nervous glance over my shoulder, then knelt on the cushion across from her. "My apologies for disturbing your meal, but what I have to say is urgent."

"It's fine—I am almost finished." She took another bite of tofu and a vegetable I couldn't name. "I never can finish these sumptuous meals."

I suppressed a wry smile. *She eats like I used to.*

Kishi set her chopsticks on their rest, then folded her hands on her lap and looked up at me expectantly.

This was it. I just needed to convince her to come with me to the island. From there . . . I'd figure it out as we went. I placed my palms on the table in front of me and bowed my head so low my nose brushed the tabletop. I held my position, praying my face wasn't as flushed as it felt. "Kishi-san, I would like you to accompany me to the island." I squeezed my eyes shut and waited for her reply.

"The island." A moment of silence. "You have already asked me to come back to the inn on short notice and—against my better judgement—I have complied with your request." She paused, and I could hear her take a sip of tea, weighing her words. "Now it is late, I am tired, and you ask me to follow you to the island? At night? Without explanation?"

I maintained my bowed position, fighting back tears with eyes clamped shut. "I would ask you to humor me for just a little longer, and then I will be able to explain everything. Please."

The sound of the door sliding open jolted me upright, and I spun around. But it wasn't Ogura. Just the evening maid coming for Kishi's dishes. My rumbling heart slowed, and Kishi and I sat in silence until the maid gathered the dishes onto her lacquer tray and left the room.

"Why can't you tell me here, now?" Kishi gestured around the room, her tone rising in pitch. "Why does it have to involve the island? I expected more from you. You, of all people, Mari-chan, know why I can't go back there. How is it that you *can*? I—"

Kishi's voice cracked, broken by her surge of emotion. Her fist pressed against her mouth, and her eyes closed as she struggled to regain control.

"Me, of all people?" I shot another nervous glance over my shoulder. "Please, we don't have much time. I am sorry you are hurting. I promise I wouldn't ask this of you for no reason. Please, just this once, put your trust in me. Please come with me." I tried to infuse my words with sincerity, but desperation crept in.

Kishi let out a long, slow breath and smoothed down the front of her kimono. "If I agree to come with you on this ridiculous excursion, you must then leave. Immediately. I'll not deal with this again. We will not see each other again."

I knew I didn't have a choice, that it didn't matter anyways—whatever was to happen, would happen tonight. Yet the finality of her declaration stung me.

"Yes, Kishi-san. I understand."

We sat in silence for a few tense heartbeats. Then Kishi said, in a tired, resigned voice, "All right. I will come with you."

Chapter Forty-Two

The air was chilly, and the sky cloudier than the previous night. The veiled moon shed little illumination on the garden's gravel paths, but I didn't dare slow my pace, knowing at any moment Ogura might notice Kishi's absence and come after us.

"Lennox-san," Kishi began, out of breath as she rushed after me down the dark path. "This is ridiculous—why weren't you more prepared for this excursion?"

I stopped walking and Kishi bumped into me from behind. I turned to her. "I'm so sorry. I should've brought a flashlight."

She didn't reply, just waved at me dismissively.

If I'd had more time to prepare . . . well, reality was never quite as glamorous as the plans in my head. I bobbed my head and started walking briskly down the dark path again.

I shot a glance over my shoulder; Kishi's lips were pressed into a tight line, her hands balled into fists. She was anxious; I would be anxious, too, if someone was dragging me to visit the site of my daughter's untimely death for the first time in almost thirty years.

At night. Without a flashlight.

When we turned a corner and the pond was within view, I saw a light up ahead near the shore.

Of course Honda would think to bring a light.

My breath hitched. *I didn't tell Kishi-san we'd be meeting Honda-san here.* I sucked air in through my teeth and kept walking.

We approached the halo of light and Honda stood up, her face softly illuminated by the camping lantern. I could hear the owner's swift intake of breath over my shoulder, and I cringed inwardly, praying she wouldn't take this surprise meeting as a betrayal, wouldn't mistake my intentions.

"Lennox-san—" Kishi hissed at me.

But then Honda approached us and bowed deeply. "It is good to see you again, Kishi-san."

"It's been a long time," Kishi answered coolly, bowing her head in response, and I found myself grateful that she was too refined to make a scene.

I glanced from woman to woman.

"I'm glad you brought a lantern," Kishi said after a moment, a faint smile gracing her lips.

Honda laughed. "Yes, Mari-chan hasn't changed much, has she? The spirit of a three-year-old persists until one hundred."

Did she just call me "Mari-chan"?

Kishi chuckled now, too. Were they sharing a moment? Over my ineptitude? I opened my mouth to say something, but then stopped cold. Wait, how well had Honda-san known child-Mari? A flash of memory: me, a child, stumbling and in pain. Crying for help. Then a flurry of movement, a woman—Honda-san—running toward me in her brown wrap top and pants. Calling my name . . .

I blinked. Honda was watching me closely. She must've seen my disorientation, because she took the reins of the situation. "I can transport you across the pond now," she said with another slight bow.

"Transport?" Kishi said, softly.

Honda set the lantern on the gravel and untied the boat's rope from the bushes.

"Oh!" Kishi exclaimed as the wooden boat was pulled out from its hiding spot. Surely she must've been wondering how we were going to reach the island, knowing she'd had it blocked off so many years ago. But then it dawned on me—I didn't know if the blocking off was Kishi's idea. I'd seen how far Ogura would go to protect the owner. Perhaps Ogura had ordered the island closed off to protect Kishi from more pain? A pang of sympathy struck my heart.

I helped Honda position the boat in the water, and then offered my hand to Kishi. She accepted it, and we both climbed in. Honda gestured that we should sit on the middle plank so she could sit in the back and control the oar.

As Honda pushed us away from shore, I turned for one more glance back toward the inn. A single spot of light wavered in the distance. Had Ogura noticed our absence? Was she coming to find us?

I smiled, grimly. Well, it was too late; she couldn't reach us now. There was only one boat.

Gliding across the water at night, with a nearly full moon peeking from behind the clouds, was a surreal experience. I think we all must have felt it; we rode in silence, save for the quiet lapping of the oar in the dark water. My mind returned to my harrowing boat trip across this pond with Suzu, to the terror that had seized me as I'd faced the dark depths of the pond and the real possibility I would plunge into them. I closed my eyes, took a deep, steadying breath. A faint breeze stirred up distant scents (rosemary, cypress), bringing with it a fresh spring chill.

I dared a glance at Kishi. She sat on the bench beside me, perfectly upright, but her arms were hugging her body, fists clenching the cloth of her padded jacket. Her anxiety was palpable; I could've sworn I saw wisps of vapor rising off her body, but it could have been a trick of the lantern light.

Soon the boat journey was over, the passage so quick compared to my agonizing attempt the night before. Kishi didn't wait for me to help her out of the boat; the moment the nose pushed up onto the far bank she was stepping out and onto the solid ground of the island.

Honda and I busied ourselves with the rope longer than was necessary, allowing Kishi a private moment before we proceeded. She was simply standing, staring into the grove of bamboo shielding the interior of the island from view. For a moment, a flicker of doubt passed over me. Was I being cruel, bringing her here? I kept telling myself this was for Kishi's sake, but I could only imagine how it must feel to revisit the location of her daughter's death for the first time.

But this couldn't be the first time. Surely Kishi-san had been responsible for the Jizō statue.

"Perhaps," I said quietly to Honda after we'd finished securing the boat, "we should take her straight to the Jizō statue."

She nodded, turned to look at Kishi.

The owner was still standing in the same spot, staring straight ahead. I hated to interrupt her, but I knew there was much to get done that night. "If you would follow us, please."

As we climbed the slight incline and passed through the bamboo border into the interior of the island, I heard Kishi-san gasp. At first, this made me smile, my insides warming with pride at the accomplishments Honda and I had made. But when I turned to catch Kishi's expression, it was pinched, angry.

"What have you done?" she demanded. "Photography is one thing. But what gave you the right to do all . . . this?" She swept her hand toward the neatly shaped azalea bushes, the pruned pines, the gravel paths free from debris.

"I-I . . ." I had been so caught up in all the improvements we'd been making, it never occurred to me that Kishi might object. Maybe in her mind the deterioration of the island was a kind of penance; whether toward the place that had stolen her daughter or toward herself, I could never say. For a moment I just stood, mouth agape, my mind spinning. But I had to trust that I could convince her this was all for the best.

I had to trust that I still believed that myself.

I pursed my lips for a moment, stood up straighter. "I promise all will be made clear soon. Please, this way." I bowed my head briefly, then turned and continued on the path that would lead us to the Jizō statue, praying she would follow.

She did.

Now that we were on the other side of water, I knew I could stop looking over my shoulder for Ogura. But, I realized with a sinking sensation, I would have to cross back across the pond. Alone.

"Honda-san," I whispered, "after we've shown Kishi-san the Jizō statue, I'll have to go back for Suzu. Think you two will be ok?"

She nodded, eyes focused on the path in front of us, illuminated in the soft light of her lantern. Honda had seemed oddly quiet ever since she stepped into the boat. Perhaps it wasn't so strange, all things considered. We all had a lot to work through tonight.

Just as we reached the final bend in the path before reaching the statue, Honda motioned as if to hand me something. Inside her palm was a rosary, just like the loop of brown wooden beads I'd seen earlier. I opened my mouth to question her, but Honda shook her head sharply, and I remained silent. I slipped the beads inside the fold of my yukata.

We turned the corner, and Honda and I stopped in front of the Jizō statue. A moment later Kishi paused next to us, taking in the sight. The statue was beautiful in the soft light of the lantern. His round, bald stone head was shiny and clean, and a new red bib was tied around his neck. The purple hydrangeas behind him glowed in the moonlight.

Kishi stood up straight and tall as she observed this scene, but her clenched hands trembled. "Lennox-san, this is too much. You should've known how unbearable this would be for me." Despite obvious effort, her voice wavered with the final words.

Honda met my gaze and gave me an encouraging nod.

"Please, look around you at the transformation that has occurred here. Honda-san and I have worked hard to restore this garden to its former beauty, to heal the damage done by years of neglect." The owner's jaw clenched tighter at the word *neglect*.

"So you brought me here just to show off the illicit gardening you've been doing? Take me back to the inn. I am leaving." Kishi's voice was harsh, and she turned to leave.

"Kishi-san," I said, stepping closer and laying a light hand on her shoulder. "We had a good reason to fix up the gardens." I paused, took a deep breath to steady my nerves. "Someone asked me to."

Kishi knocked my hand off of her. "It does not matter who asked you to do this. Yanagi Inn is my property." She frowned at me for a moment, then her gaze shifted to Honda. "Please don't tell me that Honda-san was behind—"

"Wait," I broke in. "Suzu-chan asked me to fix up the island."

Kishi's breath faltered at the mention of her daughter's name, and her body began trembling. She turned to face me head-on, her mouth morphing into a firm line and her eyes hardening. "How *dare* you."

"Kishi-san, I—"

"No, how dare you invoke my daughter's name to justify your actions. I welcomed you to my inn, hoping to put the past behind us, and this is how you repay me?"

"Please, you don't understand—"

"No, I *don't* understand," Kishi interrupted. "How can you even stand to be here, Mari-chan? Why aren't you haunted by what happened?"

I shot a confused glance at Honda, but her head was bowed, murmuring quiet prayers.

"I-I don't understand."

Kishi stared at me, eyes wild. Then her mouth went slack, understanding spreading across her face. "Do you not remember?" she said, softly.

"Remember?"

"*How can you not remember?*" Kishi's voice became an anguished cry.

She stumbled forward and I tried to catch her, but she fell to her knees, bent over, arms wrapped around herself. A low moan issued from her mouth.

I froze. "K-Kishi-san?"

Then Kishi's head snapped up, her eyes wide. Her gaze was focused on a point behind me, her lower lip trembling. "S-Suzu-chan?"

Time slowed down. Someone—Honda-san?—spoke, but all I could hear was the resounding thud of my heartbeat in my ears.

As if in slow motion, I turned around.

There, standing ankle-deep in the pond, was Suzu.

And in that moment, I remembered.

Chapter Forty-Three

"Come on, Mari-chan. Roll up your pants—your mother won't even know." Suzu beamed her lopsided smile at me as she stood ankle-deep in the pond, holding the hem of her green yukata up over her knees.

I wavered on the edge of the water, the hot summer sun sending a drip of sweat down the back of my T-shirt. "I don't know . . . it's against *your* mom's rules, too, and I really don't want to make her mad." I shot a glance over my shoulder, though I knew my mom and Kishi-san were still on the mainland and couldn't possibly see us.

"Oh come on. We can break the rules *sometimes.*" Suzu's melodic laugh made me grin, despite the queasiness in my gut.

"I don't know . . ."

But Suzu must've sensed my resolve faltering. "Come *on*! The water isn't even cold—it feels great!" She gave a big kick with one foot and it sent a spray in my direction. I shrieked and scampered away, pulling up my pant hems to avoid getting them wet.

"Mari-chan, there's even a fish! Come see the koi! Do you still have that rice cracker? Come on, bring it over. We can feed it to him."

"All right, all right." I hiked up my pants further, rolling them above my knee, and waded into the pond. Suzu was right; the water was the perfect temperature—cool to my sweaty skin, but not cold. Probably because it was shallow here. Kishi-san had always warned us that the pond got much deeper further in; that water was probably icy.

I splashed my way over to Suzu, enjoying the squish of the mud between my bare toes. The water grew murky as I stirred up the depths with each step.

"Hey, you're scaring the fish!" Suzu pointed at a flash of movement underwater, and turned, wading in deeper, up to mid-thigh, the hem of her yukata dragging in the water.

"Suzu-chan . . . I don't think that's a good idea. Just let him go. I'm sure there are other fish."

But she wasn't listening to me as she chased down the fish. "Oh c'mon, might as well enjoy it! The water is so nice and cool over here!"

"But I can't—"

Then Suzu's foot slipped and her whole body dunked under the water. My heart seized, but then she reappeared a moment later, sputtering and laughing.

I added my own nervous laughter, glancing over my shoulder to make sure we were still alone.

"What are you going to tell your mom? Your yukata is ruined!"

Suzu rose back to her feet, hair dripping down her face. "You worry too much, Mari-chan!" She laughed again and tried to swoosh a tidal wave of pond water at me, but lost her balance again, this time falling backwards.

I laughed, too, the expression on her shocked face priceless as she dunked under once again.

But this time Suzu didn't resurface.

The smile faded from my lips.

"Suzu-chan?" I called.

I waited. "C'mon, don't play games!"

I stepped forward, suddenly cold.

Bubbles formed on the surface of the pond.

"Suzu-chan!" I cried and took another step.

Nothing.

Then I was rushing, splashing through the water, my rolled-up pants forgotten as I waded deeper and deeper into the cold, cold pond. I stepped on something hard and sharp and I winced, my mind imagining a million biting creatures circling me down below. Then my hurried step reached out and found nothing, my momentum pulling me forward into the water. I went under.

Panic surged through my veins. I tried to scream, but the murky pond water forced its way between my lips. I flailed arms and legs, meeting only the slick muddy cliff I'd just stepped off in my haste.

I can't swim, I can't swim, I can't swim.

My arms pinwheeled, my fingers grasped at nothing, at mud, then at knotted plant matter. I pulled, and it held. I pulled some more, hoping I was pulling up. I had lost all sense of direction, unable to open my eyes. The pain in my lungs consumed me.

I pulled and kicked my legs and fought, even as I began seeing flashes of static inside my eyelids, and then suddenly my body surged the last few inches. My face broke the surface, cresting like a whale, and I inhaled, choking and gasping as I scrambled in the slick mud to get my footing.

I'd made it. Somehow I'd made it back up.

But Suzu-chan—where was Suzu-chan?

I spun to look behind me, but Suzu had disappeared.

Help. I needed help.

I slipped and scrambled and pushed my way to shore, still coughing and gasping. I tried to catch my breath, to scream, but my "*Help*" came out weak, like a mewling kitten. The piercing drone of cicada song filled the air around me, smothering my sounds.

Tears streamed down my face, and I tried again and again to cry out, each time getting a little stronger until a proper scream erupted. "Help! *Help!* HELP!"

There—a rustle of movement on the path ahead, behind the row of azalea bushes in full bloom. A figure, a blur of brown pants and top, a floppy straw hat.

I fell to my knees on the gravel shore.

Help was coming.

Chapter Forty-Four

The ghost girl's face was a mask of grief and sorrow as she stood over her mother. Tears streamed down her cheeks, raw and unrestrained.

"Suzu-chan!" I gasped. "How did you get here? I was just about to—"

I stopped. *Of course, she's a spirit.* Why had I thought she'd require physical transportation in a boat?

Suzu didn't react to my words at all, and I wondered if she could even perceive me. We remained in our positions for what felt like an eternity—me and Honda as silent observers, Suzu standing watch over Kishi, who was collapsed on the ground, drowning in her sorrow.

I had to say something. "Suzu, why don't you talk to—"

"No!" Honda broke in, startling me into silence, her hand raised. "Mari-san, look."

I returned my gaze to the owner, who had turned and was now staring up at the ghost of her daughter. But her face didn't register sorrow or fear, but rather her brow was knitted in confusion.

"No, Mari-san. *Really look.*" Honda gestured with her beads. It took a moment, but then I understood her intent.

I pulled the loop of beads out of my yukata, and the moment my fingers touched them it was as if a filter had been removed from the scene, and I could see clearly for the first time. Kishi wasn't looking up at Suzu-chan's ghost anymore—she was looking at . . . herself?

What?

I narrowed my eyes, clenching the beads in my closed fists. Kishi was looking up at another version of herself, a more insubstantial version. The spirit woman looked just like Kishi down to the silver kimono and long, loose hair.

But her face—looking into the spirit's face was like looking into a funhouse mirror of Kishi's, it was so stretched and distorted with sorrow. And I could feel the pulsations coming off the spirit-Kishi, the waves and waves of grief sinking under my skin.

Tears welled in my eyes, blurring the scene in front of me. The stench of rotting swamp matter assaulted my nose, and I fought back the urge to gag.

"What is she?" I whispered.

"I believe," Honda began slowly and softly, as if afraid to disrupt the scene before us, "she is an *ikiryō.*"

I turned to Honda, confusion written across my face.

"A living spirit. It is akin to a ghost, but for a person who is still alive. In this case, she would be Kishi-san's ikiryō."

"But did Kishi-san summon this spirit? Or does she think it's Suzu-chan?"

We both turned to watch Kishi and the ikiryō, still just staring at each other silently, unmoving, as if frozen to the spot.

"It is difficult to say. I believe most people wouldn't be aware of their ikiryō at all. I don't know whether she would see the spirit as the ghost of her daughter, as you did, or if it is like looking at one's doppelgänger."

I wanted to reach out, shake Kishi from her trance, but something held me back—some deep-down understanding that the scene in front of me had to play out. But the ikiryō's disfigured face was so disturbing I had to look away.

"Is this her grief? Like a . . ." I gestured toward the ghastly figure beside the kneeling Kishi, unsure how to name the phenomenon I was seeing. Grief-demon? No, that was too malevolent. I hoped.

"I believe so," Honda said softly, rotating the string of beads through her fingers. "An ikiryō is the result of an intense emotion, usually rage or jealousy. But a grief like Kishi-san's . . ." She shook her head sadly. "A part of Kishi-san's tormented soul must've been breaking away at night and taking the form of her daughter."

Snapshots of my experiences at Yanagi Inn were piecing together in my brain as Honda spoke. The bridge. The puzzle box.

"That's why the spirit didn't know about our childhood secrets, isn't it? She only knew what Kishi-san knew."

It had never been Suzu that I talked to at night while everyone else was asleep. Suzu-chan, the little girl I had known, was gone.

I pictured little Suzu-chan as she had been in life, so full of joy and vitality. But then an image of Honda rose in my mind, splashing into the pond to grab that little girl's limp body, and it sent a sharp pang through my chest. I realized how much I had been clinging to the idea that she really was a ghost. Proof that life could continue, in some form, after death. I'd been clinging to my hope that the ghost girl could be reunited with her mother in a way that would bring both of them (and me, I realized) peace. But no, Suzu-chan had been gone for decades, and she could never be brought back.

No one could be brought back. I had to accept that.

Tears welled in my eyes again, and this time I let them spill down my cheeks unchecked. My heart went out to Kishi, face-to-face with the embodiment of her grief and sorrow—and her guilt. To bottle up so much pain, to shut out everyone who could potentially hurt her again—such a thought resonated with me on a deep, deep level. The aching hole inside of me widened and I clenched a hand to my chest.

Flashes of my phantom visions of Mom—on the plane, in the baths—flickered before my eyes and I took a deep, shuddering breath.

Now that I'd seen what grief and guilt could do, I had to question what my visions of Mom had really been. Perhaps they hadn't been entirely inside my head.

I forced myself to look at Kishi-san and her ikiryō. *There but for the grace of God, go I.*

"Honda-san," I said through my tears, "What can we do? We have to help them."

She walked over to me, still rotating the beads in her fingers. "I suspect you weren't far off when you thought Suzu-chan and her mother needed to meet to reconcile. Perhaps we should encourage Kishi-san to talk to her ikiryō."

It made sense now. If the ikiryō was a splintered part of Kishi, she would never be able to heal so long as she didn't recognize the half that was tormented by grief and sorrow.

I nodded and waited for Honda to step in and say something to Kishi, but she just kept looking at me.

"What? You think I should talk to her?"

"I think it will mean more coming from you. You were the one who brought her here, and you are attuned to the sorrow that led you to the spirit in the first place."

I nodded, and then knelt down. "Kishi-san?" I said gently, laying a hand on her shoulder.

This contact seemed to startle her out of her trance, for she blinked and turned toward me. For a moment her face still held the confusion from staring at her ikiryō, but then it softened. "Mari-chan . . ."

I nodded and squeezed her shoulder. "I'm here to help. Please listen to me carefully—who were you looking at just now?"

She blinked a few times, then turned back to the spirit. This time her eyes filled with tears and she cried out, "Suzu-chan!"

She saw her daughter's ghost. A wave of poignant sorrow swept over me, and I couldn't tell if it was issuing from the ikiryō or if it was my own. I closed my eyes. Was it better this way? Better that Kishi-san have a chance to say goodbye, even if it wasn't real? Goodbyes are for the survivors, after all, for our own closure. So we can move on, learn to live our lives without our loved one in it. So we can forge a new normal for ourselves. I knew that now.

When I reopened my eyes, Kishi had risen to her feet and was embracing her ikiryō, tears streaming down her cheeks. But to my eyes, the ikiryō embracing her back was a funhouse mirror image of Kishi— the same woman but with eerily stretched skin and an impossibly long, drooping mouth. Viscous black tears oozed from the spirit's eyes, mimicking Kishi's own. I gasped, dropping the beads to the ground. The moment they left my hand, the filter returned, and I could see Kishi hugging her ghost daughter, little Suzu-chan with the twisted smile. The little girl I had befriended so many years ago.

I smiled, a bittersweet smile. Yes, it was better this way.

"Kishi-san, I think it's time to tell Suzu everything you need to tell her." I wiped my eyes with the back of my wrist.

"I'm so sorry, Suzu-chan. I should've been there, watching over you, and I wasn't. I never should have—" she broke off, sobbing and clutching the ghost girl tight to her chest.

Suzu wasn't crying now, though—her face held a serene smile, as if she were basking in her mother's love, and I could feel the hole inside me closing, healing.

"Suzu-chan isn't sad anymore," I said softly. "The island has healed, too—it doesn't have to be a sad, broken place any longer."

Kishi's sobs slowed to a sniffling trickle, and she held her daughter out at arm's length.

"It's all right, Mama, everything is all right now." Suzu's voice—it was the same as I'd heard in her room, and last night when I'd brought her to the island. I willed myself to just accept it, to embrace the illusion.

"Have you seen the island, Mama? Isn't it beautiful?" Suzu waved her arm, encompassing the blooming hydrangeas around us or perhaps the entire island. "Isn't it much better this way?"

Kishi tore her gaze from her ghost daughter to look around with fresh eyes. Honda's lantern glowed gently behind them, and the nearly round moon came out from behind the clouds, lighting the pond of stones around Jizō in an unearthly glow. "Yes," she whispered, "it is much better this way."

"I want you to be happy, Mama. Please don't grieve for me anymore." Suzu's words seared my heart, and my tears began flowing again, though I no longer knew who I was crying for.

"I'll try, Suzu-chan," Kishi whispered. "I'll try—for you."

With those words, Kishi closed her eyes. She sighed out a deep breath, and when she inhaled, Suzu shimmered like a mirage, her form dissipating into a fine mist.

Kishi was breathing her in.

For a moment Kishi looked like a double-exposed photograph, with the misty image of Suzu overlaid on top of her. Then they merged; Suzu was gone, and only Kishi remained.

Kishi's knees wobbled, and I lunged forward to grab hold of her, my arms wrapping around her angular frame. Underneath her thick kimono, she was as thin as I was when I arrived. She really needed some hearty Yanagi Inn breakfasts and healthy outdoor exercise.

"It's all right, everything's all right," I murmured, gently stroking her back like my mother used to do to me. Honda's approaching footsteps crunched along the gravel, but she remained silent.

After a few moments, I released my embrace and Kishi shuffled back slightly. She looked up at me and Honda, her hair disheveled, her face red and streaked with tears. She gave us an embarrassed smile. "I-I don't know what to say."

But that was enough. With those words, the oppressive weight in the air was lifted, and the strange absurdity of it all overwhelmed me; I found myself laughing. Fortunately, neither woman reproached me for my irreverence—they both smiled back, the lightness in the air infectious. The sweet scent of hydrangeas lilted past us in the breeze.

"Kishi-san," Honda said gently. "I have something for you." She reached into her cloth bag and pulled out a piece of red fabric. Probably homemade, for it looked like hand-knitted yarn.

Kishi accepted the item with both hands and a bow of her head, then turned the piece over quizzically. "What is this, Honda-san?"

"It's a hat. For the Jizō statue."

Kishi let out a quiet, suppressed sob and brought the tiny hat up to her face. I was unsure whether she was kissing it, or some other intimate gesture, but she held it against her skin for the length of several heartbeats. "Thank you, Honda-san."

We both stepped to the side, revealing the Jizō statue behind us. Kishi strode forward, her chin held high as if she were performing a solemn ceremony, carrying the small red cap on her upturned palms. Then she knelt in front of the Jizō statue, gently pulled the cap on his round head, and bowed.

Chapter Forty-Five

H onda, Kishi, and I agreed to reconvene after breakfast the next
morning at the no-longer-hidden boat. Despite my late night, I
got up early and was dressed and waiting for Yuna when she knocked
on my door. I'd debated what I should tell her of the strange happen-
ings in the night, but ended up spilling absolutely everything, and even
invited her to join us for the trip out to the island.

"I've always wanted to visit the island!" She squealed with delight
and agreed to join us as soon as she cleaned up and got changed. I told
her we'd be happy to wait for her.

When she strode toward us down the garden path, I did a dou-
ble-take; I realized I'd never seen Yuna in anything but Yanagi Inn's
kimono. Now she showed up in a charming Alice in Wonderland-esque
white dress covered with tiny, embroidered rabbit faces and strappy sandals. "That outfit is very you," I said with a smile.

She laughed and gave a twirl. Honda and Kishi chuckled and went
back to their quiet conversation.

Honda offered to ferry all four of us across to the island, so we all
piled into the boat and Honda sat in the rear seat with the oar.

"Honda-san," I began when we had pushed off from shore and
were floating free, "When do we have to return the boat?"

"Wait, we don't get to keep it?" Yuna exclaimed, stroking the side. "But it's so perfect!"

Honda chuckled. "I told my friend I would return it within a week."

"Your friend . . . he made this boat?" Kishi spoke up.

"Yes, he is quite the craftsman, no?" Pride shone through her voice. He was definitely her beau.

Kishi nodded, lost in thought. "It would be good to have a boat here," she said softly.

I half-turned in my seat to gauge Honda's reaction. She was beaming. "I would be happy to make inquiries," she said with a bob of her head.

I turned again to watch the scenery gliding past, to listen to the oar's soft splash as the boat slid through the pond's surface. Yes, a boat would be good to have here. It was not part of the original design (I thought of the broken bridge with its forlorn pillars erupting from the water, the submerged stones which had been so terrifying to me in the beginning), but the island needed a new normal.

I smiled. I was building a new normal for myself, too.

The front of the boat hit the far shore, and Yuna sprung out to tug the boat further up onto land. "Honda-san, can you show me how to be captain on the way back?" Her enthusiastic smile was sweet and endearing as she caught the rope Honda tossed to her.

"Of course! I'd be happy to."

Yuna knelt on the gravel, oblivious to the damage she must be doing to her stylish clothes, and tied the boat's rope to the cluster of bamboo stalks.

She reminds me of myself at sixteen.

Yuna was so open, so free, so bursting with possibilities. I could remember running around downtown Chicago with my friends at that age, newly acquired cameras in our hands, taking elaborately staged photos, laughing and feeling so very wild and alive. I recalled Yuna's words when we first met, how impressed she'd been that I was a photographer.

I should order Yuna a nice camera before I leave.

Before I leave. I stepped out of the boat and gave Honda my hand to help her onto the island. It was time to seriously start thinking about going home.

We spent a leisurely morning strolling through the island's gardens, Honda and I pointing out the changes we'd made: where an old rotting tree's stump was now a new seat from which to enjoy the view, where we'd found the bushy monstrosity of rosemary and turned it into an enormous ball of herbs. While we shared some of the funny stories from our renovation experiences, a trio of squirrels appeared, and Honda gave Yuna a handful of nuts to feed them. Yuna was thrilled.

"And then," I said dramatically, "I reached a hand up to feel *bird poop* on my head and—"

Yuna pointed to the sky and exclaimed, "Oh, a crane!"

We all turned our eyes skyward. Indeed, there was a crane gliding over our heads from the south.

I squinted my eyes, shielded them with one hand. "Is it . . . ?"

"No, I don't believe it's her. Look at the facial markings—his face is mostly black." Honda shielded her eyes, followed the crane's movements carefully.

"It's a male?"

Honda nodded. "I think so. It looks like our friend may have a new mate."

We all watched the crane glide down lower and lower and then land somewhere on the far end of the island. Near the willow trees. Near the crane's nest.

Was this new relationship our doing? The island seemed like one singular entity, an interconnected ecosystem of life in which one part of the system influenced all others. Could the changes we made lead to new beginnings?

I felt ready for a new beginning. It was time for me to give Thad a call; I had some apologizing to do.

We ended our tour of the island at the Jizō statue. In contrast to the light-hearted garden party atmosphere we'd created on the rest of our excursion, we entered his cove quietly, reverently, as if it were a sacred space. Even bubbling Yuna, who had exclaimed and rejoiced at every beautiful flower, every expansive view, was silent.

We stopped beside the pond of rocks around the statue's small island, admired the Jizō with his jaunty red bib and new knit hat. He looked so warm and secure. My heart swelled to compare his present condition to what he looked like when I first came in secret to the island.

"My mother used to visit a Jizō statue. In a park by our house." Yuna was the first to break the silence, speaking in soft, solemn tones I had not heard her use before. "Every time we'd go for a walk, we ended up there at the statue. And my mother would always bring something to leave—a little toy, a piece of fruit or candy. When I was older, a friend at school told me that Jizō protects the souls of children who die before their parents. But I've never been able to ask my mother why she visits him."

We were all silent then, all lost in our own thoughts, our own memories. But somehow the atmosphere was not sad, just nostalgic in a sweetly painful kind of way. Tears blurred my eyes.

A warm hand slipped into mine, and I glanced down to see Honda standing beside me, smiling through her own tears. She squeezed my hand, and I could feel something hard pressing into it. The beads.

"You dropped these last night," she whispered, and I remembered with a flash the moment I had let go of the beads and seen Suzu once more.

I nodded, swallowing hard, and held up the string. The beads were smooth and round, varying shades of warm browns.

"They are yours. To do with as you wish." Honda whispered, then patted me on the shoulder.

To do with as I wish. I rotated the beads of the rosary through my fingers. *Loss. Sorrow. Heartbreak.* With each bead, a different word passed my lips. *Clarity. Healing. Revival.* I closed my eyes, let the warmth of each word sink in.

Then I strode forward and knelt before the Jizō statue, brought the beads to my lips for a brief prayer, then slipped the strand around Jizō's neck.

I bowed low to the ground, then brushed off my clothes and turned back to my friends. Yuna, Honda, and Kishi were watching me, smiling as if we all understood each other better now that we'd shared part of each other's journeys.

"Oh," Honda said, reaching into her bag again, this time pulling out a packet of seeds. "I wanted to see if we could find a place to plant these on the island."

She handed me the packet and I smiled at the large, cheerful sunflower on the front. "Sunflowers!" A sweet pain stabbed me in my chest. My smile turned sad. "But I won't get to see them bloom."

Honda patted me on the arm. "You'll just have to come back."

Honda and Yuna decided to move on, vowing to go spy on the cranes' nest and report back about their findings. They went on their way, chatting quietly like schoolgirls.

Kishi and I stayed behind, silent beside the Jizō statue now decorated with the string of beads as well as the vibrant red accessories.

I cleared my throat. "Do you have to leave right away? I would love to show you the rest of my photos. I took before- and after-pictures of the island while Honda-san and I were working on it. I thought they would add an interesting dimension when I make up my grant portfolio. Do you think—"

"There is no grant."

Kishi's soft words caught me off guard.

"What? I-I don't understand."

Yet somehow Kishi's admission didn't surprise me. Deep down, maybe I'd known all along that the grant was a fabrication, but I hadn't been willing to admit it.

Kishi didn't meet my gaze, just continued staring at the Jizō statue and the hydrangeas swaying gently in the breeze around him.

"Your mother contacted me. It was only a week or two before she passed." She paused, and I swallowed back a tightness in my throat. "It was so unexpected; we hadn't spoken in many, many years. Not since—" She broke off for a moment, struggling to compose herself enough to continue.

"She told me she was dying, but that's not why she called. She called because she was worried about you, Mari-chan. Your mother knew you would need to get away, need a place to find your own peace." Now she turned toward me, looked into my eyes. "She asked if you could come here. But she said you'd never come if you felt it was charity or a pity invite, so . . ." Kishi spread her hands out in front of her, a gesture of futility.

"So she made up the grant. To get me to come here, thinking it was work." It all made sense. And Risa must've been in on it, too, the little sneak. Was the whole grant idea one of Mom's wishes she talked to Risa about in the hospital room that day? Just like she had asked me to pass on her engagement ring to Diego?

"Your mother was a lovely woman. We were . . . very close." Kishi turned away at this admission, went back to viewing the Jizō statue. "It is one of my biggest regrets in life that we drifted apart after Suzu-chan passed away. Did you know you used to play in this garden with Su-zu-chan when you were just this high?" Kishi held her hand up to just above her waist. "You girls would play whenever your mother came for tea." Kishi smiled at some long-ago memory.

I followed Kishi's gaze, and realized she wasn't looking at the stat-ue, but rather at the flowers, the purple hydrangeas.

"You sent them, didn't you? The hydrangeas in Mom's hospital room?"

She nodded, tears brimming in her eyes, though she never removed her gaze from the flowers.

The final puzzle piece fell into place at that moment. I held up my hand and inspected the ring Mom had given me in the hospital. I'd always thought of hydrangeas as big, poufy flowers. But if you looked closer at what they were truly made of, each pouf was really a cluster of cheerful little blooms. Just like the little flowers on Mom's ring. "The ring—you gave it to my mother didn't you?"

Kishi's jaw tightened, and I saw her swallow. She couldn't meet my gaze again, but she nodded briefly.

So that's what it was—a token of their secret relationship. They must've really loved each other.

There were so many things I didn't know about my mother. What dreams had she had that she never pursued? Perhaps that was why she pushed me to return to my art, to follow my own path to happiness.

To live life without regrets.

"When I show you the photos I took here at Yanagi Inn," I said slowly, "I can also show you some photos from over the years, if you'd like. I took lots of photos of her."

At this, Kishi turned toward me and smiled, her eyes shining. "I would like that."

I bowed my head, blinking back the tears which threatened to overwhelm me. I tried to spin the hydrangea ring with my thumb, but it was too tight to spin anymore. So I tugged it off my middle finger, examined it in the light for a moment, then slid it on my ring finger. It fit perfectly now.

When I turned back to Kishi, for a moment I thought I saw my mother standing beside her, smiling, wearing a cheery yellow yukata and looking out at the hydrangeas. I closed my eyes, this time savoring the image.

My mother was a complex woman, equal parts sterling and tarnished, and I could finally understand that. And accept it.

I took a deep breath, relishing the sensation of fresh spring air in my lungs, and gazed up at the clear blue sky above me.

A flicker of movement caught my eye, and for a moment I thought it was one of the cranes coming back to roost, but no, it was an airplane passing by high overhead. I smiled.

It was time for me to go home.

Epilogue

Six months later

"Now, on the count of three, open your eyes."
Risa had led me to what felt like the center of the gallery, my hands covering my face. My unaccustomed high heels and palazzo pants made it difficult not to trip over Risa's maxi dress as I'd trailed after her.

"Risa, can't I just—"

"One, two, three!" Risa pulled my hands away from my face and I squinted at the bright lights before my eyes adjusted and I took in my surroundings.

The gallery's familiar high walls were dotted with scenes from Yanagi Inn's gardens; some wall-sized blow-ups, others small snapshots of minute details. And beside each collection of themed images was an ikebana display, each flower arrangement perfectly matched in color, shape, and mood to the photographs behind it.

"Do you like it?" Risa was hopping from foot to foot in her excitement.

"Oh my god, it's—"

"Breathtaking? Gorgeous?"

"It's perfect, Risa. Truly. You're going to be the best event manager the gallery has ever seen."

Risa's eyes teared up and she threw herself into my arms for a tight hug.

"You were right about Mrs. Hamamura—she was stoked for her students to display their arrangements outside the community center. Didn't they turn out great? And did you notice—"

Risa grabbed my hand and pulled me from display to display, showing off how she'd paired each before- and after-photo of the island to highlight the transformations; I smiled at the peeling half-moon bridge next to its cheerful bright red "after." Combining the photographs, the elaborate flower displays, and the whimsical origami cranes and flowers dotting the pedestals or hanging from near-invisible wires was even better than I could have imagined. Risa really did have a knack for design.

I strolled slowly around the gallery's spacious interior, nostalgia for my time in Japan already tugging at my heart. Then I stopped in front of a wall featuring the photos I'd taken of the inn's staff.

My friends.

The photo of Yuna, laughing and leaning on her mop in the baths. Honda-san, standing triumphantly beside the newly-trimmed rosemary monstrosity with a pair of loppers in her hand. Elegant Kishi-san, kneeling beside the smiling Jizō statue, surrounded by purple hydrangeas.

"I wish I could see it. All of it," Risa said quietly, gazing up at an enormous photo of the crane in flight, flanked by a multitude of hanging red origami cranes.

"Well, I heard the room refurbishments are almost done, and they'll be opening up to guests this fall—just in time to see the autumn leaves." I reached out and squeezed her hand. Something hard pressed against my fingers.

"Wait, Risa, is that . . . ?"

Risa squealed and offered her left hand for me to inspect. "I was wondering when you'd notice! He proposed last night!"

"Oh that's wonderful, Risa! Congratulations!" I inspected the engagement ring on her finger. Diego had indeed had the diamond reset so it was now flanked by two tiny spheres of turquoise, Risa's favorite stone. "It's lovely—very you."

She beamed back at me, tears gleaming in her eyes. "Mom really planned out everything, didn't she?"

I nodded, holding back my own tears.

"Oh!" she said. "Let me show you my favorite photo." She grabbed my hand and pulled me across the room. My newly bobbed hair bounced in unison with Risa's as we raced like children.

She dragged me to the front corner of the room, where we normally displayed the star piece—usually something small, but always the crown jewel of any given exhibit. In the corner was a small table with a framed 8x10" photograph, capped on both sides by arrangements of purple hydrangeas in full bloom.

My breath caught in my throat.

I'm not even sure how Risa got ahold of the photo of Mom—it was just a casual snapshot I'd taken one morning over coffee in Mom's kitchen. Before the cancer, before things changed. Mom was leaned back in her chair, laughing, and she was full of life and energy, and looking upon the photo sent me back in the room with her, the scent of coffee and those little mandarin oranges filling the air.

It was perfect.

Beneath the frame was a placard: "In loving memory of Frances Eliza Lennox." A wave of warmth washed over my body, the sadness now manifesting as a sweet ache rather than a sharp stab of grief.

"I love it," I said softly. We stood for a long moment, looking at Mom, happy, in her own kitchen.

"Oh!" Risa exclaimed again. "I forgot. Wait right here."

She went rushing into the backroom, and I could hear her talking in hushed tones to the serving staff helping out for the opening. I admired Mom's photo a little longer, noticing the glint of a ring on the hand holding her coffee mug. I smiled, touched the silver hydrangea ring on my own finger.

Risa returned a minute later, a champagne glass in each hand.

"I thought sparkling saké would be better than champagne for this event," she said with a wide grin, and I accepted one of the glasses. "Is Thad coming, by the way?"

I shook my head. "He flew to New York for a second interview with that company. I know he's going to get an offer."

"And . . . ?" Risa raised a single eyebrow.

I chuckled. "I've already told him he should take it. He needs to do what's best for him. And I think we're both ready to move on." The pang was still there when I thought about life without Thad, but what I'd said was true—I was ready for a new start.

"Perfect! Then I would like to propose a toast," Risa said in a formal tone. "To new beginnings!" She held up her glass and I clinked it with my own. We both took a sip. The bubbles tickled my nose and I fought back a sneeze.

Risa glanced at her watch. "It's almost time. Shall we open the doors?"

I took one last look around the gallery, at the beauty of Yanagi Inn all around me, at the sign on the front easel with *Marissa Lennox: The Secret Garden of Yanagi Inn* emblazoned in bold letters, and then back at my little sister, breathless with excitement.

"Open them up—I'm ready."

THE END

Author's Note

Yanagi Inn is a fictional location, although it was loosely based on a number of real-life ryokan. Liberties have been taken with many aspects of the inn's gardens, such as the presence of the endangered red-crowned cranes so far south in Japan, and the blooming seasons for many of the flowers mentioned. Please chalk these up to artistic license. And the magic of the gardens.

Acknowledgments

It takes far more than one person to make a book, so grab some tea and settle in—I have a lot of people to thank.

First, *The Secret Garden of Yanagi Inn* wouldn't exist if it weren't for Frances Eliza Hodgson Burnett's 1911 classic *The Secret Garden*. Her story inspired me in so many ways, while still leaving fertile ground for my imagination to take root (*wait, you mean there WASN'T something supernatural going on the whole time?*).

Ah, the beauty of retellings.

Next, I'd like to express my gratitude to the entire team at CamCat Books. A debut author would be hard-pressed to find a more supportive and engaged publishing team, and I am grateful for all of you. Thank you, in particular, to my editor Helga Schier, for pushing me to go further and make my story all the stronger. Thank you, Maryann, for the novel's stunning cover and Cassandra for your mad polishing skills. And thank you, Sue, for bringing me into the CamCat family—I feel fortunate to be part of such a supportive group of authors.

I am also forever indebted to my literary agent Hannah Weatherill and the many fine people on the other side of the pond at Northbank Talent Management. I am fortunate to have you in my corner. Thank you for continuing to believe in me!

Thank you to my writer's club (the Foo Writers!) for their ceaseless encouragement, weekend writing retreats, never-ending group chats, and lots and lots of coffee. Jamie—thank you for your insightful questions and willingness to "take a quick look" at a page or a chapter. Amy—thank you for your countless hours of beta reading, your undying enthusiasm for my work, and for loving the insanity that is writing as much as I do. And thank you Heather and Kachina for reading early drafts of the novel and providing valuable feedback. A big thanks also to Brian for sharing his camera expertise, and Minori for her thoughtful cultural sensitivity read.

And, of course, I must thank my family. Thank you to my parents for the multiple trips to the Japanese Tea Garden in San Francisco's Golden Gate Park as a child. I'm convinced that garden holds as much magic as Disneyland. Thank you to my children, Fox and Willow, for their patience in always letting me take their photos in cool gardens, and for their interest in "how the book is going." I can't wait to read this book aloud with each of you someday (be warned, Willow, it has some scary bits!).

Last, but not least, thank you to my husband, Chris, who has loved me since I was a silly teenager handwriting him books. Thank you for being my first reader, my sounding board, and the love of my life.

About the Author

Amber A. Logan is a university instructor, freelance editor, and author of speculative fiction living in Kansas with her husband and two children, Fox and Willow. In addition to her degrees in Psychology, Liberal Arts, and International Relations, Amber holds a PhD in Creative Writing from Anglia Ruskin University in Cambridge, England.

When she's not writing, Amber enjoys trips to Japan, eating unusual vegetarian foods, and reading Haruki Murakami. Although she was once a professional landscaper, Amber has no time for garden maintenance, and her own backyard is unfortunately reminiscent of Yanagi Inn's forlorn gardens.

If you enjoyed

Amber A. Logan's *The Secret Garden of Yanagi Inn*,

you'll enjoy

K. L. Murphy's *Her Sister's Death*.

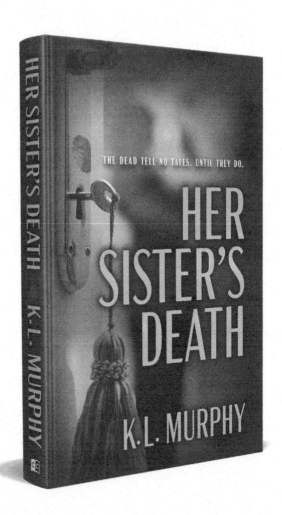

CHAPTER
1

VAL

Monday, 9:17 a.m.

Once, when I was nine or maybe ten, I spent weeks researching a three-paragraph paper on polar bears. I don't remember much about the report or polar bears, but that assignment marked the beginning of my lifelong love affair with research. As I got older, I came to believe that if I did the research, I could solve any problem. It didn't matter what it was. School. Work. Relationships. In college, when I suspected a boyfriend was about to give me the brush off, I researched what to say before he could break up with me. Surprisingly, there are dozens of pages about this stuff. Even more surprising, some of it actually works. We stayed together another couple of months until I realized I was better off without him. He never saw it coming.

When I got married, I researched everything from whether or not we were compatible (we were) to our average life expectancy based on our medical histories (only two years' difference). Some couples swear they're soul mates or some other crap, but I consider myself a little more practical than that. I wanted the facts before I walked down the aisle. The thing is, research doesn't tell you that your perfect-on-paper husband is going to prefer the ditzy receptionist on the third floor before you've hit your five-year anniversary. It also doesn't tell you that your initial anger will turn into something close to relief, or that all that perfection was too much work and maybe the whole soul mate thing isn't as crazy as it sounds. If you doubt me, look it up.

My love of research isn't as odd as one might think. My father is a retired history professor, and my mother is a bibliophile. It doesn't matter the genre. She usually has three or more books going at once. She also gets two major newspapers every day and a half dozen magazines each month. Some people collect cute little china creatures or rare coins or something. My mother collects words. When I decided to become a journalist, both my parents were overjoyed.

"It's perfect," my father had said. "We need more people to record what's going on in the world. How can we expect to learn if we don't recognize that everything that happens impacts our future?" I'd had to fight the urge to roll my eyes. I knew what was coming, but how many times can a person hear about the rise and fall of Caesar? The man was stabbed to death, and it isn't as though anyone learned their lesson. Ask Napoleon. Or Hitler. My dad was right about one thing though. History can't help but repeat itself.

"Darling," my mother had interrupted. "Val will only write about important topics. You know very well she is a young lady of principle." Again, I'd wanted to roll my eyes.

Of course, for all their worldliness, neither of my parents understand how the world of journalism works. You don't walk into a newsroom as an inexperienced reporter and declare you will be writing about the environment, or the European financial market, or the latest domestic policy. The newspaper business is not so different from any other—even right down to the way technology is forcing it to go digital. Either way, the newbies are given the jobs no one else wants.

Naturally, I was assigned to obituaries.

After a year, I got moved to covering the local city council meetings, but the truth was, I missed the death notices. I couldn't stop myself from wondering how each of the people had died. Some were obvious. When the obituary asks you to donate to the cancer society or the heart association, you don't have to think too hard to figure it out. Also, people like to add that the deceased "fought a brave battle with (fill in the blank)." I've no doubt those people were brave, but they weren't the ones that interested me. It was the ones that seemed to die unexpectedly and under unusual circumstances. I started looking them up for more information. The murder victims held particular fascination for me. From there, it was only a short hop to my true interest: crime reporting.

The job isn't for everyone. Crime scenes are not pretty. Have you ever rushed out at three in the morning to a nightclub shooting? Or sat through a murder trial, forced to view photo after photo of a brutally beaten young mother plastered across a giant screen? My sister once told me I must have a twisted soul to do what I do. Maybe. I find myself wondering about the killer, curious about what makes them do it. That sniper from a few years ago—the one that picked off the poor folks as they came out of a concert—that was my story. Even now, I still can't get my head around that guy's motives. So, I research and research, trying to get things right as well as find some measure of understanding. It doesn't always work, but knowing as much as I can is its own kind of answer.

Asking questions has always worked for me. It's the way I do my job. It's the way I've solved every problem in my life. Until now. Not that I'm not trying. I'm at the library. I'm in my favorite corner in the cushy chair with the view of the pond. I don't know how long I've been here. How many hours. My laptop is on, the screen filled with text and pictures. Flicking through the tabs, I swallow the bile that reminds me I have no answer. I've asked the question in every way I can think of, but for the first time in my life, Google is no help. Why did my sister—my gorgeous sister with her two beautiful children and everything to live for—kill herself? Why?

Sylvia has been dead for four days now. Actually, I don't know how long she's been dead. I've been told there's a backlog at the M.E.'s office. Apparently, suicides are not high priority when you live in a city with one of the country's highest murder rates. I don't care what the reason is. I just want the truth.

While we wait for the official autopsy, I find myself re-evaluating what I do know.

Her body was discovered on Thursday at The Franklin. According to the maid, the *Do not disturb* sign had been on the door for three days before she was found. The hotel claims my sister called the front desk after only one day and asked not to be disturbed unless the sign was removed. This little detail could not have been more surprising. My sister doesn't have trouble sleeping. Sylvia went to bed at ten every night and was up like clockwork by six sharp. I have hundreds of texts to prove it. Even when her children were babies with sleep schedules that would kill most people, she somehow managed to stick to her routine. Vacations with her were pure torture.

"Val, get up. The sun is shining. Let's go for a walk on the beach." I'd open one eye to find her standing in the doorway. She'd be dressed in black nylon shorts and neon sneakers, bouncing up and down on her toes. "I promise I won't run. We'll just walk."

Tossing my pillow at her, I'd groan and pull the covers over my head.

"You can't sleep the day away, Val." She'd cross the room in two strides and rip back the sheets. "Get up."

In spite of my night owl tendencies, I'd crawl out of bed. Sylvia had a way of making me feel like if I didn't join her, I'd be missing out on something extraordinary. The thing is, she was usually right. Sure, a sunrise is a sunrise, but a sunrise with Sylvia was color and laughter and tenderness and love. She had that way about her. She loved mornings.

I tried to explain Sylvia to the policeman, to tell him that hanging a sleeping sign past six in the morning much less all day was not just odd behavior, but downright suspicious. He did his best not to dismiss me outright, but I knew he didn't get it.

"Sleeping too much can be a sign of depression," he'd said.

"She wasn't depressed."

"She hung a sign, ma'am. It's been verified by the manager." He'd stopped short of telling me that putting out that stupid sign wasn't atypical of someone planning to do what she did. Whatever that's supposed to mean.

The screen in front of me blurs, and I rub my burning eyes. There are suicide statistics for women of a certain age, women with children, women in general. My fingers slap the keys. I change the question, desperate for an answer, any answer.

A shadow falls across the screen when a man takes the chair across from me, a newspaper under his arm. My throat tightens, and I press my lips together. He settles in, stretching his legs. The paper crackles as he opens it and snaps when he straightens the pages.

"Do you mind?"

He lowers the paper, his brows drawn together. "Mind what?"

"This is a library. It's supposed to be quiet in here."

He angles his head. "Are you always this touchy, or is it just me?"

"It's you." I don't know why I say that. I don't even know why I'm acting like a brat, but I can't help myself.

Silence fills the space between us as he appears to digest what I've said. "Perhaps you'd like me to leave?"

"That would be nice."

He blinks, the paper falling from his hand. I'm not sure which of us is more surprised by my answer. I seem to have no control over my thoughts or my mouth. The man has done nothing but crinkle a news-paper, but I have an overwhelming need to lash out. He looks around, and for a moment, I feel bad.

The man gets to his feet, the paper jammed under his arm. "Look, lady, I'll move to another spot, but that's because I don't want to sit here and have my morning ruined by some kook who thinks the pub-lic library is her own personal living room." He points a finger at me. "You've got a problem."

I feel the sting, the well of tears before he's even turned his back. They flood my eyes and pour down over my cheeks. Worse, my mouth opens, and I sob, great, loud, obnoxious sobs. I cover my face with my hands and sink lower into the chair, my body folding in on itself. My laptop slips to the floor, and I somehow cry harder.

"Is she all right?" a woman asks, her voice high and tight.

The annoying man answers. "She'll be fine in a minute."

"Are you sure?" Her gaze darts between us, and her hands flutter over me like wings, nearing but never touching. I recognize her from the reference desk. "People are staring. This is a library, you know."

I want to laugh, but it gets caught in my throat, and comes out like a bark. Her little kitten heels skitter back. I don't blame her. Who wouldn't want to get away from the woman making strange animal noises?

"Do you have a private conference room?" the man asks. The wom-an points the way, and large hands lift me to my feet. "Can you get her laptop and her bag, please?"

The hands turn into an arm around my shoulders. He steers me toward a small room at the rear of the library. My fading sobs morph into hiccups.

The woman places my bag and computer on a small round table. "I'll make sure no one bothers you here." She slinks out, pulling the door shut.

The man sets his paper down and pulls out a chair for me.

I don't know how many minutes pass before I'm able to stop crying, before I'm able to speak.

"Are you okay now?" I can't look at him. His voice is kind, far kinder than I deserve. He pushes something across the table. "Here's my handkerchief." He gets to his feet. "I'm going to see if I can find you some water."

The door clicks behind him, and I'm alone. The man is gone. My sister, my best friend, is gone, and I'm alone.

"Do you want to talk about it?" the man asks, setting a bottle of water and a package of crackers on the table.

Sniffling, I twist the damp, wadded up handkerchief into a ball. I want to tell him that no, I don't want to talk about it, that I don't even know him, but the words slip out anyway. "My sister died," I say.

"Oh." He folds his hands together. "I'm sorry. Recently?"

"Four days."

He pushes the crackers he's brought across the table. "You should try to eat something."

I try to remember when I last ate. Yesterday? The day before? One of my neighbors did bring me a casserole with some kind of brown meat and orangey red sauce. It may have had noodles, but I can't be sure. I do remember watching the glob of whatever it was slide out of the aluminum pan and down the disposal. I think I ate half a bagel sometime. My stomach churns, then rumbles. The man doesn't wait for me to decide. He opens the packet and pushes it closer. For some reason I can't explain, I want to prove I'm more polite than I seemed earlier. I take the crackers and eat.

He gestures at the bottle. "Drink."

I do. The truth is, I'm too numb to do anything else. It's been four days since my parents phoned me. Up to now, I've taken the news like any other story I've been assigned. I've filed it away, stored it at the back of my mind as something I need to analyze and figure out before it can be processed. I've buried myself in articles and anecdotes and medical pages, reading anything and everything to try and understand. On some level, I recognize my behavior isn't entirely normal. My parents broke down, huddled together on the sofa, as though conjoined in their grief.

I couldn't have slipped between them even if I'd wanted to. Sylvia's husband—I guess that's what we're still calling him—appeared equally stricken. Not even the sight of her children, their faces pale and blank, had cracked the shell I'd erected, the wall I'd built to deny the reality of her death.

"Aunt Val," Merry had asked. "Mommy's coming back, right? She's just passed, right? That's what Daddy said." She'd paused, a single tear trailing over her pink cheek. "What's passed?"

Merry is the youngest, only five. Miles is ten—going on twenty if you ask me—which turned out to be a good thing in that moment. Miles had taken his sister by the hand. "Come on, Merry. Dad wants us in the back."

I'd let out a breath, crisis averted.

My sister has been gone four days, and I haven't shed a tear. Until today.

The man across the table clears his throat. "Are you feeling any better?"

"No, I'm not feeling better. My sister is still dead." God, I'm a bitch. I expect him to stand up and leave or at least point out what an ass I'm being when he's gone out of his way to be nice, but he does neither.

"Yes, I suppose she is. Death is kind of permanent."

I jerk back in my chair. "Is that supposed to be funny?"

Unlike me, he does apologize. "I'm sorry. That didn't come out right. I never did have the best bedside manner for the job."

I take a closer look at the man. "Are you a doctor?"

He half-laughs. "Not hardly. Detective. Former, I mean. I never quite got the hang of talking to the victim's families without putting my foot in my mouth. Seems I've done it again."

My curiosity gets the best of me. He's not much older than me. Mid-forties. Maybe younger. Definitely too young for retirement. "Former detective? What do you do now?"

"I run a security firm." He lifts his shoulders. "It's different, has its advantages."

The way he says it, I know he misses the job. I understand.

"I write for The Baltimorean. Mostly homicides," I say.

"That's a good paper. I've probably read your work then."

Crumpling the empty cracker wrapper, I say, "I'm sorry I dumped on you out there."

He shrugs again. "It's okay. You had a good reason."

I can't think of anything to say to that.

"How did she die, if you don't mind my asking?"

The question hits me hard. What I mind is that my sister is gone. My hands ball into fists. The heater in the room hums, but otherwise, it's quiet. "They say she committed suicide."

The man doesn't miss a beat. "But you don't believe it." He watches me, his body still.

My heart pounds in my chest and I reach into my mind, searching for any information I've found that contradicts what I've been told. I've learned that almost fifty thousand people a year commit suicide in the U.S. Strangely, a number of those people choose to do it in hotels. Maybe it's the anonymity. Maybe it's to spare the families. There are plenty of theories, but unfortunately, one can't really ask the departed about that. Still, the reasoning is sound enough. For four days, I've read until I can't see, and my head has dropped from exhaustion. I know that suicide can be triggered by traumatic events or chronic depression. It can be triggered by life upheaval or can be drug-induced, or it can happen for any number of reasons that even close family and friends don't know about until after—if ever. I know all this, and yet, I can't accept it.

Sylvia was found in a hotel room she had no reason to be in. An empty pill bottle was found on the nightstand next to her. She checked in alone. Nothing in the room had been disturbed. Nothing appeared to have been taken. For all these reasons, the police made a preliminary determination that the cause of death was suicide, the final ruling to be made after the M.E.'s report. I know all this. My parents and Sylvia's husband took every word of this at face value. But I can't. Sylvia is not a statistic, and I know something they don't.

"No. I don't believe it," I say, meeting his steady gaze with one of my own.

He doesn't react. He doesn't tell me I'm crazy. He doesn't say I'm sorry again. Nothing. I'm disappointed, although I can't imagine why. He's a stranger to me. Still, I press my shoulder blades against the back of the chair, waiting. I figure it out then. Former detective. I've been around enough cops to know how it works. It's like a tribe with them. You don't criticize another officer.

You don't question anyone's toughness or loyalty to the job. You don't question a ruling that a case doesn't warrant an investigation, much less that it isn't even a case. So, I sit and wait. I will not be the first to argue. It doesn't matter that he's retired and left the job. He's still one of them. In fact, the more I think about it, I can't understand why he's still sitting there. I've been rude to the man. I've completely broken down in front of him like some helpless idiot. And now, I've suggested that the cause of death that everyone—and I mean everyone—says is true is not the truth at all.

He gets up, shoves his hands in his pockets.

This is it. He's done with me now. In less than one minute he'll be gone and, suddenly, I don't want him to leave. I break the silence.

"I'm Val Ritter."

"Terry Martin."

I turn the name over in my brain. It's familiar in a vague way. "Terry the former detective."

"Uh huh." He shifts his weight from one foot to the other. "Look, I'm sorry about your sister. You've lost someone you love, and the idea that she might have taken her own life is doubly distressing."

"I'm way past distressed. I'm angry."

"Is it possible that you're directing that anger toward the ones that ruled her death a suicide instead of at your . . ." his words fall away.

"My sister?"

"Yes."

"I might be if I thought she did this." I cross my arms over my chest. "But I don't. This idea, this thing they're saying makes no sense at all."

Terry the former detective's voice is low, soothing. "Why?"

My arms drop again. I'm tempted to tell him everything I know, which admittedly isn't much, but I hold back. This man is a stranger. Sure, he's been nice, and every time I've expected him to walk out the door, he's done the opposite. But that doesn't mean I can trust him.

"I'm sorry if my question seems insensitive," he says. His voice is soft, comforting in a neutral way, and I can picture him in an interrogation. He would be the good cop. "No matter how shocking the, uh, idea might be, I have a feeling you have your reasons. You were close—you and your sister?"

"We were." I sit there, twisting the handkerchief in my fingers. The heater makes a revving noise, drops back to a steady hum. "We talked all the time, and I can tell you, she wasn't depressed. That's what they tried to tell me. 'She must have been depressed.' I know people hide things, but she was never good at hiding her emotions from me. If anything, she'd been happier than ever." I give a slow shake of my head. "They tried to tell me about the other suicide and about the pills and the sign on the door and—" I stop. I hear myself rambling and force myself to take a breath. "If something had been wrong, I would have known."

Terry the former detective doesn't react, doesn't move. He keeps his mouth shut, but I know. He doesn't believe me, same as all the others. I can tell. There is no head bob or leading question. He thinks I'm in denial and that I will eventually accept the truth. He doesn't know me at all.

The minutes pass, and I drink the water. I realize I feel better. It's time to leave. "I should be going." I hold up the crumpled rag in my hand. "Sorry I did such a number on your handkerchief. I can clean it, send it to you later."

He waves off the suggestion. "Keep it."

I gather my items and apologize again. "Sorry you had to witness my meltdown out there."

"It happens."

I'm headed out the door, my hand on the knob, when he breaks protocol.

"What did you mean by the other suicide?"

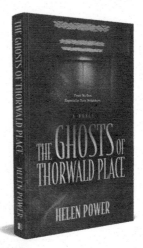
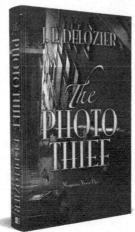

CamCat
Books

VISIT US ONLINE FOR MORE BOOKS TO LIVE IN:
CAMCATBOOKS.COM

SIGN UP FOR CAMCAT'S FICTION NEWSLETTER FOR
COVER REVEALS, EBOOK DEALS, AND MORE EXCLUSIVE CONTENT.

CamCatBooks   @CamCatBooks   @CamCat_Books   @CamCatBooks